ALL YOUR TWISTED SECRETS

DIANA URBAN

HARPER TEEN
An Imprint of HarperCollins Publishers

To Bryan, for every hour

HarperTeen is an imprint of HarperCollins Publishers.

All Your Twisted Secrets
Copyright © 2020 by Diana Urban
All rights reserved. Printed in the United States of America.
No part of this book may be used or reproduced in any manner whatsoever without
written permission except in the case of brief quotations embodied in critical articles
and reviews. For information address HarperCollins Children's Books, a division of
HarperCollins Publishers, 195 Broadway, New York, NY 10007. www.harperteen.com
Library of Congress Control Number: 2019950095

ISBN 978-0-06-290821-6

Typography by Corina Lupp
20 21 22 23 24   PC/LSCH   10 9 8 7 6 5 4

❖

First Edition

Dear Amber Prescott,

Congratulations! It is our pleasure to inform you that you have been selected as a recipient of the Brewster Town Hall Scholarship in the amount of $20,000. We commend you for your musical talents and contributions to the community.

To celebrate your achievements, we invite you to dine with Mayor Timothy Meinot and the other five scholarship recipients on Tuesday, February 4th, at 7 p.m. at the Chesterfield.

Again, congratulations, and we look forward to meeting you at the Chesterfield.

Sincerely,
Scholarship Chair
Brewster Town Hall Scholarship Committee

I spent the last hour wondering if I would die tonight.

You can drop dead from a heart attack at seventeen, right? The prospect of tonight's dinner party made my heart ricochet off my rib cage so fiercely I was convinced my days were numbered.

What's so bad about a dinner party? Let's start with the fact that my boyfriend, Robbie, was also invited to this little shindig, and we were on shaky ground. Our post-graduation plans were at odds, to say the least—and as senior year dwindled, the tension mounted. It didn't help that soon-to-be-valedictorian Diego scored an invite, too. Our friendship had recently morphed into something else—something that made my cheeks flush, my nerves tingle, and my heart swell like a submerged sponge.

Putting the three of us in the same room could be catastrophic. If Robbie suspected I liked the class nerd, he'd introduce

Diego to his fist in front of everyone. I had bigger issues with Robbie than another boy. But strike a match in a room doused with lighter fluid, and you're bound to get burned. If I were even slightly capable of hiding my emotions, I might get through the night unscathed. Unfortunately, I'm a crap liar, so splitsville with a side of bruising was basically inevitable.

Yep. A heart attack was imminent. I just had to get tonight over with, and everything would work out.

Hopefully.

I cranked up the *Harry Potter* score in an attempt to quell my nerves and ransacked my wardrobe, quickly determining that everything I owned looked hideous. I could either go ultra-casual or concert black (or funeral chic, as Sasha liked to call it) and either option was downright depressing.

After most of my clothes were heaped into a pile on the floor—much to the delight of my cat, Mittens, who swiftly nestled in—I discovered an old emerald sequined number I wore to a piano recital years ago. The dress now ended well above my knees, but it was the only garment within reach that wasn't a complete waste of space.

"Amber, you look great!" Mom said as I raced up the stairs from my basement bedroom, tugging at the dress's hem.

"You're only saying that because you're my mom."

"Don't get all self-deprecating on me." She scrunched one of my red curls, which already threatened to go limp. Her own red, stick-straight hair was cut in a typical mom-bob. "You look sophisticated. Though that dress could stand to be a little longer—"

"Is Robbie here yet?" He was already ten minutes late. I peered out the front door's stained-glass window, searching for his black SUV while fidgeting with my amethyst bracelet. Mittens rubbed against my ankles, getting his white fur all over my black velvet peep-toe shoes.

"You're not allowed to date 'til you're forty-seven," Dad shouted from his office down the hall.

"Is this a bad time to point out we've been dating for like a year?" I said. Even Mom mirrored my exaggerated eye roll.

Just as I rattled off a text to Robbie, his headlights flooded the driveway. I dropped my phone into my purse, and Mom handed me a jacket and kissed my cheek before I could bolt out the door. "Text me when you get there."

"God, Mom." I wiggled into the coat. "In a few months, I'll be in college. Should I text you whenever I go anywhere then, too?"

"That'd be great, thanks for offering!" Her eyes twinkled mischievously, though with the flicker of sadness that never really left them. "Love you."

"Bye!" I called over my shoulder as I raced into the unseasonably muggy night and down the front walk, my unzipped coat flapping behind me. Mom wasn't *exactly* overprotective. She let me do whatever, as long as I constantly let her know I was still alive.

I couldn't say she didn't have a good reason.

Robbie tossed his baseball mitt into the backseat. "Hey, babe—"

"Fifteen minutes late, Robbie? Really?" I slammed the

passenger door and clicked on my seat belt in one fluid motion. I wasn't usually one to pick a fight, but my nerves had me on edge.

"Amber. Chill. Practice went a little late." His go-to excuse. Robbie leaned over and kissed me, the sweet scent of soap and hair gel flooding my senses. He gripped the back of my headrest and backed down the driveway. Mom gave a little wave from the living room window, and the curtains fluttered shut as Robbie floored the gas. "Besides, I had to stop at home to grab your present." He reached behind my seat without taking his eyes from the road, grabbed a small box, and tossed it onto my lap.

"My . . . present? For what?"

"Open it." He grinned, the corners of his gray eyes crinkling as dimples creased his cheeks. Curious, I plucked open the red ribbon securing the small white box and found a charm bracelet inside. Several tiny silver music notes dangled from an amethyst-beaded band. "I thought it'd go with your other bracelet." He motioned to my grandmother's amethyst bracelet on my right wrist.

My anger dissipated, replaced by a confusing mix of joy and dread. "But what's this for?"

"What, I can't get something nice for my girl for no reason?" His smile widened—that infectious grin that always made me feel like I was somehow the brightest star in his sky. It seemed genuine. Everything about Robbie was genuine. He wore his heart on his sleeve, which was a blessing and a curse—I never had to wonder how much he loved me . . . or how annoyed he was with me, especially recently. But the musical theme of his gift caught me off guard.

My music had been a sore point for us lately. Robbie wanted me to follow him and his baseball scholarship to Georgia Tech, as if ditching my dreams of studying music at USC or Berklee wasn't that big a sacrifice. "But you can play music anywhere," he'd insisted. A couple of months ago we had a huge fight about it, and he convinced me to apply to Georgia Tech, suggesting we put off the discussion until I heard back from them.

Then I got my acceptance letter. That's when I knew we were going to break up.

I might've fallen in love with Robbie, but I'd been in love with music for as long as I could remember. I couldn't let him tempt me into abandoning my dreams. Despite my resolve, I hadn't figured out how to break the news.

But this was a shocking turn of events. I ran my fingers over the music note charms. It was such a thoughtful gift. Did he finally see my point of view? Was he willing to compromise?

As if on cue, he said, "I know we haven't talked about school and stuff in a while." School and stuff. How neatly all of my musical ambitions could be packed into one word. "Stuff." He smoothed back his short dirty-blond hair. "Have you heard from Georgia Tech yet?"

My shoulders tensed. "No. Not yet." Fortunately, the darkness obscured my flushed cheeks. I was so pale, my own blood always ratted me out: *Liar.*

"Well, it has to be soon. I want to be with you." Keeping one hand on the steering wheel, he entwined his fingers with mine. "We can figure this out together. I love you, Amber."

"I . . . me, too." Oh, God. What should I do? He kissed my hand and released it, and I fumbled with the clasp on my new bracelet, securing it on my left wrist. I leaned against the window, watching identical two-story colonials whip by. We drove the rest of the way in silence until fat raindrops pelted the car, drowning out my thoughts.

"Ah, crap." I zipped my jacket under the seat belt. Just like washing a car, using a curling iron on my hair pretty much guaranteed rain. If we moved to California, I could singlehandedly resolve the drought crisis.

The corner of Robbie's mouth quirked up. "It's only water."

"Explain that to my hair, would you?" I brushed aside my bangs.

Robbie glanced at me as he slowed in front of the Chesterfield. "Hey. You look beautiful. Hair included."

My cheeks flushed again. "Thanks." I shook away my anxiety and scanned the street for a parking spot. The Chesterfield was an upscale restaurant in the basement of an old warehouse converted into high-end retail space. On the weekends, locals bustled around this area pretending they lived in a vibrant city, when in reality, three square blocks constituted our entire "downtown."

There was no fooling anyone. We were lame upstate New York suburbanites, through and through.

Fortunately, it was a Tuesday, and there were plenty of spots around the corner. Once Robbie parked, I unclipped my seat belt and bolted out the door. I held my hood over my head as I rounded the corner, careful to avoid any puddles. The sidewalk was deserted except for two middle-aged women dashing to a nearby car under huge black umbrellas. I hustled down the steep steps to the Chesterfield's front entrance without waiting for Robbie to catch up.

God forbid he rush to anything besides home plate.

I shook the water from my jacket in front of the host podium. Beyond, crimson velvet booths lined either side of the dimly lit room, and a bar stretched across the opposite wall. A pyramid of wine and liquor bottles towered behind the bar, light streaming out between them to create a halo effect. Classical music flitted from speakers dotting the ceiling above the tables.

Empty tables.

The room was deserted.

"Are you sure this thing's at the Chesterfield?" Robbie asked from behind me.

"Yeah. Look." I pointed to a sign taped to the host podium. *Brewster Town Hall Scholarship Event in the Winona Room.* An arrow pointed to the right. "This way."

"Where the hell is everyone?"

My heart fluttered as I stepped farther into the room. "Probably in the Winona Room, where they're supposed to be."

"No, I mean everyone else—"

"Come on, let's go." *Let's get this over with.* I grabbed Robbie's calloused hand and led him across the empty dining room. A familiar throaty laugh floated through an open doorway next to the bar.

I walked in to find a smaller but equally elegant room. A

7

long mahogany dining table stood over an intricate red Oriental rug, which covered most of the gleaming, almost-black hardwood floor. Since most of the room was underground, there were only two small windows nestled close to the ceiling. Matching mahogany sideboards spanned the walls under the windows and next to the door. Two china cabinets filled with glasses and trinkets sandwiched a redbrick fireplace on the left, reflected in a giant brass mirror hanging on the opposite wall. Faux candles flickered in a brass chandelier hanging low from the center of the ceiling. The room felt medieval, and positively claustrophobic.

Sasha Harris and Diego Martin were already seated, laughing over some joke that must have had nothing to do with her perpetual need to one-up him. Robbie coughed, and Sasha paused mid-chuckle, peeking around the back of her chair. Spotting me, her eyes lit up. "Hey, lady!" She zipped around her chair and stretched out her cheek, kissing the air on either side of my face. "Thank God you guys won this, too. Otherwise tonight would be such a drag," she said under her breath.

Sasha was everything everyone else wanted to be—cheer captain, drama club director, class president, and potential valedictorian. "Sleep" wasn't exactly in her vocabulary. In a bizarre twist of fate, she also happened to be my best friend at the moment. Tonight she wore a form-fitting strapless red dress, and her shining chestnut hair flowed in loose waves over her bare shoulders, not a single strand out of place.

"Getting to meet the mayor is kind of cool, though," I said. "Is he here yet?"

She released Robbie from a hug. "Nope, not yet. But he's the opposite of cool, just FYI. I mean, come on. Who grows up wanting to be mayor of Podunk?"

I shrugged off my damp jacket, hung it on the ornate coatrack next to the door, and smoothed back my bangs. The curls I'd coaxed into my hair already fell limp. Damn rain. "Ick. It's like an oven in here."

"Ugh, I know." Sasha flapped her hand like a fan. "C'mon, you're next to me." She pointed to the seat closest to the door. Eight high-backed chairs surrounded the table—three on each side, and one on either end. On my empty gold-rimmed plate sat a place card for *Ms. Prescott*. Hers had one for *Ms. Harris*. Fancy. I pulled out my tall chair and glanced across the table, locking eyes with Diego.

Oh, here we go.

Strands of black hair fell over his forehead, and as he held my gaze with his intense copper eyes, a smile slid onto his lips. "Hi, Amber." My mind flashed back to a few weeks ago, when those eyes were mere inches from mine. Let's face it—you could pretty much fry an egg on my face.

"Hi." The word came out like a breathy wisp of wind. I set my purse on the floor and sat, silently cursing myself for being so obvious. After all, nothing ever happened between us. It almost did a few weeks ago. But almost doesn't count.

"Congratulations," he said. "Let me guess . . . you won because of your music?"

I laughed nervously, fidgeting with the music note charms on

9

my new bracelet. "Yeah. Mr. Torrente must've nominated me. I mean, I've basically been teaching his orchestra class for the last four years," I rambled.

Oh, God. If Robbie caught wind of the weirdness between me and Diego, tonight would be a nightmare. I faked a cough and covered my mouth, trying to hide my flaming cheeks. Thankfully, Robbie was oblivious as he fiddled with his phone next to the coatrack, shaking his head.

"Can you believe they'd give Diego one of the scholarships?" Sasha whispered when Diego pulled out his phone. "Twenty thousand dollars must be chump change to him now."

As if being ridiculously smart wasn't enough, Diego was sort of a celebrity in our school. He'd invented a weird sponge that changed colors when it got wet, and was on the show *Bid or Bust*—a reality TV show where inventors try to win funding from wealthy entrepreneurs—the summer before our freshman year. After getting bids from all of the investors and securing a deal, he and his dad sold millions of SpongeClowns.

"Well, he's *probably* going to be valedictorian," I whispered back.

Sasha tilted her head and grinned, though there was fire in her eyes. "Not if I have anything to say about it."

"I can't get a signal in here." Robbie took his seat next to me, unbuttoning the top button of his plaid shirt. "Is it just me, or is it like ninety degrees?"

I reached for my water and took a small sip. "Yeah, it's hot."

"Ugh," Sasha groaned, and I followed her gaze over my shoulder—Priya Gupta walked in, scanned the room, and visibly cringed. Saying that Priya used to be my best friend was an understatement. She'd been like a sister to me. She avoided my gaze now, casting her doe eyes to the floor as she hung her jacket and tugged down the loose sleeves of her white boho dress. When Robbie greeted her, she merely grunted in reply. Grief settled on my chest like a pile of stones, but I remained silent as Priya took her seat next to Diego. They muttered their hellos, and she busied herself examining her fingernails.

"Hi, Priya," Sasha said in a singsong voice.

Priya's jaw set in a rigid line. "Hi." I smiled at her, but she wouldn't look at me. My throat constricted. Would she ever talk to me again? Didn't she know how much I missed her?

"Congratulations! I had no idea you qualified for a scholarship," said Sasha. Priya was no valedictorian, but her grades were stellar.

Priya quirked her eyebrow. "Oh, you mean you cared who else would win?"

Sasha's smile faltered. "What's that supposed—"

I elbowed Sasha. "Leave it." She scrunched her eyebrows at me. "You don't want the scholarship people to hear you fighting." Sasha nodded, and Priya made a *psh* noise and went back to scrutinizing her fingernails.

Diego met my gaze again, and my insides pooled into a puddle around my feet. Just then, Robbie reached for my hand under the

11

table, and I jolted. He laughed. "Didn't mean to scare you." His hand was cool despite the warmth of the room, and he kissed my cheek as Diego watched. Oh, God. How was I going to get through this night?

"I'm starving," said Priya, fishing through her purse. "Ugh, I forgot to bring a granola bar."

Diego grabbed his backpack from the floor. "I have a candy bar somewhere in here. Want it?"

She waved him off. "No, no, it's fine. Thanks, though." As she eyed the ornate silver platters dotting the table, Scott Coleman—stoner extraordinaire—loped into the room. He wore his standard outfit—a black leather jacket over a black T-shirt and torn jeans, topped off with a black beanie.

Sasha gaped. "What are *you* doing here?"

"Same as the rest of you, methinks," said Scott. He grinned at Priya, who offered a shy smile in return.

"No way, man." Robbie scrunched his nose. Scott reeked of cigarette smoke. "You won a *scholarship*?"

Scott tugged at the collar of his leather jacket. "Seems so."

"Bullshit," said Robbie, and Sasha clucked her tongue.

Wow. Nobody was going to get along tonight, were they? "Guys. Be nice," I said, trying to lighten the mood. "Maybe he's a closet genius."

Scott winked at me. "Hey, Red. What's shakin'?"

"Bacon." This had been our customary greeting ever since we used to play together as kids, before we realized how little we had in common.

He nodded approvingly as he extracted a folded letter from his pocket. "I got this letter. It said to come here. So here I am."

"But how'd you qualify?" said Sasha, smiling sweetly. "Do you have some secret talent you've been hiding from us?"

"Nope." Scott shrugged and moseyed along the table. "But who the hell cares?" He plopped in the empty seat next to Priya and unwrapped a stick of gum. "Twenty kay is twenty kay. Besides, I had no plans tonight, and I like free food, so no rind off my orange."

Sasha cringed. "That's not an expression—"

The massive oak door behind me slammed shut with such force it reverberated through my chest, and the glasses in the china cabinets rattled. Everyone jumped, and a few people gasped.

"Wind tunnel?" I scooted my chair back and stood to open the door as thunder clapped outside.

"Oh, right." Robbie's shoulders relaxed. "The storm."

As I squeezed past Sasha, she tossed her hair back and focused on Scott again. "Anyway, they don't just arbitrarily hand out twenty thousand dollars." Leaning on her armrest, she perched her chin on her fist, like the mere concept of Scott winning anything was utterly fascinating. "Like, Robbie has baseball, Amber's a music prodigy, and I'm the director of the drama club. There has to be *some* reason you won."

"Yeah?" Scott's lips slapped with each chew. "Well, I'm director of the give-zero-fucks club. Maybe that counts for something."

"Uh . . . guys?" I jiggled the doorknob. It turned in my grip, but the door wouldn't budge. "I think the door's stuck."

"Seriously?" Priya glared at me, like being trapped in a room together was her version of hell.

"You're just a little weakling." Robbie strutted over and gave me a playful shove.

"I am not," I muttered, returning to my seat. I fished my cell phone from my purse. No signal.

As Robbie fought with the door, I scanned the table. Diego was the only one not looking at his phone. He stared at one of the windows as lightning brightened the alley outside. Robbie cursed and gave the doorknob a final shake. "Dammit. It really is stuck."

I rolled my eyes. "Told you."

"Shit." Sasha waved her phone above her head. "I have no signal."

"Me neither," I said.

"I haven't had one since we got here." Robbie took out his phone and shook it, like that would help.

"Same here," Priya chimed in.

"Well, the mayor's going to show up at some point, right?" asked Diego.

"Yep." I nodded. "He'll be able to let us out, or get help, or whatever."

"Shouldn't he be here by now?" Sasha checked her watch.

"He's probably just running late," said Diego.

Sasha eyed Robbie, who slammed his fist against the lock and jiggled the doorknob again. "But what if he had to cancel?" Her voice quavered. "What if he tried calling to let us know, but couldn't get through? What if no one's coming—"

"Sasha, chill out," I said. Diego trained his eyes along the table with a frown.

"If he couldn't get through," said Scott, "his office would send some secretary here to tell us, right?"

"Huh, weird," said Diego. "The table's set for six." Priya pointed at each place setting as she silently counted. Diego was right—there were eight chairs, but the ones on either end had no place settings, plates, or glasses laid out.

"Yeah? So?" said Scott.

Diego and I exchanged a look. "That's bizarre," I said. "If the mayor's having dinner with us, why is the table only set for six?"

"Are you saying nobody's coming to let us out?" Sasha said, an octave too high.

"Someone'll be here to serve food and stuff," said Scott. "A waiter or something?"

"It looks like they already did." Diego motioned to the covered trays lining the table. "But why would they serve dinner before we got here?"

Scott lifted the lid on the tray closest to him, revealing a whole roasted chicken and steamed veggies. "Is it just me, or is this kinda weird?"

"For once, it's not just you," Robbie muttered, uncovering a salad platter.

"Well . . ." Priya licked her lips, eyeing a bowl of roasted yams. "We might as well eat, right?"

"I guess so . . ." I bit my lip.

Robbie dropped the lid on the floor behind him. "Whatever.

Let's get this party started, shall we?" He uncovered another chicken platter. "They got any booze in this joint?"

"Yeah, but it's all at the bar out there," said Sasha, uncovering a platter of deviled eggs. "Gross. How long have those been sitting out?"

I stood and lifted the lid from the biggest platter in the center of the table.

Sasha and Priya both shrieked, making me almost drop the lid. My heart fell into my stomach as everyone gaped at the contents of the tray.

A syringe.

An envelope.

And something that looked an awful lot like a bomb.

"What the actual fuck?" said Robbie. A shiver coasted down my spine as I stared at the syringe. It was filled with a pale beige liquid, and the needle was uncapped, glinting from the chandelier lights overhead.

"What the hell is that . . . that *thing*?" Sasha cried.

A couple of plastic canisters the size of milk cartons were strapped to half a dozen brown logs wired to a small digital clock and stack of batteries. Each canister was half full of some sort of yellow liquid. The clock faced the ceiling, its red numbers counting down from fifty-nine forty-five. Fifty-nine forty-four. Fifty-nine forty-three. Fifty-nine forty-two.

"Looks like a bomb," said Robbie, clenching his jaw.

"I started the timer . . ." I said to no one in particular, gripping the lid in both hands. "When I lifted the lid, I must have started the timer."

"That can't be real," said Priya. "Can it?"

"And what's with the syringe?" asked Sasha.

"It's labeled." Diego leaned over to read, "'Botulinum toxin'— holy shit." He blanched.

"What's butool—what's that?" asked Priya. She clutched his arm so hard her knuckles turned white.

Diego kept reading. "It says, 'Warning: Avoid contact with skin. A single drop can be fatal. Full injection causes immediate death.'"

We all exchanged baffled expressions. "What's in the envelope?" asked Robbie. Nobody moved.

Fifty-nine thirty. Fifty-nine twenty-nine.

I set the lid under the table and plucked the envelope from the tray, opened the flap, and pulled out a sheet of paper. Unfolding it, I cleared my throat and read aloud.

"'Welcome to dinner, and again, congratulations on being selected. Now you must do the selecting. Within the hour, you must choose someone in this room to die. If you don't, everyone dies.'"

I YEAR, I MONTH AGO

JANUARY OF JUNIOR YEAR

I'd spent the last three years avoiding bitches like Sasha Harris.

But I had a favor to ask of her, and my future depended on it.

As director of the drama club, she chose each semester's play, and I wanted to compose the score for the next one. It was my only shot to get into USC's film score program. Dad had recently broken the news that he couldn't afford to fly me to auditions in the fall, so I had to think of some way to impress the pants off the college admissions officers—something the other two thousand virtual applicants wouldn't attempt. With only three undergraduate film score programs in the country, the competition was fierce. Scoring our school play set to a live orchestra and sending in the recording was the best plan I could hatch.

But it meant I had to talk to *her*, Sasha freaking Harris, basically royalty at Brewster High—haughty, pretentious, and intimidating as hell, yet inexplicably revered. We hadn't met until freshman year; our town had two middle schools that merged into Brewster High, and Priya and I had gone to Crompond while Sasha and her friends went to Hampton. But I'd heard whispers of her mean streak, how cutthroat she could be. Had I witnessed her nastiness myself? No. Had I gotten close enough to? Don't be ridiculous. I wasn't about to risk being her next victim.

Until now.

So here I was on the first day back after winter break, watching her cross the cafeteria, plotting my approach. Her besties, Amy and Maria, hovered around her like gnats, wasting away the minutes by chewing over the latest gossip. I wasn't sure what scared me more: rejection from USC, or Sasha.

"My hands are shaking." I raised my hand to eye level, showing off trembling fingers. "Dammit, I can't do this."

My best friend Priya's posture relaxed. "Oh, thank God. Let's get out of here." She spun to leave, her long, shiny black hair whipping my arm.

"Wait!" I grabbed her wrist. "You're gonna let me wimp out that easily?"

"You're not wimping out—you're coming to your senses," she rationalized, darting a glance at Sasha and her crew. "You don't need to score the stupid play. I'm sure your recordings will get you into any music program you want."

"All the other applicants will have recordings, too." I wiped sweat from my upper lip as the trio finally settled at an empty table in the middle of the cafeteria. "But they'll all submit the standard stuff—you know, tracks for commercials, movie trailers, that sort of thing. I have to do something *epic*. Something to stand out."

Priya raised her eyebrows. "What, your ten thousand YouTube followers won't make you stand out?"

"Ten thousand's nothing. Some other kids have way more. I *have* to do this."

"What makes you think Sasha's even going to *consider* it? They always pick some Broadway play, and the music's already done. Asking Sasha to compose new music for the play is like asking if I could join the freaking cheerleading squad. It won't happen."

Priya had always wanted to be a cheerleader. Problem was, she never had the guts to try out. "If I get her to agree, you're *so* trying out for the cheerleading squad."

Her eyes widened like saucers. "I am *so* not. Sasha's captain now. She'd never let me in."

I glanced at Sasha again. How had she hooked her talons into everything? It was like the girl was determined to be the center of attention at all times. And nobody said no to Sasha Harris.

Now I had to make sure she didn't say no to me.

Taking a deep breath, I paused before tugging out the earbud lodged in my right ear, soaking in a last bit of energy from an epic fantasy battle scene track. Some people needed liquid courage, but I only needed a shot of music. The powerful chords and crescendos made me feel like I was bravely facing my foe, ready for combat.

"I'm doing this."

"I'm officially not letting you." Priya clutched my elbow as I started toward them. "As your best friend, I can't let you put yourself in Sasha's warpath. Right now she barely knows we exist, and we should keep it that way. Remember what happened to your sister? Remember what people like Sasha can do?"

My throat constricted at the mere mention of my sister, and I yanked my elbow from Priya's grip. "Like I need the reminder?"

My sister Maggie's death taught me to avoid girls with mean streaks like the plague. I knew what it meant to be the brunt of their jokes, victim to their cruelty. I didn't know what Maggie endured until things went too far—four years stood between us (she was a senior when I was in eighth grade), so we hadn't attended the same school since elementary school. Guilt stifled me whenever I thought of Maggie, and how oblivious I'd been to those girls' abuse.

By the time I learned the truth, it was too late.

After she died, I withdrew from my clique of girlfriends. Part of me was terrified they'd eventually turn on me, too. But mostly, I couldn't stand their pity. Most people were awkward as hell around someone in mourning. They'd stare at me with these wide, sorrowful eyes, and their uneasiness made me feel like I should've been the one comforting *them*.

At the time, I couldn't handle it. It was bad enough watching my parents grieve, and needing to be strong for them. Priya was the only one who acted normal around me, letting me pour my heart out without getting that disquieted look in her eyes, refusing to leave my side.

So instead of partying or flailing at school dances, we camped out in my room for movie marathons or "jam sessions"—I'd work on a song at my keyboard with huge red headphones glomming my skull, while she'd sprawl on the carpet with Mittens, reading a fantasy novel or learning David Thurston's magic tricks from his Netflix show *Manic Magic*. As a textbook introvert, Priya was living her best life, but sometimes I missed being part of a big group.

"I'm sorry." Priya's voice was strained. "I just don't want to see you get hurt." She eyed Sasha and her friends huddled over their table, whispering animatedly. They seemed prepped for the runway compared to their neighboring table, where Becky Wallace and our old clique donned a mix of too-big glasses, sweatshirts, and poorly executed French braids.

Suddenly, Sasha slapped the table, threw her head back, and laughed heartily. I couldn't imagine having such boisterous self-confidence. People turned to gape, like they wanted in on the joke. If Sasha Harris thought something was funny, it must be worth hearing.

As long as it wasn't about you.

My stomach clenched. I could let fear rule my future and keep being afraid of girls like Sasha. Or I could rise above this petty high school crap and do whatever I could to get into music school and someday produce epic movie and TV scores.

I had to do this. I *had* to.

Besides, what was the worst that could happen? She could say no. She could make fun of me. Torture me. Turn me into an object of ridicule and make me want to—

"Oof." Someone behind me collided hard with my arm, tearing me from my thoughts.

"My bad!" Zane Carter called over his shoulder as he headed for Sasha's table.

As I rubbed my arm, Priya ogled him. "Oh my God. He touched you."

"That's kind of an understatement."

Priya had worshiped Zane for years. He was the spitting image of her favorite magician, David Thurston. And with those blazing green eyes, shaggy chestnut hair, defined cheekbones, and perma-smirk, who could blame her?

Well, I didn't get the appeal of the perma-smirk.

Either way, she turned wide-eyed and mute whenever he appeared, which made it kind of difficult to have any sort of meaningful interaction. I thought she'd finally forgotten about him over winter break (I certainly had) until a couple of days ago, when she went to the grocery store with her mom and spotted him examining a protein shake nutrition label in aisle seven. I knew it was aisle seven because Priya told me about it seventeen times.

"You know . . . if we go over there," I said, "you might get to talk to Zane." I had to get this over with, and it'd be much easier if I didn't have to approach Sasha alone.

"What?" Priya gasped. "He'd never talk to me. No way."

"Why not? I heard he broke up with his girlfriend last month." I nudged her with my elbow. "Maybe he'll be into you."

"Yeah, right!"

"C'mon, let's go see." I grabbed Priya's wrist and, ignoring her frantic protestations, dragged her to Sasha and Zane's table. Zane typed on his phone, elbows on his knees, as the girls giggled over something. "Hey, guys—"

Oh. Oh, no. Zane's baseball teammate Robbie Nelson sat next to him, scribbling last-minute answers on a homework assignment. I hadn't noticed him with his baseball cap shading his face. He glanced up at me, and my stomach gave a small lurch.

Robbie had one of those faces you couldn't help staring at— well defined, with a high-bridged nose, angular jaw, and these wolfish gray eyes that made you go all deer-in-headlights when they landed on you. While I was invisible to Sasha, which was exactly how I wanted it, Robbie's eyes would flick to mine in the halls, his head tilting like a question mark as he offered a shy grin. I'd always look away first, flustered to be caught gawking. Since we didn't have any classes together, he probably didn't even know my name.

But I couldn't let him psych me out. I had to talk to Sasha.

"So, um, hey," I started again. I tossed my hair back and flashed a wide smile, ignoring my wobbly legs. "How was your winter break?"

The five of them only offered vacant stares. I kept smiling, forcing down the heat threatening to creep up my neck. My mind went blank, and words seemed like an altogether foreign concept. All the scenarios I'd concocted in the shower this morning for what to say jumbled in my brain. What did popular people even talk about? Oh, hell. These people were the rulers of the roost, and we were like worms wriggling into their coop. What was I thinking?

Finally, Robbie broke the silence. "It was nice. You're Amber, right?"

So he *did* know my name. Warmth spread through my veins. He reversed his cap, and his gray eyes sparkled under the fluorescent lights as he gave me his usual lopsided grin. His two front teeth were a little crooked, somehow making his smile even cuter.

He stood and swung over two chairs from a neighboring table like they were light as feathers. "I don't think we've ever met before."

"I know, crazy!" I said, taking a seat. "Our class isn't *that* big. But better late than never, right? That's, you know, a thing people say." I was totally blabbering, and despite my best efforts, I blushed profusely. Priya, of course, had reverted to her mute state. She stared at Zane, practically drooling.

Amy's and Maria's smiles didn't reach their eyes, betraying their suspicion. Why had we barged onto their turf? Before I could say anything else, Sasha reached over and ran a lock of my hair through her fingers. "Oh my God, I love your hair color." Her voice was so melodic, I couldn't tell if she was mocking me. "Which is it?"

"It's . . . um . . . red?"

She laughed throatily. "Obviously. I mean the swatch. The dye you use."

"Oh." I smoothed my hair back. "I don't dye it, actually."

Her eyes narrowed. "Bullshit. That's virgin hair?" I stiffened, biting the inside of my cheek. Did she think I was lying? She leaned back in her chair, draping her elbow over its frame. "You lucky bitch." Her own chestnut hair fell in loose waves over her shoulders, sleek and shimmering, and the mole next to her left eye disappeared into the crinkles when she smiled brightly enough to warm the room. She was giving me a compliment. Snarky, but genuine.

"You guys, I'm having a brain fart," said Amy, twirling a strand of shoulder-length blond hair. "Are cheerleading tryouts today or tomorrow?"

"Today." Sasha cracked her knuckles one at a time. "I can't believe Emily and Ellie moved to Wisconsin. What the hell's in Wisconsin?"

"Potatoes?" Maria popped a bite of a muffin in her mouth and flicked a crumb from her periwinkle lace dress.

"That's Idaho, idiot." Amy looked down her sharp nose at Maria. "Wisconsin has cheese or whatever."

Robbie rolled his eyes at them. "Either of you cheer?" he asked us.

Priya shook her head automatically, but I said, "Priya does." Her eyes widened, the cords in her neck bulging. "Well, she wants to. She took gymnastics lessons for years." I nodded at her encouragingly, but she seemed to be willing herself out of existence.

"Hey, so did Sasha," said Amy, suddenly interested in us. "That gives you a leg up."

"But Sasha qualified for the Olympics when she was *twelve*," Maria chimed in, her brunette ringlets bobbing. She always starred in our school musicals, and once even made it to the final casting round of some singing reality TV show.

"Guys, stop it," Sasha said bashfully, but her smile faltered. "You have to be sixteen to qualify; I just scored high enough to be able to."

"Wow!" I said. "Will you compete?"

Sasha shifted in her seat and clenched her jaw. "No."

"Why not? Seems like an amazing opportunity—"

"I can't." The words left her lips as a whisper. "I broke my leg in a car accident. Needed surgery." Lines creased her forehead as she cringed at the memory. Suddenly it was like the girl who had everything had nothing at all. The transformation was staggering. I had no idea about her accident. By the time high school started, Sasha seemed on top of the world.

"It's fine now"—she waved off my concerned look—"but it took a while to recover. I can do stunts and stuff again, but . . . it's not the same."

"Still . . . I'm so sorry—"

Zane suddenly tossed his phone onto the table. "Good news. My folks are outta town this weekend." He pointed at himself with both hands. "Party at my place on Friday."

"Nice." Robbie bumped fists with him.

Sasha perked up, the glimmer returning to her eyes. "Do you have any booze? I thought your parents locked up their stash after last time."

"Yeah, they did. We'll have to get some."

I cleared my throat, eager to sidle into their conversation again. "If you can't, you could always have a game night or something. You know what's hilarious?" I was about to say Apples to

Apples, my favorite game, but thought better of it. "Cards Against Humanity. You can borrow my deck."

"When's the last time we had a game night?" said Sasha. "What were we, like, twelve?" Was she mocking me or reminiscing?

"I love Cards Against Humanity." Robbie grinned at me, dimples creasing his cheeks. "I'd be down for that." His smile was infectious, and I found myself beaming back.

Zane punched Robbie's arm. "Lame!"

"Whatever, man." Robbie shook him off. "Better than sitting around staring at each other." Zane shrugged and fiddled with his phone again. Robbie scooted his chair closer to me and wagged a finger between me and Priya. "You two should join. Bring over that deck yourself."

Oh. My. God. Robbie Nelson just invited us to a party. My heart skipped about twenty beats. I should probably be dead. "Sure! We're free," I managed to say.

"Nice."

"I guess we shouldn't get too wasted, anyway." Sasha snapped her fingers at Amy and Maria. "Don't forget, my mom's taking us to see *Phantom of the Opera* on Saturday."

"On Broadway?" I asked. "I love that musical. It's so sad."

"Her sister dropped out of college to be one of the ballerinas," Amy said to me, pointing at Sasha, "and now she's understudy for the lead—"

"Can we *not* talk about my perfect sister right now?" Sasha rolled her eyes. "Bad enough we'll have to fawn over her this weekend."

"At least we have backstage passes," said Maria.

Sasha nodded. "True. The guy who plays the Phantom is so hot." She scrolled through her phone and leaned over to show me a picture of the dark, brooding Phantom.

"Oh my God, I'm so jealous," I said. "Oh, and . . . speaking of plays . . ." My heart thrummed wildly, but this was a perfect segue. "I have a question for you. It's about the school play. You know, in the spring. I was wondering if you'd considered putting on a play with original music."

"Why would we do that?" Maria asked a little defensively. As the drama club's perpetual prima donna, she'd probably hate this idea. But Sasha was the one I had to convince. As director, she got to help the drama club supervisor, Mr. Norris, choose the play.

I swallowed hard. "I'd love to score the spring play. An entirely original score."

"Whoa, seriously?" said Sasha. "That'd be so much work . . ."

"Please, hear me out." I licked my lips. Sasha *had* to be stuffing her résumé to get into some Ivy League college. I knew what angle to take. "Directing a play with an original score and a live orchestra would be way more impressive on your transcript than putting on some Broadway play."

"Maybe . . ." Sasha groaned. "But the sheer amount of coordination that would take—"

"Sasha, chill," said Robbie. "Let her finish." He threw me a reassuring smile. Was it weird that I wanted to throw myself in his lap? Probably.

But I was on a mission here. I took a deep breath and focused on Sasha. "I'd compose all of the music myself based on your stage direction, and I'd coordinate with the orchestra. Mr. Torrente already agreed to this."

"What, you think you could compose an entire musical?" Maria crossed her arms and scrunched her brow. "Like, yourself?"

"Not a musical. It'd be a play, with an orchestral score—"

"Oh, hell no," said Maria.

But Sasha sat silent, arms crossed, glancing between me and Maria.

"We don't even have to do something *completely* original," I went on. "We could pick something like *A Streetcar Named Desire*, or *Romeo and Juliet*, and set it to new music."

"No way," said Maria.

"It's a great idea. Truly, it is." Sasha shook her head. "It'd just be too much work."

Frustrated, I huffed. "But now that you're the director, don't you want to do something unique?"

"I'm sorry," said Sasha, her tone uncertain. "But we can't." She watched Maria slump back in her chair, relieved.

"But—"

"She said no!" said Maria.

"Well, who the hell made her queen of the universe?" The words tumbled out of my mouth before I could stop them.

Oh, God. What did I do?

My cheeks reddened as Sasha frowned and tilted her head, narrowing her eyes at me. Maria's jaw dropped. Priya looked like she was literally about to start seizing. But Robbie looked impressed, and Amy struggled to stifle her laughter. Even Zane finally looked up from his phone.

After a moment so long it broke the laws of physics, Sasha threw her head back and burst out laughing. Everyone else followed her lead.

"Oh my God! The look on your face!" Sasha finally said, wiping her eyes with her pinkies, careful not to smudge her mascara.

I let out a nervous chuckle, gripping my quivering fingers in my lap. Sasha rested an elbow on the back of her chair, poking her cheek with her tongue, sizing me up. Maybe she was impressed I'd challenged her when everyone else sucked up to her all the time.

When everyone else quieted, Robbie said, "C'mon, Sasha, I think it's a good idea. Nobody wants to see *Bye Bye Birdie* anyway."

"That's true," said Amy. "That's some lame shit."

Sasha raised her eyebrows. "You said you loved *Bye Bye Birdie*!"

Amy slinked back in her seat a bit. "Er . . . I kinda lied. Sorry."

"Well," said Sasha, "I *do* love *Romeo and Juliet*. So dark and romantic. I'd be down for that."

Whoa. Might this really happen? Hope blossomed in my chest as Robbie threw me a conspiratorial wink.

"Yeah, I guess that'd be fun," said Maria unconvincingly. I felt kind of bad to deprive her of her singing glory, but she'd dazzle as Juliet.

"Can I play Romeo?" asked Zane.

Robbie scoffed. "Dude, you're not even in drama club."

The warning bell rang, and Sasha stood and draped her messenger bag over her shoulder. "Alright, alright. Let's talk. But we'll need to get the rest of the drama club on board . . . everyone loves doing Broadway." She snapped her fingers. "I have an idea."

"What is it?" My heart leapt into my throat.

"I'll invite them to Zane's party on Friday. And it'd be amazing if you could bring some booze. You know, loosen them up a bit. I'm sure they'll at least hear you out."

My stomach twisted in a knot. "Booze? You want *me* to bring alcohol to a party?" I had no idea where to get drinks.

"Tequila would be great."

"Or vodka." Zane smirked. "Off-brand is fine, we're not picky."

Priya and I exchanged a wary look. "But . . . I don't have a fake ID or anything." I stood and stumbled after them. "Where am I supposed to get booze?"

Sasha gave an exaggerated shrug. "I mean, you could show up empty-handed. But if you want to impress them, you'll just have to figure it out."

59 MINUTES LEFT

My pulse raced as I stared at the syringe of poison and the bomb atop the gleaming silver platter. *Within the hour, you must choose someone in this room to die. If you don't, everyone dies.*

"That's one sick prank," said Robbie. "Who the hell would do this?" He grabbed the note from me, his eyes darting across the page. Diego leaned against the edge of the table, studying the bomb.

"Wait, wait, wait." Sasha clutched her throat. "Does that mean . . . if we don't kill one of *us*, that bomb will go off in an hour?"

Scott burst out laughing.

"What the hell is so funny?" asked Sasha.

He leaned back in his chair. "It's obviously a joke, and you fell for it like an anvil."

"Doesn't seem very funny to me," muttered Robbie.

"Who would do this?" Priya cried. "Who would think up something so awful?"

"Did anyone see who shut the door?" I asked. Priya and Scott shook their heads.

"No." Diego slumped back into his seat. "I didn't see anyone."

"Me neither," said Sasha. "I was too busy talking to that creep." She motioned toward Scott, and he scoffed.

"Someone probably stood behind the door and pushed it closed," said Diego.

Priya visibly shivered. "Does that mean someone was hiding behind the door the whole time?"

"And are they still out there?" My voice shook slightly.

Robbie slammed the note on the table and scooted his chair back with a screech, making me jump. "This is ridiculous." He rounded his chair and pounded on the door. "Hey! Unlock the door!" His jaw tightened when nobody replied. "This isn't funny. Unlock the door now!"

"Oh my God," said Priya. Sasha took slow, deep breaths, trying to keep calm, but her eyes darted around the room frantically.

"Robbie." I rushed toward him, grabbing his hand. "Calm down. It's just some morbid joke. I'm sure they'll get bored and let us out."

He shook me off and knelt, peering with one eye into the large keyhole below the doorknob. "There's no key."

"I didn't hear a lock click or anything," Sasha added.

"It all happened so fast." I touched the oak door, the wood

cool under my palm, and turned back to the group. "Think they're still out there?"

Robbie shrugged. "Who the hell knows?"

"Hello?" I called out. "Is anyone there?"

"This is bullshit." Robbie kicked the door. "What kind of sick psycho would—"

"Shhh." I waved him off and pressed my ear against the door, but all I could hear was Priya muttering, "Oh my God, oh my God," over and over again. "Priya, shut up," I said. She clamped her lips shut, her eyes glassy.

I pressed my ear against the door again, straining to hear something. A voice. Footsteps. Someone breathing. Anything. But all I could hear were the muffled baritones and strings from the orchestral music playing in the main dining room.

"Nothing?" asked Diego.

I shook my head and knelt, peeking through the keyhole. My heart raced as I held my breath. Years of watching horror movies had trained me to expect an eyeball to appear on the other side. My whole body tensed, ready to leap backward.

But all I could see was one of the red-cushioned booths across the main dining room. There was no movement of any kind. "There's nobody there." I stood and turned back to the group. "I don't see anything."

"Damn, it's so hot in here." Sasha touched the back of her hand to her forehead.

"It really is." I wiped my upper lip and scanned the walls. "Crap. The thermostat must be out in the main dining room."

"It's gotten worse since we got here." Priya tugged on her hair. "I just want to go home."

I gasped and bit my lip. *Home.* I forgot to text Mom when Robbie and I got here. "Oh, no." I grabbed my phone from the table and raised it toward the ceiling, but I had no signal whatsoever. Sasha tried the same thing, stretching toward the windows facing the alley.

"Nothing," she confirmed. "I can't get anything."

"Crap, crap, crap." My chest tightened like a vise squeezing my heart. What if something terrible did happen here tonight? What was the last thing I said to my mother as I ran out the door? Did I tell her I loved her? When was the last time I told my parents I loved them? A chill tore through me despite the room's warmth, and I shook the morbid thought away. This was just a prank. It wasn't real.

"Oh my God." Sasha hunched over, hugging herself around the middle. "This can't be happening."

"So what do we do?" asked Robbie.

Sasha straightened and rubbed her forehead with trembling fingers. "I can't believe this is happening. What if we're really going to have to do this? What if they really make us kill one of us?"

1 YEAR, 1 MONTH AGO

JANUARY OF JUNIOR YEAR

"Priya, you're killing me." I slumped over my keyboard, racked with giggles as Priya scrambled to pick up the fifty-two playing cards she'd shot all over my room.

"Sorry, sorry!" She threw herself across my bed, nearly knocking over the camera's tripod to recover a card that slid between the mattress and the wall.

I slipped off my headphones and toggled the camera's Record button. "Oh my God, you're such a klutz." I'd agreed to help Priya film and score her latest magic act, which she supposedly spent the last week perfecting. We'd produced several videos for her fledgling YouTube channel, but this was Priya's first foray into playing card flourishes.

"I swear I'll catch them next time."

"You only swore that the last dozen times," I teased, stealing a glance at my phone. Nine thirty. Zane's party started a half hour ago, but we couldn't head over until I had alcohol in hand. And that couldn't happen until my parents went to bed.

I planned to swipe some of their booze since they hadn't touched the stuff in years. They used to have a glass each night together, but one time Dad got so blackout drunk after Maggie died, Mom and I thought *he* died. He'd passed out on the living room floor, and Mom screamed at me to dial 911 when he wouldn't wake up. After he got his stomach pumped, he vowed never to drink and scare us like that again.

"Think they'll go to bed soon?" Priya asked, reading the stress on my face.

I often found Mom working at the kitchen table on her free-lance editing projects when I padded in for water at three in the morning, but usually not on Fridays. "Yeah, they usually turn in by nine to watch Netflix. Can't be long now."

Priya adjusted the camera on its tripod. "Think we have time for one more take?"

"Maybe practice that waterfall thing a couple times first." Apparently making the cards waterfall from one hand into the other before the reveal would make the trick more impressive, but so far the cards found themselves in every possible square inch of my room except for Priya's other hand.

"Sorry! I swear I did it right a bazillion times before. But as soon as someone else is watching, I mess up." She positioned the deck in her hand. "Ready? Ready? I can do this."

I held my breath as she squeezed the edges of the deck to create a half-moon. She released the deck, and the cards flew toward her other outstretched hand, hit her palm, and scattered in every direction. She gave me a sheepish look as I pressed my lips together, struggling to contain a laugh. But it was no use—after a moment's pause, we both collapsed into a fit of giggles.

"I think you're supposed to catch them," I said, catching my breath.

"Obviously."

"You sure you're not feeling dizzy?"

"Positive." She held out her hands, checking for tremors. "I just had a granola bar a half hour ago." Priya had the misfortune of having non-diabetic hypoglycemia. She constantly munched on trail mix or nutty granola bars, otherwise she'd get all dizzy and trembly. In her words, it made her a "perpetually hangry klutz."

She rubbed her eyes. "Maybe you can just write the music, and I can plan my reveal around it?"

"Well, I have it most of the way there, but I need to see the final beats of the act. Here's what I have so far." I unplugged my headphones from the keyboard so she could listen. "The music will be discreet—sort of light and ethereal." Priya nodded along as my fingers danced across my keyboard. "We mainly want it to emphasize key moments, without being distracting. And a crescendo will cut to silence at the reveal, but I can't get the timing right until we record the whole act."

"Ah, that's great." She wiped a hand down her face. "I can try it without the waterfall."

"No, no, no." I crossed my arms. "This all hinges on the waterfall. Besides, I've watched you toss those cards like fifteen times. You're not giving up on it now—"

Mom rapped on my open door. "Hey, guys. Need anything before Dad and I turn in?"

Oh, God. It was almost time. I rolled my eyes, hiding my anxiety. "Fortunately, I've been blessed with the talent of microwaving popcorn myself."

Mom snorted. "Aren't you so clever?" She had dark rings under her eyes, and had probably been editing all night. I used to think she was escaping into words like I escaped into music, but when I heard her and Dad fighting about dipping too deep into their retirement savings, I realized she was taking on more clients to supplement his reduced income. I'd offered to get a job last year to help out, but Mom insisted I focus on school and my music. "Hey, weren't you two going to a party tonight?"

Priya and I exchanged a look. "Yeah," I said, "but we want to finish up this project first."

"Okay. Just remember, text me when you get there." Ever since Maggie died, Mom constantly needed reassurance that I was still alive, and my phone buzzed with check-ins throughout the day. "And if you need me to come pick you up, you call me, no matter what time it is."

"I know, I know. Night, Mom."

"Night, honey. You two have fun doing . . ." She glanced at the camera on its tripod and the cards all over the place. ". . . well, whatever it is you're doing."

When she disappeared, Priya whispered, "How long should we wait?"

"Like, five minutes?" My heart was already trying to jam itself through my throat. "She was already washed up."

"Is that long enough?"

I checked my phone. "We can't wait any longer. I don't know how late Zane's party will go." My insides jittered. It wasn't just that I had to be on point with the drama club—I'd also never been to a real high school party before, let alone one with the most popular kids in school. A mix of nerves and excitement buzzed in my veins.

I put on my jacket and slipped my messenger bag over my shoulder. "Okay, so first I'll get the key from my dad's desk. Then I'll sneak into the living room and grab a bottle. You keep a lookout at the staircase, and start coughing if my parents open their door. Then we'll head out the back door."

"Got it."

"Oh, wait." I grabbed my new deck of Cards Against Humanity from my desk in case Robbie was serious about playing. My stomach wobbled . . . and it wasn't just from nerves. "Okay. Ready."

We tiptoed upstairs, and I waved Priya toward the other staircase while I slipped into my dad's office. I inched toward his desk in the darkness, arms outstretched, my heartbeat thundering in my ears.

Careful not to make a peep, I slid open the drawer. Suddenly, something thudded to my left. I gasped and leapt back. Two glowing eyes stared up at me.

"Mittens," I whispered. He'd jumped down from the bookshelf. "Silly cat." I patted him on the head as he slinked between my legs, purring.

Using the light from my phone, I quickly pocketed the right key and tiptoed to the living room, nodding at Priya as I passed. Her eyes were wide, but she nodded back. Muffled voices from my parents' TV floated downstairs. I edged across the living room, the dim light from the streetlamps filtering through the curtains, and unlocked the liquor cabinet.

As I opened the door, the hinges squeaked like they hadn't seen use in ages. Just then, Priya burst into a coughing fit, signaling a warning. I froze. Oh, God. Did my parents hear that noise? *I'm so busted*, I thought as Dad called down the stairs, "Everything okay?" How was I going to explain this? My fingers tingled with fear.

"Yeah, totally fine!" Priya called back up, somehow managing to keep her voice steady. "Just choking on my own spit." She coughed for emphasis. "Going to get some water."

"Alright. G'night, kiddo." The staircase glowed as he flicked on the bathroom light, and dimmed as he shut the door.

Priya peeked into the living room. "Hurry!" she whispered.

I grabbed the first bottle within reach and dropped it into my bag—the drama club would have to make do with whatever it was—locked the liquor cabinet, and returned the key to my dad's desk. Priya followed me outside through the kitchen to grab our bikes.

Zane's house was only a few blocks away. He lived in a generic three-story colonial with perfectly groomed shrubberies dotting its front lawn, and a rusty old basketball hoop at the end of the driveway. The booming bass of a rap song seeped through his front door. I texted Mom to let her know our bikes hadn't committed murder as Priya rang the doorbell.

"Well, well, well." Sasha opened the door, her smile instantly calming my nerves. "I didn't think you were going to make it."

I looked past her to the empty foyer. "Where is everyone?" Priya asked. Laughter floated from somewhere down the hall, as if in response.

"In the basement."

"Ah." Shifting my weight on my feet, I swallowed hard, unsure what to do next. I reached into my messenger bag to pull out the bottle, but Sasha leapt forward and grabbed my wrist.

"Not here! Do you want the neighbors to see?" Giggling, she pulled me inside, beckoning for Priya to follow. "Your timing's perfect—we just ran out of beer. So, listen . . . nobody from the drama club could make it tonight. Well, except for Maria."

My stomach dropped. "Seriously?" I'd stolen booze from my parents for nothing?

"Yeah . . . but that's okay—we should talk strategy first anyway. And I should probably listen to some of your music."

"Right, of course. I have plenty of samples you could listen to." I pulled out my phone and scrolled through my library.

"Awesome. Email me some, and I'll listen later, okay? Let's just have fun tonight." She threw her arms over her head. "You ladies ready to party?"

I grinned, trying to hide my surprise. "Sure!" I couldn't believe Sasha still wanted to hang out with us even though the drama club hadn't shown. Maybe she wasn't such a bitch after all. I'd assumed those rumors about her were true—but maybe I should have given her the benefit of the doubt. She entwined her arm with mine and led us downstairs, where a couple dozen kids were lounging around in clusters holding red cups or cans of beer.

Robbie, Zane, and a couple girls from the cheerleading squad sat cross-legged in a circle. Robbie stared at his phone with a surly frown, his thick brows furrowed. But when he glanced up and spotted me, a grin broke out on his face. "Heyyy!" he called over. "You made it! Did you bring the game?"

My insides turned to mush. "I did!" He pumped his fist. "Hey, Zane, you're in, too, right?" I said, hooking my arm through Priya's so she felt included. I wanted to make sure she had a good time. "It's fun, I promise."

Robbie slapped Zane's shoulder. "C'mon, man."

"Okay, okay," said Zane.

As they stood, Sasha extended two red Solo cups to me and Priya. "Awkward shot glasses, but whatevs."

Priya shook her head and clasped her hands behind her back. Her mother would homeschool her if she ever caught her drinking. I bit my lip. "Er . . . no thanks."

"Aw, c'mon." She shoved a cup into my hand. "If you're gonna party with us, you're gonna *party*." Amy and Maria whooped, and something in my chest fluttered.

Priya and I used to have dorky sleepovers with friends like Becky Wallace, but our version of "partying" meant playing Truth or Dare (mainly Truth, because we were all wimps) and using

44

Becky's pink karaoke machine. But this was a *real* party. I never imagined the cheerleaders and jocks would be so welcoming to a couple of nerds.

Sasha sidled close, rested her forearm on my shoulder, and flicked my messenger bag. "So, what've you got?"

I freed the bottle from my bag and handed it to her. "Here you go."

"Ooh, Jack Daniel's." Sasha examined the label. "Nice. My parents love this stuff. Our pantry's full of it."

"Oh, cool. Did you bring some, too?"

A sly smile inched across her lips. "What, and risk getting caught?"

57 MINUTES LEFT

"Let's not panic, okay?" I said to Sasha. "Nobody's going to make us kill anyone. This has to be a prank."

"How do you *know* that?" said Sasha, her voice trembling. "It can't be me. It *can't* be. I don't want to die!"

"Oh my God!" Scott suddenly shrieked at the top of his lungs. Everyone jumped a mile high. He stood and approached Sasha. "Can I . . . can I get your autograph?" he pleaded with wide eyes, clasping his chest.

Sasha furrowed her brow. "What the hell are you talking about?"

"It's just . . . I never thought I'd meet the person the world revolves around."

Her expression soured. "Oh, for the love of God," she muttered, raking back her hair with shaking fingers.

"Will you stop kidding around, man?" Robbie shoved Scott away from Sasha.

"Yeah," Sasha agreed. "You don't know this is a joke."

Scott wiped the starstruck expression off his face. "And you don't know it's real."

I set a reassuring hand on Sasha's shoulder. "You're being ridiculous. This is just some stupid prank. We're not killing anyone. So let's just calm down and find a way out of here." I glanced around the room. There weren't any other visible exits besides the door and two windows.

"You read the note." Sasha shoved Scott out of her way and plucked the note from the table. "*Within the hour, you must choose someone in this room to die. If you don't, everyone dies.* Who would joke about something like that? We'll have to pick someone." Her eyes were wide and frantic.

A wave of nausea rolled over me. She truly believed this was real. But I could never kill anyone. I'd seen death before. I shuddered to think of that instant the soul leaves a body. That instant when a person becomes nothing more than an empty shell, a decaying carcass. Besides, this was just a sick joke. And we had an hour—well, fifty-six minutes—to figure this out. But panicking was the worst thing we could do. Panicking solved nothing.

"Listen," I said, "even if it's not a joke, it's probably some sort of test to see how we'll react."

Diego met my gaze. "You mean . . . you think it's part of the scholarship?"

"Exactly."

"Nifty prize." Scott took off his beanie and threw it on the table, ruffling his hair. "Maybe next year they'll lock the winners in a graveyard and convince them zombies are after them." He chortled. "That sounds way more fun than this."

"No, it's not the prize, obviously." Diego rested his elbows on the table, steepling his fingers. "Maybe they're running a scenario to see who has the best leadership qualities. Who can see past the threat and find a way to get everyone out safely."

"I dunno . . ." Robbie rubbed his jaw. "That's a little far-fetched."

"Is it?" I raised my eyebrows. "You don't think it's *more* far-fetched for that poison and bomb to be real? Maybe it's like one of those Escape the Room games."

"Yes!" said Diego.

"What's that?" asked Priya.

"I love those games." Diego whipped out his phone and scrolled through his apps. "I've got a few of them here. You're trapped in a room and need to find enough clues to open the door, or the elevator, or whatever. Usually you need to solve a few puzzles to get out."

We all glanced around the room. "Should we start looking for clues?" I asked.

"What if there are no clues?" said Sasha, her voice laced with panic. "What if some psycho put us in here wanting to torture us, and this is just what the letter says it is?"

"Oh my God," Priya whispered, squeezing her eyes shut.

I shook my head. "No way. It has to be some sort of test or game, like in that app."

"I agree," said Diego.

"Yeah, okay, I buy that," Robbie nodded, rubbing my back. "I say we look for clues."

"Alright." Sasha stood along with everyone else, taking a deep breath. "Let's do it."

I traced the edge of the sideboard next to the door, trying to spot anything that could pass as a secret panel or serve as a clue. The china cabinets sandwiching the fireplace were crammed with glasses, decorative trinkets, and figurines. Anything in there could be interpreted as a clue in some way.

Priya turned in a slow circle. "What kinds of things are usually clues in that app?"

"Well, it could be anything." Diego scratched his head. "A key in a grate. Numbers in a painting that correspond with a combination lock. And it's not just an app anymore—they have real-life Escape the Room venues now. People pay like forty bucks to get locked in a room and find their way out, it's nuts."

"People pay fifteen bucks for a sponge," I quipped. "People are dumb." Diego tilted his head, like he was trying to puzzle out if I'd wrung out that grudge.

After all, my dad lost his job over Diego's stupid sponges.

Diego finally lifted the corner of his mouth. "Touché." He knelt, running his fingers over the Oriental rug. "There could be a clue behind a painting, or under the rug." He flipped over the corner, but there was nothing but gleaming hardwood underneath.

I scoured the area near my seat at the table. Robbie knelt next to the door, peering through the keyhole.

"See anything?" said Diego.

Robbie shook his head. "Nah, man. Nothing."

Priya dashed to the coatrack and dug through her jacket pockets.

"Maybe there's something in one of the china cabinets?" I scrutinized one of them, which mostly contained rows of glasses and dainty dishes. The top shelf was lined with small figurines, but there didn't seem to be any patterns.

Scott picked up an incense vase from one of the sideboards and sniffed the bamboo sticks. He shrugged and set it back down. "Hey maybe . . ." He pointed at the bamboo sticks, then scratched his head. "Yeah, yeah, that's it. Maybe it's the number of sticks, and the number of plates, and the number of chairs . . . maybe that's the combination for a lock."

Sasha brandished her arms. "Do you see any combination locks?"

"Oh wait, sorry, that's not right." Scott tapped his chin. "It's not the number of chairs. It's the number of assholes in the room."

"Oh, go to hell—"

"Wait, you guys," Priya said, an octave too high, gripping her dinner invitation. "Nobody signed the invitation. There's no signature or anything."

"So?" I asked.

"It's from the mayor's office, right?" Sasha pulled her invitation from her purse.

"Well," said Priya, scanning the invitation, "it says 'Scholarship Chair, Brewster Town Hall Scholarship Committee.' But why wouldn't they sign a name to it? Shouldn't the mayor at least have signed this?" Almost everyone shook their heads, baffled.

"Also," said Diego, "don't they usually give out this scholarship in May?"

"I don't exactly keep a calendar of these things," said Robbie.

"You're right, they do." Sasha rubbed her forehead. "I thought it seemed early, but didn't think much of it . . ." She trailed off.

Scott threw his head back and laughed.

"What the hell's so funny?" said Robbie.

"We're obviously being punked. There's no scholarship."

"Yes, there is," said Diego. "They give it out every year."

"Yeah, well, whoever did this knows that, too," said Scott. "And the *real* scholarship doesn't even have winners yet. This was no scholarship dinner. There's no test. No clues. It's just some prank to freak us out."

"Or a ploy to *kill* one of us." Sasha gripped her throat.

"Oh, stop it," I said. "Even if it has nothing to do with the scholarship, it has to be a test or prank or something."

"Well, that bomb over there sure as hell looks real to me," said Sasha, pointing to the table with her invitation.

"Have you ever seen a real bomb before?" asked Diego.

"Uh, yeah."

"Movies and TV don't count," I said.

Sasha crossed her arms. "Well, then, fine. I haven't. But that thing's got an awful lot of wires and . . . what are those brown things?" A few of us approached the table to examine the bomb. "Those." Sasha pointed at the half a dozen brown logs wired to a small digital clock and stack of batteries.

"Are those . . . dynamite sticks?" said Robbie. "I dunno, guys, this looks pretty real to me."

"I think so, too," said Priya.

"Oh, please." Scott bent over the table, squinting at the wires feeding into the dynamite sticks. "Anyone could Google what a homemade bomb looks like and rig something like this together."

Priya scrunched her nose. "Have *you* Googled it?"

Scott shrugged. "Sure. I remember looking up how to make a pressure-cooker bomb after that bombing in Boston. I was curious how those psychos did it. There are instructions on how to make all sorts of homemade bombs."

"Wait." Robbie narrowed his eyes at Scott. "So you're saying you know how to make one of those?"

Scott raised his hands. "No. I'm just saying there are all sorts of pictures of bombs online. Anyone can piece together a fake bomb based on those."

"Or," said Sasha, "they can piece together the real deal. Like you said, the instructions are out there." Her eyes flicked to the poison on the tray. "And that syringe looks pretty real, too."

"It could be fake, or a prop," I said.

"No way," said Priya, gripping her stomach as she leaned forward to examine the syringe. "It's totally real. It's exactly like the ones at my doctor's office."

"Well, of course they'd make it *look* real," I said.

"Well"—Robbie pushed past Scott—"there's only one way to find out for sure." Before anyone could stop him, he grabbed the syringe from the tray and pressed his thumb on the plunger.

I YEAR AGO

I was going to be suspended. After all, that's what happens when you walk into the winter ball with a bottle of tequila in your purse.

Why the hell did I agree to this? If I got busted, my parents would take away my laptop, and maybe even my phone, and all of my music was on there. Going through life without my music would be like breathing air without oxygen.

I pulled my bike over a block away from school and yanked out my earbuds. Maybe I should go back home. If I kept this up any longer, my parents would notice their old bottles going missing, even if they hadn't touched them in years. After all, there's no way the liquor cabinet could empty on its own.

But I was so close to getting to score the school play—I just had to get buy-in from the drama club. Sasha promised they'd be at the dance tonight, and that we'd corner them with tequila. I wasn't sure why she seemed to think we needed to bribe them with booze, but she *was* the queen bee, so she must've known a thing or two about how to get her way.

I stuck in my earbuds again and blasted one of my favorite movie scores as I sped to the dimly lit commuter lot on a low hill behind the school. If I went in through the back entrance, I could avoid any security guards patrolling the front lobby.

The racks there were empty. I zipped past the tennis courts and glided into the first spot, closest to the dirt path winding down the hill to the back of the school. A street lamp flickered overhead, casting eerie shadows into the woods behind the lot. Humming to the fast-paced strings and percussion, I unclipped my helmet with shaking fingers and secured my lock to the rack.

A car door slammed behind me. "That's from a battle scene in *The Lord of the Rings*, right?" someone asked. I whirled and gasped, and my helmet tumbled off my head. Oh, no. It was Diego Martin. He was tall and lithe, with warm, tawny skin, like a sunset on the sand, and these intense copper eyes.

As he approached, I clenched my tote bag under my arm, the tequila bottle digging into my rib cage. I couldn't let him see what I was up to. Diego was a straightedge nerd. If loyalty were a family trait, he'd rat me out in a heartbeat.

Or would he?

Diego and I used to go to different schools, but when our fathers worked together at a consulting firm they'd co-founded, we'd see each other at client events and family barbecues next to Brewster Lake. We used to slip away to the fishing pier to escape the boring adult talk and Maggie's mood swings. I'd sit dangling my legs over the splintered edge of the pier, my toes skimming the glassy water as I listened to music while Diego read next to me, wisps of black hair falling across his forehead. Those memories were hazy, but I did remember how his eyes gleamed in the sunlight, and the funny flutter in my stomach whenever he looked at me.

I guess you could say he was my first crush. But we hadn't exchanged more than two words in years.

"Sorry," he said as I clutched my chest, catching my breath. A few strands of his disheveled hair fell between his eyes. "Didn't mean to scare you."

I tugged out my earbuds and paused the track. "It's fine. And . . . it's not."

"It's not fine?"

"No, no. The song." I huffed. "It's when they're running from the Balrog. You know, the fire demon thingy in the first movie." I couldn't help it—resentment bubbled in my stomach. If it weren't for Diego's stupid sponges, Dad could have afforded to fly me to USC auditions, and I wouldn't be scrambling to score the school play.

Dad and I used to watch *Bid or Bust* every Friday night—until the night Diego and his dad appeared on our flat-screen. Mr. Martin had been shirking his responsibilities at my dad's company for months. *He doesn't have a kid to mourn,* Dad would say in an uproar, *what the hell is his excuse?* Suddenly, he had his answer—our jaws dropped as they pitched a sponge that changed colors when it got wet. Apparently it was Diego's idea, and Mr. Martin handled manufacturing. The show producers obviously loved the adoptive teen and father angle—the camera panned across the teary investors when Diego recalled meeting his father as a four-year-old, knowing he was finally home.

After they landed their massive deal, I'd texted Diego with a gazillion scream emojis, congratulating him, and begging for details. But he never texted me back. The next day, his father quit Dad's company, and when Dad couldn't find anyone with the same skill set to replace him, the business collapsed. And Diego never talked to me again.

I guessed mediocrity was a potent repellent.

"Ah." He scooped up my fallen helmet and looped the straps through my handlebars. "Well, it all kind of sounds the same, doesn't it?"

"No, it doesn't." I hugged my arms to my chest, warding off a chill. Why did he suddenly think I was worth talking to again? Maybe he thought it would be more awkward to say nothing. "Those two scenes just share the same motif."

He glanced up from my bike, his copper eyes piercing mine as a car's headlights swiped across us. The main lot must've just filled up. "Motif, huh?" Under a flannel button-down, he wore a black T-shirt with the words "Expressions of Vader" over nine identical images of Darth Vader. Everything about him screamed über dork.

"It's the theme." My words came out terse, laced with bitterness. After Diego made it clear I was no longer worth talking to, I'd avoided him at school, skirting around him in the halls, and sitting on the opposite side of the room in any classes we shared.

I was bleeding friends like a stab to the heart, and the flicker of a flame between us made Diego's cut the deepest. And while I lost Diego, Dad lost *everything.* He had such a hard time landing freelance gigs now, he spent his free time running food deliveries just to pay the bills. I hated seeing him so miserable. All thanks to some pathetic sponge.

"I know what a motif is." Diego took an expensive-looking camera from his backpack and slung the strap over his head. He was a photographer for our school paper, and was probably covering the dance.

"Oh." I fluffed up my side bangs, which my helmet had flattened, lost for words. Could he make out the shape of the tequila bottle in my purse? I edged it behind my torso. "Anyway, I need to get going."

I set off down the dirt path, but Diego followed right behind. "So . . . *The Lord of the Rings* is your jam, huh?"

Frowning, I gave him a wary look. Sometimes when I passed him in the halls, I'd swear he was about to say something, but then he'd clam up, letting me pass without a word. Or maybe he never meant to say anything at all. After a while, resentment filled the hole in my heart where hope had dissolved. Maybe our friendship was a mere convenience to him when our fathers were close—and now that he was filthy rich, I wasn't worth his time.

But maybe he missed me, and finally mustered the guts to say something now that he'd caught me alone.

"Yeah," I finally said, curious. "I have a thing for movie soundtracks." I'd never told him what I was really listening to when he asked years ago. I wasn't embarrassed, per se. Listening to movie scores nonstop gave my mundane life its own vibrant soundtrack. But it wasn't exactly mainstream.

"Really? What's your favorite?" He sounded genuinely intrigued.

"Anything by Hans Zimmer, Howard Shore, or John Williams."

He nodded appreciatively. "Nice." Wow. Usually that answer got me nothing but blank stares and vacant frowns, so I'd started telling people my favorite musician was Taylor Swift. People liked her, right? He pushed his hair from his eyes again. "I listen to the *Star Wars* scores while I study. Original trilogy, mostly."

My jaw dropped. "Seriously?"

"Sometimes I throw in some *Gladiator* or *Blade Runner*, if I'm feeling adventurous."

"I totally love you." My stomach plummeted as Diego's eyebrows shot up. "*Those*. I love *those*. It's just, I didn't know you listened . . . and, I don't know anyone else who, you know, listens to soundtracks like I do . . ." Flustered, I clamped my lips shut to keep more word vomit from spewing out, while his lips curved into a smile.

"Trust me, you're not the only person who likes movie soundtracks."

"Right. Obviously." Mortified, I watched for fallen branches in front of my feet as we descended the hill toward the back doors. But Mr. Turner, one of our school security guards, was standing outside the back door, smoking a cigarette. I gasped and froze. What if he asked to check my bag? I'd have to take my chances and go through the front lobby instead.

"What's wrong?" asked Diego.

"I don't want to go in through the back doors." I turned to backtrack.

"Uh . . . why not?" His tone was annoyed. So much for thinking he'd missed me. False hope at its worst.

I swallowed hard. I couldn't admit the truth about the booze. "It's . . . it's my first school dance" was all I could come up with.

"So?"

"I've never been to one before."

He furrowed his brow. *"So?"*

"So! This is, like, a major milestone. I'm coming out of my shell. Putting myself out there. Going to . . . school dances!" I jabbed a finger toward the front of the building. "And I want to walk in through the front doors." God, he probably thought I was even more pathetic than he realized.

Diego considered me, frowning. "Okay then." He brushed past me to walk alongside the building. "To the front doors it is."

Heaving a sigh, I jogged to catch up, and settled into stride beside him. When we reached the front doors, I started to push one open, but he blocked me with his arm.

"What is it?" My heart raced in my chest like a wild stallion escaping its captor. He spotted the tequila in my bag, didn't he?

He closed his eyes and took a deep breath. "This is it."

"What?"

"We're about to cross the threshold onto the next stage of your life."

I gave him a deadpan look. "Are you seriously mocking me right now?"

"Wait, wait . . . do you smell that?" He gave a big sniff.

The air smelled faintly of exhaust and evening dew. "No."

"It's the smell of new beginnings!"

"Oh, shut up." I rolled my eyes and shoved his arm away.

"Alas!" He rushed after me as I sped through the door. "It's the dawn of a new era!"

I shook my head and barreled across the vestibule, trying to put as much distance between us as possible. Naturally, I collided with the other security guard, Mr. Garcia. My heart bypassed my stomach, dropping directly into my uterus.

"Whoa, slow down, Amber," said Mr. Garcia, gripping my shoulders to steady me. "You're gonna knock someone out."

"Oh my God, I'm so sorry." I straightened myself out and swung my purse behind me, the strap cutting into my shirt between my boobs. *Please don't check my bag. Please don't ask to check my bag.*

"That's okay." A friendly smile spread under Mr. Garcia's black mustache.

"You alright?" asked Diego. He touched the small of my back, and I adjusted my purse again, edging the bottle away from his hand. But now Mr. Garcia could probably see the weight of my purse as it sagged toward the floor, heavy with a thousand pounds of guilt.

"Yep. I'm fine."

Mr. Garcia looked between us and winked. "You kids have a good time." My cheeks were on fire, but Diego looked nonplussed.

We headed into the gym and hesitated near the doors, taking

in the scene. I always thought the winter ball would be fancy like prom. But at Brewster High, there were no fancy dresses and no decorations save the balloons half-heartedly strewn about the gym, courtesy of the student council. The girls swayed to the thumping bass in form-fitting jeans and sparkly tank tops, and the boys looked the same as always: preppy jock or über dork.

As I scanned the crowd for Priya or Sasha, Diego motioned toward the DJ's booth. "Sorry they're not playing *The Lord of the Rings* soundtrack. Should I make a request?"

"I don't think everyone else would be thrilled with that selection," I said as he unzipped his backpack and pulled out a second camera. "Er . . . exactly how many cameras does it take to cover a school dance?"

He tapped the one dangling from his neck. "Just the one, but—"

"Oh, well look at you, being all fancy," I said, trying to throw back some shade. "Too bad the rest of us have to settle for coin collections."

A smile crept onto his lips, and I bit back a grin. "I just have two cameras, alright? This was my mom's. It's a Polaroid."

"Oh, huh. I didn't realize they made those anymore."

"You can still order the film online. You can find anything online, really. C'mere, let's memorialize this milestone of yours." He raised the camera at arm's length, aiming the lens toward us.

"Oh, no, I don't think—"

"Say cheese." Okay, so this was happening. I obliged, not wanting to look caught off guard, and flashed my biggest smile as the camera's flash blinded us. A small white strip immediately ejected from the camera.

I blinked the violet flash dots from my view. He held out the strip, and we watched as the gray smudges morphed into grinning versions of us.

"Ha, I look like such a dork." I hated seeing myself in pictures. The image staring back at me never quite matched how I pictured myself—the smattering of freckles on my cheeks was more pronounced than I thought, and my hair never sat quite right.

"You look great." He shoved the camera back in his bag, but before I could read his expression, someone opened the door behind us, and a stream of light behind him obscured his face in shadow.

Priya poked her head inside the gym. "There you are!" She bolted over.

"There *you* are."

"Why haven't you been answering your texts?" Oh, crap. I always kept my phone on silent when I biked so I didn't get distracted. "Come on!"

"Come where?"

Priya glanced at Diego warily. "Just . . . come on."

"Okay. Well, see you." I gave Diego a small wave and raced after Priya.

"Everyone's this way." She led me toward the band practice room, her eyes wide with anxiety. "I hate being so shy," she said. "I never know what to talk to Sasha about."

"Talk about cheerleading," I suggested. "You have that in

common now." Emboldened by my small victory with Sasha, I'd convinced Priya to try out for the cheerleading squad, and to her utter shock and delight, she made it. But it hadn't seemed to bolster her self-esteem.

"Yeah, I guess."

After we slipped into the band room, Sasha rushed over. "Look who finally showed up!" She kissed the air beside my cheeks. Priya and I exchanged a tentative glance as I dug out the tequila. Sasha grabbed it. "Half a bottle? I hope it's because you pre-gamed on your way over."

I couldn't tell if she was joking or annoyed. Before I could reply, she dashed behind the drum set.

"Well, halle-fucking-lujah." Zane peeked at us over the cymbals, his eyes shadowed under his baseball cap, and threw us a roguish grin. "Thirsty?"

Priya and I rounded the drum set and found a whole group huddled on the floor. Amy and Maria were hunched over one of their phones, giggling at something. Sasha sat back-to-back with Robbie, holding her phone at arm's length for a selfie. And I recognized a few kids from drama club, including Asher and Dan, who watched Zane divvy the tequila into red plastic cups and pass them around. Sasha flicked my ankle and gave me a meaningful look, nodding toward them.

"Hey, guys," Sasha called to them. "You know Amber, right?"

"Sure." Dan waved, then stuck his hands in his pockets. He usually played the lead opposite Maria, who watched us with narrowed eyes. "You write music, huh?"

"Yep! I want to produce movie scores someday."

"Sweet," said Dan.

"That's awesome," said Asher, another actor. "Hey, maybe you'll score a movie I'm in someday."

I grinned. "That would be incredible."

"So, Sasha told us about your *Romeo and Juliet* idea—"

"Let's get turnt!" Zane interrupted, passing me a cup. I'd never tried booze before, unless you counted the time Dad let me try a sip of his beer. Nasty stuff. Each time we hung out with Sasha's crowd, Priya turned down drinks point-blank, while I'd sneakily avoid them by faking sips and draining my cup in the kitchen or bathroom sink when nobody was looking. But there was nowhere to do that here. I sniffed my cup and winced as Zane held one out to Priya. "Here you go, gorgeous."

Her face turned a deep shade of crimson. She tried to thank him, but it came out as "Thaaa," and she made an odd choking noise as she tried to recover.

"Cheers." Robbie stretched toward me and tapped his cup against mine, giving me a crooked-toothed smile. I couldn't help but smile back.

Sasha tipped the liquid into her mouth and swallowed with barely a grimace. I gingerly took a sip, trying to hide my cringe as the liquid burned all the way down my esophagus. I clutched my throat. "Woo! That's . . . interesting."

Sasha raised an eyebrow at Priya, who watched me with her mouth agape. "Well?"

Priya took a tentative sniff, screwed up her face, and held the cup out for someone to take. "No, thanks."

Zane smirked at Priya. "Haven't you had tequila before?"

"I've never drunk anything before," said Priya. "My mom would ground me in a millisecond if I got wasted."

"Trust me, you won't get wasted from one shot," Sasha said reassuringly. "Drinking that much just gives me a nice little buzz for a couple hours. And I'm much smaller than you, so."

"Oh," said Priya, taking in Sasha's frame, which wasn't any more petite than her own. "Still. I'd rather not . . ."

"At least try it," said Amy.

"It's not going to kill you," Maria piped up.

"Do iiiiit," said Zane. "C'mon, it's just a little drink." Priya still hesitated, torn between wanting to impress Zane and not wanting to disobey her mother. "It's not like we're making you turn over to the dark side of the Force."

I laughed along with everyone else and played a few chords of the Imperial March theme from *Star Wars* on the upright piano.

"Whoa, that's awesome!" Robbie grinned, dimples creasing his cheeks.

"Thanks," I squeaked.

"She can play the theme from any movie." Priya lowered her cup, clearly grateful for the distraction. "Literally, any. Name one."

Asher set his untouched drink on the piano and nodded toward the keys. *"James Bond."*

I couldn't help but smirk. Easy. I sat at the bench and played about twenty seconds of the *GoldenEye* theme. Everyone crowded around me. Maria stood off to the side, her arms crossed.

Robbie nudged my arm. "Play *Jurassic Park*." I played the most iconic bit of the main theme as he watched my fingers course over the keys, transfixed. The others shouted out more movies and TV shows, each more obscure than the last. I played them all, transitioning smoothly from one theme to the next. When I finally stopped playing, Robbie and Sasha whooped, and I blushed furiously.

"That was amazing," said Asher. "Can you play some of your own stuff?"

"Ooh, pull up YouTube." Sasha pointed at my purse. "Play one of your actual recordings."

I whipped out my phone. "Okay, so, here's one." I pressed Play, and basically broke the record for longest breath held as everyone listened.

When the song ended, everyone showered me with compliments. Even Maria said, "You did that yourself? All of those instruments? That's pretty sick."

Priya gave me a giddy smile, mouthing, *Yay!*

"So." Sasha turned to the actors as Robbie and Zane bashed on the piano keys. "I'm thinking we do a modern rendition of *Romeo and Juliet*. We can Americanize some of the lines, you know? Add some humor, maybe a bit of satire . . ." As she blabbered on, my heart swelled with gratitude. I couldn't believe I ever thought she was a bitch.

Suddenly, the doors burst open. I gasped and stood fast,

making the bench topple backward. At the same moment, Zane dropped the empty tequila bottle, and it shattered. Maria tugged Sasha's wrist, yanking her behind the piano as the boys ducked behind the drums. We all huddled low, eyes wide, hands clasped over mouths to suppress giggles and gasps. Robbie's arm somehow made its way over my shoulder, clutching me close. I didn't mind.

"I know you're back there," a voice called out. It was Mrs. Burr, the librarian. "I heard something break. And I heard the piano from down the hall." None of us replied. Nobody knew what to do. We were busted. "What's going on in here?"

Shit, shit, shit, Sasha mouthed as she grabbed the nearby cups and stacked them. Priya started to stand, but Zane tugged her by a belt loop and yanked her back down. He pointed toward the side door, which led into the auditorium. We could make a run for it. Mrs. Burr was too old and feeble to be able to catch us. Maybe she wouldn't see our faces.

Hunched over the shattered bottle, Sasha grabbed the piece with the nozzle intact and raised it like a dagger, the jagged edges glistening. What the hell was she going to do with that? Was she going to try to *stab* Mrs. Burr? If we got caught drinking on school campus, the cheerleaders and baseball players could get thrown off their teams. How far was she willing to go to get away with this?

But before I could do anything, Sasha wound back and threw the glass across the room, creating a distraction. "Run!"

53 MINUTES LEFT

Robbie clenched the syringe of poison over one of the empty plates on the table, his thumb on the plunger, his grip tensing like he was about to squeeze. I cringed, instinctively holding my breath.

"No!" Diego yelled, flailing his arms at Robbie. "You could kill us all!"

Robbie relaxed his grip. "What? How would I—" Diego lunged at Robbie, grabbed his wrist, and plucked the syringe from his fist. "Alright, alright! Geez."

"We can't release any of this toxin." Diego pinched the syringe between two fingers like it was something filthy and set it back on its tray. "Nobody touch it. It says right here"—he pointed at the label—"'Avoid contact with skin. A single drop can be fatal.' What if you get some on yourself? And who knows what'd happen if it goes airborne? We don't know how concentrated this is. You could kill us all by accident."

Sasha raised her eyebrows. "So you *do* think it's real?"

Diego scrutinized the syringe. "I don't know for sure. I mean, the syringe itself *looks* real. But I don't know about the stuff inside." He rotated the syringe with the tip of his pinkie, inspecting the light beige liquid. "Botulinum toxin can be extremely dangerous."

"I've never heard of it," said Priya.

"It's literally the most lethal known toxin. The label doesn't say what type it is, but if it's type H, it's the deadliest substance in the world. A single drop *could* kill you."

Priya's eyes were as big as saucers, and Sasha clapped a hand over her mouth.

I raised my eyebrows. "How do you know all that?"

He shrugged. "I don't remember exactly—I read about it somewhere once. Or maybe it was in a documentary." If any of us were to geek out over science documentaries, it'd be Diego.

"Would it be instant death?" I said. "What happens, exactly?"

"I think so." He scrunched his brow. "It's a neurotoxin. It blocks the nerves controlling your vital organs. Your lungs would stop sucking in air. Your heart would stop beating."

Hearing him describe it made my stomach turn over. He caught my terrified expression. "It wouldn't be very painful. At least, not for long. On the other hand, if this is type A or B, there might only be enough in here to kill one person with a full injection." Diego shook his head. "But without knowing the type for sure, or the concentration, there's no way to know until . . . well, you know. Until we use it."

"How would anyone in our town get their hands on something like this?" asked Priya.

"I have no idea." Diego raked back his shaggy hair. "Some black market online? Or maybe they're not from here."

"I don't get it," said Robbie, wrapping a protective arm around me. "Why poison? Why not a gun, or a dagger, or something?"

"Those things are harder to fake, right?" said Scott.

"How are you so sure it's fake?" said Sasha.

He tapped his skull. "Using my noggin. They want us to think it can kill you with one drop or whatever, so we won't risk testing it. They obviously don't want us testing to see if it's real, cuz it's not, but they don't want us to know that. It's backward psychology."

"Reverse psychology," I said.

"Whatever. I still say this is a prank."

"Or maybe it's because they only intend for one of us to die"— Sasha pointed at the bomb—"or for *all* of us to die."

Scott furrowed his brow. "I don't follow."

"With a knife or gun . . . who knows what can happen, right? How many of us could get stabbed or shot or whatever? But maybe the poison *isn't* the most lethal type, and there's only enough to kill *exactly* one of us." I nodded, following her train of thought.

"But why? At this point, why would they care what happens to the rest of us?" said Priya.

"Because," I said just above a whisper, "they want the rest of us to live with what we've done."

Sasha nodded. "Exactly."

"Jesus." Robbie wiped his forehead.

"Oh my God," said Priya. "This can't be happening. This *cannot* be happening."

I started toward her, instinctively wanting to comfort her, but she cowered away from me. I swallowed the rock that swelled in my throat and turned to Diego. "Are you sure the syringe is real?"

Diego tugged at his shirt collar. "I mean, there's no way to test it. Like Scott said, we can't risk it. I don't even want to let out a drop. If it is the super-dangerous kind, and it goes airborne, inhaling it could kill us, too."

"I think we have to assume it's real," said Robbie. "Right?"

I exchanged a glance with Diego, who rubbed his jawline. "I don't know. It could be real. But I don't know."

"No, no, but I mean . . ." Robbie licked his lips and furrowed his brow, like he was struggling to articulate his thoughts. "We have to assume this whole scenario's real. The poison, the bomb, everything. Like, if it's not real, great . . . we inject someone with that stuff, but nothing happens. But we've got to pick someone, and we have to poison them, in case the poison and bomb are *both* real." He motioned to the bomb. "Because we can't risk the bomb killing everyone."

Everyone stilled. Were everyone's hearts beating as rapidly as mine? I clutched my chest, and my collarbone was clammy with sweat. The room seemed to be getting hotter by the minute.

"So what do we do?" Priya croaked.

"We'll have to go through with this," said Sasha. "We'll have to pick someone."

71

11 MONTHS AGO

FEBRUARY OF JUNIOR YEAR

I tried to survive for as long as I could. But here I was, crawling toward Sasha on my hands and knees, begging her to save me.

"I'm dead in forty-five seconds," I cried. "Forty-four, forty-three. Revive me, revive me."

But Sasha was too busy avoiding getting slaughtered herself. "Hang on a sec. These assholes won't die!" She ducked behind a plank wall she'd constructed, narrowly dodging a burst of rifle fire. After a moment of silence, she built a ramp, peered over the wall, aimed her shotgun, and fired. "Dammit! Come on, that was a head shot."

"You two are useless," said Robbie. "I got you." He raced over to revive me, hovering his hand over my head. In ten seconds, I was back in action.

Not that I was much use. We'd been playing Fortnite for over an hour, and so far all I'd mastered was chopping down trees, stumbling across ransacked treasure chests, and generally getting in the way.

"Thanks." I glanced over at Robbie. We sat cross-legged on Sasha's bed, laptops on our laps, while Sasha sat at her desk pummeling her keyboard, spraying bullets at our enemies. So much for showing Sasha my new tracks for the first act of *Romeo and Juliet*. When I'd arrived, Robbie was already there, laptop and gamer headset in hand. I turned to leave, thinking I'd have to come back another time, but they asked me to join their squad. My jaw dropped open. Maybe I'd misheard them? But Sasha said, "C'mon, you brought your laptop, right? Sit." She pointed at her bed. "Play."

If you'd told me a month ago that I'd be sitting on Sasha Harris's bed playing video games with her and the hottest guy in our grade, I would have keeled over laughing. But I was thrilled to be included.

Until I realized how much I sucked at this.

"No prob." Robbie dropped some health kits at my avatar's feet. "I got your back."

After my avatar bandaged itself up, Robbie lifted his hand from his keyboard for a fist bump. I tapped my knuckles against his, and heat rushed up my arm. Suddenly I became very conscious of how our knees were almost touching. I bit my lip, watching him play. His eyes sparkled as they danced across his screen, the light illuminating flecks of silver around his pupils. His strong brows scrunched in concentration as he aimed his missile launcher. I must have stared a moment too long, because he met my gaze, a smile playing on his lips. "You gonna come?"

"What?" I focused on my screen again, my cheeks flushing. His and Sasha's avatars were barreling down the hill toward an outcrop of buildings. "Oh, yeah. Sorry." I raced after them. But my neck prickled with heat, and I was pretty sure Robbie's eyes were lingering on me. I dared a quick glance.

Yep. I wasn't the only one staring.

"You guys," said Sasha. "Enemies are building on that hill. To the right." Sure enough, scaffolding rose into the air at a fast clip. It looked like they were trying to construct a bridge from one hill to the next.

"Alright," said Robbie. "Let's head around back over here—"

But I fired at the enemies' bridge. The scaffolding disappeared, and two of our enemies fell to the ground. A message popped up: *AmberOnFire eliminated DeftAssassin and Warrior045.*

Sasha whooped. "That was badass! Bad. Ass."

"Nice!" Robbie gave my arm a playful shove. "Those were your first kills, right?"

"Yep." I beamed. I'd forgotten how much I loved playing video games. Maggie and I used to play together all the time.

Grief choked the air from my lungs. Maggie would have loved this game. The last-person-standing element was just like *The Hunger Games*, which Maggie snuck under my pillow after Mom refused to let me read it, saying I was too young. We'd fangirled over the series together, and if she were still alive, we might've played Fortnite together—me in my bedroom, her at some Ivy League school, shouting instructions at each other through our headsets.

Suddenly, Sasha's door burst open. I nearly jumped out of my skin. A stern-looking woman stood in the doorway, a hand on her hip. "What on Earth is going on in here?"

"Mom!" Sasha threw off her headset. "We're just playing a game. What're you doing home so early?"

Her mother raised a thin, arched eyebrow at Sasha. "My last two patients canceled. I thought I'd get a head start on dinner. Clearly you didn't think to get a head start on your homework." Robbie and I exchanged a glance as Sasha's mother clucked her tongue, narrowing her eyes at Sasha's screen. "How could you waste any more of your time? And on something so stupid."

"It's not stupid—"

"The SATs are just around the corner."

"I know, Mom. I've been studying nonstop, you know that. And we still have two months—"

"Two months is nothing." Her mother crossed her arms. "If you want to get into Harvard, there's no time to waste. When your sister wanted to be on Broadway and had auditions in two months, you think she sat around playing video games? No. She practiced, constantly. She sacrificed her degree. She never squandered any opportunity. Now she's in *Phantom of the Opera*."

"I *know*, Mom," said Sasha. "We went to see her *together*, remember?"

"Well, I'm just saying, you ought to take a page from her book." Jesus. If Mom ever compared me to Maggie like this, I'd be crushed. But Sasha sat there stoically. Only her glistening eyes betrayed any pain.

"It's my fault, Mrs. Harris," said Robbie, whose bravery clearly extended beyond the digital realm. He shut his laptop and scrambled to his feet. I glanced at my screen as an enemy squad took our avatars out in one fell swoop. "Sasha and Amber were going to work on the school play. But I convinced them to play Fortnite instead. It's my bad."

Mrs. Harris looked me over like she'd only just noticed me. "Well, you two might as well stay for dinner. It'll be ready in an hour." With that, she left the room, leaving the door open behind her.

Robbie and I stared at Sasha, who slumped back in her chair and crossed her arms. "You okay?" asked Robbie.

"Whatever," Sasha muttered, blinking at the ceiling.

"You know, you can't constantly work, work, work," said Robbie. "Everyone needs to take a break once in a while." When Sasha didn't respond, he went on. "Besides, the SATs are dumb. Life's biggest victories have nothing to do with school."

"You think I don't know that?" Sasha snapped. "Why do you think I do the play? And cheerleading? And everything else?"

Robbie raised his hands. "Sorry. I'm just trying to help."

"Yeah, well." Sasha stared out her window, facing away from us. "You guys should just go."

"Wait," I said. "Don't you want to hear those tracks we talked about?" Without hearing them, she and the drama club couldn't finalize their decision to do *Romeo and Juliet* in May.

She let out an exasperated sigh. "Not now, okay? She's right . . . I should be studying." She rubbed the stress from her eyes. "Just email them to me, and I'll listen later." Her voice shook like she was holding back tears. Maybe she didn't want us to see her cry.

"Okay." I felt so bad for her. No wonder she was always trying to be perfect at everything. We weren't exactly close, but I felt weird just leaving her like this. "I could stay and help you study, if you want," I said as Robbie slid his laptop into his backpack.

"Really?" she said. For a moment, I thought she was going to say yes. But then her eyes watered even more, and she pulled a tissue from a box on her desk. "No, it's okay. Just go, okay? Please?"

Robbie nudged my arm. "C'mon."

I packed up my stuff and followed Robbie out the door. He closed it behind us, and we trooped down the stairs. "Bye, Mrs. Harris," he called in the kitchen over the sound of clattering pots and pans.

"Bye, now," she replied, not even bothering to encourage us to stay.

"Yeesh," I said as we walked down Sasha's front stoop.

"Yeah."

"If her mom's so strict, how is Sasha always going out and partying and stuff?"

Robbie chuckled. "You think she tells her mom the truth? She probably says she's going to someone's house to study, or to the library, or some shit."

"Ah." I never lied to my parents like that. At least, not until I started swiping booze from them. Robbie walked me to my bike, which I'd left leaning next to their garage door. I wiped a hand down my face.

"You okay?" Robbie asked.

"Yeah. I'm just stressed about the play. If she doesn't listen to those tracks soon . . . well, we're running out of time. I need to know if we're officially doing this. It'll take a ton of work to get everything ready in time for May, but it's possible . . . as long as we don't waste any more time."

Robbie leaned against the wall, considering me. His eyes lingered on mine a beat too long, and my heart stilled. "This play really means a lot to you, doesn't it?"

"Yeah. It means everything. It's my best shot at proving I can write a full-length score for an actual orchestra. When else am I going to get this chance again?"

"I know how much it means to have a shot at something. Something big." He rested a hand on my shoulder. "I'll talk to Sasha. I'll make sure she listens."

I perked up. "Really? You'd do that for me?"

"Sure. I mean, I can't guarantee the drama club will agree to anything. But I'm sure she'll be willing to help you out."

But after seeing how stressed she was, I wasn't so sure of anything.

51 MINUTES LEFT

This was the second time Sasha insinuated we'd have to choose someone to die.

"No." I balled my hands into fists, willing myself to stop trembling. My muscles ached from shaking so much despite the heat. "There's no way it'll come to that. It *can't* come to that."

Sasha threw out her arms. "Well, what are we supposed to do?"

"Let's just . . . stay calm and try to find a way out of here. This isn't exactly the Tower of London. There has to be a way out." But nobody agreed. Nobody said anything. Everyone stared at me and Sasha.

I met Diego's gaze, pleading with my eyes. "Come on! We have to at least try to find a way out."

He nodded. "I'll try the door. Someone open the windows!"

He rounded on the door and twisted the knob until his knuckles turned white, straining to force the lock open. Everyone followed his lead and sprang into action. Robbie joined Diego at the door, while Scott and Priya each dragged a chair to either end of the sideboard under the two windows nestled near the ceiling. Sasha dashed to the fireplace, and I paced the perimeter of the Oriental rug, looking for God knows what. Maybe a hidden door or panel? I opened every drawer I could find, searching for a key.

"The fireplace is fake." Sasha stooped and leaned into the fireplace, pounding on a panel above her head where the opening for a chimney should be. "Completely fake."

Priya grunted as she tried to pry open the lock on the window from atop her chair. "The lock is stuck."

"Same," said Scott. Sweat glistened on his forehead and upper lip. "Someone painted it shut at some point. And the windows are barred, anyway."

"We might be able to unlock those, too. Keep trying!"

Robbie watched Diego rattle the knob, but after a minute, he shoved him aside and threw himself against the door. The great oak door didn't budge. He reared back and rammed his shoulder into the door again, putting his full body weight into it, but stumbled back, gripping his shoulder. "Dammit!"

"Maybe try to kick it down?" Diego suggested.

Robbie's foot connected with the middle of the door over and over again. *Pound. Pound. Pound.* Each kick reverberated in my chest, but I kept digging through the drawers in the side table. *Pound. Pound. Pound.* All I could find were tablecloths, napkins, doilies, forks, spoons, plates, and decorative candles. *Pound. Pound. Pound.*

Sasha climbed on the table and frantically looked around. "I need a broom or a stick or something."

"For what?" I asked. *Pound, pound, pound.*

"To bang on the ceiling. Maybe there's someone upstairs."

I pointed at Robbie. "You think they wouldn't hear that?" *Pound, pound, pound.*

"I don't know—Robbie, that isn't working!" cried Sasha, covering her ears. "You're not helping."

Diego glanced around the room. "Maybe there's something we can use to break down the door."

"Like what?" asked Robbie, trying to catch his breath.

"I don't know . . . anything."

Robbie picked up the nearest chair and reared back, bucking like he was surprised by the weight of it. After regaining his footing, he hurled it at the door. Diego jumped back with a shout. The chair clattered feebly against the door, falling on its side. "Dammit!"

I tugged at the collar of my sequined dress, which scratched at my sticky skin. "God, it's boiling in here." Crossing the room, I examined the grille lining the wall under the large brass mirror. Was there a way to shut the vents? I touched the edge of the grille and flinched. "Ow!" It was scalding. "Is this supposed to get this hot?" But everyone ignored me, focused on searching for a way out.

"Does anyone know how to pick a lock?" Sasha asked. A few people shook their heads.

"Er . . . I could try," Diego said. "Does anyone have a paper clip? Or a . . . a hair clip thingy?"

"A bobby pin?" I asked.

"Yeah, one of those."

Sasha plucked a bedazzled barrette from the front compartment of her purse and offered it to Diego. "Would this work?"

He examined it. "No, I don't think so. I'd need something thin and pointy."

"Let me check my purse." I raced back to my chair and fished through my purse, pawing at the bottom, but there was nothing sharp and pointy he could use. "Priya," I shouted over the table. "Do you have a bobby pin?"

"No," Priya grunted, straining to twist the lock on the window. She finally let go, breathing hard. "You know I don't use bobby pins." That's right. She always used banana clips in her thick hair.

"Well, or anything else pointy? A paper clip or something?"

"I brought my phone and lip gloss. That's it."

"Helpful." Scott leapt down from his chair. "You never know when you'll need shiny lips in a pinch." He fished random objects from his jacket pockets and set them on the table—cigarettes, a lighter, gum, his wallet, a wad of tissues.

"You're not exactly doing much better," I said. He shrugged and climbed back onto the chair to struggle with the window again.

Sasha cried, "I found a bobby pin!" She dropped her purse and ran it over to Diego. "Robbie, move."

Robbie backed away, panting. Diego knelt next to the lock. "I don't know if this will work."

"Try it anyway," said Sasha.

"Dammit!" Priya released the window lock and shook out her hand. "It's really stuck." She set her palms against the window. Raindrops streaked down the glass, obscuring her view.

"Lemme try," said Robbie. Priya hopped down from her chair, and he climbed up.

"Why would anyone paint over the locks?" Scott strained to pry open the other window's lock. "This is ridiculous."

"It's a . . . goddamn . . . fire hazard . . . is what it is." Robbie's biceps bulged with strain under his button-down shirtsleeves.

"Can you break the glass?" Sasha suggested.

"No, don't," I said. "This is pointless. The windows are barred anyway."

"But we might be able to unlock the bars," said Priya.

Robbie eyed me, the most petite of the group. "We could boost you through. You could run and get help."

I brushed back my bangs, frustrated. "I don't think I could fit through there, even if we could unlock the bars."

Diego focused on the lock, his tongue peeking out as he tried different angles with the bobby pin. He heaved a sigh and leaned back on his heels. "I have no idea what I'm doing here."

Scott wiped his brow. "Gimme a chair."

Sasha frowned. "You're . . . already on one?"

He pointed frantically. "Another chair! Obviously."

I sighed. This was pointless. But I stood closest to him, so I passed him the nearest chair, straining to lift it. It was heavier than I expected.

He took it from me, grunting as he raised it above his head, and rammed its back legs against the window. The glass was thick, but after a few well-placed hits, a large crack spidered from the middle.

"Yes! That's it!" Priya shouted.

Scott bashed the window one last time, and the glass shattered. I scrambled back against the table as glass rained down on Scott. A large shard caught his cheek, and a surprised howl of pain escaped his lips. He lost his balance and waved his arms like propellers, his fingers searching for anything to grip on to. But there was nothing but air, and I couldn't move fast enough to reach him.

He stumbled off the chair and landed on the floor with a sickening crack.

10 MONTHS, 2 WEEKS AGO

MARCH OF JUNIOR YEAR

"Do you see them?" I asked Priya, scanning the crowd at the Chesterfield for Sasha. I'd only been here once before. Maria's parents owned the place, and last weekend Sasha asked me to be lookout while she and Maria snuck in to swipe booze. I thought I was going to puke the whole time—until the two of them strolled out with full tote bags, eyes hidden behind matching huge sunglasses, like they'd just performed a heist. We'd crammed into the backseat of Amy's car and burst into a fit of giggles. It almost seemed worth it for that moment alone.

Now most of the junior class was packed into the restaurant like sardines, and I could barely hear myself think over the music and chatter. Priya scrolled through her phone, the hair I'd curled for her cascading around her face.

"Ugh, there's no signal in here. But look," she said. "Sasha posted on Instagram twenty minutes ago—looks like she'd just finished getting ready." She angled the screen toward me, and my whole body went rigid. My head instinctively snapped back, nearly giving me whiplash. Maggie's lifeless face flashed in my mind, and my breath hitched painfully in my lungs.

"Oh my God." Priya powered off her screen. "I'm so sorry."

I clasped my chest, struggling to slow my breathing. "It's okay—"

"No, I'm an idiot. I can't believe I forgot."

After Maggie died . . . after what I saw on social media . . . my parents urged me to see a therapist, but I refused, and they didn't force the issue. But sometimes I wondered if that was a mistake. I couldn't lose it like this every time I saw a social media site.

"Do you want to leave?" Priya's forehead crinkled in concern.

I shook my head. "No. It's fine, it passed—"

A hand suddenly clasped Priya's shoulder. "Ladies!" Zane shouted as someone cranked up the music, and Priya's face brightened. Zane held three flutes of bubbly liquid with one hand and motioned for each of us to take one.

"Thanks." I grabbed one, my stomach still twisting in knots. "Um . . . it's not champagne, is it?"

"You wish," he said. "Sparkling cider." I took a small sip as he edged a metallic flask from his pocket. "But I made things a little more interesting."

"Hey." Robbie joined my side as someone cranked up the music.

I coughed as spiked apple cider went down the wrong tube. "Hi," I sputtered.

"You okay?"

I hacked one last time before clearing my throat. *Smooth, Amber. Smooth.* "Yeah. I'm fine."

"Your . . . ear . . . pretty." The middle of his sentence was lost in the din.

"What?"

He reached out and tucked a strand of hair behind my ear, then gently ran his finger over one of the earrings I'd chosen for tonight. They were gold dream catchers dotted with tiny bits of amber. He must have been complimenting them.

My pulse quickened. "Thanks."

He said something else, but I shook my head, unable to hear him. He leaned close to my ear. "C'mon, let's find somewhere quieter." His warm breath on my neck set my nerve endings aflame.

Priya was too busy making googly eyes at Zane to care if I left, so I let Robbie take my hand and lead me across the room. We squeezed through the crowd past the bar, and Robbie pushed open a large oak door standing a crack open. After flipping on the light, he shut the door behind us, cutting the noise to a low muffle. It was just him and me.

Alone.

In some fancy private dining room in the back.

By ourselves.

My heart swelled like a balloon ready to pop. I still couldn't figure out what a jock like Robbie would want to do with a music nerd like me, but each time we hung out, the current running between us intensified.

"So . . . what's up?" I asked.

"I just wanted to get away from everyone for a little bit. It's hot in there."

"Yeah, it's pretty packed." I took a sip of cider to have something to do.

"And loud," he said. "Maybe you could play the piano. That'd shut them all up." I giggled as blood rushed into my cheeks. "So I talked to Sasha about your tracks."

"Oh, really?" Ah, so he'd only brought me in here to talk about the play. Since the last time we spoke, I'd sent Sasha recordings for all of acts one and five of *Romeo and Juliet*, impatient to make more progress. But I didn't know if she'd listened yet.

"Yep. Then I nagged her again earlier today, and she said the drama club's on board. You're doing *Romeo and Juliet*!"

"What?" I shrieked. I couldn't believe it. It was happening. It was really happening. "Oh my God, thank you." I launched myself at him, somehow hugging him while simultaneously jumping up and down. He laughed, and I pulled back, embarrassed from my outburst of emotion.

"I'm happy to help," he said. "I know what it's like to dream big."

I flapped my hand like a fan in a useless attempt to cool my face. "Baseball's your dream, right?"

He grinned. "Yep."

"Don't your brothers play, too?" It made the local news when one of his brothers got called up to the majors last month.

"That's right. Liam plays ball for Georgia Tech, and Paul's on the Red Sox now. I can only hope things go so well for me."

"Do family connections help with that sort of thing?"

"I dunno." He stuck his hands in his pockets. "My brothers . . . they were big shots. I always kinda felt like they were on another level. I wanted to be just like them, though—whenever they practiced in the backyard, I tagged along. But they're only a year apart, and I'm four years younger than Liam. So they treated me like the world's biggest annoyance. I was always the baby brother, you know?"

"But that clearly didn't stop you."

"No way. Whenever they gave me shit, I handed it right back." He grinned, his dimples reappearing, and my heart wobbled precariously. "You got any brothers or sisters?"

Maggie. Bile crept up my throat. I didn't want his pity. One thing I loved about hanging out with his and Sasha's crowd was that since they went to Hampton, we hadn't met in middle school, and they hadn't connected the dots between me and the Brewster High senior who died when we were in eighth grade. They didn't know I was Maggie's sister. And people look at you differently when they find out you're the sister of that girl who died.

"No." I smiled as naturally as I could. "It's just me."

"That must be nice. But, you know, if you ever get lonely . . . you could come over." He hooked a finger around one of my belt loops and pulled me closer, and a shiver coasted through me. "My parents go to Paul's games in Boston a lot now. So I get kinda lonely, too, sometimes." With his other hand, he tucked that stray hair behind my ear again, holding my gaze. "You know, there's something I've been wanting to do for a while."

My heart was beating so fast I was sure he could hear it thrashing against my rib cage. "What's that?"

His eyes lowered, settling on my mouth. "I think you know."

Oh my God. This was going to happen. Right now.

But I'd never kissed anyone before. What if I did it all wrong? Were my lips too chapped? Were my palms sweaty? What was I supposed to do with my tongue? Anything? Nothing? What if my heart exploded before I could find out? What if—

Before I could freak out any more, he put his other hand behind my head and pulled me toward him. Our lips touched lightly. He closed his eyes as he moved his mouth against mine. Heat rushed through me, making my fingers and toes tingle.

As he deepened the kiss, he pushed me back against the china cabinet. I dropped my plastic flute, spilling cider all over my peep-toe shoes. But I didn't care. I wrapped my arms around his neck, a small sigh escaping as he ran his tongue along my upper lip. I always thought French kissing would be gross, but somehow, it was electrifying and exhilarating—he wanted to explore all of me, and I wanted to let him.

Well, maybe I didn't want to let him explore *all* of me. As his fingers started working their way down my thigh, I gently pushed him away. "Maybe we should get back to the party."

"Alright." He gave me one more long kiss, and I smiled sheepishly as he moved to open the door.

But the door was stuck.

"What the hell?" he said, rattling the doorknob.

"Did it lock?"

He ran his fingers over the door around the knob. "There's a lock, but no key." He pounded on the door. "Hey! The door's stuck!" I face-palmed. Everyone would know we were hooking up in here. "Is anyone out there—"

The door flew open, revealing Maria and Priya on the other side. "Ha! Sorry about that." Maria took a large brass key from the door and dangled it in front of my face. "Door locks on its own." She inserted the key into the keyhole on the inside of the door and winked at me. "Just in case." She grinned and fluttered back toward the bar.

I coughed awkwardly. "You go ahead," I said to Robbie, desperate to tell Priya what just happened. "I'll catch up with you later."

He grinned at me before heading back into the main dining room. "Sorry I ditched you—" I started saying to Priya.

"Oh, please. Don't apologize." She grinned widely. "Did you guys make out?"

My face flushed. "Yeah."

We both squealed, and she hugged me. "Oh my God, he's so hot. You're so lucky."

I tried not to grin like a baboon. "What about you and Zane?"

Her smile dissolved. "The moment Sasha showed up, I turned into chopped liver."

My heart twisted at the sadness in Priya's eyes. "I can drag her away from Zane. But you can't just stand there and look pretty."

I adjusted one of her curls over her shoulder. "You have to participate in the conversation a bit."

She pinched the bridge of her nose. "He wants nothing to do with me."

"That's not true! You're just being shy. Loosen up a bit." I grabbed her arms and wiggled her around. "You're so silly and fun. Let him see that."

She laughed. "Okay, okay."

"Good. So let's get you back to Zane, shall we? Where are they?"

"Over by the bar—"

Before she could finish her sentence, I squeezed through the crowd toward the bar, dragging Priya behind me. I spotted Sasha giggling with Amy and Maria over something Zane said. "Sasha!"

"Hey, lady." Sasha kissed the air on either side of my face. "I have news for you."

Over Sasha's shoulder, I spotted Becky Wallace standing with Phil Pratt and a couple of her friends, staring at me with a flabbergasted expression. She was the one who first warned me off Sasha back in eighth grade as we speculated about the new classmates we'd get next year. Maybe she was jealous of the popular girl she'd heard everyone adored.

When I didn't reply, Sasha followed my gaze. "What on Earth is she staring at?" she said under her breath. "And what is she wearing? Didn't she hear? This is a birthday party for a seventeen-year-old, not a seven-year-old."

Becky wore a hot pink maxi dress with a tiny white unicorn

print. As Amy and Maria burst out laughing, Becky's eyes widened behind her thick glasses, and seeing everyone staring at her dress, she self-consciously wiped at it like she could brush off the unicorns. Phil, who was on crutches, glared at Sasha and tightened his jaw.

"And what the hell is Phil Pratt doing here?" said Priya a lot less quietly, glancing at Zane. Phil's face reddened under his mop of greasy brown hair. "Don't you need to shower to score an invite to these things?" My jaw dropped. That is *not* how I meant she participate in the conversation. How could she say something like that, even to impress Zane?

"Right?" Sasha looped her arm through Priya's. "Maria," she said in a low voice. "What were you thinking, inviting them?"

Maria rolled her eyes. "My mom made me invite everyone in our class. She didn't want anyone to *feel left out*. But I figured, whatever, we don't have to talk to them."

Becky glared at me like she thought I was making fun of her, too. But I'd never make fun of her. We used to be friends . . . until I couldn't handle being her friend anymore. And that wasn't her fault.

Eager to get everyone's attention off of Becky, I tugged Sasha's sleeve. "Robbie told me about the play!" I clapped my hands giddily.

She hugged me. "Yay! I'm so excited. When I listened to the 'Drinking Poison' track, I kid you not, I literally started crying. Like, ugly crying. You are severely talented." She grabbed a pretzel from the bar and doused it in spinach dip. "I can't wait to do this."

My attempt at a response came out as a squeak.

"But we need to wait until next winter. I know you were pushing for May—"

"*What?* That'll be too late!" My heart sank. "I wanted to send in the recording with my college applications."

She reached for another pretzel. "It's just that it takes a ton of work to put on a play with original music. And *Romeo and Juliet* will be a lot harder to pull off than *Bye Bye Birdie*." She paused to chew. "We'll have to finalize the script, nail down the stage direction, all of it. Besides, this'll give the orchestra more time to learn your music."

Panic bubbled in my gut. "But the winter play is always right before the holidays. That'll be too late."

"When are the application deadlines?"

"Mid-December, I think."

She licked some dip off her thumb. "Well, we can make sure the first showing is before your deadlines. Don't worry, we'll work it out, I promise!"

But that meant we'd have to be lucky enough for the first showing to go perfectly. This was my entire future on the line. And I didn't like depending on luck.

When you depend on luck, something's bound to go wrong.

48 MINUTES LEFT

"Scott!" Priya shrieked.

Scott landed on his back, and the chair toppled on top of him. He wheezed and gripped his stomach, the wind knocked out of him. Blood streaked down his face from a cut on his forehead.

I raced toward him. "Are you okay?" He grimaced and yelped. "What is it? What hurts?"

"Everything." He propped himself on his elbows with a grunt. His right foot was pinned under his left leg. Diego raced around the table as I dragged the chair out of the way. We all crowded around Scott.

Priya crouched next to him, dabbing a long gash on his forehead with a red cloth napkin. "Ah, this is deep. Hang on, there's some glass in there—"

"Wait. Stop." He pushed her away. "My ankle." He bent his

left knee and yanked his right foot free with his hands, groaning in pain. He slid up his pant leg, revealing an ankle twisted at an unnatural angle.

My stomach clenched, and I looked away, covering my mouth. Robbie gripped my shoulders, and I clasped one of his hands. While I could handle blood, displaced body parts were more than I could take. Oh, God. This couldn't be happening. This could *not* be happening.

"Damn," said Diego. "What do we do?"

Robbie brushed past me and knelt next to Scott. "Lemme take a look—" He reached for Scott's foot, but Scott shrank back, howling in pain.

"Don't touch it!"

"I want to see if it's broken," said Robbie.

"It's obviously broken," said Scott.

"It could be dislocated. See how the joint seems to be poking out?" He pointed to something that looked like a round knob pushing against the inside of Scott's skin. "Same thing happened to Zane during a game a couple years ago. If that's it, I can try to pop it back—"

"No!" Scott dragged himself back against the wall, wincing as his palm slid over a shard of glass. "Ahh. Get away from me." Priya crouched next to him, cupping her cheeks, staring in horror at Scott's ankle. I reached for her shoulder, wanting to comfort her, but she noticed the movement and edged away from me. My fingers caught air and dropped limply by my side.

"C'mon, man," said Robbie, kicking some of the glass away from Scott. "It won't hurt as much if you let me pop it back in."

"You're no doctor." Scott pressed back into the wall, sweat glistening on his forehead. He started wiping his hands on his jeans, brushing off the glass fragments, but froze when he noticed the maroon streak he left behind. One of his palms was bleeding. "Dammit."

"Here, let me help." Priya examined his hand, picking out a tiny glass shard.

"Have you ever popped a bone back into place?" Diego asked Robbie.

"No . . ." said Robbie. "But I watched Coach do it for Zane."

Scott shook his head; his face had a gray pallor. "No way." He waved Robbie back. "That doesn't count."

Robbie stood and ran his palm over his hair. "Dammit," he muttered, watching Priya tie a napkin around Scott's hand. Then she got to work on the gash on his forehead, clamping her mouth shut like she was trying not to be sick. I passed her a glass of water from the table.

"Thanks." She dipped the napkin in the water and gave me a look that said, *How is this happening?*

"You guys," cried Sasha. "We need to get out of here. Now." I glanced at the bomb's timer. We had about forty-five minutes left. Forty-five minutes . . . until what? Until everyone settled on one person to kill? Or until one of us attempted murder single-handedly? Would we work together to find a way out of this? Or

97

would we chance the bomb being fake, and wait it out? Scott's fall made this all seem terribly real. And if it got much hotter in here, could we suffocate before the hour ran out? Was that even possible?

Either way, we couldn't just stand around waiting for something to happen. Someone had to do something. I dragged the chair Scott had been standing on closer to the window, stepping over the largest glass shards. Clambering onto the chair, I leaned against the wall, peering out. Rusted iron bars crisscrossed the window, making it impossible to slide anything larger than a fist outside, let alone a person. As I searched for a lock or lever to open the bars, Sasha poked my leg. "C'mon. You're skinny as a pencil. Try climbing out."

I ran my fingers along the iron bars where they met the outer bricks of the window frame, feeling for a hinge. "It's useless, Sasha," I said. "These bars are cemented into the wall . . . I don't see any way to open them."

"Dammit," she said. "Is anyone out there?"

All I could see were sheets of rain in the narrow alley between the Chesterfield and the long brick building across from us. A large blue garbage bin stood to the left, blocking my view of the side street. To the right, there was nothing but brick wall and pavement—the building across the way had no windows facing us.

"Help!" I leaned as close to the jagged edges of the window as I dared. "Help us!" But my voice didn't carry over the pouring rain. Another clap of thunder rattled the alley. I screamed for help once more, but my cries went unanswered.

I turned to Robbie. "No one's out there. No one." He took

my hand and helped me step down from the chair, and wrapped me in a bear hug. I didn't know if he wanted to comfort himself or me. But his body heat smothered me, and I backed away from his embrace. "God, it's so hot in here." I never thought it could get this hot this fast, but the room was small, and the body heat from six panicked people probably wasn't helping. "It's so muggy and gross out, none of the hot air is escaping."

"It is," said Diego. "Just not fast enough."

Sasha leapt onto the chair and gripped the crisscrossed iron bars, as though she could shake them loose. Sweat coiled the hair at the nape of her neck. When her efforts proved fruitless, she shrieked at the top of her lungs, cupping her mouth to direct the sound out the window. Priya sat beside Scott, absentmindedly tracing the scar on her upper lip as she watched Sasha rage.

"Sasha, it's no use." I nudged her calf. "There's nobody there."

"My phone." She hopped down from the chair, out of breath, and leaned across the table to grab her phone. After climbing back onto the chair, she stuck her arm out the window, waving her phone around. Hope and dread mingled in my gut. Would that really work? Maybe we weren't getting reception because we were underground. Would Sasha be able to call for help?

"Anything?" asked Robbie, his hands on his hips. I fidgeted with my amethyst bracelet as we waited.

Finally, she pulled her arm back, her hand and phone glistening from the rain. "No. Still no signal. It's a dead spot." She climbed down and gripped my arm, her eyes brimming with tears. "My parents . . . Zane . . . what if I can never say goodbye?" Her lower lip quivered. Priya briefly narrowed her eyes at Zane's name, but said nothing.

I pulled Sasha into a hug, trying to ignore the unease seeping through my veins. We were less than fifteen minutes in, and despite the rising temperature, it chilled me to the bone that someone so headstrong was already crumbling. "Listen, you're going to see them again. There's no need to say goodbye. We'll be fine." But I wasn't so sure anymore. Her whole body trembled as she nodded.

"There has to be another way out of here." Diego scanned the room as I released Sasha, raking his fingers through his hair. "An emergency exit or something."

Scott shook his head. "I checked. There's nothing."

"There has to be something!" My voice came out high and scratchy. Leaning against the edge of the fireplace, I peered behind one cabinet, then the other. The air was thick with heat, and I wasn't sure if I was imagining it, but it seemed to be getting harder and harder to breathe.

"I told you, there's nothing," said Scott, wiping sweat from his brow with the back of his hand. "There aren't any secret doors."

"No trap panels?" Robbie kicked at the corner of the Oriental rug.

"We're already in the basement," said Diego.

"And we're not in some old mansion," said Sasha. "We're in the fucking Chesterfield. And we're totally trapped in here."

"Oh my God," Priya whined, tugging at the collar of her dress. "It's so freaking hot."

"Let's try to break down the door again," Robbie suggested.

"No way." Diego rubbed his forehead. "It's too heavy-duty—"

"Try again!" Sasha cried. "We have to do *something*!"

As they argued about the door, I slid down the wall next to the fireplace, gripping the sides of my head, damp with sweat. I scanned the room—there were no drop ceiling panels or gratings or closets or anything. Panic crept over me, and the sweltering room spun as the rising temperature made my cheeks pulsate with heat. How long did it take for heatstroke to set in? How hot would it have to get? As Robbie pounded on the door, I pressed my hands over my ears. The walls were closing in, the hot air rank with sweat and roasted meat and eggs suffocating me, and there was nothing I could do to stop drowning in my own panic. No way to claw myself free. No way to escape.

4 MONTHS AGO

APRIL OF JUNIOR YEAR

My stomach gnawed at itself as I peeled off my raincoat and lifted it toward the hook inside my locker. I missed, the soggy jacket flopping onto my books and binders. So much for thinking I could function off three hours of sleep.

Staying up until four in the morning to finish the track for Tybalt and Mercutio's duel in *Romeo and Juliet* seemed like a brilliant idea . . . until I hit snooze on my alarm clock seven times this morning. By the time I stumbled out of bed, I didn't have time to shove a Pop-Tart down my throat, let alone apply makeup. I dared a glance at my reflection in the locker mirror.

Yep. Whoever invented the snooze button should rot and die. In that order.

As I plodded toward the girls' bathroom to attempt damage control, Sasha barreled toward me, her eyes bugging out, nearly knocking over Phil Pratt. "Watch out!"

Phil scowled at her as he trudged away.

"Ugh. Doesn't that kid ever shower?" Sasha dumped a thick stack of papers in my arms. "Take this." She opened her tote bag, fished out a stapler and Scotch tape, and dropped them onto the stack. "And this and this."

"What're these?"

"I need your help putting up flyers . . . I don't have time—oh geez, who punched you in the face?" She narrowed her eyes at the purple rings under mine. I wiped at them self-consciously.

"I, uh, didn't get much sleep."

"Story of my life." She dug through her tote bag again and unwrapped a piece of gum. "Here. Caffeinated gum." Since my hands were full, she edged it into my mouth. "It'll help." She tapped on the stack of papers. "And then put these up? Please?"

"Why should I?" I mumbled, chewing on the sour peppermint chemical-laced gum. "You insulted my face."

"You look fresh-faced and fabulous, okay?" she said, eyes wide. "Just do it, please? I have to cram for our bio test during every free moment today." She clasped her chest over her heart, pleading. "I have cheer practice tonight and like zero free time ever."

"Are you alright?"

"I'm fine. Just stressed." She clutched my arm. "Please, pretty, pretty, please, help me out. You'll be my hero forever."

Laughing, I shoved her off. "Alright, alright." I scooted the stapler with my chin and read the top sheet. The words *Sasha Harris for Class President* formed an arc over Sasha's headshot, her loose brown waves cascading around her shoulder, her smile so white it looked Photoshopped. "You sure you have time to be class president?"

"I need to beef up my résumé. I'm getting into Harvard if it's the last thing I do." As if her résumé wasn't jam-packed already.

"Hey, wait . . ." I adjusted my grip to flip through the stack. Some of the flyers were nasty rumors about Jason Goding, her opponent, including one reading, *Jason Goding stole class funds last year. Vote for him if you want our senior prom stolen.* Another read, *Jason Goding cheated on his history final. Don't let him cheat our class, too.* "These are all lies."

Sasha frowned. "So?"

"*So?* I'm not helping you spread fake news."

"Oh, come on. It's not a big deal—"

"Amber!" Priya skirted the crowds milling about before the warning bell rang, rolling a poker chip over her knuckles. She'd been practicing nonstop since our "jam session" last Sunday, when she taught herself one of David Thurston's magic tricks.

Sasha scrunched her brow. "What are you doing?"

The chip fell from Priya's grasp and bounced across the floor, coming to a stop near Scott Coleman's feet. "Oh, crap. Sorry," she said as Scott handed her the chip.

"No worries. Happy to be of service." He flashed her a goofy grin. Scott had asked Priya out at least once a semester since eighth grade, but she could never date the class stoner—her mother would ground her for life if she even said the word "weed."

"Thanks," she said, blushing. Shy little Priya had a thing for dangerous boys.

"Hey, Red, what's shakin—"

"She said thanks," Sasha snapped, flicking her hand in a shoo-ing motion. He snorted and walked away, and she glanced back at Priya. "So what's with the poker chip?"

"It's for a magic trick," said Priya. "I was practicing on the bus, I didn't even notice I was still doing it—"

"You took the *school* bus?"

Priya flushed. "Yeah, well, it's pouring, I didn't want to bike—"

"Oh my God, you're *so* adorable." Sasha smiled brightly.

Priya chuckled awkwardly.

Sasha turned to me and clutched her forehead. "Dammit, I really have to go study for bio. I'm coming over tonight after practice. We'll study together." She motioned to all three of us.

"I don't need to study anymore," I said. We'd spent most days together recently, which was fun—I'd never had such a bustling social life, especially with all the parties Sasha invited me to—but it was exhausting. "Can't you study with Amy and Maria? Or Robbie?"

She snorted. "Those girls have zero interest in their GPAs, and all Robbie ever wants to do is play Fortnite."

"Well, I really have to focus on the *Romeo and Juliet* score."

"No worries. Priya and I will listen while we study." Before I could protest, she bumped her cheek against mine, then against Priya's, and strolled off.

I grumbled under my breath, but I had to admit, her manic drive was motivating. We were overachievers who fed off of each other's intensity. Sometimes I'd play an in-progress track for her, and she'd offer surprisingly good feedback—albeit delivered with a dash of snark. But then she'd smile brightly, as if to show she was just pushing me to be the best I could be.

Priya shook her head as she watched Sasha disappear down the hall. "I don't understand." Her voice rattled. "Why does she hate me so much?"

"What do you mean? She doesn't hate you," I said as we meandered toward our French class. "She invites you to all of her parties. She literally just invited you to study with us."

"Seriously? Did you not hear her? I'm *adorable*?"

"Yeah, so? You are."

"That's not what she meant," Priya moped, tugging on her shimmery blue scarf. "She was being condescending. You know, she's sidelined me every game so far."

"Really? I didn't know cheerleaders got benched."

"Not benched. Sidelined. I'm just supposed to cheer and rile up the crowd instead of doing stunts. But she *knows* I'm bad at being loud."

"Well, maybe that's the point. She's pushing you to do better. She's trying to help." I dropped the stack of flyers on the floor under a bulletin board and held up one with Sasha's headshot. "She knows you wish you weren't so shy. And you *have* been more outgoing lately."

"I guess . . ."

Grinning, I flicked her arm. "That's what friends do for each other. They help each other." I brandished Sasha's stack of flyers as proof.

Her eyes widened. "Oh my God. If she's been trying to help me this whole time—I mean, she *did* let me onto the team— shoot, what if I seem ungrateful? Maybe that's why she's mad at me." She bit her lip.

The warning bell rang, and the milling crowds broke apart to head to their first class.

"She's not mad at you," I said. "Seriously, I think you're read- ing too much into what she said."

Priya nodded, but she still looked worried. As we headed to class, I paused at a trash bin. Should I dump the flyers that lied about Jason? Friends helped friends, and that meant keeping them from getting caught in a lie. I dropped the incriminating flyers into the trash bin and headed to class.

After the final bell rang, I shuffled to my locker, eager to get home and take a nap before Sasha came over. As I tugged open my locker, Priya dashed over, whisper-shouting my name. "Amber! You've got to help me!"

"Why are you whispering all weird?"

"I did something bad." Priya's voice shook. "Really, really bad." Her eyes, wide and watery, darted around the hall.

"What did you do?"

She unzipped her backpack and tugged out the edge of a manila folder. "I stole the answers to our bio exam."

"You did *what*?"

"I did it after fifth period—I knew Mrs. Tanner didn't have class then. That's when she has office hours. So I found the folder on her desk. I thought I'd just snap pics of the answer key, but then the janitor came in, and I panicked and hid the folder in my binder. You know, I've been practicing sleight of hand . . ."

"And what, you thought you could *magic* the folder back onto her desk?"

"I don't know! Like I said, I panicked."

"But . . . what . . . why . . ." I didn't even know where to begin. "Did anyone else see you?"

She shook her head. "No. The janitor didn't even see; he was busy listening to music and taking out the trash. I just slipped out."

"Why did you do this?"

"For Sasha!" Priya shoved the folder back into her bag. "She was so stressed about our bio midterm, and you said she's been trying to help me, so I wanted to do something to help her, too."

"That doesn't mean you should have stolen an *exam*. God, Priya—"

"I know, I know."

"Did you send the answers to Sasha?"

Priya cringed. "I figured I might as well." She grabbed my wrists. "But please . . . *please* . . . you have to help me."

"How?"

"I need to get the folder back on Mrs. Tanner's desk, in the same spot, but she's in there now with a bunch of people. I think she's supervising some club." She wiped sweat off her upper lip. "But I have to do this before the end of the day, before she notices."

"Maybe she already has! She's already had a few periods to notice it's gone."

Priya choked back a sob. "I know. I know!" She rubbed her forehead. "I went back between every period after history, but she was always there. She must have a bladder of steel." She let out a hybrid squeal and growl sound. "Maybe I should just toss it. She'd never know it was me."

"No, no," I said. "You can't throw it out. Then she'll *know* someone took it, and if she questions everyone, you'll get caught for sure. You're an even worse liar than I am." I rubbed my eyes.

"Oh my God," said Priya. "My mom is going to kill me if she finds out. What if this goes on my permanent record?" Her eyes widened, and she gripped her throat. "What if I get *expelled*?"

"Priya." I clutched her shoulders. "Calm down, okay? We'll fix this. Can't you just wait around until whatever club it is lets out?"

She bit her lip. "I thought about that—but what if she goes to make copies of the test right after, before she goes home? She'll know it's gone."

I slammed my locker shut. "Alright. Let's scope out the situation."

"Thank you, thank you . . . I'm so, so sorry." Priya whispered apologies all the way to the science wing. "We need to distract her somehow. Maybe we should pull the fire alarm? No, then we'd get in bigger trouble."

"We? Who's *we*? You're the one who stole the test. I'm not doing anything that extreme." Mrs. Tanner's classroom door was wide open, and voices and laughter floated into the hall. I stood behind the row of adjacent lockers and leaned over, peering into the room.

Mrs. Tanner wasn't at her desk, which was next to the door. She stood writing something on the chalkboard running along the adjacent wall—I couldn't tell what with the glare from the windows—while a bunch of people sat around two of the lab tables. Diego was speaking. "I think we should build an aquifer prototype."

Amanda, a sophomore I recognized, screwed up her face. "Ugh, that's so boring, though. What about my 3D virtual reality idea?"

"Yeah, I liked that one," someone else chimed in.

Diego shook his head. "But better groundwater management could help so many developing countries. People are *dying* of thirst, every day."

"I think it's the Science Olympiad club," I whispered to Priya. She nodded, her lips puckered as though to keep herself from puking. I pulled my bio notebook from my backpack and rifled through the pages. "Okay, here's the plan. I'm going to ask Mrs. Tanner a question and try to get her to face the windows. While she's distracted, drop the exam on her desk when nobody's looking."

Priya nodded again so vigorously she looked like a bobble-head.

"Let's get this over with."

"Wait—" Priya whispered, but I was already knocking on the open door. All eyes in the room shifted to me, and Mrs. Tanner stopped writing on the blackboard. "Um, sorry, Mrs. Tanner? Do you have a sec? I have a quick question before our midterm tomorrow."

"Ah, sure thing." Mrs. Tanner set down the chalk and clapped the dust off her hands. "Melissa, can you take over up here? You guys keep brainstorming."

Mrs. Tanner started toward us, but I made a beeline for an empty desk at the far end of the room, next to the windows, nearly barreling over poor Melissa, who stood to transcribe while her fellow Olympiads shouted out ideas. "Sorry to interrupt."

"No, it's no problem." Mrs. Tanner pinched the bridge of her nose. "I should have rescheduled the Olympiad meeting and held extra office hours this afternoon. So what's up?"

She seemed frazzled, maybe a little overworked, but showed no signs of concern or anger that her midterm had been stolen. Maybe she hadn't gotten around to making copies yet. I stood at the farthest lab table from the desk and set down my notebook, so Mrs. Tanner and I both faced the windows to look at my notes. "I had a question about . . ." I frantically scanned my bullet points for something believably confusing. "Osmosis. I wasn't sure if I wrote this down right. What's the difference between hypertonic and hypotonic solutions? I think I might've mixed them up?"

Mrs. Tanner raised her eyebrows. "Did you look up the definitions in your textbook? Or online?"

I grimaced. Of course, finding a definition online would have been way faster than asking her for help. "I . . . well, yeah, I did, but . . . well, I guess I'm more confused about how we'd know which is which? You know, in a . . . practical application? I couldn't find a good explanation . . ."

"Ah"—she lowered her voice—"well, that's more than you'll

need to know for the test. I only ask for the definitions." She gave a sly smile, like she was divulging classified intel. "But since you asked, I'll tell you anyway." As Mrs. Tanner babbled on about cells shrinking or swelling, I glanced over my shoulder and gave Priya a pointed look. She inched her way to Mrs. Tanner's desk, keeping an eye on the Olympiads, who watched Diego and Amanda argue about the merits of aquifers like a tennis match.

"Nobody wants to do aquifers," said Amanda. A few other people nodded in agreement.

Diego pressed a clenched fist against his lips, shaking his head like he couldn't believe Amanda's stupidity. "Listen," he finally said, "taking on a project that ends human suffering will get us more points. Water depletion is killing people. Killing *babies*. Better aquifers can save lives and make entire regions more socially and economically stable. None of the judges care about 3D virtual reality. Maybe augmented reality . . . but those are such first world problems."

"You're one to talk about first world problems," said Amanda. "Who the hell needs a sponge that changes colors?"

Diego wiped his hand down his face, like he was tired of hearing about his own invention. "I came up with that years ago, okay? This has nothing to do with SpongeClown . . ." As a few people snickered, Priya lifted the edge of a stack of folders on the desk, clutching the stolen midterm folder in her other hand.

"Face it, Spongeman," said Amanda, her tone haughty. "Your idea's *boring*. We should go with mine instead." A few people cackled at her jab. Why was Diego letting her steamroll him like this?

"Guys, let's keep things civil, shall we?" said Mrs. Tanner, turning toward the group. Priya leapt back, still gripping the folder, looking guilty. Time seemed to slow, and panic settled on me like acrid fog as I visualized what would happen next. Mrs. Tanner would spot the folder in Priya's hand and understand what we were doing. I'd get suspended, and my parents would punish me by taking away everything that made me whole—my keyboard, my violin, my computer, my music. I wouldn't be able to work on the play, and Sasha would change her mind about letting me compose it. The walls felt like they were closing in on me.

But I couldn't let myself dissolve in a panic. I had to do something to get out of this.

"AQUIFERS!" I practically shrieked. Mrs. Tanner jumped, and everyone turned to stare at me. Heat flowed into my cheeks, and I knew I was red as a tomato. "Um . . . I think you should go with Diego's aquifers idea."

Amanda scowled. "Why should we listen to *you*?"

"Because . . . because . . ." I swallowed hard, my legs shaking, trying to think of something as Priya edged back to the stack of folders. "Because Diego's right—every other school is going to do flashy projects like VR or 3D printing or whatever. Things that mostly matter to people who are already well-off. If you go with the aquifer idea, you'll be doing something that can help people who are suffering every day, who aren't in a position to help themselves."

Diego raised his eyebrows, surprised. After a moment, he nodded. "Exactly. And if we can create an efficient, cost-effective aquifer prototype, companies in Africa and Asia can replicate the design."

"Oh, sure." Amanda rolled her eyes. "A bunch of high schoolers are going to be able to design something better than actual engineers."

"Why not?" I said. "If you don't think you can make a real difference, what the heck are you doing here?" A smile slid onto Diego's lips, and something fluttered in my chest.

Priya gave me a thumbs-up from across the room. Unfortunately, Diego turned to follow my gaze and saw Priya's thumbs-up, too. His head whipped back toward me, his smile gone, and I froze. Crap, crap, crap. How much did he see? Did he know what she did? Was he going to say something?

I grabbed my notebook. "Well, anyway, I have to get going. Lots of studying to do. Thanks for explaining all that, Mrs. Tanner." I bustled across the room, avoiding Diego's gaze, but his eyes bored into the back of my skull as Priya and I hurried out the door.

44 MINUTES LEFT

"Hey," said Diego. My eyes flew open to find him kneeling beside me as Robbie pummeled the door with a chair. Priya huddled under the open window next to Scott, watching Robbie's fruitless efforts, while Sasha circled the room, looking for clues. I released my ears, but flinched when the chair connected with the door again. "You okay?" Diego asked.

I hugged my knees close as waves of nausea rippled through me. "Just . . . feeling claustrophobic."

Diego leaned back, his eyes wide with worry. "Want me to leave you alone?"

Oh, God. I had to get a grip. "No, no. It's fine." I swallowed hard and rested my head back against the cool bricks lining the fireplace. "It's getting so hot. You don't think we could suffocate in here, do you?"

He rubbed my upper arm reassuringly, shaking his head. "I doubt it. I'm sure the thermostat isn't set that high."

"What if the boiler's busted or something?" I wiped my forehead with the back of my hand. "What if it *can* get that high?"

Diego furrowed his brow, considering it. Across the room, Robbie wound up for another hit, and the sound of splitting wood filled the room. Was he finally getting somewhere? "Dammit." Nope. The frame of the chair split down the middle. He cast aside the busted chair, which landed with a thud on the Oriental rug.

"Aargh!" Robbie slapped his palms against the door. "It's no use." He swiveled and found me on the floor with Diego, and clenched his jaw. "Still think this is some psycho scholarship test, Spongeman?" he asked Diego, balling his hands into fists.

Diego glanced at Scott, who grimaced in pain while he peeled off his leather jacket, and shook his head.

"There has to be some way out of here." Sasha opened the bottom drawers of the china cabinet I'd already searched earlier, only finding tablecloths. "There *has* to be." Her eyes darted around the room like a trapped animal's.

"You don't think killing someone's the only way out of here, do you?" I asked Diego in a low voice.

Diego shook his head. "Ugh, I don't know what to think anymore." He stood and extended a hand toward me. I grabbed it, and he helped lift me to my feet. "It *is* getting hotter in here, even with that window open. Maybe we should break the other one, too. And the glass on these"—he tapped on one of the china cabinets—"in case there's something useful inside—" He froze when something in the cabinet caught his eye.

I followed his gaze and spotted a tiny red glow in the back of the top shelf. "What the hell is that?"

"What is it?" Robbie joined us.

I rested the tips of my fingers on the glass. "We're . . . we're being watched."

"What?" Sasha rushed toward us.

I pointed into the cabinet. "It's a camera. Someone's watching us." A small lens—it looked like a webcam—was nestled between two rows of crystal goblets, covered by a dark red cloth napkin. It blended in with the mahogany shelves.

"So it is a test." Priya scrambled to her feet. "They're watching to see how we'll react."

"No," said Diego, clasping his hands behind his head. "If anything, it means it's not just a test. The poison's real, the bomb's real . . . this is really happening."

Priya blanched. "Why?" I asked. "Why does the camera mean it's real?"

Scott let out a groan of agony. He pressed his back against the wall, his legs splayed out in front of him.

"Because of that." Diego motioned to Scott. "If they're watching, and this was just a joke, or a test, they wouldn't let Scott lie there injured for the rest of the hour. They'd have stopped this when he broke his ankle so we could get him to a hospital."

"Oh my God," Priya whimpered. "That means they're waiting until . . . until . . ."

"Until we kill someone," Sasha finished, her voice trembling.

Robbie nodded and said through clenched teeth, "She's right. This is real. We're gonna have to kill someone." Scott threw me a worried look, pinching his lips as if to keep himself from howling in pain again.

Robbie pushed Diego out of the way and peered at the camera. "Fuck you!"

I shoved Robbie's arm. "Robbie, stop it. That won't convince whoever it is to let us go."

Priya gasped. "Do you think we *could* convince them?"

"How?" Scott grunted through shallow breaths. "We don't even know who they are."

"Well," I said, "let's think. Who do we think it could be? Who'd hate us enough to do this?"

Sasha nudged my arm. "You don't think it could be Maria, do you?" I raised my eyebrows.

"Maria . . . cheerleader Maria?" Diego asked. Sasha nodded, swallowing hard.

Robbie shook his head. "No way. Maria wouldn't do this to us."

I ran my fingers over my lips, considering this, taken aback that the first person Sasha would suspect of locking us in here was someone she considered a best friend. Was she thinking of something she did to piss Maria off? Sasha's eyes were wide and panicky as she watched me mull this over. "I don't know," I said. "Why would she do this? What would her motive be?"

"Well . . ." Sasha licked her lips, like she was holding something back. "Her parents own this place. It'd be easy for her to set it up."

I frowned. "True. But that's not a *reason*."

"She couldn't set this up, anyway, right?" said Robbie. "She's in the middle of the ocean somewhere."

Maria's parents had pulled her out of school for two weeks for their biannual family reunion, and she'd been on a cruise for the last week and a half. "Lucky bitch," Sasha kept saying to her before she left.

Sasha slapped her forehead. "I didn't even think of how the restaurant should have been closed."

I gripped my throat, shaking my head. Maria's family always shut down the Chesterfield when they went on vacation so their staff could take time off, too. "Me neither. Didn't think of it at all."

"When do they get back?" asked Priya.

"Saturday, I think," I said.

"Okay, so it wasn't Maria . . ." Priya bit her thumbnail, staring at the camera. "Maybe it's some serial killer. Remember those murders a few years back over at the park?"

"Oh, right," said Robbie. Back when we were in seventh grade, a few young women disappeared within weeks of each other. Each of them had been out jogging in Brewster State Park, and each washed up within a week in Brewster Lake. I didn't know any of them, but terror flooded our town like a tsunami. At school we had a buddy system in place whenever we set foot outdoors for gym or lunch. Mom and Dad wouldn't let Maggie and me bike to school by ourselves, and Maggie, then a junior, put up a huge stink about having to take the school bus.

The killer turned out to be the manager of our local grocery store. Apparently when his wife left him for his best friend, he went berserk and preyed on redheads who resembled her. Once the cops connected the dots, they were able to make the arrest pretty quickly. But even after he was behind bars, Mom made me carry pepper spray in my purse at all times. She was especially freaked out since we were redheads. "That could have been one of us," she'd say each time a news report aired.

"They caught that guy." Robbie scoffed. "Stupid son of a bitch."

"More like murderous piece of shit," Scott muttered, tugging a pack of cigarettes from his coat pocket with trembling fingers. One of the victims had been his cousin.

"Maybe he escaped from prison," said Sasha.

Scott laughed, though it sounded more like a croak. He dangled a cigarette between his lips, his head resting against the wall as he fished through his pockets for a lighter. "He's a serial killer, not a petty thief. He's in some maximum-security prison now. There's no way he escaped."

"And we would have heard about it," said Robbie.

"Right." Scott cast aside his jacket. "Besides, it's not his MO."

"His what?" asked Priya.

"His MO." Scott lit up, the flame wavering as he touched it to his cigarette. "You know . . . his pattern. Don't you watch *Law and Order?*"

"No."

"It stands for modus operandi," said Diego.

Scott pointed at Diego with his extinguished lighter. "Yeah, that. Like his method; his *style*. He went after girls who looked like his ex." He paused to grimace against a fresh wave of pain. "Why would he suddenly want to torture a bunch of teenagers?"

"You really shouldn't smoke in here." Sasha eyed the trail of smoke streaming out from between Scott's lips.

"Oh, c'mon, throw me a bone over here." He motioned toward his broken ankle.

"What if something catches fire?"

Scott flicked the ash off the end of his cigarette. "Don't be so paranoid." Scott took a long drag. "We're all gonna die anyway."

"Nobody's going to die," I said, standing between them. "We're going to figure this out."

Catching a whiff of Scott's cigarette, I cringed. His face glistened with sweat, and streaks of blood stretched from the gash on his forehead down his temple to his chin. Between puffs of smoke, he breathed with wheezing gasps—I couldn't imagine how much pain he was in. "Scott, maybe you shouldn't smoke. It's already kinda hard to breathe in here."

Scott snorted. "Only for you, Red." He held the cigarette over his head, and I plucked it from his fingers and tossed it out the window between the crisscrossed bars.

Priya ran her tongue over her front teeth as she contemplated something. "So if it wasn't the grocer serial killer, who could it be? Who on Earth would want any of us *dead*?"

"Maybe they don't," said Diego. I raised my eyebrows.

"Seriously?" Sasha said.

"We've been through this," said Robbie. "Those things are probably real." He motioned at the tray with the bomb and poison. "Someone's out for blood."

"Wait a minute, hear me out," said Diego. "So either way, the whole scholarship thing was a ruse to get us in the same room. That much is pretty clear. But maybe this is some sort of psychological experiment."

I furrowed my brow. "What, like . . . by some mad scientist?"

"Or the government."

"Oh, geez." Sasha balled her hands into fists. "We don't have time for one of your stupid conspiracy theories."

"No, really—" he started.

"What conspiracy theories?" Robbie scoffed.

"He's obsessed with UFOs and secret military bases and stuff," said Sasha.

Diego's jaw tightened. "I'm not obsessed—"

"How do you even know that?" I asked Sasha.

She rolled her eyes. "I had to peer review his AP Research paper last year. He also thinks we're in the matrix, like we're all being controlled by computers."

"I do not!" Diego glanced at me, his face reddening. "I wrote about the psychological factors driving conspiracy theories, and how not enough information or scientific evidence exists to disprove certain ones. That's all." Despite everything, I had to stifle a smile. With his valedictorian status, sponges, and sci-fi-themed wardrobe, his nerd flag was already flying. There was no need to hide it.

"Well, anyway, I don't think this is just an experiment," said Sasha. "Some psycho wants to blow us to bits, and torture us first."

Robbie shook his head. "It can't be some rando. It has to be someone we know. Or someone who knows us, at least. Someone who knows we all know each other."

"And someone who knew Maria's family would be out of town," said Priya.

The back of my neck prickled, and I exchanged a wary glance with Sasha. "So do you think it's someone from school?" I asked.

"It'd have to be, right?" said Robbie. "It's the only thing we all have in common."

"And we're all in the same grade," said Priya.

"That's true." Diego rubbed his chin. "But other than that, I don't see a way we're all connected. It's not like someone wants to wipe out a group of popular kids, or smart kids, or jocks, you know?"

I nodded. All of us together didn't fit any single mold. If I were to classify us, I'd say we were the queen bee, the jock, the brains, the stoner, the loner, and the orchestra geek. Each of us was so different. "Right . . . I don't understand why each of us was invited, either. Maybe we all have some enemy in common?"

Diego raised his eyebrows. "Someone with an individual vendetta against each of us?"

"Exactly," I said.

"Well, who here has the most enemies?" asked Robbie.

"It has to be him." Sasha glared at Scott.

He opened his mouth to say something, but Robbie cut him off. "Yeah. C'mon, fess up. You get in too deep with a drug deal gone bad?"

"I don't buy drugs," he croaked. I threw Sasha a look, but she avoided my gaze. "I swipe most of it from my dad's stash. Sometimes I sell some to kids at school, but we're only talking enough for a couple joints. I don't know anyone who'd do this."

"That doesn't even make sense," I said to Robbie. "Even if he did have dealers, why would they want the rest of us dead?"

Sasha flicked her hair behind her shoulder. "Well, none of us have enemies. At least, none who'd want to kill us."

"That's not true," said Robbie. He met my gaze, a look of fear in his eyes. "I can think of someone who'd want Amber dead."

9 MONTHS AGO

MAY OF JUNIOR YEAR

Kneeling at my locker, I swapped out a few notebooks and stood to find Robbie standing next to me. My heart jolted aggressively. He was saying something, cradling a notebook and textbooks under his arm, but I couldn't hear him over *The Tudors* score blaring in my ears. (Hey, it made Mr. Baskin's lectures about medieval England infinitely more interesting.)

I yanked out my earbuds. "Sorry, what'd you say?"

Robbie cleared his throat and rubbed the back of his neck. "I just wanted to know . . . if you were free Friday night."

"Oh!" Warmth spread through my veins. Robbie and I hadn't been alone together since Maria's birthday party over a month ago. When I asked Sasha about him recently, she said his baseball team's schedule was super packed. That made sense—I knew what it was like to be ludicrously busy. But more likely than not, I'd hallucinated our entire make-out session. Yep, that was the most logical conclusion.

But now here Robbie was, with his toned biceps, adorable smile, and killer dimples, asking me out on a date.

And there I was, melting into a puddle the janitor would have to mop up later.

"Yeah, sure." I grinned like an idiot and blushed as memories of his kisses raced through my brain. "I'm free."

"Great." His posture relaxed. "I just inherited my brother's car, so I can pick you up." He wiggled his eyebrows. "It's a piece of shit, though."

"Better than nothing, right?" I didn't even have my license yet. Since I was working nonstop on *Romeo and Juliet*, I hadn't had time to take driving lessons this year. But I was in no rush—my parents couldn't afford to get me a car. Not even a beat-up used one. I could think about taking lessons this summer.

He shrugged. "True. Anyway, six okay?"

"Six what?"

"Six o'clock. On Friday."

Oh, God. My brain was malfunctioning. "Oh! Yes. That . . . definitely. That good." Me Jane, you Tarzan. Oh, brother. Now my cheeks were scalding.

"Nice. So I figure six'll give us time to catch a movie after dinner. Is there anything out—"

"'Scuse me." Phil Pratt stood behind Robbie, his mouth set in a frown. His mousy brown hair was greasy as always, with an accompanying low-level rank smell. I'd had to hold my breath around him for years; since his last name was right before mine alphabetically, he always had the locker next to mine, or the seat in front of me if they were assigned. His eyes were heavily lidded and dark, and he always wore the same black hoodie. His backpack bulged behind him, and he gripped the straps as if to keep them from digging into his shoulders.

Robbie was blocking his locker, and clearly hadn't heard Phil, because he kept talking. "—you want to see? There's that action flick with Matt Damon, but—"

Phil cleared his throat and said louder, "Can you move?" My eyes lingered on a yellowing bruise under Phil's left eye. I vaguely wondered if it was Zane's doing. I recently saw him "accidentally" bump into Phil in the hall; maybe he'd "accidentally" elbowed him in the face, too. Though I shouldn't have assumed the worst—Zane had even bumped into me before. Maybe he was a legit klutz.

Robbie followed my gaze and finally noticed Phil. "Do you mind, dude?" Robbie leaned against Phil's locker, holding his ground. "We've having a conversation here."

Phil furrowed his brow and gritted his teeth, staring at the locker behind Robbie. "Do you mind?" His voice was monotone. "I need to get to my shit."

Robbie glanced back at the locker. "Oh, crap. Sorry." He shifted closer to me to give Phil some room.

"Anyway," I said. "That Matt Damon movie sounds great, I've been wanting to see that."

Robbie grinned. "Awesome." He tucked my bangs behind my

ear and brushed his lips against mine. Electricity rippled through me, and I could feel his kiss all the way down in my toes. "I'll catch up with you later," he said.

"Sounds yes. Is good." My God, what was wrong with me? Robbie spun to head down the hall, accidentally crashing into Phil with his shoulder. Phil's backpack was so heavy he nearly toppled over.

"Oh, shit, sorry, man," said Robbie. "I was just, you know . . ." He motioned toward me, then ran his hand over his short hair. He laughed awkwardly, gave me a final wave, and strode away.

Oh my God. I made Robbie Nelson get all flustered. *Me.* What was even happening?

"Whatever," Phil muttered after regaining his balance. I opened my mouth to apologize, but before I could say anything, Priya dashed over, with Sasha, Amy, and Maria in tow. All four of them were squealing.

"OhmyGoddidRobbiejustaskyouout?" Priya spoke so fast it sounded like one word.

I grinned. "Yeah. We're going on a date on Friday."

She squeaked again and threw her arms around me, while Amy and Maria launched question after question about the venue, my outfit, whether we'd get to second base. I blushed furiously. It was like having my own pep squad, and I wasn't used to all this attention.

Sasha opened my locker door all the way and checked her lipstick in the mirror. "I told him you wanted to go out with him."

My eyes widened. "You did what now?"

"Well, you asked me about him last week." She nudged me with her elbow. "It's because you like him, right?"

I bit my lip. "Maybe . . ."

"Oh, please." She fished through her purse and uncapped her tube of rose-tinted lipstick. "Don't play coy. He's gorgeous, sweet, loyal—"

We both jumped when Phil tossed a heavy textbook into his locker. Sasha cringed at him and pinched her nose, miming passing out from his stench. Amy giggled.

"Gawd, Sasha," said Maria. "Why don't *you* date Robbie?"

My stomach dropped. "Oh . . . is that something you'd want?"

"Oh, God, no," said Sasha. "He's like a brother to me. You know, our dads are BFFs, so we've been friends forever. And I could never date anyone who saw me throwing up next to the kiddie pool half naked when we were five." Sasha dabbed some more color onto her bottom lip. "But you'll be good for him; he needs something to fawn over besides his baseball mitt." She gave me a conspiratorial wink. "So I helped you two along. It all worked out, didn't it?"

"Yeah, I guess . . ." Diego and I had also been friends since we were little, but that never kept me from thinking maybe someday I'd feel his lips on mine. That maybe someday we'd end up together. But that spark had extinguished when he started ignoring me.

"Who is your latest boy toy, now, anyway?" Amy asked Sasha.

"You know I don't kiss and tell." Sasha winked, throwing me a mischievous look. "I don't need any of you fools spreading gossip."

I cooed. "Are you seeing someone?"

"On and off. Nothing serious." She shrugged, smoothing gloss over her lipstick. "Honestly, I don't have time for a relationship, anyway."

"You're so lucky," Priya said to me. "You're going on a date with the hottest guy in our year!" She bit her lip. "Well, second hottest . . ."

I gasped and grabbed Priya's wrist. "Oh my God, I have an idea. Let's make it a *double* date."

Her eyes widened, while Sasha's narrowed in the mirror. "What do you mean?" Priya asked.

"I'll ask Robbie to bring Zane, and then I'll bring you! It'll be so much fun." Having Priya there would take some of the pressure off. Besides, she'd been mopey ever since Sasha started coming over so often. This would cheer her up.

"Really?" she asked. "Do you think he'd even want to go on a date with me?"

"Of course! I mean, come on. He totally thinks you're cute. He calls you 'gorgeous,' right?"

Priya squealed and threw herself at me for a hug. "We should go shopping tonight and pick up cute outfits."

"Seriously?" Sasha said to Priya as I knelt to retrieve the trig textbook I needed for next period. "You've got to practice for our meet on Saturday. Your form needs work."

"Womp, womp," Amy muttered to Maria, who grinned.

After Priya stole the bio exam for her, Sasha let her start doing stunts, but apparently Priya had a lot of catching up to do. It was nice of Sasha to take extra time to train her—with everything else she was working on, I didn't know how she managed it.

But Priya crossed her arms. "But I can take a couple hours off to go shopping." As they debated their schedules, I leaned out of Phil's way—he was frantically chucking the contents of his backpack into his locker. Annoyed, I glanced over. As he rummaged through his locker, I caught a glimpse of something shiny in his backpack. Whoa. Was that a . . .

No. It couldn't be.

But it was. I knew what I was seeing.

Phil looked up and met my gaze. My heart froze. My fingers went numb.

Did he know I saw the gun?

I couldn't say anything. What if he took it out and started *shooting*? No. That wouldn't happen. That *couldn't* happen. Could it? This couldn't be real. This could *not* be real. The blood drained from my face, and his jaw tightened as I continued digging around in my locker, pretending everything was fine. I couldn't tell the girls. They'd freak out. And then he might panic. No. Best to pretend I didn't see anything and go get help.

I pulled out my trig notebook and slammed my locker shut. Sasha flinched back. "Hey!" She'd been examining her eye makeup in my locker mirror.

"I have to go to the bathroom," I said.

"I'll come with—" Sasha started.

"No, it's fine. Go to class." *Go to class now before Phil goes ballistic!* I wanted to scream, but I couldn't set him off. Phil zipped his backpack, shut his locker, and speed-walked down the hall.

Her brow furrowed in concern. "Are you okay?"

"Go!"

Sasha flinched, and her eyes widened. I'd scared her. The other girls watched the exchange with raised eyebrows, saying nothing. I didn't know if they went to class right away, or watched me spin and bolt down the hall, past the girls' bathroom, toward the principal's office. I didn't care if they thought I was nuts. I had to tell someone about the gun. What if Phil was about to shoot someone? He *did* get shoved around a lot, accidentally or not. Maybe he wanted revenge. Oh, God. Maybe I should have grabbed for the gun right then. What if he started shooting people right now? What if people *died*? It would be all my fault, because I could have stopped it.

As the bell rang, I turned a corner and nearly collided with Mrs. Burr. Her deep wrinkles furrowed into a frown. "No running in the halls—" But I raced past her. Telling her would be useless—it would take her forever to hobble down the hall to find Mr. Garcia or Mr. Turner, the school's security guards.

Mr. Garcia's desk outside the principal's office was empty. While we didn't have fancy metal detectors like other schools, he usually sat there facing the front doors, monitoring the stream of people coming and going throughout the day. Where was he? I dashed into the principal's office. Mr. Garcia was filling his water bottle at the cooler, laughing at something Ms. Anderson, the principal's secretary, was telling him. The principal's door was closed.

"Mr. Garcia!" I put my hands on my knees, catching my breath.

He turned and spun the lid of his bottle shut. "Hey there, Amber." His smile dropped at the expression on my face. "What's wrong?"

"Gun!" I blurted between gasps. "Phil Pratt has a gun in his backpack. I saw it when he was at his locker. His is next to mine, and I saw a gun in his backpack. Please, you have to do something—"

But he didn't have to hear another word. "Cheryl," he said to Ms. Anderson, unhooking his two-way radio from his belt. "Look up what class Phil has now." He held the radio to his lips. "Precinct, I need immediate backup at Brewster High. I have a report of a student with a gun."

"Ten-four," a woman said on the other end. "Sending the request now."

"He's in Mrs. Lanish's trigonometry class." Ms. Anderson squinted at her monitor, pushing her wire-rimmed glasses up her nose. "Room 309."

"Alright," he said. As she bustled over to the principal's door and stuck her head in, Mr. Garcia put his hands on my shoulders. "Does he know you saw the gun?"

"I . . . I don't know . . ."

Mr. Garcia shook my shoulders gently. "I need you to tell me the truth. Did he see?"

"I . . . yeah. Yeah, I think he saw me looking at it."

"Then what did he do?"

"He zipped up his bag real fast and left—oh my God, and I should be sitting behind him in class right now. He'll know for sure I saw when I don't show up."

"Alright. I'm going to confiscate the gun. I need you to go straight to the parking lot, away from the school, and don't come back inside, whatever you hear. Got it?"

I nodded, swallowing hard. Was I in danger? Would Phil come after me now? Since I got him busted, would I be a target? We both left the office, and I bolted down the hall toward the front doors and didn't stop running, leaving the school and God knew what was happening inside behind me.

39 MINUTES LEFT

"So wait . . ." Priya crinkled her brow. "You think *Phil* locked us in here?" She sat on the floor on her folded legs next to Scott, glass shards glittering on the floor around them.

"Yeah," said Robbie. "He blames Amber for ratting him out."

At the time, I'd been hailed a hero. But I sure didn't feel like a hero. I was only terrified of what would happen if I said nothing.

Mr. Garcia had pulled Phil out of class under the guise of getting a phone call from home—a family emergency. Once out in the hall, he'd confiscated Phil's backpack and unloaded the gun. Nobody saw what happened, and nobody was the wiser until Sasha cornered me later and asked what happened earlier. I was so shaken, I had to tell her. Of course, Sasha blabbed to Maria and Amy, and word quickly spread that I'd prevented a mass shooting.

"I don't think Phil did this." I brushed back my bangs, pacing between the table and the door. "I mean, I'm sure we can all think of someone who holds a grudge against one of us."

"Well, Phil sure holds one against you," said Robbie.

"But he doesn't hate Amber in particular," said Sasha. "He hates everyone."

"Even more reason to suspect him."

"He doesn't hate *everyone*," I said.

Sasha cringed. "Of course he does. He's always scowling at everyone, giving them dirty looks. Hence the gun."

Anger bubbled in my stomach. She acted like Phil was the only bad guy, when she was constantly ragging on him behind his back. "You sure gave him plenty of reasons to scowl at you."

Her eyes narrowed. "Me?"

"Yeah, *you*. You always made fun of him behind his back."

Sasha pursed her lips and crossed her arms. "That's no reason to bring a gun to school. That's no reason to *kill* people."

"Dammit, Sasha." I clenched my fists at my sides. "You know it was just a BB gun."

"So?"

Robbie rubbed my upper arm. "A close-range BB shot can still kill someone."

"But he wasn't going to open fire in the hallway or anything," I said.

"How do you know that?" Robbie asked. I swallowed hard. I knew why Phil had the gun, and I'd kept his secret for months. I hadn't prevented a mass shooting at all.

Sasha shook her head at me. "I don't get it, Amber. Why the hell are you defending him?"

"He never meant to hurt anyone." My throat constricted.

Robbie furrowed his brow. "What do you mean? Why else would he bring a gun to school?"

Turning away, I folded my arms as a chill ran through me, despite the heat. I faced Diego, who stood at the end of the table watching me with his head slightly inclined, like he was trying to piece together a jigsaw puzzle.

"Amber?" Robbie asked.

Oh, God. I had to tell them the truth.

7 MONTHS AGO

JULY AFTER JUNIOR YEAR

Something about this crescendo didn't sound right. I narrowed my eyes at the screen, examining the notes as the chords played in my headphones. It needed more resonance. I could try using a crossfading legato . . .

Without taking my eyes from the screen, I grabbed my glass of pink lemonade and took a sip, trying to audiolize a modification, when someone tapped me on the shoulder. I jumped, and lemonade sloshed over the glass onto my PJs. "Ahh!"

"Ahh!" Dad leapt backward.

I tugged off my headphones. "Oh my God. You scared me to death."

He laughed. "Well, there's no other way to get your attention. You're deaf to everything but music. The doorbell. Your mother shouting. The house could be burning down and you'd still be sitting there, happy as a clam."

I gripped my knees, waiting for my heart to slow. I hated when people snuck up behind me. Not because of the jump scare. But because it reminded me of Maggie.

It reminded me of the last time we ever spoke.

I'd been learning to use a multitrack sequencer and was on something like my fiftieth attempt to sync a piano and violin medley when a hand suddenly gripped my shoulder. I'd jumped and flailed my arms. "Ahh!"

"Whoa!" Maggie had backed up, laughing nervously. "Sorry, it's just me."

"What the heck, Mags." I tore off my headphones and groaned. "I was almost done with this track. It was almost perfect." I clicked the Stop button, slamming harder on the mouse than I had to, and the recording stopped.

Maggie's eyes widened, and she tucked her wiry brown hair behind her ears. "I'm sorry! Geez, don't have a panic attack."

"What do you want?" I'd snapped, not in the mood to fight with her again. She'd been nothing but sulky and snarky over the past year. Despite our age gap, we used to hang out all the time; we'd geek out over the latest fantasy fad, have all-weekend movie marathons, gobble up fan fiction, and listen to the scores—some of the greatest ever composed. It's how I discovered my love for movie scores. But then I'd become more of a nuisance to her than a sidekick.

Maggie shifted her weight on her feet. "There's something I wanted to give you." She reached into her pocket and plucked out her amethyst bracelet—the one my grandfather had given Grandma Betty as a wedding present. "Here. It's yours."

I swiveled my chair around to face her, staring dumbfounded at the bracelet. When we were little, we'd take turns sitting on Grandma Betty's lap, counting the misshapen beads, trying to pick which of them was our favorite. When she died last year, she left it to Maggie. I shook my head. "But you wanted to wear it with your prom dress. Mom was going to help you find a purple dress to match—"

"I know. But I don't want to go to prom." She inched closer, dangling the bracelet in front of me. I held out my hand, and she dropped the bracelet onto my open palm, the amethyst beads warm from her pocket.

"Why not?"

She shrugged. "No boy will take me. What's the point?"

"You don't need a date to go to prom, do you?"

"I just don't want to go, alright?" She raised her voice, and her chin quivered slightly. "Here, let me help." She grabbed back the bracelet and draped it over my wrist, securing the clasp for me. "There."

I ran my fingers over the beads, unsure what to think. "Thank you."

"You're welcome." She turned back to the stairs.

"Wait!" I called after her. She paused without looking back. "Do you want to hang out or something? Maybe we could watch a movie?"

"You're busy with your music. I'll let you get back to it."

I glanced at my keyboard—I wanted to finish this track tonight. But maybe Maggie was reaching out, trying to be a real sister to me again. I missed spending time with her. But when I looked back up, she was already out the door, sprinting back up the stairs.

I didn't follow.

It was the last time I ever saw her alive.

Now Dad stood next to me, crossing his arms and squinting at the stanzas on my screen. "Lookin' good."

I snorted, shaking away my sad memories. "Really?"

"I have absolutely no idea." We both laughed. "So, that free software's working out okay?" Worry etched across Dad's forehead. When my laptop crapped out last year, I'd refused to take Maggie's old one, so had to get a refurbished one my state-of-the-art notation software wasn't compatible with. And the best compatible programs were too expensive.

"Yeah, it's totally fine. I'm almost done with this track, actually—the end of act three."

"Oh, good." His posture relaxed. "Just one more to go after that, huh?"

"Yep." I grinned. Dad knew I'd already completed act five— he liked getting updates on my progress. He was baffled I was scoring an entire Shakespeare play, and even reread it so he could listen and have a general sense of what was happening.

"Amber!" Mom shouted from upstairs.

"Oh yeah." Dad wiped his upper lip. "Someone's at the door for you."

"Really?" Who could it be? Everyone had scattered for the summer. Priya went to India to visit her grandmother, and Sasha,

Maria, and Amy were counselors at some cheerleading camp in Pennsylvania.

"Yeah. Now, remember. You're not allowed to date until you're forty-seven." I raised my eyebrows. He raised his to mirror mine, and when he didn't offer any more information, I bounded upstairs.

When I reached the foyer, I locked eyes with Robbie, who stood *in my house* holding a single red rose. Presumably for me. My lungs seized up, making it somewhat impossible to breathe.

"Hi," I finally managed to choke out. Mom stood next to the stairs, grinning from ear to ear. I hadn't seen Robbie since school let out for the summer. After the Phil Pratt incident, I'd canceled our date, too shaken to think about dating or kissing or generally having a good time.

But after that, Robbie made it his personal mission to make me laugh. He'd slip notes into my locker with jokes that were so bad, I couldn't help but crack up, like, *What do you call fake spaghetti? An impasta!* I especially loved the jokes he attempted to draw, like one muffin being terrified of another talking muffin. We also texted for hours each night, seeing how long we could converse purely with emojis. I was convinced Robbie was a dork disguised as a jock. A particularly hot jock.

"Um . . . what's up?" I glanced at the rose. Mittens was already having his way with Robbie's ankles, rubbing his face all over his jeans, but despite the cuteness overload, Robbie held my gaze.

"I'm taking you to the carnival. You know, for your birthday."

I was pretty sure I heard Mom squeak.

"My birthday's not until tomorrow—wait, how'd you know it was my birthday?" I'd deactivated my Facebook profile in eighth grade, and I was pretty sure I hadn't mentioned the date to him.

He grinned. "Priya texted me."

Our town hosted this cheesy carnival every Fourth of July weekend, and Priya and I always went together on my birthday. When we were little, it was the most magical thing in the world, like Disney World was coming to visit. Then our families took a trip together to *actual* Disney World, and we realized, nope. Still, we went every year, and even though Priya was halfway around the world, she'd made sure I'd carry on the tradition.

"Anyway," Robbie said, "I figured you already had plans for tomorrow, so I'm stealing you for myself tonight." He handed me the rose, and I took it, biting back a grin. My insides got warm and tingly, and my fingers trembled slightly, like I'd drunk a cappuccino too fast.

Mom looked like she was about to spontaneously combust from glee. Oh my God. How embarrassing. I turned to her and Dad, who'd finally made his way upstairs. "Is it okay if I go?" Dad's jokes aside, I wasn't sure if my parents were cool with me dating yet—I hadn't mentioned Robbie to them in the spring.

"Of course!" said Mom. "Since when do you have to ask for permission to go out with your friends?"

Since before Maggie died. I didn't have to say the words out loud for Mom to hear them. Her smile collapsed.

After Maggie died, it was like my parents' ground rules vanished. I thought they'd get more protective, but instead they

143

let me do whatever I wanted, as long as I texted Mom every so often. It was like they were walking on eggshells around me, terrified to upset me.

"Great," said Robbie, the moment going over his head. It seemed to fly over Dad's head, too—he was too busy sizing up Robbie. "So . . . you want to get changed first?"

I glanced down at my plaid pajama bottoms and fuzzy bunny rabbit slippers, both stained with pink lemonade. At least I was wearing a bra, but that didn't stop me from turning bright red. "Right. Be right back." I raced to my room, set the rose on my desk, and changed into jean shorts, a sparkly T-shirt, and Converses, and raced back upstairs before Dad could warn him that I wasn't allowed to date for another thirty years.

"Text me when you get there," Mom called after me.

It was only a few-minute drive to the carnival. When we arrived, Robbie bought my ticket and a huge mass of pink cotton candy. I hated cotton candy, but took it anyway, hoping my fluttering stomach could handle the sickening sweetness.

"Feel any older yet?" he asked.

I grinned slyly. "You'll have to ask me tomorrow."

"It's close enough."

I shrugged. "I don't love the idea of getting older."

"What!" He shoved my arm playfully. "Come on. You're seventeen!" Yes. Seventeen. The same age Maggie was when she died. "You're, like, not even a fifth of the way through life."

"True," I said, biting back my morbid thoughts.

"So how's the play coming along?" he asked.

"Pretty good." I pinched a clump of cotton candy and let it dissolve on my tongue, practically feeling the sugar disintegrate my teeth. "I'm trying to finish before Sasha comes back from cheerleading camp."

"Good thing you guys put it off 'til December, huh?" he said as we wandered past the spinning teacup ride—the one so nauseating it turns your insides to slime.

"Yeah, I guess." My progress had stalled this spring—it was hard to focus as my mind reeled with gory images of what might have happened at school if I hadn't busted Phil. But I didn't want to talk about that now.

"Oh hey look, there's an actual roller coaster this year!" I pointed to it, eager to change the subject. "Though you'd have to have a death wish to ride it."

I turned back in time to catch Robbie's eyes roaming up and down my body. Oh my God. He was checking *me* out. "Nah, I'm sure it's safe."

"Um, no. It could get stuck upside down. Or derail. You see stuff like that in the news all the time. People have *died*."

"Yeah, but that wouldn't happen to us." He chuckled, waving off my concern, like death was only something that you saw on the news—something that only happened to other people.

I took another bite and offered the pink cloud to Robbie, but he waved it off. "Oh, come on," I said. "I can't eat all this myself."

He grinned. "What, you can't put away a square foot of pure sugar?"

"No way. Am I weird for thinking cotton candy is gross?"

"Not even slightly." He grabbed it and tossed it into a nearby trash can. "Everyone else is weird for liking it."

"So you assumed I was some weirdo, huh?"

"My bad. What else can I get you? An artery-clogging funnel cake? A mystery-meat corn dog?"

I cringed. "Uh-oh, are you some sort of health freak?"

"'Uh-oh'?" He clasped his chest, feigning offense. "I take pride in my freakishness, thank you very much."

I laughed. "I guess you can be a freak if I can be a weirdo."

"Mm'kay." He took my hand, and butterflies wreaked havoc on my innards as we loped through the aisles of carnival games and food vendors, the pungent smell of fried dough and meat wafting from the stalls.

My mind raced for something clever to say, but all I could come up with was, "So what've you been up to?" Earth-shattering, I know.

He shrugged. "I've been hitting the gym a bunch." I tried not to glance at his biceps, which I hadn't stared at the entire car ride over.

Okay fine, I stared. Sue me.

"You haven't been playing baseball?"

"I'm going to baseball camp next week. It's local, though, so we can still hang out." The butterflies raged. He wanted to spend more time with me. *Me.* "And I'm playing in the county baseball league in the fall, since I still haven't been recruited for college yet." Worry lines etched his forehead.

"*Still?* It's not even senior year."

"Yeah. You usually get recruited junior year." We paused at a stall to watch some middle school boy chuck bean bags at three milk bottle pyramids and fail miserably. "My brother Paul was actually recruited sophomore year."

"Whoa, seriously?"

"Yep. But he only went to college a year before getting drafted to the minors." His voice was strained. I thought I was running out of time with college applications due in December. I'd be devastated if I felt like I'd already lost my chance.

"It's not too late or anything, is it?"

He rubbed the back of his neck. "To be honest, it might be. But I'm not giving up. There's no way I can give up." Wow. I admired his perseverance. Before I could tell him so, he approached the middle schooler. "Hey man, lemme show you how it's done." He swapped cash for three bean bags from the balding man running the stall. The boy backed toward his older sister, who I hadn't noticed before. It was Becky Wallace. Her expression soured as her eyes darted between me and Robbie.

Robbie tossed me two of the bean bags and stood back from the stand, holding the remaining bean bag behind his back, like he was lining up a pitch.

"Don't you play third base?" I teased, trying to ignore Becky's stare.

"Doesn't mean I don't know how to pitch." He stepped forward and hurled the bag at one of the pyramids, knocking over all six bottles. I cheered. He curled his pointer finger at me in a come-hither motion, and I tossed him a bean bag, giggling.

He easily toppled the last two pyramids and whooped, and

picked me up for a hug, twirling me around. Becky's little brother cried, "That was badass!" but Becky grabbed his forearm and marched him away, ignoring his protestations. What was her problem, anyway?

"So what'll it be?" asked the balding man, sounding bored. "The giant dog, the giant dragon, or the giant cat?" He motioned to the stuffed animals dangling over his head.

Robbie glanced at me. "Lemme guess. You want the cat, right?"

My eyes widened. "How'd you know?"

He glanced at his legs; his dark blue jeans were coated with Mittens's white fur. "Just a wild guess, really."

"Well, I'm going with the dragon." I crossed my arms. "Call me mother of dragons." The man started fishing the dragon off its hook with a long pole. "No, wait. The cat. Definitely the cat."

"Ha!" Robbie guffawed as I hugged my new oversized cat.

"Shut up."

"Okay." He pulled me around the last stall in the aisle and tucked my bangs behind my ear. Before I knew it, his lips were on mine, and I was pretty sure my heart was about to burst out of my chest. His hands cupped my face, and with my free hand I clutched a bunch of his shirt, pulling him close as he deepened the kiss. Heat tore through my veins, and my entire body tingled, like every nerve ending was on fire.

A few people shrieked nearby, pulling us from the moment, and I gasped. But it was just the roller coaster soaring past. Robbie grinned. "C'mon, let's do it."

"I dunno . . . I don't exactly have a death wish."

"Neither do I!" Laughing, he led me toward the line, right behind Becky and her brother. Oh, no. Becky was still glowering at me—not quite a glare, but more like I'd just stabbed her in the gut and she couldn't fathom the betrayal. Had she been watching us kiss? Was she jealous or something?

Back when we were friends, she'd crushed on every boy in our grade at one point or another, even Phil Pratt. At each slumber party, she initiated the game Kiss, Marry, Kill to gauge whether any of us liked the same boys.

Robbie checked his wallet. "Crap, I'm out of cash. There were ATMs near the entrance. Lemme hit that up real quick."

"I have some cash—"

"No, no, today's on me." He gave me a peck on the cheek. "Hold our place in line."

As he jogged off, Becky openly gawked at me. I awkwardly shifted my weight from one foot to the other. "So much for going Dutch, I guess?" I laughed feebly. But she said nothing. Guilt clenched my chest as I remembered Sasha and her friends, and even Priya, mocking Becky's outfit at Maria's birthday party, while I stood by and did nothing.

I met her gaze, wanting to make amends. "Listen, I'm sorry . . ."

"*I'm* not the one you should be apologizing to," she said. Her little brother stood behind her, ignoring us as he played a game on his phone.

Now it was my turn to gawk. "What? What do you mean?"

She fiddled with the end of her braid looping over one shoulder. "I just . . . I don't understand you. You think you're so high and mighty now. What happened to you?"

Whoa. Oh, no. Had she been holding this grudge since middle school? Maybe she thought I was social climbing now that I was friends with Sasha and Robbie. But that wasn't why we'd bonded at all.

"Listen, Becky . . ." I hugged the oversized cat close to my chest. "I never meant to hurt you. You know that, right? I wasn't in a good place for a long time—"

She dropped her braid and balled her hands into fists. "This isn't about me."

"Then what are you talking about?"

She glanced at her little brother, but he was still in his own world. "This is about Phil."

I gasped. "Phil, as in Phil Pratt? God, Becky, how were you even friends with him?"

"I am friends with him. *Am.* Present tense."

"But . . . why?"

"He's not a bad person. You don't know anything about him."

I shook my head, unable to believe what I was hearing. "He brought a gun to school. That's all I know."

Her expression darkened, the resentment in her eyes magnified by her thick glasses. "Of course it's all you know. You never bothered asking him anything. You don't know why he had that gun."

I cringed at her tone, like I was the one who did something wrong. "Then why did he?"

Becky clamped her lips, considering me for a moment. "His reasons aren't mine to tell. I promised him I wouldn't . . ." She swallowed hard. "But you don't know him. You don't know anything. Phil didn't deserve to be expelled. And now he's trapped at home with . . . with . . . he's trapped at home, and it's all your fault."

"Hey!" Robbie squeezed past people behind us in line and stepped in front of me like a shield. "What the hell's the matter with you?" He towered over Becky, and her eyes widened as she cowered backward. But Robbie went on. "Don't talk to Amber about Phil. Do you have any idea how traumatic that was? She saved all our lives."

"No, she didn't." Her voice shook, and her lower lip trembled. "She didn't save anyone."

"Bullshit."

"Phil never would have hurt anyone. Not like how you and your friends hurt him, all the time."

Robbie screwed up his face. "We didn't hurt him."

Becky shook her head, her eyes brimming with tears. "Now I'm calling bullshit." Without another word, she grabbed her brother's arm, yanked him from the line, and ran off, while the hate in her eyes seared into my mind like a hot iron branding my skull.

38 MINUTES LEFT

I let out a deep sigh. "Phil told me why he had the gun, alright? But he swore me to secrecy—"

Robbie grabbed my arms. "You let that psycho talk to you?"

I broke free from his grip. "He saw me in Starbucks once, after the carnival." Becky must have told him what happened. She might have even encouraged him to tell me the truth. "He sat at my table while his mom ordered coffee. I couldn't just pack up my stuff and leave. I can't run away every time I see him."

"Yeah you can!"

"But he's not dangerous. Not really."

"What did he say?" asked Priya. She straightened to get a clear view of me over the table.

I hesitated, gritting my teeth. I hadn't told anyone this. Phil asked me not to, and his life was already in pieces. But now I had no choice. "He said he only had the gun to protect himself from his father. And to protect his mother." I'd never forget the look on his face when he rolled up his sleeve and showed me the cigarette burns. The way his lower lip trembled when he spoke about the pain. The coldness in his eyes when he looked into mine. Like I'd knowingly betrayed him, subjected him to a year at home with his drunk, violent father.

Guilt ensnared my heart. I knew I did the right thing snitching on Phil. You see a gun in school, you report it. And it was absolutely wrong of him to bring a BB gun to school. But I had no idea things were so bad at home. How was I supposed to know he had an abusive father? It wasn't exactly like he'd confided in me before.

But Becky was right—it wasn't like I ever asked, either.

I'd seen the bruises on Phil's face. I'd seen him hobbling around on crutches last year. But I hadn't cared to ask what happened. I hadn't cared about anything but the play and my bustling social life. Maybe if I'd been more observant, more empathetic, I could have helped him escape his abusive situation, even if it just meant tipping off our school guidance counselor or something. Instead I blinded myself to his pain and wrote him off him as a loser who could use a shower more often.

Priya climbed to her feet. "Was his dad beating him or something?"

"Yeah," I said. "He was. All the time."

"Bullshit," Sasha snarled. "That's probably just a sob story he came up with." She pointed at the door. "I bet that sniveling little cockroach is out there right now, laughing at us." I winced, startled by her tone.

Robbie swatted her hand down and whispered, "Don't say that," throwing a pointed look at the camera.

"It wasn't just a sob story," I said. "I told our guidance counselor what Phil told me, and now he's living with his aunt."

"That doesn't mean it's true," said Sasha.

"I don't think he was making it up," said Diego. We all looked at him. "I've seen bruises on him before."

"I did, too," I said. "Right before I saw the gun in his bag. At first, I thought it was because Zane pushed him in the hall. Or maybe even you." I glanced at Robbie. "I thought that was why he had the gun. To shoot one of you."

Robbie gave me a pained look. "I never touched him."

"Oh, c'mon, Robbie," I said, my voice trembling. "I've seen you knock into him before. Was it always really an accident?" I'd never confronted him about it before. Maybe I should have called him out the first time I saw him collide with Phil. But I'd assumed it was as he made it appear—an accident. I was dazzled by him, and wanted him to like me. To love me. Back then, he looked at me like I was the only girl in school worth looking at, even next to Sasha, and I didn't want to ruin that. But I was stupid. I knew the toll bullying could take on someone.

Robbie reddened and rubbed his neck. "So I might've pushed him around a bit. But I didn't mean anything by it."

"Yeah, but still," said Diego. "Even if it wasn't Phil, maybe

154

someone else you 'pushed around' put us in here." He made air quotes at "pushed around."

"You think it's *my* fault we're stuck in here?" Robbie tensed and flexed his hand. The syringe's needle gleamed on the silver platter mere inches away. I'd seen Robbie's temper flare before, but he wouldn't reach for the syringe in anger . . . would he?

I touched his arm with trembling fingers. "This isn't your fault. We're just trying to figure this out, okay?" Robbie's nostrils flared, but after a few moments, he nodded. "And anyway, I think it's more likely that someone more conniving would put us in here."

"Think it was Becky?" said Robbie. "She clearly hated both of us."

"Wait, what was this?" asked Sasha.

"We were at the carnival last summer . . . I went to get cash, and when I came back, Becky was yelling at Amber like a fucking psycho."

"Becky knew the truth about Phil," I explained. "She was angry . . . well, I think she was angry for a bunch of reasons, but especially because I turned in Phil and got him expelled without knowing why he had the gun. And when Robbie stood up for me, she turned on him, too."

Sasha nodded along with this. "Alright, Becky seems plausible." She raised her hand like it was her turn at the podium. "She hates Amber because she busted Phil. She hates Robbie because he took Amber's side." She kept tally on her fingers. "She hates Diego because he's Diego."

"Hey," said Diego. "What's that supposed to mean?"

"Oh, shut up," Sasha snapped. "You're already a millionaire because of a stupid sponge. *Everyone* hates you." Diego opened his mouth to protest, but Sasha kept talking. "So that leaves Scott and Priya."

"What about you?" Priya glowered at Sasha. "She hates you, too." I raised my eyebrows, impressed. I'd rarely seen her talk back to Sasha before.

To my surprise, Sasha nodded. "Yeah . . . she's always staring at me like some freaky bug-eyed stalker." She shuddered at the thought. "She's always been jealous of me."

"Oh, come on, Sasha," I said. "It's not just jealousy. You know that, don't you?"

Sasha frowned. "Well, what else would it be?"

"Oh my God." I clasped my forehead. For a borderline genius, Sasha could be incredibly thick.

"Maybe she hates you because you're a total bitch to her?" said Scott. "Just a theory."

"She's a total bitch to everyone," Diego muttered.

Sasha's mouth dropped open, and after a moment, she pursed her lips, as though to hide her surprise. "That's not true. I'm a nice person." She turned to me, and the pleading look in her eyes caught me off guard. "You don't really think I'm a bitch, do you?"

6 MONTHS AGO

AUGUST BEFORE SENIOR YEAR

"Zane asked about *me?*" Priya asked for the third time.

I laughed mid-sip, and water dribbled down my chin. "I swear to God, yes. And why wouldn't he? He hasn't seen you all summer." I grabbed a napkin and wiped my chin and shirt. We were sitting in Mike's Diner—I'd been avoiding Starbucks ever since my run-in with Phil.

"So what did you say?"

"The truth. That your grandmother was trying to set you up with every eligible Indian boy in town."

Priya stretched across the table and shoved my shoulder. "Shut up, no you didn't."

I laughed again. "What? If anything, it made him jealous."

"No way—"

"Hello, ladies." Scott appeared at our booth, wearing a white apron over his usual all-black attire, and set down two huge cappuccino mugs. "On the house."

"Aw, that's so nice! Thanks," said Priya, grinning up at him.

I glanced around the quiet diner—only two other customers occupied the booths next to the windows. "Are you allowed to give this to us?"

He shrugged. "Whatever. I'm bored out of my skull. There are only so many times you can wipe down an espresso machine." He picked up our empty mugs from earlier. "See? I'm so bored I'm cleaning up your shit."

"That's kind of your job, isn't it?" I teased.

Before he could reply, Sasha burst into the diner and, spotting us, squealed. "Hey, lady!" She rushed over, and I stood for a hug. After cheerleading camp, she'd gone straight to Paris with her parents for a week, so I hadn't seen her all summer. She kissed the air on either side of my face, and then gave Priya a hug.

Scott still hovered, as though waiting for his greeting. "'Sup."

Sasha lifted her sunglasses, perching them atop her head. "Ugh! Why are you always everywhere?"

"Why are you never nowhere?" he retorted. He returned to the bar, shaking his head.

"Oh my God," she muttered. What was Sasha's problem with Scott, anyway? This wasn't the first time I'd seen her snap at him. "Listen." She nudged Priya's shoulder. "Can you scram? I've got to talk to Amber about *Romeo and Juliet* stuff."

Priya glanced at her fresh cappuccino. "But we're still catching up."

"Yeah, well, this is important." Sasha put a hand on her hip. "And time sensitive."

"But I haven't seen Amber all summer."

"You can catch up later. I mean, you *could* stay, but you'll be bored out of your mind. We're just going to be talking about the play."

Priya glanced at me. "Did you know she was coming?"

I bit my lip. I'd forgotten to tell Priya, but I didn't think Sasha would boot her like this. "Yeah, I invited her. But I'll text you when we're done, and you can come over."

"Ugh, fine." She grabbed her purse and slid from the booth, and Sasha took her place.

"So." Sasha leaned forward, placing her elbows on the table. "I have some updates about *Romeo and Juliet*."

"My summer was fantastic, how was yours?"

Sasha clucked her tongue. "Hardy har har. No seriously, you'll want to hear this ASAP." Her brow furrowed, like whatever she had to say wasn't good news. My stomach lurched. Oh no. "I just came from a drama club meeting." I never went to those meetings. "Amber, you have so much on your plate," Sasha had said last spring when I'd asked if I should attend. "You handle the orchestra, and I'll handle drama club. It's the least I can do."

"Oh, God." Panic flooded my veins. They hadn't decided against *Romeo and Juliet*, had they? I'd just sent Sasha the finished score two weeks ago, and I was so proud of it. But what if all that hard work was for nothing? "They don't hate the music, do they?"

"No, no!" Sasha said. "The music is fantastic . . . it's just that, well, people think doing a straight-up Shakespeare play is kinda boring."

Oh, God. No, no, no. Did they think my composition was *boring*? I'd worked so hard on it; I'd put every ounce of my soul and energy into it. How was it not enough? "What do you mean?" My voice shook. "I thought everyone was on board. And we're doing a modern rendition. It's more like a retelling, anyway. And you've already written the script—"

"Amber." Sasha reached across the table and grabbed my hand. "Calm down. We can still do the play if we add a few singing numbers."

I snatched my hand back. "Wait, what?"

She scrolled through her phone and pulled up her notepad app. "We've decided on a few scenes that we think would be great as songs." She glanced up at my startled expression. "Just a few! The balcony scene, the beginning of act four where Juliet threatens to kill herself, and Juliet's suicide scene."

"But . . . but . . ." My mind raced. This was completely out of left field. The majority of the work was done. The orchestra was supposed to start learning the music next week when school started, and we'd only have to adjust for tweaks to the script or stage direction. "Adding just a few random singing parts will sound ridiculous. Besides, I'm no Lin Manuel. I've never scored a song to lyrics before."

"Well, then this will be a fun challenge," Sasha said enthusiastically.

"No! It won't!" I said so loudly that the three other people in the diner turned to stare. Scott raised his eyebrows.

Oh, God. This was a disaster. I wanted to send a recording of a gorgeous, haunting, ethereal score off to colleges, not some hacked-together score smattered with random singing numbers.

Sasha picked up Priya's full cappuccino, her pinkies extended. She took a sip as she stared at me over the lip of the mug. "Listen, I tried arguing against this, but I was very much in the minority. The thing is, if you don't agree, I'm afraid everyone's going to insist on doing *Grease* instead."

I felt my face drain of blood. She must have seen me go pale.

"I didn't want to have to tell you this," she went on. "But they already wanted to switch."

"What?" I felt like I was going to puke.

"But I convinced them we could make *Romeo and Juliet* more fun . . . more *vibrant* . . . if we add these few singing numbers, and some more jokes to the dialogue." She rubbed her eyes and let out a great sigh. "I would feel horrible if you lost this chance. You already did so much work. I'd hate for it to be for nothing. But, I mean, if you really are against this, I'll let everyone know—"

"No. Don't." I took a deep breath. "I'll do it."

"Really?"

"Yeah." My stomach churned. This was going to be so much extra work—and I wasn't even sure I'd be able to pull it off. But I had to try. "Thank you, Sasha. Seriously. Thank you for fighting for this."

"Of course." A smile crept across her lips. "We're in this together. I'm not going to let some drama geeks ruin this for us."

36 MINUTES LEFT

I stared at Sasha, unsure how to answer her. Did I think she was a bitch? After everything she'd done over the past year, absolutely. But her total lack of self-awareness shocked me to my core.

Unless she knew, and she was faking.

"Guys," said Diego, stepping between us. "Let's focus here. Does Becky have a reason to hate you?" he asked Sasha, who vehemently shook her head.

"Sasha," said Robbie, "you know I love you, but you've been mean to Becky, too. I mean, come on." He shoved his fingers in his pockets. "We all have."

I took a wary step forward. "Just think about all the things you've said about her behind her back. About her outfits, her glasses . . . does any of that ring a bell?"

Sasha glared at me, poking her tongue into her cheek.

"Alright. Fine. So what about you?" she asked Priya. "Does Becky have a reason to hate you?"

Priya shook her head, dumbfounded. Sweat dampened her hairline. Then she tilted her head. "Well, we used to be friends with her," she said, looking at me. "But then . . ."

I nodded. "Yeah. We both kinda ditched her. But I don't think she *hated* us—or hated *me* at least—until we started hanging out with Sasha."

Sasha crossed her arms. "Oh, please. You can't think she hates me enough to hate you by association. At least, not enough to kill you."

"I wouldn't put it past that freak show," Robbie muttered.

"Okay, so let's say she does. That just leaves you." Sasha spun on Scott. "What does Becky have against you?"

Scott shrugged, a small smile playing on his lips, his head lolling back against the wall. "Don't know. Can't think of anything."

"Nothing?" said Sasha. "You can't think of a single time you might've pissed her off?"

"Nope."

"Then why the hell are you here?" asked Robbie.

Scott's grin widened, and what he said next sent a chill running down my spine. "I dunno. Maybe Becky thought I'd be the one psycho enough to kill one of you."

4 MONTHS, 1 WEEK AGO

SEPTEMBER OF SENIOR YEAR

The warning bell shrieked, jolting everyone from their blissful five-minute reprieve from boredom. I edged open the girls' bathroom door and peeked into the hall. Except for a few stragglers racing toward their fifth-period class, the coast was clear.

I slinked out of the bathroom toward the nearest stairwell. But before I could reach my destination, Priya rounded the corner down the hall, coming from the junior wing. I dodged into the next doorway. Crap, crap, crap. If she spotted me, she'd want to have lunch together.

Guilt coiled around my heart. I hated avoiding my best friend like this. But I needed this hour to write a new song. With only three months left until opening night of *Romeo and Juliet*, I had to finish those new singing numbers.

In the biggest upset of drama club history, Sasha had secured the lead role over Maria. Since there were only a few singing numbers, she finally had her shot. She was bursting at the seams when she told me the news.

I could only cringe. I hadn't made much progress on the new songs, since I was so busy. Between leading orchestra practices (under Mr. Torrente's supervision), going to Robbie's baseball games, doing homework, and studying—not to mention juggling Sasha's and Priya's demands to hang out—I was lucky to get five hours of sleep a night. Plus, I wasn't exactly eager to write these songs. I still thought they were a ridiculous idea.

"You can still back out if you want," Sasha had said. "But everyone might decide to switch to *Grease* instead. They've all got the words memorized anyway. I mean, we all do. It's *Grease*! But Maria would definitely get to play the lead . . ." I couldn't let her down. I couldn't let *myself* down. I'd already put so much work into this play.

So now I was in a race against the clock, and this was my only free hour all day thanks to orchestra practice and a date with Robbie tonight. Should I break my plans with him?

After our carnival date, Robbie came over whenever he didn't have practice or games at his summer baseball camp. Mom was thrilled she could keep an eye on us since she worked from home, but Dad would grunt, "You can't date until you're forty-seven," whenever Robbie showed up with his swim trunks or laptop and gamer headset. But after a few weeks, Dad fired up the grill next to the pool each night and asked Robbie to stay for dinner. They even threw around a baseball a few times, and Dad installed Fortnite on his own laptop. It was kind of adorable.

But once school started again, our packed schedules meant squishing impromptu dates between other commitments. We didn't both have another night free until the week after next, so I didn't want to cancel on him tonight. Priya had to be the one I ditched this time.

With my back pressed to the side of a locker, I peeked around its metal frame, waiting for her to turn right toward the cafeteria. If she saw me, she'd guilt-trip me—

"Can I help you?" Mr. Baskin asked from the doorway. I whipped around. His entire class had been watching my little performance.

Someone snickered, and heat crept up my neck. "Uh . . . no."

"Great. I suggest you get going then." He bristled his mustache. "Unless, of course, you'd like another rehashing of the French and Indian War, hmm?" He motioned for me to enter the room.

"Er . . . that's okay. I got the gist this morning." Becky giggled from the first row. I shot her a scathing look. Her smile collapsed, and she started erasing the corner of her blank notebook page. Remorse immediately flooded my veins, but I stepped out of the way, letting Mr. Baskin shut the door. I peered down the hall. No sign of Priya.

I hurtled into the stairwell and collapsed in the alcove behind the stairs. Muted daylight filtered through the tiny window in the back door, dimly lighting the space. It was pouring, so hopefully nobody would pass through here to go outside.

Heaving a sigh, I fished my earbuds from my messenger bag, cursing the limited number of hours in the day. Too bad I didn't have any of that caffeinated gum Sasha carried around. Setting aside my exhaustion, I got to work on sequencing the double bass loop with violins, flutes, and percussion, creating soft, subdued harmonies. As the stanzas whizzed by on my screen, Scott's face materialized next to my laptop.

I jumped so hard my laptop slipped and fell. "Whoa. You scared me to death!" I yanked out my earbuds.

"Back atcha', Red." Scott stuck a cigarette between his lips and dug through the pockets of his beat-up leather jacket. "Didn't expect to see you here."

I paused the track and shut my laptop as a clap of thunder rattled the door. "Right. I'll go."

"No worries." Scott flicked on the light. "Hang out. I won't tell if you won't." He wiggled his cigarette.

I eyed him warily and opened my laptop again. "Okay. Deal."

He nodded toward the laptop as he lit the cigarette. "So, what's shakin'?"

"Bacon."

He smirked. "No, really. What're you up to, hiding out here?"

"Mind your own business," I huffed, wanting to get back to work.

He quirked an eyebrow. "Perusing illicit websites, huh? Didn't think you were the type, Red." He shook his head and took a drag.

"What? No! I'm not . . . I'm . . ." I hesitated, considering whether to tell him the truth. If Priya found out I was hiding in stairwells to avoid her, she'd be crushed. She took everything way too personally.

"Well, you're clearly hiding some dirty little secret." He held his breath for a few moments and finally blew out a puff of smoke, watching my expression. Suddenly, his face fell. "Oh, shit, Red. Are you hiding from Phil? They'd never let him into the building, you know."

My stomach plunged, remembering Phil's stony expression as I spotted the gun in his bag, and when he told me the truth about his abusive father. He wouldn't try to get revenge on me for turning him in, would he? I shuddered. "No, no. It's not that. I'm . . . I'm working on something. I just needed somewhere to focus."

Scott's face relaxed. "Oh." He plopped down next to me, cross-legged, and eyed my laptop. "Wish I had one of those. I have to use my pop's old PC from like the '90s or something."

"Seriously?"

He shrugged. "Nah, it can't be *that* old. All I know is it crashes more often than it starts up. Figure that one out." He took another drag. "So what're you working so hard on?" Before I could answer, he hooted. "Ha! Hard on."

"Oh, geez." But I had to bite back a grin. "I'm working on a composition, if you must know."

"I must indeed! A composition . . . as in, music? For the play?"

"Way to connect the dots."

"Well, you could be composing an *essay*. Or *literature*."

I scoffed. "People don't say that."

"So where are your instruments?"

"I use a program to write music." I tilted the laptop toward him so he could see the stanzas on the screen.

"Ah, okay. So you write the music for each instrument, and it puts it all together, right?"

I grinned, impressed. Most people were clueless about composition. "It's more nuanced than that, but yeah, that's the idea. Once you like what you've got, you can record the song with a keyboard modifier, or with real instruments, like we'll do at the play." I scrunched my nose. "Ugh. Whatever you're smoking smells like skunk—" Oh, God. Was he smoking *weed* in here? I smacked the laptop shut and shoved it into my bag. "Dammit! Scott!" I lowered my voice to a whisper. "Are you *trying* to get me suspended? I didn't realize you were smoking pot."

He laughed. "You're hanging around Sasha's crowd, and you're still that naïve?"

I eyed the joint and scanned the ceiling for smoke detectors. There was one in the far corner near the door to the hallway, its red battery light blinking like a threat. "They don't do drugs. At least, not around me. They only drink."

"Not even Sasha?"

"Nope."

He raised the joint to his lips. "This is a shocking development."

"Why?"

He rested his elbows on his knees, flashing me a coy smile. "Just is."

What did he mean by that? Did he know something about Sasha that I didn't? I smacked his arm. "Why're you shocked? Tell me."

"Hey, you want me telling her *your* dirty little secret?" He nodded toward my laptop and took a long drag.

"It's not my *dirty little secret*. Sasha's the one who asked me for these tracks. I've got nothing to hide." I bit back the irony of that statement, being that I was literally hiding in a stairwell.

He let out a puff of smoke. "And what Sasha wants, Sasha gets." His voice came out bitter, which was weird for him. He was usually so blasé.

I furrowed my brow. "What do you mean?"

"Nothing. Forget it."

"You obviously mean something."

He slowly rolled his joint between two fingers, pondering something. "Well, let's take you, for instance. I may or may not have overheard part of your conversation at the diner . . ."

"Yeah, whatever, it's fine."

"Okay. Well, think about how you caved to her in like two seconds. That didn't seem weird to you?"

"I didn't cave to *her*. I caved to the drama club. Sasha was helping me. If I didn't agree to those new tracks, they would have switched the play to *Grease* instead."

"Sorry, do you need to lie down?"

I glanced at the floor. "Why?"

"I didn't realize you were recovering from spine removal surgery."

I scowled at him. "Well, what else was I supposed to do—"

Someone swung open the door to the hall and clopped up the stairs. I mouthed, *Put that thing out*, pointing frantically at Scott's

170

joint. He squished the tip between his fingers and put it in his pocket, but the stairwell reeked of pot. When the stairwell door slammed upstairs, I scrambled to my feet and slung my bag over my shoulder. "I'm leaving. Whoever that was might tell a teacher what they smelled."

He patted his pocket. "Geez, you need this stuff more than I do." He grinned. "Wanna buy some? I give discounts for newbs."

"No! Ugh." I headed for the door.

"Wait." Scott climbed to his feet. I hadn't noticed his blood-shot eyes before.

I swatted at the wisps of smoke lingering in the air. "What is it?"

"I just wanna say . . . I think you're giving that girl too much power."

I tilted my head. "No, I'm not . . ."

"You are. It's not just you, though. We all do it." He screwed up his face and shook off some thought. "I mean, c'mon, Red, think about it. Did you even talk to the rest of the drama club about their bizarre ask?"

My eyebrows shot up. "Wait, what do you mean?"

He guffawed. "They really think it's a good idea to turn Juliet's suicide monologue into a *song*? Who the hell breaks into song before offing themselves?"

When Sasha asked me to compose those singing numbers, I panicked, agreeing right away for fear that all my hard work the past few months would be for nothing. But maybe I should have asked to join a drama club meeting. "Wow, you're right. I should have tried to talk them out of it." I pressed a palm to my forehead. "But it's probably too late now."

Scott leaned back against the opposite wall, watching me with glassy eyes, a smile creeping across his lips. "Nah. You still don't get it."

"Well, what do you mean, then? I caved to them quickly. Sure. I get that. Next time they ask for something dumb, I'll meet with them and convince them there's a better solution—" I paused when Scott slapped his knee, hooting. "What is it?"

"Poor innocent little Amber Prescott. Red, you have no idea how the world really works, do you?" He hunched over, laughing like he'd just heard the most hilarious joke on the planet.

"Oh my God. You're high as a kite, aren't you?"

He more lolled his head than nodded, zoning out toward the wall behind me. "Well, yeah. But that doesn't change the fact that you're naïve as a pebble."

I crossed my arms. "That's not an expression. So what am I so naïve about? Care to enlighten me?"

He chuckled, clapping a hand on my shoulder. "I already told you, Red. What *Sasha* wants, *Sasha* gets."

God, this was so frustrating. He was talking in circles. "Will you stop speaking in code? If there's something I'm missing, just tell me. It's not even what Sasha wanted—"

"Eh? *Eh?*" He pointed at my face, almost touching my cheek, and I swatted him away.

"Oh my God, what the hell is wrong with you?"

But he just laughed. "Looks like Sasha has more than one dirty little secret."

The way he said it sent a chill down my spine.

Sasha was the queen of everything, but she'd been nothing but kind to me—befriending me without question, helping me with the play, setting me up with her best friend. Still, I knew she wasn't as perfect as she let on. She was guilty of underage drinking, and on school grounds—but so was I. She cheated on that bio exam Priya stole the answers to—but I helped Priya get away with it. As far as I'd seen, Sasha hadn't done much worse than I was willing to do. So what was I missing? Was Sasha in some kind of trouble? Or was she hiding something from me? Had I been wrong to trust her so implicitly?

I prodded Scott's arm. "What's her other secret, then?"

He grinned. "I can't just tell you. Otherwise she'll know I blabbed. You'll need to catch her in the act."

"But I don't even know what *it* is. How can I catch her?"

"I dunno yet." He seemed to be having trouble focusing. "I don't know when the next time will be. When I do, I'll text you." Without another word, he strolled into the hallway, leaving me more confused than ever. What "dirty little secret" could Sasha Harris possibly have?

35 MINUTES LEFT

Everyone gaped at Scott like a herd of gazelles that spotted a tiger ready to pounce. His words echoed in my brain. *Maybe Becky thought I'd be the one psycho enough to kill one of you.*

Scott was the outsider. The outlier. And he was arguably a little off-kilter. But did that make him a potential killer? No. It didn't.

"Why would you say that?" I asked, my voice strained.

"One of these things is not like the others," Scott said in a singsong voice, motioning to one of us with each syllable. But his grin dissolved as he took in everyone's wide-eyed looks of fear.

"Just because you're kind of an outcast doesn't make you a psychopath," I said.

"He's not just an outcast," said Robbie.

"Oh, right, I forgot." Scott narrowed his eyes at Robbie. "To you pretentious assholes, I'm nothing but a stoner. A drug dealer—"

Before he could say anything else, Sasha suddenly lunged toward the table and swept up the syringe. "Sasha!" I screamed. "What the hell are you doing?"

She clenched the syringe in her fist, angling it toward Scott. "I'm protecting us. He's dangerous. That's why he's here. He'd kill one of us." Her hair tumbled wildly over her shoulders. A few stray strands were matted across her forehead.

"Holy shit. I was kidding." Scott raised his hands and pressed himself back against the wall, his face contorting with pain.

"Why the hell would you kid around about something like that?" she screeched. "Are you insane? That just proves you're crazy enough to kill us all."

Diego tilted his head. "Does it, though?"

"I can't even stand right now!" Scott shouted, breathing hard. Beads of sweat dropped from his chin onto his shirt. "You're the one pointing that toxic shit at me. You're not exactly in a position to question anyone else's sanity."

"Oh, no. Don't you turn this around on me. *You're* the one who's messed up in the head. You've probably blasted your brain cells with weed and God knows what else."

"Sasha." I inched toward her. "Put the syringe down. Scott wouldn't hurt us."

"How can you be sure of that?" She stepped away from me, shaking her head, fighting back tears. "Why do you trust him?"

Scott stared at the syringe in Sasha's grip, a grimace etched on his face. "Why don't *you* trust me?" he cried. "You of all people have every reason in the world to trust me!"

Robbie frowned. "What're you talking about?"

"I don't know. He's nuts." Sasha's eyes flicked to Robbie again. "Maybe . . . maybe he should be the one we choose."

"What?" Priya cried.

Sasha's eyes brimmed with tears. "If we have to do this . . . if we have to choose someone to kill . . . it should be him."

I shook my head, repulsed that she would suggest killing Scott—especially because I knew why. And it wasn't because he was dangerous.

"Fine, I shouldn't have cracked that joke." Scott's hands were trembling. "I was just throwing out a wild theory for why Becky or whoever would have invited me. But I have no clue why I was really invited, I swear."

A tear trailed down Sasha's cheek. "I don't believe you." She moved closer to Scott, each footstep like an explosion in my ears. Nobody dared move an inch. But Scott wasn't the psychopath Sasha was painting him as. He only knew her "dirty little secret." Maybe she wasn't just crying at the thought of killing Scott—she was also terrified he'd spill the beans.

"What is it?" Robbie asked, noticing my expression.

But I ignored him and approached Sasha. "Killing him won't fix this."

Sasha's eyes widened. "What do you mean?" She licked her lips. "I don't want to have to do this. But if it's the only way out . . . killing him will stop the timer. It'll get us out of here—"

"That's not what I mean, and you know it. Killing him won't bury your secret . . . because I know it, too."

3 MONTHS, 3 WEEKS AGO

OCTOBER OF SENIOR YEAR

"Mike's Diner okay?" I secured my seat belt, my stomach grumbling at the prospect of a milk shake. Robbie had an hour to kill before his baseball game since the opposing team was stuck in traffic, so he promised me a quick dinner date.

"I'm not really hungry, are you?" Robbie put the key in the ignition without turning it, his eyes lingering on mine.

I shrugged. "Well . . . I guess not. We can sit here and talk for a while."

The corner of his mouth quirked up. "Sure. Let's *talk*." He trailed his fingers over the back of my hand, sending shivers to the base of my spine. I knew where this was going. Lately we spent most of our dates huddled in his SUV. I'm not going to lie; I enjoyed our make-out sessions immensely, so that was fine by me. But I wasn't ready to go any further—especially not in the middle of the school parking lot.

Not that we hadn't come close before. He'd cup my face in his hands, and start each kiss so softly, so carefully, like I was some prized treasure he wanted to protect. Then he'd run his hand under my shirt, his skin hot against mine, and it was hard not to melt into him completely. But sex was a big deal. I was terrified to give myself so completely to another person . . . no matter how fiercely my nerve endings tingled at his touch. I'd never so much as kissed another boy before Robbie. I just wasn't ready yet.

I clasped his roaming fingers, holding them still as my heart pounded in my chest. "So there's something I've been curious about."

"What do you call a curious musician?"

I grinned, and as I mulled it over, he brought my hand to his lips and kissed my fingers one by one. Finally, I said, "I don't know, what?"

"An in-choiring mind."

I shoved his chest. "Oh my God, that's terrible." But I laughed anyway as he cracked up. "No, but seriously."

"Yeah?"

"If you suddenly couldn't play baseball anymore, for what-ever reason, what would you do instead after you graduate?" Now that college applications were looming, and he still hadn't been recruited to a college baseball team, I was curious what he had in mind as a fallback plan. Maybe he could apply to some schools in Southern California. "You know, for a career?"

"Ugh." He furrowed his brow. "To be honest, I don't know. Baseball's been it for me, you know?" He ran his fingers along my neck, leaning closer. "I can't think of anything else I love as much."

"Why do you love it so much?" I prodded. Maybe some elements would translate to another field.

He grinned. "Ah, man. Where do I even start? I love the anticipation of each pitch. The tension released at every swing of the bat. The smell of the grass on the field. I love how it's a game of inches, how hitting the ball in a slightly different spot can change the course of an entire game. I love the precision of it, you know?" My mind whirred. Maybe math? Or physics? "But also how sometimes when everything goes right, like when you end the game with a walk-off homer, or when everyone's in sync with base hit after base hit, it seems like fate. Or destiny." Wow. I never knew he could be so poetic. "I dunno. It's hard to explain."

I smiled. "You're doing a pretty good job."

"Yeah?" Without warning, he unclipped my seat belt and tugged me toward him by one of my belt loops, so I was sitting on his lap. "I can think of something else I'm pretty good at, too." He brushed back my hair with one hand and cradled my cheek with the other, bringing his lips to mine.

If he was implying he was a good kisser, he was one hundred and fifty percent correct.

Robbie's phone suddenly blinged, jolting us back to reality. I disentangled myself from him and slumped back in my seat as he dug his phone from his pocket. "Um . . ." He furrowed his brow at his screen. "It's your mom. 'Is Amber with you? Is she okay? Please reply ASAP.'"

"Oh, shit." I fished my own phone from my purse. I was supposed to text to let her know we got to Mike's Diner, but we'd never left the parking lot. Sure enough, I'd missed a few calls from her and about fifteen texts, which devolved from a basic check-in to about a bajillion red angry face emojis. I unsilenced my phone and let out an annoyed huff—she'd promised she'd only use Robbie's number in an emergency, and this definitely did not classify as an emergency.

As I rattled off a reply to let her know I was fine, a new text popped up. It was from Scott. *Back door, junior wing. Outside. 10 minutes.*

I sat up straight. It had been two weeks since Scott hinted at Sasha's secret, and I still had no idea what it was. Curious and concerned, both for Sasha and the trust I'd placed in her, I'd texted Scott every day since, prodding him to tell me her secret, but all he'd text back was either the joy or wink emoji. But it seemed he was finally ready to show me whatever it was, and I was lucky I was still on school grounds. I had to go see.

"I'm sorry, I have to go."

Robbie groaned. "Well, I can drive you home."

"No, that's okay . . . I biked in."

"Alright." We got out of the car and headed toward the school. Robbie entwined his fingers with mine. "You sure you can't come to the game?"

"Sasha's coming over in a bit. She's freaking out about the SATs on Saturday."

He rolled his eyes. "She would be. Uh . . . bike rack's over there?" He pointed toward the bike rack we just passed.

"Oh, I—I have to use the bathroom first." My cheeks flamed, but he didn't question me. After crossing the vestibule, I gave Robbie a peck on the lips. "Good luck tonight. Or break a leg?"

"Luck works." He waved and headed toward the boys' locker room. Once he disappeared around the corner, I jogged through the deserted halls toward the junior wing, past empty classrooms to the back door. I inched it open and peeked outside. The floodlights lit up the baseball field in the distance, casting a lavender glow on the dusky sky, but the closer football field was deserted. There was no sign of Sasha.

"Hey, Amber!" someone called behind me. I let go of the door and whirled. Oh, God. It was Diego. He carried a large tripod, and a camera dangled from his neck. "Heading to the game?" He adjusted his camera strap as he approached, his dark hair falling over his eyes.

"No, not tonight." I glanced down the hall, but there was no sign of Sasha. "You?"

"Yep. I'm filming this one. Need to create a montage for the County League's website."

I quirked an eyebrow. "You have time for that kind of thing?" He nodded. "No."

I couldn't help but laugh, and his copper eyes sparkled.

"It's fun, so I make time," he said. I wasn't surprised—years ago he'd made these viral videos for SpongeClown that helped it take off. Resentment clenched at my gut, and my smile withered away. "But I clearly chose the wrong game to film. The other team's still a half hour away. So what're you doing here so late?"

"Nothing. I mean, I was . . . studying." Dammit, I was a crap liar. But I didn't have time for this—I couldn't miss whatever was about to go down outside. "Anyway, I need to get going." I swung the door open again, but he followed me outside.

"You parked in the commuter lot, too?" He motioned to the path leading up the hill.

"Um . . . no."

"Okaaay." He tilted his head, probably thinking I was a total nimrod. Couldn't he just leave? I cringed against the frigid air seeping through my leggings—it was freezing for October. Was Scott planning to meet me here? Or did he only know where Sasha would be? The bleachers were still empty, and only a few players tossed around balls on the field. Scott must have been mistaken.

Or maybe I was too early.

"Oh, I just remembered, I forgot something in my locker. I'll see you later—" I tried to open the door and return to the warm hallway, but it had automatically locked behind us. "Ah, crap."

Diego laughed. "You seem to have a problem with doors, don't you?"

I grimaced. "God, can't you just—" I pinched my lips, stopping myself from saying something I'd regret. "I'll go around front. I'll see you tomorrow, okay?"

He shrugged. "Okay, then." I bit my lip as he climbed the hill toward the commuter lot. Why did he always show up at the most inopportune moment? It was almost like he was looking to bust me for something.

Or maybe he was just looking for a chance to talk to me, just like before the winter ball. Maybe he really did want to be friendly again.

Ignoring the fluttering sensation in my stomach, I glanced around, but there was nothing to see. Maybe I was actually too *late*. Dammit.

A couple of pigeons darted out of the way as I trudged through the mud past the bleachers toward the front of the school, getting muck all over my boots. Suddenly I caught movement under the bleachers.

I gasped as Sasha ducked through the side frame of the bleachers, still in her gym clothes from cheerleading practice. She started toward the school, and when she spotted me, her eyes widened. She darted over and grabbed my forearm. "Shit, hi. What're you doing here?" She smacked her forehead. "I didn't tell you drama club was meeting tonight, did I?"

"No." I'd wanted to go to last Friday's meeting, but Sasha told me it started at four when it really started at three, so I'd missed it. She was so busy lately, she couldn't keep her schedule straight. "I was just with Robbie . . . what were you doing back there, anyway?" I twisted toward the bleachers in time to see Scott climb out, too. He wore his usual leather jacket, his dark curly hair poking out from under a black beanie. He winked at me and fished a box of cigarettes from his jacket pocket. "Holy shit, Sasha. Were you hooking up with *Scott*?"

A look of disgust crossed her face. "No, don't be stupid. I like Zane. And I'd never . . . no! Ugh!"

She and Zane had been obnoxiously flirting ever since I started hanging out with them, but they'd been friends since forever. Did she really have feelings for him? Or was she trying to make me believe she wasn't hooking up with Scott? "Then what were you doing?" I prodded.

"Nothing," she snapped. "Just forget it. Let's go to your place. I'll drive."

She dragged me toward the parking lot. I glanced back at Scott, who leaned against the bleachers. He watched us go as he flicked his lighter, cupping his hand to ward off the breeze. If they weren't hooking up . . . what else was she doing with Scott under the bleachers? She couldn't have been doing drugs with him . . .

But if she had some sort of dirty little secret, drugs would fit the bill. The only question was: What the hell was she on?

34 MINUTES LEFT

"What's Amber talking about?" Robbie asked Sasha, who shrank against the table, the syringe shaking in her grip. "What secret are you hiding?"

Sasha shook her head, eyes wide. "Nothing. I have no idea." Priya exchanged a knowing glance with me and I nodded, confirming her suspicions.

Robbie watched this exchange. "What is it?" he asked, his forehead wrinkled in concern. Sasha would be mortified if Robbie learned the truth. She'd constructed such a sturdy façade of perfection, she hadn't even confided in him.

Scott let out ragged breaths as he stared at the syringe, sweat running down his temples. I had to say something. Sasha couldn't really think her secret would die with Scott. I'd asked her about it point-blank months ago, and she'd denied it, thinking she'd put it to bed. But if she didn't realize I knew . . . if she thought Scott was the only one safeguarding her secret . . . would she actually plunge the syringe into his shoulder?

I couldn't risk that. It was too soon. There was still time. I had to reveal her secret.

"Sasha's been buying drugs off Scott," I said. Sasha shot daggers at me with her eyes, pursing her lips.

Robbie balked. "What kind of drugs?"

I shook my head. "That, I don't know."

"Wow," he muttered. "That kind of explains a lot."

Sasha lowered the syringe. "What the hell is that supposed to mean?" Scott sank against the wall in relief.

"Well . . ." Robbie rubbed the back of his neck. "You've been acting real antsy and panicky. And your eyes get all bugged out and stuff, just like they are now." Sasha blinked rapidly, trying to de-bug her eyes. "I knew you were stressed. We've all been stressing about next year." He gave me a meaningful look. "So I chalked it up to excessive coffee or something. I never thought you'd do *drugs*. I mean, Jesus." He shook his head, his mind clearly blown.

"That's why I needed something," said Sasha. "I had to stay awake. You have no idea how stressed I've been. No idea! I had too much on my plate . . . and I had to keep my grades up for Harvard. I had to stay awake. I had to focus." Her voice cracked. She still hadn't received a response from them, and each passing day left her more anxious than the last. "The stress was too much."

186

"But there are other ways to cope." Diego shook his head. "We're all under stress, right? I mean, try running a business and going to school at the same time."

"Oh, please," Sasha snapped. "You're already a millionaire. You don't need to worry about school anymore."

Diego scrunched his brow. "Says who? I want to become a biomedical engineer, so I need to worry about *lots* more school. I'm just saying, you're not the only one with a zillion things on your plate. And either way, Harvard's not worth becoming an addict. There are plenty of other schools."

Sasha narrowed her eyes at him. "Easy for you to say. You already got in." She clenched her jaw so hard I thought the vein in her neck might explode. "Harvard's the best of the best. I have to get in. I have to."

The *best of the best*. I didn't get it. She'd do whatever it took in her perpetual quest for perfection—cheating, lying, taking drugs, or worse. It seemed to stem from more than just pressure from her mother—but where was it coming from?

"Anyway," Sasha said, glancing at the bomb's timer, "we don't have time now for a freaking intervention."

"So what've you been selling her?" Robbie rounded on Scott, his nostrils flaring.

Scott opened his mouth to answer, but Sasha cut him off. "I've been taking speed, alright? It's no big deal."

"No big deal?" Robbie yelled. "You could be in deep shit if you're busted for taking meth!"

Scott scoffed. "Don't get your knickers in a bunch—" He

winced, glancing at his knotted ankle. "I've been selling her Ritalin, not speed."

"WHAT?" said Sasha.

"Whoa, whoa, whoa," I said. "You *lied* to her about what you were selling her?"

"Hey, I was doing her a favor." Scott's voice was low and gravelly, like each word took effort. "One day, she asks me if I've got any speed to sell. Like I'm some bona fide drug dealer."

"You are," said Sasha.

He screwed up his face. "Selling a few joints doesn't count."

"Anyway, go on," I prodded.

He hesitated and darted a quick glance at Sasha. "So at the time, I'd just finished weaning off Ritalin, but I still had a 'scrip. So I figured, no rind off my orange to keep refilling it. I let her think she was getting speed, sold her something less dangerous, and made a few extra bucks. It was a win-win-win."

Sasha raised the syringe like a dagger above Scott's shoulder. "You *tricked* me!" she hissed.

Scott leaned away and yelped from the pain the movement caused. "For your own good!"

She took a step closer. "I didn't even know what I was taking. Don't you know how dangerous that is?"

"Not as dangerous as doing meth." He wiped his bloodied forehead with the back of his hand. The syringe wavered in Sasha's grip as she mulled this over.

Robbie shook his head. "I can't believe either of you." He kicked the chair next to him, making Sasha flinch. Oh, God.

What if she accidentally pressed down the plunger? The liquid would get all over Scott's arm.

"Sasha, put the goddamn syringe down!" I balled my hands into fists to keep them from trembling.

"Yeah, put it down," said Scott. "I thought I was helping you."

Now that was a stretch. "Seriously?" I shook my head at him. "You sold her a drug that was illegal for her to take. She really could have hurt herself!"

"She clearly already did." Priya stared at Sasha's shaking frame.

"And you did nothing to help her," I said. Scott pursed his lips. "You just kept letting her hurt herself, when you could have gone to someone for help."

"Oh, please, Red. You didn't, either."

"I didn't know the whole truth! You wouldn't tell me anything concrete. You just played coy about some *dirty little secret* she had. And when I confronted her, she denied it . . . just like she denies everything else."

3 MONTHS, 2 WEEKS AGO

OCTOBER OF SENIOR YEAR

"Sasha, I literally can't keep my eyes open anymore." I rubbed my burning eyes. Our SAT prep notecards were spread across my bedroom floor. The last time I'd dared a glance at my alarm clock, it was after two in the morning. Priya had already nodded off twice, and we'd cycled through my "Top Original Scores" playlist three times. My parents didn't mind if I hung out with friends until the wee hours of the morning, even on a school night, as long as we were under their roof. Their leniency was a blessing and a curse, since it meant I didn't have a good excuse to kick anyone out.

"Shut up and tell me the definition of *transitory*." Sasha waved a notecard under my nose.

"No more." I slammed my head back against my mattress.

"We have to keep going." Sasha wiped the sheen of sweat from her upper lip, and I narrowed my eyes at her. I'd been watching for signs that she was on something, but so far it was hard to tell what was stress, and what could be something else. "This is my last shot at retaking the SATs. I need to beat Diego."

It was common knowledge to everyone who would listen that Sasha scored a 1540 on the SATs. But Diego scored a 1560, so as far as she was concerned, she'd flunked.

"Why do you need to beat him so badly?" asked Priya, grabbing another handful of trail mix. In an attempt at a continuous sugar rush, she'd added M&Ms, though she'd probably regret it when she crashed in the morning. Thanks to her hypoglycemia, her mother wouldn't even let her in the same room as a candy bar. But once a chocoholic, always a chocoholic, so she'd sneak some sweets here and there—and would pay for it later with an epic headache.

"Harvard rarely accepts two students from the same school," said Sasha. "I can't risk that." Mittens chose that moment to edge open my bedroom door and prowl between us. He plopped belly-up onto the cards littering the carpet, stretching his paws, clearly asking for belly rubs. I was pretty sure he was a dog in a past life.

"Get off of those!" Sasha snapped, making a shooing motion. Mittens scrambled to his feet.

"Hey!" I scooped up Mittens and hugged him close. "Don't yell at my cat."

Sasha rolled her eyes. "Whatever." She flicked my arm with the notecard. "C'mon, don't be an idiot. This is an easy one. *Transitory.*"

I glared at her. "My patience will be *transitory* if you keep being a bitch." Priya raised her eyebrows and silently munched on her trail mix.

Sasha threw the card down. "Good enough. Next one. *Abscond*—" She narrowed her eyes at Priya. "Ugh, I'm so jealous."

Priya froze, her head tilted back, a fistful of trail mix hovering in front of her lips. "What?"

"I wish I could eat that much sugar, but it'd go straight to my thighs." She slapped her skinny jeans. "I've gained weight just looking at it. You're so lucky a fuller figure looks good on you." Priya's face fell, and she lowered her hand. Sasha turned back to me and practically shouted, *"Abscond."*

"Why don't *you* abscond?" I shot back, unsure if that even made sense.

"Fine. I gotta pee anyway." She hopped up and dashed to the door. I set down Mittens, and he followed Sasha upstairs. Stupid cat.

"She just called me fat," Priya grumbled.

"Priya, no she didn't. She was calling herself fat."

She shook her head. "Whatever." She chucked the rest of her trail mix in the trash. "How the hell does she have so much energy, anyway? I'm ready to pass out. And now my stomach hurts."

I stood to shut off the music and collapsed on my bed. "I was ready to pass out like two hours ago."

"Can't she study on her own?" Priya grumbled. She snatched one of the pillows from under my head and lay on the floor. "Why'd you have to make us her study slaves?"

"Oh, stop it. You know she invited herself over." Splitting my time between the two of them was like a tug-of-war, and there was only so much of me to go around.

"Couldn't you say no for once? She could study with Amy and Maria, or Zane, or someone, *anyone* else."

I bit my lip. The mention of Zane made me wonder for the hundredth time if I should tell Priya about Sasha's feelings for Zane. Maybe she lied to cover for whatever she was doing with Scott under the bleachers. I didn't want to get Priya upset over nothing. After a few minutes, I propped myself onto my elbows. "What's taking her so long?" Priya grunted, half asleep. I stood, shuffled out the door, and headed upstairs to the bathroom next to the kitchen. But the door was wide open, the lights off. "Sasha?" I whispered. My parents were asleep, so I didn't want to yell. No reply. Maybe she wanted to use the bathroom upstairs? That would be weird.

As I headed for the stairs, something clattered overhead. It sounded like it was coming from . . . *shit.*

I raced up the stairs, quiet as a mouse. Maggie's door was open a sliver, light streaming into the hall. My heart dropped to my feet. *No, no, no.* Mittens sat outside the door, his green eyes glowing in the dark, staring at me. He let out a single meow, like he was reporting the intrusion. Like he knew that room was off-limits.

I slipped into the room and shut the door behind me. Sure enough, Sasha hovered over my sister's vanity. I couldn't stand to see anyone in here with Maggie's things. "What the hell are you doing in here?" I whispered.

"I was looking for mouthwash, the downstairs bathroom

didn't have any." She smacked her lips with a sour look on her face, like she still hadn't found any. "I thought this was the bathroom. Whose stuff is this?" Sasha gripped a bottle of my sister's most expensive perfume, staring at her vanity cluttered with makeup and hair accessories. The bookshelves were filled to the brim with fantasy and science fiction novels, and the walls were lined with posters of Legolas, Captain America, and Thor. Mom wouldn't touch anything in here, as if Maggie would come home and be upset if she noticed anything out of place.

"It's my sister's. It's her room." I nervously thumbed my amethyst bracelet.

Sasha started to spray her wrist with the perfume, and her eyebrows shot up mid-spritz. "Seriously? You have a sister?" Oh, geez. If Mom smelled Maggie's perfume on Sasha, she'd go ballistic. The lavender and mahogany teakwood scent was unmistakable.

"Don't touch that! I'll get in so much trouble—"

"Chill, it's just perfume." She dropped the bottle on the vanity and scanned the corkboard overhead. Maggie never hung pictures of herself—she hated how she looked in photos, just like me. "I . . . I thought you were an only child." She stepped toward her desk, running her fingers over Maggie's old laptop. Seeing her step on the spot where Maggie died sent shock waves through my soul, triggering memories—such awful memories. It was like watching it happen all over again, as clear as though almost four years hadn't passed.

Our parents had been out to dinner that night, and I'd been in the kitchen getting water when I'd heard something crash upstairs. "Mags?" I'd called out. No reply. Then I'd heard another strange noise. It sounded like . . . retching. Was Mittens coughing up a hair ball? I'd glanced into the living room, where Mittens was perched on the couch, his tail dangling over the back cushion.

There was the retching sound again. It was definitely coming from upstairs. A chill ran down my spine. "Maggie?" I'd raced up the stairs. The bathroom door was ajar, and I pushed it open. The room was empty, greeting me only with the *plip, plip, plip* of water dripping from the leaky showerhead. I ran down the hall and tugged on Maggie's doorknob. It was locked. I pounded on the door. "Maggie? Are you okay?" No response. Maybe she had headphones on. I cupped my mouth and shrieked as loud as I could at the door, "MAGGIE!"

Nothing was louder than the silence that followed.

"Maggie!" Frantic, I rattled the doorknob. But the door locked from the inside, and there was no key, just a pinhole for picking the lock with a screwdriver in an emergency. Where did Dad keep his toolbox? In the garage? I had a strong feeling I didn't have time to find it. Would I be able to kick the door down? Our house was over a century old. The walls and doors had so little insulation you could hear everything going on in the next room. I was probably strong enough to kick down the brittle door.

But what if she was blasting music through her headphones? What if I was freaking out over nothing? She'd be furious with me, and Mom and Dad would sure be upset if I broke the door. But the chill racing along my vertebrae told me I wasn't wrong. I reared back and kicked the door just to the left of the knob. Pain stabbed at my heel, but when the door didn't give, I kicked it again. This time, the wood splintered, and I pushed the door open.

The room was dark. The only light came from the laptop screen on her desk, illuminating her empty bed in an eerie glow. I switched on the light.

Maggie was splayed across the floor, her face a terrifying shade of purple. "Maggie!" Her desk chair had toppled over with her in it. I crossed the room and knelt over her. Her eyes were closed, and an awful gurgling noise was coming from her throat. She was alive. Was she choking on something?

My mind raced. What should I do? I'd learned about the Heimlich maneuver in class—you were supposed to stand behind a choking person and thrust your fists into their abdomen below the rib cage. But I wouldn't really know what I was doing. No . . . I should call the police. They'd send help. They'd know what to do. I dashed to her desk—her cell phone was next to her laptop.

That was when I saw the pill bottles—a dozen empty orange bottles with prescription labels, and several other white ones with names I recognized: Advil, Tylenol, Excedrin. All empty. Like she took every pill we had in the house.

I'd called 911, but she was dead before the dispatcher could walk me through rolling her onto her side. She'd drowned in her own vomit on the very spot Sasha was standing now, while I'd hunched over her, hoping more than I'd ever hoped for anything in this world that she'd take another breath.

"We have to get out of here," I managed to croak at Sasha. Suddenly, a scratching sound came from the door. Mittens was clawing to get in. My parents were bound to hear the noise across the hall.

"Come on," I shout-whispered.

But Sasha only shook her head. "I can't believe I didn't know you had a sister. Is she in college?" Sasha scanned the walls for any sign of college insignia. Her eyes fell on a pillow on the bed with Maggie's name embroidered among flowers and leaves—we all had to make one in sixth-grade art class. She mouthed Maggie's name, her eyes widening in what looked like . . . was that recognition?

Did she know about Maggie? When she died, Sasha and I were in different middle schools, but her older sister—the one who dropped out of college to be in *Phantom of the Opera*—might've known Maggie. She might've known about the girl who died halfway through her senior year.

She also might've known the girl who made Maggie do what she did.

I opened my mouth to ask Sasha her sister's name when a door shut down the hall, and I froze, my heart pounding. "We really shouldn't be here. Mom'll kill me if she finds us." I grabbed Sasha's wrist and shoved her toward the door—the door my parents replaced and never opened again.

I led Sasha down the hall. The nerves in my fingers tingled as we tiptoed past my parents' bedroom. Once we were back in my room in the basement, I let out my breath, folding my arms over my stomach. "God, Sasha. You can't just snoop around other people's houses."

197

She ignored me and nudged Priya with her foot. "Did you know Amber has a sister?"

"What?" Priya's eyes flew open. "A sister? Yeah, of course."

"*Of course?*" Sasha turned to me, breathing fast. "How does Priya know about your sister? You've never mentioned her to me."

"We've been best friends for like thirteen years." Priya climbed to her feet to stand by my side, suddenly wide awake and defensive.

Sasha's face reddened, and her lip curled. "I'm her best friend now, too," she nearly shouted, her eyes bugged out and glassy. I never thought she'd find Priya's greater knowledge of my family tree so hurtful.

"Sasha, calm down." I eyed the door, nervous my parents would come downstairs to see what all the fuss was about. "Did you take something? Something to stay awake, maybe? You're acting so weird."

"No!" She flinched her head back and balled her shaking hands into fists as though to hide the tremors. "I'm just . . . shocked!"

"What's the big deal? So, I have a sister. She's never around. So what? It's just never come up." Priya threw me a look, but I ignored her. I didn't want to tell Sasha Maggie's story. Not now. Not ever, really. Reliving it in my own head was hard enough. Telling someone what happened—that I was the one who watched her die, that I was the one who couldn't save her—was a living nightmare.

Sasha screwed up her face like she was about to burst into tears. "I just . . ." Without another word, she grabbed her bag and barreled out the door, leaving her books and notecards behind.

"Whoa," said Priya. "What the heck was *that* all about? She totally hates me, doesn't she?"

"No." I sighed and rubbed the back of my neck, remembering her and Scott climbing out from under the bleachers. "I don't think that had anything to do with you. I think she's high."

32 MINUTES LEFT

"I denied it because it's none of your business," said Sasha, taking slow, deliberate breaths. "My choices about what I put into my body have nothing to do with you. It's not hurting anyone else." I crossed my arms and raised an eyebrow, but she ignored me. "But we're all going to die if we don't figure out what to do next. So can we focus on that?"

"Oh, God." Priya hugged her chest. "What *do* we do next? We've looked everywhere; there's no way out."

"Right. We have to choose someone," said Sasha. "And he's proven he can't be trusted." She pointed at Scott. "He lied to me about what he was selling me."

"No way." I swallowed the nausea threatening to creep up my throat. How could she be so ready to kill someone? "He was wrong to sell you his Ritalin, but that doesn't mean he should *die* for it.

This isn't up to you. We should all get a say in this. And I say we figure out a way to get *everyone* out of here alive."

"But how?" Priya asked.

"Whether that poison's real or not," said Diego, "someone's waiting for us to pick someone and inject it." He pointed toward the camera in the china cabinet. "Someone's watching us, right? So maybe we could reason with them."

"Do you think Phil or Becky, or whoever it is . . . do you think they can be reasoned with?" asked Priya.

"I still don't think it's Phil." Diego kept a wary eye on Sasha, who still gripped the syringe, her thumb on the plunger. "Or Becky."

"Why the hell not?" said Robbie. "He brought a gun to school. And she defended him."

Diego wiped his forehead with the back of his hand. "Honestly, I don't think either of them are clever enough." He motioned to the tray with the bomb and the note. "This is too . . . elaborate."

"Yeah, I don't know about Becky," said Priya. "But Phil's definitely not smart enough to pull off a stunt like this."

"But who else hates all of us?" said Robbie. He turned to Scott. "Er . . . almost all of us. You sure Phil and Becky don't have anything against you?"

Scott only shook his head. Sweat mingled with blood on his forehead, and he grimaced against the pain of his twisted ankle.

"Does it have to be someone who hates all of us?" I glanced at Sasha. "Maybe whoever it is has a particular target in mind."

Priya's eyes widened. "If that's true," she said breathlessly, "how could they do this to the rest of us? And how could they even know it would go the way they want it to?"

Sasha finally set the syringe back on its tray. "Yeah, that's nuts."

"Well, hang on," I said. "Can you think of anyone who might hate one of us fiercely enough to do all of that? To take that chance? Think of all the people you've wronged in some way." My pulse pounded in my ears. "Sasha, what about—"

"I know someone who hates me," said Diego, and his eyes shifted to meet mine. "Maybe even enough to kill me." My breath caught in my throat, and I took a step back.

Priya frowned. "Who?"

"Amber's father."

Swallowing hard, I gripped the chair in front of me to keep my balance. "How could you say that?"

Sasha looked between us, confused. I never told her about my history with Diego. She had no clue our fathers used to be business partners.

Robbie leapt to stand next to me, scowling at Diego. "What the hell is wrong with you, man? There's no way it's Amber's dad."

"We're listing the people who hate us, right?" said Diego. Sweat glistened on his neck. "Well, her dad hates my whole *family*."

"He doesn't hate you, Diego," I lied. "He hates your dad, not you. Your dad's the one who screwed him over. He's the one who left their business without any warning."

"Because of SpongeClown. Because of me."

For a moment, I could only stare back. Diego blurred in my vision as tears filled my eyes. "That's crazy."

"Yeah, it's crazy," said Diego. "This whole fucking night is crazy. But maybe he put you guys in here so you'd all have a reason to kill me. It's like Sasha said . . . everyone hates me."

"That's not true!" I stepped forward.

He shook his head. "You know what they say, Amber. It's lonely at the top. Maybe your dad finally found a way to get revenge on mine."

3 MONTHS, 1 WEEK AGO

OCTOBER OF SENIOR YEAR

School was the absolute last place I wanted to be on a Saturday, but Dad insisted on taking me to the college fair—as though my heart hadn't already been branded with USC insignia. He must have figured he wasn't doing his parental duties correctly otherwise.

As we roamed the aisles packed with classmates and students I didn't recognize from neighboring towns, Dad pointed out a few state school booths. I shook my head. "None of these look interesting?" he asked.

"Nope."

"Good. You're not allowed to go to college 'til you're thirty-three, anyway."

"Ha, ha."

But the more booths we passed, and the more he pointed out, the more I shook my head. "Come on, Amber." He clapped a hand

204

on my shoulder. "You're not going to learn about any of these places by scowling at them."

"But I already know where I want to apply," I said. "Definitely USC, but in case I flop auditions, also Berklee, UCLA, NYU, Oberlin—"

"I already told you"—he wiped a hand down his face—"we can't afford to fly you out for auditions."

"I know. They let you do online auditions now. Like on Skype." Each school encouraged in-person auditions, and I had a feeling those boosted your chances of getting in, but I didn't want to belabor the point. "And I have to send recordings, too." Naturally, opening night of the play was literally twenty-four hours before the first application deadline. Kill me now.

"Alright." Dad steered us toward the end of the aisle, where it was less crowded. "But, listen . . . I think you should apply to some state schools, too."

I bunched my eyebrows. "What? Why?"

"Well, these schools are much less expensive." He plucked a pamphlet from the nearest booth and flipped through it. "See? This one's commuting distance, and it's twelve thousand a year. USC is seventy-four thousand. *Each year.*"

"Why . . . why are you only bringing this up now? Why not ages ago?"

Dad blew air between his lips. "I hoped I'd never have to. I hoped things would turn around. But they haven't. I'm sorry, Amber."

The ground seemed to give way beneath me. "But . . . I could take out student loans."

"Absolutely not. I won't let you graduate three hundred thousand dollars in the hole."

"Are you *serious* right now?" I couldn't believe we were having this conversation.

Dad's nostrils flared. "Don't give me attitude."

"Don't treat me like I'm five! We've been through this. If I'm producing music for movies, I'll make good money. But I'll never make the connections I need in Hollywood if I'm not in the right program."

Dad shifted uncomfortably, glancing at the recruiters eyeing us at a nearby booth. "Being in the right program is no guarantee. You know how competitive the entertainment industry is?"

My heart sank. "What, you don't think I have what it takes?"

"Of course I do . . . you know I love your music. I just want you to finish college without decades' worth of debt like I did. If I hadn't, I might've been able to start saving earlier. Losing my business wouldn't have hurt us so badly. No"—he shook his head, his resolve set—"I won't let you become a starving artist. If you don't get a scholarship at any of those music schools, you'll have to go to a state school instead. And . . . well, your grades aren't really good enough to get a scholarship."

"Well, sorry I'm not Maggie," I snapped.

Her name hung in the air between us, heavier than her lost dreams. Maggie was the one who got all the scholarships. She wanted to be a doctor since before she could ride a bike. While

Priya and I played dress-up and dolls and teatime, Maggie would chase us with her stethoscope and a tiny rubber mallet. If you were her next victim, she'd force you to shut up so she could listen to your heartbeat or tap your knee to make your leg shoot straight out. Years later, when she'd gotten her first acceptance letter—and full scholarship—to Johns Hopkins, Dad had been so proud.

The acceptance letters kept coming after she died.

Dad exhaled slowly, staring at the ceiling, as though keeping himself from tearing up. The fluorescent lights accented new wrinkles that had spidered across his temple at an alarming rate. He'd aged a decade in a couple of years. "You think this is easy for me? To tell my baby girl that I can't help make her dreams come true?"

I fought back the tears welling in my own eyes. "No." Dad had always been so supportive—he always wanted the best for me. That's why he drove me to piano practice three days a week for years before buying me a keyboard of my own. That's why he gave up his man cave in the basement, so I could have a space to play my music. That's why he took time off from work after Maggie died, so he could spend time with me and make sure I was okay.

"I wish more than anything that I could pay for whatever school you want to go to."

"I know, Dad."

He pulled me into a hug. "So what do you say? Can we at least take a look? You don't have to decide where to apply today. Just browse. See if any of them have a music program you might like."

"Okay," I muttered, wiping my eyes to make sure there was no leakage.

We roamed the aisles again, a rock swelling in my throat. I picked up brochures from any school that had some semblance of a music program. As Dad and I perused the pamphlets at one of the booths, a flash went off next to us, and I glanced up. Oh, crap. It was Diego—the last person I wanted to see right now. I glanced warily at Dad, who was already on his way to the next booth.

Diego grinned and stepped closer, looking at the display on his camera. "Great candid shot." He leaned close to show me. It was a great father-daughter picture, like something you'd see on the college fair's website. "I can email it to you."

"Sure. Whatever." My voice shook. I'd resented Diego and his ridiculous sponges for toppling Dad's business, but I never imagined he'd toppled my plans, too.

"You okay?"

I didn't know what to say, and I wasn't sure if I could keep my disdain from tumbling out.

Diego glanced at the stack of booklets in my hand. "What schools are you looking at?"

My stomach twisted into a knot. "Well . . . I want to go to music school . . ."

"Ah, yeah. I heard you were scoring the school play."

"Yeah, well, it might all be for nothing."

"What? Why?"

"Turns out, I have to go somewhere less expensive. My dad wants to make sure I can support myself once I graduate from college." I glared at Diego, unable to hold back. "He doesn't want me to lose everything, the way he did."

His eyes widened, and he raked back his shaggy hair. "Shit," he muttered.

"Yeah."

He pressed his palm to his forehead. "Amber. I . . . that sucks. I didn't realize you were in such a tough spot."

A fireball started forming in the pit of my stomach. "Well, maybe if you didn't ignore me for three years, you would have realized." I was so shaken from my conversation with Dad, I couldn't stop myself. "You know, if my dad didn't lose his business thanks to your stupid sponges, none of this would be happening."

An incredulous look crossed over his face. "Wait a minute. *I* ignored *you*? You were the one who spun around whenever you saw me in the halls. You were the one who stopped talking to me. I thought you hated me."

I cringed. "Are you for real? I texted you that night, after you were on that stupid show. You never texted me back, and then your dad left my dad in the fucking dust. And then you never spoke to me again."

"I—"

"Did you think you were too good to talk to me anymore? Was that it?"

His eyes widened. "Not at all—"

"Beat it, kid." Dad came up behind me, narrowing his eyes at Diego. "Can't you see you're upsetting her?"

Diego's mouth opened and closed, like he couldn't figure out how to respond. "Mr. Prescott. I'm sorry, I was just—"

Dad's face reddened, and a vein bulged in his forehead. "You've interfered enough in our lives. Now back off." He jabbed a finger at Diego. "And I don't want to see you anywhere near my daughter again."

30 MINUTES LEFT

The idea of Dad locking us in here was so ludicrous it was almost comical. He'd never carry out this elaborate scheme to off some kid inventor out of jealousy. Diego suggesting it was both obnoxious and tragic—the fact that he suspected I'd be willing to murder him broke my heart.

"How could you say that?" I shouted at Diego, my whole body trembling. "First of all, my dad would never risk my life like this." I motioned to the bomb. "Never in a million years. And you can't possibly think I would ever want to kill you." A tear slipped down my cheek.

He cringed. "I didn't say that. I said your *dad* wants you to kill me." Everyone else watched us like a tennis match. Sasha stared with her jaw agape.

"But that means he would've had to include me in his scheming to make sure we'd choose you. Meaning *I* would've had to *agree* to it. Do you really think I'd ever agree to killing you?"

"No . . . of course not." He took a step back. "That's not . . . that's not what I meant . . ."

I clenched my fists, breathing hard. "Well, maybe you're not as smart as you think you are."

He recoiled like I'd slapped him in the face. But I felt like he'd stabbed me in the chest with that syringe.

Robbie let out a growl. "This is freaking ridiculous. There's no way Amber's dad's behind this. I've spent loads of time at her house. He's a cool guy. None of our parents would do this to us. That's just sick." Gratitude flooded my chest.

Sasha slapped her hip. "Guys, we don't have time to debate this!"

Robbie growled again and kicked the door.

"That helps exactly no one," Diego muttered.

"Yeah, well screw you, too, Spongeman." Robbie took a couple steps toward Diego, and I raced between them.

"Guys." I set a hand on Robbie's chest. His shirt was damp with sweat. The room was sweltering. "Cool it. Okay? Let's get back on track." I glowered at Diego, shaking my head.

"I'm sorry, alright?" Diego gestured broadly around. "It's just, all this . . . well, it has to be someone we know, right? And he's the first person I could think of . . ." He trailed off, wiping his upper lip. "I'm sorry."

Maybe he really didn't mean it. Maybe the stifling heat was making us all a bit crazy. "Whatever," I said. "It's fine."

"Okay, okay," said Sasha. "He's sorry, you're sorry, we're all sorry. So who else could it be? Does anyone have any enemies you're not telling us about?" Everyone stared at each other, waiting to see who would volunteer first.

"What about you?" I asked Sasha. "You're the star of every-thing . . . best at everything . . . you must have made *someone* mad along the way."

Sasha shook her head. "No." Her eyes darted toward Priya. "I mean, nobody we haven't already talked about."

Scott pointed a finger at Sasha, his head lolling. "Ha! Bullshit. You use people left and right." His words slurred like he was drunk with pain. "You get people to open up to you, and then you use what they tell you against them."

Robbie scoffed. "That's ridiculous."

But this wasn't the first time Scott suggested Sasha had taken advantage of people. *What Sasha wants, Sasha gets.* "What do you mean?" I prodded. What knowledge had Sasha used against Scott?

"Oh, wouldn't you like to know?" Scott glared more around me than at me, his eyes losing focus. He grasped his leg and clenched his jaw, and his shirt collar was dark with sweat. "You hate me. Just like she does."

I jerked my head back. "*What?* I don't hate you—"

"Yes, you do. You hate me for selling drugs to Sasha. You

said . . ." His eyes fluttered. "You said it yourself. You think I'm a creep." He motioned vaguely toward Priya, who tilted her head, confused.

I bit my lip, and guilt spread through my chest like ink oozing across oil. But before I could reply, Scott's eyes rolled up in his head, and he slumped back against the wall.

3 MONTHS AGO

NOVEMBER OF SENIOR YEAR

I finally did it. After weeks of trying to convince Robbie to pull the trigger, we were finally going on a double date with Priya and Zane. Part of me wondered if Sasha would care . . . what if she really did have feelings for Zane? But I figured I didn't need her permission—she'd said herself that she didn't have time for a relationship, so he was fair game.

At least, I hoped he was.

And besides, Priya'd had feelings for him since the dawn of time.

Robbie and I huddled on a bench outside Mike's Diner, bouncing our knees to ward off the cold as other kids we knew from school filed in and out. Zane was supposed to pick up Priya, but according to the texts she sent me every ten seconds, he was running late.

"I have something to show you." I pulled up a video file on

my phone, leaned into Robbie's arm, and positioned the phone so we both could see.

He instantly recognized the first frame. "Holy shit, you already finished it?"

"Yep." I pressed Play, and we watched Robbie's updated baseball recruit reel, complete with rock-influenced background music. He already had a reel he'd been sending to colleges since sophomore year, but since Georgia Tech was now considering him, he added new footage from his summer baseball camp—things like him hitting home runs, or stealing third, or diving into second on a base hit. When he showed me the reel last week, I cringed at the cheesy background music and offered to create a new track and clean up the editing.

When it ended, he beamed at me. "Shit, Amber. Thank you so much."

"You're welcome." I leaned in for a kiss, and he obliged. But then he pulled away and heaved a sigh. "What's wrong?"

"Ah, it's nothing."

I bit my lip. Was the track not good enough? Was the timing too rough? "No, really. What is it? I can fix whatever it is."

"No, no. The reel is perfect. I just hope it's not too late."

I frowned and swiped my phone back. "But you have this new interest."

Robbie rested his elbows on his knees, holding his head. "Yeah, but it's my last shot. If Georgia Tech doesn't bite, that's the end." He stared at the parking lot across the street, unable to meet my eyes. "I just wish . . ."

"What?" I took his hand. "What is it?"

"Well . . . my dad hired these recruitment companies to help Paul and Liam their sophomore years. They got in touch with tons of scouts, had super-professional reels made, things like that. But he's been so busy going to their games, he didn't do any of that for me." He kicked at some loose gravel. "I guess he figured two out of three wins was enough."

I squeezed his hand. "But you're winning, too. You got a scout's attention without any of that extra help."

"Still, I just feel like, I dunno . . . no matter what I do, it's never good enough for Dad. He flies to Boston to see Paul play more often than he goes to my games down the street. I told him the scout from Georgia was coming to watch me play, and he didn't even care." He rubbed his face again. "Ah, I don't know. It's like, Paul and Liam already made it, you know? I'm like the runt of the litter. The one who doesn't matter."

Seeing his pain brought tears to my eyes. I hated seeing him hurting like this. I stared at our clasped fingers. "I know how that feels. To feel like you don't measure up to your siblings . . ."

Robbie glanced at me. "I thought you were an only child."

I took a deep breath, shivering against the cold. I hadn't told Robbie about Maggie yet, and he hadn't connected the dots. It had been such a relief, not being pitied. But I could tell Robbie. I could *trust* Robbie. "I wasn't always." The words came out as a whisper. "I had an older sister. She died when we were in eighth grade."

His eyebrows shot up. "Oh, wait a minute. Shit. That girl who died when we were in eighth grade . . . that senior . . . she was *your* sister?"

I stared at the ground, nodding slightly.

"I'm sorry. I had no idea." He put his arm around me and pulled me close. Her lifeless face flashed before me, and I squeezed my eyes shut, burying my face in Robbie's jacket as my shivering turned to shakes of anguish. He hugged me as I struggled to hold back tears, hoping the crowds of people hovering near the front door wouldn't notice.

"She wanted to be a doctor, and she got scholarships to all these great schools," I finally said, wiping a lone tear that managed to escape. "My dad doesn't think I can get scholarships like she did. So he wants me to apply to state schools that cost less. He doesn't think I can make it as a producer, that I could pay off my student loans. Not the way she would have made it." My voice caught in my throat, and I swallowed hard. "So I kind of get what you're going through. It's horrible. And I'm sorry."

"I'm sorry, too." Robbie kissed my cheek and kept holding me close. "But hey . . . we're not going to let them stop us. We're not going to let them hold us back." He shook my shoulder so I looked up at him. "If I want to play baseball, one way or another, I'm going to play baseball. And if you don't want to go to a state school, you don't have to go to a state school. If you want to take out student loans, that's your choice. It's our lives. Screw what they think."

I smiled. "That's right. Screw what they think—"

"Why so serious?" a voice boomed nearby. Robbie and I

looked up to see Zane and Priya approaching. I wiped my cheeks one more time as we stood to greet them.

She scanned my face as we parted from a hug. "You okay?"

"Yeah, totally. We were just having a deep conversation."

"Barf." Zane smirked. "No wonder you're upset. Listening to this fool talk is agony."

"Shut up, man," said Robbie, but he laughed.

Zane opened the door to Mike's Diner and ushered us all through. The hostess led us to a booth in the middle of the diner and set out menus for each of us, throwing Zane a flirtatious smile. Priya gave her side-eye as we sat.

But Zane was oblivious. "Sorry I was so late, you guys." He rubbed his eyes. "I almost didn't make it."

"What happened, man?" asked Robbie.

Zane gave Robbie a dark look. "It's my brother again." Zane's brother was a sophomore. I'd seen him around their house a few times, usually hobbling around on crutches. He broke his leg in three places in a skiing accident last year. I'd had a hard time finding space to write on his cast since so many people had signed.

"Ah," Robbie said, like he knew what Zane meant.

Priya looked as confused as I felt. "What happened?" She must not have questioned him on the car ride over.

He waved her off. "I don't wanna get into it."

"His brother has a drug problem," Robbie volunteered. "Opioids. His mom keeps finding his stash and flipping out."

"Oh, shit," I said.

Zane glared at him. "I said I don't wanna get into it."

"It's nothing to be ashamed of," said Priya. "It's, like, a huge problem in this country right now. Tons of people are hooked. I saw on the news that—"

Zane slapped the table, making the people in the booth behind him jump and glare over their shoulders. "I *said* . . . I don't wanna fucking get into it."

"Well, well, look at this motley crew." Scott came to our table with a notepad, as though ready to scribble down our order. My stomach clenched. I still wasn't a hundred percent sure what he and Sasha were doing under those bleachers, but I'd bet my electric keyboard he was selling her drugs. "Hey, Red. What's shakin'—"

"What, you work school nights now, too?" My words dripped with sarcasm.

He grinned. "Anything I can do to make a bit of cash, I do." As if I should be impressed. Instead, a sour taste filled my mouth. Zane glared at him with sheer loathing. Oh my God. Did he think Scott sold his brother those pills? "So what can I get you fine folks this lovely evening?"

Zane kept his mouth shut except to order a burger and fries, and other than the occasional grunt and "Yep," he was quiet throughout dinner. He spent most of the time texting someone, and once when an alert brightened his screen, I spotted Sasha's name. I was pretty sure Priya spotted it, too, because she left in a huff to use the ladies' room. She insisted I didn't have to come when I nudged Robbie to let me out of the booth.

Ten minutes later, she still wasn't back.

220

"Where'd she go, anyway?" Zane asked, slurping his milk shake. "I agreed to come out, didn't I? And she freakin' disappears?"

"You haven't exactly been Prince Charming," I shot back. "More like Oscar the Grouch."

"Yeah, yeah." He wiped a hand down his face. "It's been a rough night."

"Well, I'll go check on her." I flicked Robbie's arm, and he stood to let me out. I headed toward the restrooms, but instead found Priya leaning against the old-fashioned jukebox near the kitchen talking to none other than Scott Coleman. She laughed at something he was saying, like she didn't have anywhere else to be.

"What's going on, guys?" I said, throwing Priya a confused look.

"Oh hey, Red," said Scott. "Just chillin'—"

"Shouldn't you be working?" I said pointedly. "We're in the middle of a *double date*. So I'm going to have to steal Priya back."

A pained look crossed Scott's face. "Oh—"

"It's okay," said Priya. "I'm not in any rush to get back."

"Zane asked where you are."

I expected her to brighten at this, but instead she raised a skeptical eyebrow. "Really?" Dammit. Priya had wanted to go on a date with Zane for years, and he was totally ruining it.

"Yeah. Go on back. I need to use the bathroom first."

She shrugged with a sigh. "Alright. Bye, Scott." She gave him a little wave and headed back to our booth.

When she was safely out of hearing range, I glared at Scott. "Stay away from my friends."

His eyebrows shot up. "What?"

My chest tightened. "You were selling Sasha drugs under those bleachers, weren't you? That's her *dirty little secret*, isn't it?"

He shrugged. "I dunno—"

"Enough with the coy act." I shoved his shoulder. "Do you know what those drugs are doing to her? She's becoming a mess— she's shaky, and agitated, and freaking losing her mind." And now that I knew about Zane's brother, it was no wonder she was hiding it from her friends. They'd already seen the consequences of drug abuse, so they might try to stop her. And Sasha wouldn't stand for anyone stopping her.

He scoffed. "Yeah, well, that's her choice."

"But it's yours, too. Just stop selling her whatever it is."

"I . . . I can't." So that confirmed it. He *was* selling her something.

"What do you mean, you can't? You're *hurting* her."

"The only person hurting Sasha is Sasha. I had no choice. No fucking choice." He held his fist to his lips, like he'd said too much. "Listen, you don't know what you saw—"

I balled my hands into fists. "I saw enough. So stay away from my friends. Stay away from Sasha. And stay away from Priya. She's always going to turn you down." Even as the words escaped my lips, I regretted them. But I was so angry. "You're just some gross, creepy, drug-dealing stalker who won't leave her alone. So get lost."

29 MINUTES LEFT

We all stared in horror as Scott slumped over. "Scott!" Priya stooped next to him and gripped his shoulder with trembling fingers.

His eyelids quivered, and his head lolled in her direction as he reached for her hand. "I can't . . . it hurts . . ."

Robbie grabbed a glass of water from the table, and handed it to Priya. "We've got to keep him hydrated. Make him drink this whole thing. When he finishes, give him another one."

She nodded and took the water. "Does anyone have any aspirin or anything?" We all shook our heads. If any of us had medicine, we would have offered it to him already. I wanted to prod Scott to finish his thought from before he nearly passed out. How had Sasha used some secret against him? But his hands shook so fiercely as he tried sipping from the cup, water spattered over the edge. He clearly needed a minute.

"You guys, we're running out of time," Sasha said, staring at the bomb. She covered her ears, white as a sheet, like the bomb could blow at any moment. The timer attached to the mess of wires and tubing silently counted down. Twenty-eight minutes, thirty-nine seconds left. Thirty-eight. Thirty-seven.

"Okay, okay." I held my forehead as Priya helped Scott sit straight against the wall again, though she appeared on the verge of passing out herself. A wave of anxiety flooded my gut. "Let's think. Let's think of another way out of this. Can we defuse the bomb somehow?" A pregnant pause filled the room as everyone stared at the jumble of wires. "God, it's like whoever assembled it threw in a few extra wires just to confuse us."

"Yeah, maybe we shouldn't mess with it," said Robbie. "I don't think this is like the movies. And I don't know shit about defusing bombs." He eyed the bomb and ran a hand over his hair. "Maybe we should move it."

"Move it . . . where?" I asked.

"Can we shove it out the window?" asked Priya. Scott was sipping from the glass of water on his own.

"It wouldn't fit through the bars," I said.

"Oh, I have an idea!" Robbie snapped his fingers and held them to his lips, thinking. "We can put the bomb in a corner"— he pointed at the corner between the closed window and the large brass mirror—"and drag over the cabinets, the table, the chairs. We'll stack everything we can in front of it." Sasha nodded along. "Then we can huddle on the other side of the room—"

"In the fireplace!" Priya exclaimed, leaving Scott's side and dashing across the room. "We can try to squeeze in here . . ." She stooped and shuffled into the fireplace. "Hmm, maybe not . . ."

"We couldn't all fit in there," said Sasha. "I don't know. Wouldn't everything we piled on the bomb explode into a zillion pieces and become shrapnel?"

"Exactly." Diego nodded. "And in case you haven't noticed, we're locked in here. Even if the blast doesn't kill us, we'll burn to a crisp."

I crossed my arms. "Or die of smoke inhalation."

Diego inclined his head. "No . . . I don't think you get it. Those are huge sticks of dynamite. And God knows what that liquid is. It could take down the building. Smoke won't be the issue."

"You don't know that for sure," said Priya.

"No, I don't." Diego shook his head. "Tonight, I don't know anything for sure. But I really don't think sticking it in the corner and covering it with some chairs and tablecloths is going to help much, either."

"Too bad for the bars on the windows . . ." I tugged on my bottom lip. "What if we put the bomb in the fireplace?"

Diego shook his head. "This is a moot point."

"No, wait, listen! What if we put the bomb in the fireplace, and blocked off the fireplace with everything in here? Wouldn't that force the blast up—?"

"There is no 'up.'" Diego leaned into the fireplace, knocking on solid wood where the empty space for a chimney should be. "It's a fake fireplace. There's nowhere for the blast to go. Let's say you're right, and that did contain it . . . *then* we'd die of smoke inhalation."

I joined him at the fireplace and touched his shoulder. "Maybe there's a chance it'd blow a hole through the wall, and we could climb out."

"Most of this room's underground." He faced me. "Even if the blast took out the top of the wall, we'd have to hoist people up over a fire."

"Shit," said Sasha, eyeing the syringe on its tray.

My chest tightened. "Why are you being like this?" I asked Diego, lowering my voice to a whisper. "If we don't try everything we can—she might try going after Scott again. But we can find another way. You know it's the right thing to do. We have to at least try. We have to at least take a stand."

"I know . . ."

"So why are you just shooting everything down?"

He gripped my arms. "Because, Amber, this isn't going to work! Not everything can go exactly the way you plan, no matter how much you want it to."

2 MONTHS, 3 WEEKS AGO

NOVEMBER OF SENIOR YEAR

Time was running out. I scowled at the clock over the classroom door. I had only twenty minutes to get this stupid history assignment done before the first-period bell rang. But no matter how loudly I blared *Hamilton* in my ears, I wasn't any quicker at finding the right Revolutionary War battle dates in my textbook. And nobody else had shown up yet, so I couldn't beg the answers off anyone.

My grades had been slipping since I'd been spending so much time rewatching *Romeo and Juliet* rehearsals. Sasha always roped some freshman into recording rehearsals, thank God—I'd need to split myself in half to go to those *and* orchestra practice. But every time they tweaked the script, I had to adjust the score to time the music to their cues. And there were only so many hours in the day.

As I scribbled answers in my worksheet packet, someone plopped next to me and, without a word, plucked out one of my earbuds with an audible *pop*. I jumped and glanced up as Diego stuck it in his ear. Recognizing the song, he closed his eyes and smiled.

I hadn't spoken to him since the college fair, and was mortified by how I'd blown up at him. He took out my earbud and tapped my worksheet packet. "Didn't you get Mr. Baskin's email? He's out sick today. You have an extra day."

"Oh!" I whipped out my cell and restarted my email app. Lo and behold, an email from our history teacher popped up. "Nice." I cringed. "I mean, it's not nice that he's sick. Obviously."

"Yeah, yeah, I get it." He handed back my earbud. "So, listen. I . . . I wanted to apologize."

"For what?" He must have been living in some alternate universe, because I definitely was the one who should have been apologizing.

He blew air between his lips. "For not texting you back. For all of it. For making my dad quit your dad's company."

My eyebrows shot up. "You did?"

Diego's Adam's apple bobbed as he swallowed. "Well . . . sort of. After SpongeClown sales started taking off, I wanted to turn it into a real business. Dad was too busy with work to put in more time, but I needed help—an adult's help—and I needed cash for more inventory. So I applied to *Bid or Bust* without telling him.

"When they invited us to audition, Dad couldn't say no. It was an *insane* opportunity. And he's always gone over the top to make me happy. I think it's because I'm adopted . . . it's like he wants to prove he loves me extra or something. And then when we got on the show, the investors put us on the spot, asking how I'd manage a business while still in school. I'd assumed one of the investors would assign their team to run it or something. But Dad offered to run the company full-time, on air."

"Yeah. I remember that," I said, my voice flat.

"That's why I didn't text you back. My dad told me he was about to quit your dad's company, and he knew your dad wouldn't take it well. And I just felt so damn guilty."

My heart seized up. I was stunned.

"But I had no idea the impact it'd have on your family," he went on. "I felt so bad when I found out the business went under. I didn't think things all the way through. Then the guilt just kept on piling up, so I just . . . I couldn't bring myself to say anything. And I didn't realize things were still bad. I definitely didn't do it to hurt you." He rested a hand on my arm. "I'd never do anything to hurt you." His eyes were so earnest, I knew he was telling the truth. I'd spent all those years resenting him for thinking I was worthless, but he'd spent those years resenting himself.

I let out a sigh. "But that wasn't your fault. You were a kid with an amazing opportunity in front of you, and you took it. How were you supposed to know what the fallout would be?"

His posture relaxed, and he let out a nervous chuckle. "Well, I wish there was some way I could make it up to you."

I bit my lip. "Actually . . . there might be."

"Yeah?" Such a hopeful look crossed his face that I almost laughed.

"Yeah. You're into filming stuff, right?"

"Sure."

"So . . . we're putting on *Romeo and Juliet* in a few weeks, you know, for the school play. And, well"—I threw him a sly grin—"I still want to apply to those music programs. Maybe one of them will give me a scholarship after all. I'll never know if I don't try."

Diego grinned. "Nice."

"So I need to film the play to send the recording with my applications. I have all the equipment to film it and record the audio, but I can't record it myself since I'm playing in the orchestra, and the other week you filmed the baseball game, so maybe—"

"I'll do it. Whatever you need."

"Really?" I beamed.

"Of course. But listen . . ."

"Yeah?"

"I want to make sure you know . . . I'm not just sorry because of your dad, and the business, and all that. You need to know that I'd never, ever think I was better than you. Not in a million years. And I'm sorry if I ever made you feel that way. You're . . . you're so wonderful, Amber."

I basically stopped breathing. All these years, I'd always felt like whatever I did was never enough. I wasn't good enough to score the play without singing numbers. To get scholarships for college. To split my time between everyone wanting a piece of me. To save my sister's life. I was never, ever enough. So hearing someone tell me I was wonderful floored me.

"I know how hard you've been working to get into music school," he went on. "And the fact that you're going for it anyway, despite all the obstacles you're up against? You're a freaking rock star. You deserve this so much."

His words took my breath away. As he held my gaze with those intense copper eyes of his, it occurred to me how easy it would be to lean over and kiss him. So easy.

Wait, *what*? What was I thinking? I broke eye contact, pulling away from him. I liked Robbie. I *loved* Robbie. What the hell was I doing, thinking about kissing Diego? Maybe I was just grateful he was willing to help, and relieved that we'd aired everything out. That had to be it. I was just overwhelmed with emotion. That's all.

"Thank you" was all I could say.

"You're welcome." He put my earbud back in his ear, fished a spiral notebook from his bag, and started writing, swaying slightly to the beat of the song. But for once, my thoughts drowned out the music, racing with excuses for why the hell I just wanted to kiss a boy other than the one I loved.

27 MINUTES LEFT

Diego's eyes were wide with fear as he glanced at the bomb.

"What if putting it in the fireplace gives us a chance?" My eyes watered, and I clasped his forearms, my face mere inches from his. "A chance to get everyone out of here alive? We can stack enough layers of stuff to block the shrapnel."

"I guess . . ."

"It's better than the alternative." I stared into his piercing eyes, pleading with mine. "It's better than killing someone *now*. Isn't it?"

Robbie clapped his hands. "Doesn't hurt to try, right?" Diego and I sprang apart, and Robbie narrowed his eyes at Diego. *Oh, shit.* What was he thinking? What did he know? But he looked away to glance at Sasha, who stood in the corner, arms crossed.

"It sure will hurt if someone drops the bomb," said Priya.

"Nobody's going to drop it," I said, my pulse quickening.

"A few people should carry it," Sasha suggested. "Just to be sure."

"Fine." I nodded. "So . . . who should carry it?"

Everyone was silent. Nobody wanted to touch the thing, let alone pick it up. Nobody wanted to find out what it'd feel like to have a bomb go off in their arms. Nobody wanted to find out whether they'd be torn apart so fast they wouldn't feel anything, or whether they'd feel the intense, searing pain of burning alive.

"I'll help carry it," Diego volunteered, raising his hand.

"Me too," Robbie piped up. He rushed toward the bomb, as if to prove he was braver than Diego.

"Wait a minute." I glanced at the windows nestled near the ceiling and approached the fireplace. "Why don't we try to raise it on a platform near the top of the fireplace. That way it might blow out the section of the wall aboveground, and maybe the smoke can escape."

"It goes up that high?" asked Priya. She approached the fireplace and knelt to peer up inside it. "Oh yeah, it does . . ." She lost her balance and wobbled on her feet.

I grabbed her shoulders to hold her steady. "Are you okay?" A worried look crossed Diego's face as he stood next to me to get a closer look at her.

"I'm fine." She wiped her forehead with the back of her trembling hand. Her eyes were hazy.

"Priya, maybe you should eat something." To Diego I said, "She has blood sugar problems."

"I'm fine." Priya waved us off. "I think we should do the platform thing. Try to blow out the top of the wall."

Robbie scanned the room, looking for anything we could use to raise the bomb. "Is there anything we can stack?" Everyone glanced around.

"The drawers," Scott grunted, waving his empty water glass toward one of the china cabinets. "In the china cabinet and the sideboards."

"Will they stack evenly, or that high without wobbling?" asked Priya, handing him another glass of water.

"There's one way to find out," said Robbie. He flung out the drawers of the china cabinet closest to the door, dumping tablecloths, napkins, spoons, forks, and doilies onto the floor behind him. Sasha took care of the drawers in the second china cabinet, and Priya and I took the sideboards. Most of the drawers in the sideboard under the window were empty.

"The sideboard drawers aren't as wide," said Diego. "Those should go near the top."

Robbie flipped over the china cabinet drawers and started stacking them. They were pretty level, but only came up to his hips. "This isn't going to be tall enough."

"It's better than nothing," I said. Robbie handed Diego two sideboard drawers. Diego placed them on top. They weren't as sturdy, so he shifted a few drawers to steady the top ones.

"This is like goddamn Jenga," said Sasha.

Scott set his empty glass on the floor. "It's actually nothing like Jenga."

"Shut up." Sasha glared at him.

"Nope." At least he seemed lucid again.

"Wait, wait." Diego motioned for Robbie to stop. "If we stack everything out here, it'll be too tall to push into the fireplace. We have to continue stacking them once they're inside the fireplace."

"Right," said Robbie.

"How'll we set the bomb on top?" Priya asked.

"Yeah . . . we shouldn't tilt it or anything, right?" said Robbie.

"No." Diego shook his head. "Here's what we do. We stack it this high"—he pointed just below the top of the opening of the fireplace—"slide the bomb on top, and—keeping it level—lift the stack and slide the next drawer underneath."

"It *is* like Jenga," Sasha hissed at Scott.

He folded his arms. "Still not even slightly like Jenga."

"Alright," said Robbie, "let's do this." He and Diego tag-teamed removing drawers from the stack and reassembling them inside the fireplace. Once the stack nearly reached the top of the brick mantel, they turned toward the bomb. "You ready?"

Diego wiped his forehead. "Don't have much of a choice."

I squeezed Robbie's arm as he brushed past me to the table to get the bomb, and he paused to kiss the top of my head. The girls gathered under the windows next to Scott while Diego and Robbie took their positions next to the silver tray.

I flicked Scott's shoulder. "You okay?"

His eyes focused on mine as he drained his glass of water. "I'll survive." Then he glanced at Robbie and Diego. "I hope."

Robbie pushed up his sleeves. "Pick it up from either side?"

"Yep." Diego cracked his knuckles.

"Careful . . ." As Robbie and Diego gently lifted the tray and slid their fingers underneath, Priya uttered a small cry next to me. I put my arm around her shoulder, and she let me keep it there, nestling close despite our sticky, sweaty skin.

Sasha grabbed my other hand with trembling fingers. "I physically cannot deal with this."

"It'll be fine. We'll be fine," I said. The three of us huddled together while Diego and Robbie lifted the tray.

"Hold it off to the side, I don't want to walk backward," said Robbie. Diego shifted his position, and they inched toward the fireplace, one careful step at a time. Sweat ran down Diego's temples; his jaw was set in concentration. Robbie's eyes darted between the bomb and their destination. And the red counter ticked down. Twenty-five minutes, forty-nine seconds. Forty-eight. Forty-seven.

The boys reached the fireplace and lifted the bomb chest-level to slide it on top of the stack. Sasha cupped her mouth with her free hand. When they edged it onto the stack, everyone let out a collective breath. "Okay, man. Now for the hard part," said Robbie.

"Right." Diego puffed out his cheeks.

"Seriously?" Priya whined. "*That* was the easy part?"

"Wait," I said, releasing Sasha's and Priya's hands. "Let's make sure we have the time right."

"Oh, crud." Scott clapped his forehead. "We won't be able to see the timer."

"It's okay, we don't need to." I strode to the fireplace and leaned close to the tray. Twenty-five twenty-two. Twenty-one.

"I'll set the timer on my phone." Diego joined me and took his phone from his pocket, matching the time on the bomb to his timer app. "All set."

Priya whimpered and collapsed back against the wall, gripping her knees, her forehead slick with sweat.

"Let's finish this," said Diego. "You lift the stack, and I'll slide in the drawers." Robbie nodded.

I nudged Priya's arm and motioned to the pile of drawers. "C'mon, let's help."

Priya nodded and scooted past Sasha to pass Diego the drawers, but Sasha grabbed the back of her dress. "Stay out of their way," she said. "You'll make them drop it." She yanked her back so hard Priya stumbled backward, landing on her butt.

Priya yelped in pain. She tried scrambling to her feet, but fumbled, struggling to regain her balance. I grabbed her hands and helped her stand, and she smoothed down her white boho dress before rounding on Sasha. "What the hell is your problem? I can pick up a freaking drawer."

"You can't even stand up on your own," said Sasha.

"Stop it—" I tried getting between them, but Priya elbowed me away. I could practically see smoke fuming from her ears.

"Can't you even see yourself?" said Priya. "You're so mean . . . so *cruel*. If we have to kill someone, I hope *you're* the one to die!"

2 MONTHS, 2 WEEKS AGO

NOVEMBER OF SENIOR YEAR

"Priya, get it the fuck together." Sasha's voice carried from the field all the way to the top row of the bleachers, through the *Star Wars* score roaring in my ears. I'd promised Robbie I'd go to this game—it was a big deal since a couple of college scouts would be there. So far he'd gotten a base hit and a strikeout. Last week he struck out and slammed his bat against the ground so hard it shattered. Luckily this time he held it together. But after two more uneventful innings, I was using my lonesome bleacher time to cram for a physics exam.

But Sasha's shouting cut through my attempts to memorize Newton's laws of motion. When she heard Robbie's fall league would be playing their next home game at our school, she latched on to the chance to get her squad to practice their newest routines in front of a crowd before their upcoming competition. Now she stood in front of the cheer squad's diamond formation, hands on her hips.

Priya balanced Amy on her shoulders at the edge of the formation, facing the crowded bleachers. Amy swayed precariously, but kept her fists raised high, a determined smile frozen on her face.

"What are you trying to do, grope her?" Sasha yelled at Priya as I plucked out my earbuds. "You're supposed to grab her ankles, not her calves."

Why was she yelling at Priya like this, in front of everyone? Even from my vantage point I could see that Priya visibly flushed. Zane watched as he stood at bat, waiting for the next inning to begin, while Robbie knocked dirt off his sneakers with his bat in the on-deck circle.

Amy wobbled as Priya tried shifting her grip, her smile turning into a grimace. She was about to crumble. Before she lost her balance entirely, Amy vaulted off of Priya's shoulders, landing on her feet with a small sidestep. She beamed and waved at the crowd, like nothing went wrong. They ate it up, cheering and hooting.

Sasha glanced at the crowd, then grabbed Priya's wrist and dragged her behind the bleachers, while Amy led a "boom dynamite" chant to amp up the crowd as the game resumed. Since I was in the last row, I peeked over the railing, down at Sasha and Priya.

"We've been through this routine a million times," said Sasha. "You're the only one who still can't do basic moves. It's pathetic. I never should've let you onto varsity."

"I'm sorry," Priya muttered.

"Sorry my ass. If you can't handle this"—she jabbed a finger at Priya—"you're off the squad." Priya screwed up her face like she was about to burst into tears.

"Oh, no," I muttered under my breath. All these months, I thought Priya was being oversensitive thinking Sasha didn't like her. But now, seeing her tear into Priya like this—I didn't know what to think. I abandoned my things and ran with long strides down the wide bleacher steps.

"I said I'm sorry, alright?" Priya said as I rounded the bleachers, jogging toward them. "Can't we just try it again?"

"What"—Sasha folded her arms—"so you can drop Amy on her ass in front of the whole crowd?" I rushed over and dragged her away from Priya. "Hey!" she cried. Priya screwed up her face again, shaking her head, and stalked back around the bleachers.

"Sasha, what's the matter with you?"

She wiped her forehead with shaking fingers. "I just can't deal with her. I can't freaking deal." She clenched and unclenched her fists, breathing fast. "We've been through this routine a zillion times. Literally more times than I can count. And she still can't get it right. She's making us look ridiculous."

"But it didn't go *disastrously* wrong. She didn't drop Amy. Do you think maybe you're overreacting?"

"No, I'm not. Do you know how much time we put into this routine? She's ruining *everything*, after all our hard work." She dropped her voice to a hiss and clenched her fists again.

It was like she was trying—and failing—to contain her anger.

This was clearly more than dissatisfaction with Priya's performance. "Jesus, Sasha, are you high or something?" I grabbed her wrist, which trembled in my grip.

"No! Why would you think that?" She wrestled her arm back and turned to the bleachers, crossing her arms. A vein bulged in her neck as she tried slowing her breathing. "Because you're acting insane," I said, deciding not to bring up what Scott hinted at when she was already so agitated. "I'm worried about you, Sasha. You're taking on too much. Can't you see that? Why don't you drop cheerleading for a couple months, just until the play is over—"

"Who the hell do you think you're lecturing?" Sasha narrowed her eyes at me. I flinched, shocked by her tone. "Like I said, I'm not taking anything. I'm fine."

"You don't seem fine." Heat rushed up my neck. "And you're being a mega bitch to Priya." We'd never argued like this before, and my voice cracked under the pressure.

She threw me a look of disgust. "I don't get why you're friends with her. She's pathetic."

A lump formed in my throat, and icicles snaked around my heart. That was my best friend she was talking about. It was like she'd shed her friendly façade to reveal something vile underneath, and I was horrified to see it. "No, she's not," I croaked.

She screwed up her face and waved me off. "Too many freaks, not enough circuses. Why don't you go back to the nosebleed section and mind your own business?" Before I could respond, she spun on her heel and raced back to her squad.

I hadn't seen Sasha lash out like that before. But I couldn't have been so wrong about her. It had to be the drugs talking. It *had* to be.

And I had to help her. She'd gone out of her way for me and for Priya—convincing the drama club to let me score the play, and letting Priya onto the cheerleading squad, helping her learn their routines. But she was taking on too much . . . partially because of us. Maybe it was my fault she felt so overwhelmed. I had to help her. Whatever demons she was battling, I had to help kick their asses.

"Ow." I grimaced—Priya's bony butt was digging into my leg. Four of us were crammed into the back seat of Maria's Prius. I tried shifting closer to Amy, but she was already squished next to her girlfriend, Lisa.

"I'm sorry," said Priya. Her voice trembled like she was on the verge of tears. She was clearly still shaken from Sasha's tantrum earlier. Sasha, on the other hand, acted like nothing happened when she texted me after the game: *Get down here, we're gonna celebrate the win at Zane's.* Now she and Maria were scream-singing some Taylor Swift song while Amy and Lisa laughed along, their hands clasped in Lisa's lap.

"It's okay," I said.

"You guys," said Sasha when the song ended. "I think I'm going to let Zane get to third base tonight." She laughed. "No pun intended."

Maria squealed, and Priya threw me a confused look. Oh, God. I hadn't told her about Sasha's confession that she liked

Zane. I thought she'd only said it to throw me off whatever she was doing with Scott under the bleachers. "Are you two officially dating?" I asked innocently.

"Yep!" she said.

"When did this happen?" I said. "Why didn't you say anything?"

"She's bashful about boys," Maria said in a squeaky voice, and Sasha swatted her arm.

"I *told* you I liked him." Sasha threw me a pointed look, as if to say, *See? I didn't hook up with Scott.* I wanted to ask, *So what drugs did he hook you up with?* but didn't want to make accusations in front of everyone.

"I mean," she went on, "we've been hooking up on and off for years. But we went on our first real date last night!" She glanced in the rearview mirror at Priya, whose expression had morphed from confused to aghast. Sasha knew Priya liked Zane and let her obliviously pine over him this whole time.

"I can't believe you two haven't screwed yet," said Amy.

"I'm not that easy." Sasha shrugged like it was no big deal.

Maria twisted in the driver's seat to wiggle her eyebrows at us. "C'mon, Sasha. Give it up. How easy are you, exactly?"

Sasha flicked Maria's leg. "Keep your eyes on the road, would you?"

"Then answer the question."

Sasha sighed. "I think of myself as a third-date kind of girl."

"Oh, come on!" said Amy. "You said it yourself, you've been hooking up with Zane for *years*."

When nothing but Taylor Swift's voice filled the car for several moments, Maria yelled, "Holy shit. Are you still a virgin?" She and Amy shrieked with laugher.

Sasha mumbled something unintelligible. For once, she wasn't the first or best at something, and blotches of pink stained her cheeks. "Well, what about you guys?" she finally said. "Priya's obviously still a virgin."

Priya crossed her arms and shot me a dirty look, like I was the one who made the jab.

"Amber, have you and Robbie done it yet?" Sasha quickly switched focus to me.

Now it was my turn to flush. "No." Robbie and I had pretty epic make-out sessions, and had gotten close a couple times. But sneaking a quickie in the backseat of his SUV or in one of our bedrooms with parentals in the house didn't seem particularly romantic, so I always pumped the brakes. I still wasn't ready, and wanted to wait until the moment was right, and thankfully, he respected that.

"And neither have you, Amy," said Sasha.

"Um." Amy cocked her head. "You know I have."

"But you . . . you've never had sex with a *boy*," said Sasha. "That makes you a virgin."

Lisa gave a huff and poked her cheek with her tongue, but didn't say anything. Amy smacked Sasha's seat. "Sex with girls counts, you fuckturnip."

"Don't bother," muttered Lisa.

"Besides," Amy went on, giving Lisa's knee a reassuring squeeze, "sex with boys would be *so* boring. They don't know where the important bits are—"

"Can you *not* overshare right now?" Lisa swatted at Amy's hand.

"What?" Amy pouted. "They're my best friends, I tell them everything."

Lisa crossed her arms. "Your *best friends* don't think sex with girls counts."

Sasha sank back in her seat, nibbling on her thumbnail. Even in the dark, I could see her face was fully flushed now. Somehow, I didn't think she meant what she said—she just didn't know how to handle not winning at something. After an awkward stretch of silence, I piped up, "For what it's worth, I think it counts." But nobody said anything else until we arrived at Zane's. I scrambled out from under Priya's thighbone, shivering from the night chill, and followed the girls around Zane's house.

In the backyard, Zane's dad tossed patties onto a grill while he and his mom dragged over heat lamps for us to huddle under. The moment Zane's parents went inside, Sasha wasted no time— she dragged him over to a picnic table, planted herself on his lap, and initiated some very public displays of affection.

"Oh, geez," I muttered. I grabbed Priya's arm. "Listen, Priya, I'm really sorry—" I started, but Robbie jogged over, interrupting us.

"Where's my victory kiss?" He wrapped me in a sweaty hug and kissed me. I shoved him back playfully.

245

"Ew, you're all sweaty."

"Well, that's what happens when you hit a game-ending home run."

"You did?" I must have missed it. He released me, his expression unreadable, and my stomach clenched. "I mean, yeah, that was awesome! Great job!"

"You didn't see, did you?"

Crap. "I'm so sorry . . . I had to cram for our physics exam during the game. I must've been really in the zone."

He kicked at the gravel, his jaw clenched. "Well, the scouts saw. That's what matters." Just then, Sasha giggled as Zane whispered something in her ear. Priya huffed and raced back toward Zane's front lawn. Oh, no.

I backed away from Robbie. "Listen, I'm really sorry. But Priya's upset. I have to go talk to her."

"Fine, fine."

I ran after Priya, catching up to her on Zane's driveway. "Priya!"

She spun. "What the hell, Amber? Aren't *I* your best friend? Or has she got me beat there, too?"

"Of course you are—"

"She reams me out in front of everyone." She jabbed her finger toward the backyard, where Sasha was glomming onto Zane's face. "And then yells at me like I'm a five-year-old, and you go comfort *her*?"

"Wait—*that's* what you're upset about? This isn't about Zane?"

"No, this isn't about a stupid boy."

"But . . . wait, so you're not upset he's with Sasha now?"

"I mean, kind of? But I haven't liked him for ages. It's painfully obvious he doesn't give a crap about me. He'd *never* like me back."

For ages? My brain scrambled to recall the last time Priya brought up Zane before our disastrous double date, the last time she babbled endlessly about him . . . it must have been months ago, and I hadn't even noticed she'd stopped. "*You're* the one who's been trying to set us up," Priya went on. "What were you thinking, anyway? You knew they were hooking up. Were you *trying* to get my hopes up?"

"No! I'm so sorry. I didn't—"

"And what the hell's up with you taking Sasha's side at the game when I was the one getting shit on?"

"Priya, I was trying to calm her down. You know, so she'd stop screaming at you. I told her to stop being such a bitch."

"Sure you did."

I blanched. "You don't believe me?"

"Maybe I don't." Her lower eyelids were rimmed with tears. "You two are besties now. You go to all her parties. You're dating one of her best friends. *You're* one of her best friends now. You're in her circle."

"So are you!"

Priya threw her arms out. "Are you blind? She hates me. She hates everything about me. She thinks I'm totally pathetic."

"That's not true . . ." But Sasha did use that exact word. I brushed back my bangs. "She let you start doing stunt work."

"Yeah, because I stole a midterm for her." Oh, God. That was true, too.

"Can't we all just—"

"Just what? Get along? I tried that, Amber. Remember? I tried sucking up to her, just like you did." A tear trickled down her cheek. "I wish . . . I wish we never tried to be friends with her. I wish none of this had ever happened. I wish she didn't *exist*."

24 MINUTES LEFT

Sasha's eyes flashed, tremors shook her arms, and her cheeks flushed—whether from heat or anger at Priya's suggestion that she be the one to die, I couldn't tell. "How could you say that?" she thundered. This had escalated faster than I'd imagined.

"Because you're a complete bitch." Priya gripped the backrest of one of the chairs so hard her knuckles turned pearly white. "You'll do anything to get your way—"

"Oh my God," said Sasha. "You're so jealous of me, you want to get rid of me!" Diego slid another drawer into the middle of the misshapen platform, so the bomb was now hidden behind the mantel.

"Oh, no," said Priya. "This is *not* jealousy talking."

"Guys, stop it." I rushed to Priya's side and glared at Sasha.

"Priya doesn't really want anyone to die. It's just this room . . . it's making us all go crazy."

"How do you know?" Sasha asked.

"Because I know her better than anyone else in this room," I said, "and I'd be willing to bet my life on it." Priya's expression softened, but she still gripped the chair as though she depended on its support. "Listen, we still have"—I glanced at my watch— "about twenty-four minutes left. There's still time. Let's focus on stacking stuff in front of the fireplace."

Diego crossed his arms, shaking his head at the stack of drawers. "I really don't think this is going to work."

"Maybe we should at least start talking about who to choose," said Robbie, cringing as though disgusted he had to suggest it. "What if we *do* have to do this?"

I shook my head, my heart racing so fast I thought I might have a heart attack. "But how can we decide something like this? How can we choose one of us to *die*?"

He wiped a hand down his face. "I don't know. But we don't want to wait until the last minute to choose, do we?"

"I still say it should be Scott," said Sasha. I tilted my head. Her secret was already out. But then I remembered something Scott said earlier, before he almost passed out. He'd hinted that she'd used something he'd told her against him. And months ago, when I'd cornered him at Mike's Diner, he said he had no choice whether to sell her drugs. What did he mean by that?

"God, Sasha," I said. "Why are you still so dead set on killing Scott?"

Sasha crossed her arms. "Why do you *think*?"

"What, the Ritalin thing?" I turned to Scott. "Or . . . is there something else?"

Sasha folded her arms tighter, staring at the door. "There's not."

"So you didn't blackmail me?" said Scott, his nostrils flaring.

We all stilled and gaped at Scott. The room went so silent I could almost hear the bomb ticking in the fireplace. Sasha pursed her lips and shook her head, the vein in her neck bulging again. "You liar."

"It's not a lie, and you know it," said Scott.

"She *blackmailed* you?" I repeated. "How? What happened?"

He rubbed his eyes. "None of this leaves this room, okay?"

"Dude, *we* might not even leave this room," said Robbie.

"We won't tell," I assured Scott.

"No—" Sasha started.

"Shut up!" I yelled. She flinched.

Scott took a deep breath. "Well, one day after detention, I was waiting for my dad to pick me up, but he didn't show. No shock there. But Sasha walked by, and I really didn't feel like walking home, so I asked her for a ride. Dumb move." He shook his head. "So in the car, she acts all concerned, asking me what's wrong. And she's being all nice, giving me a ride, and I'm all vulnerable and shit, so I tell her what's up. That my dad's constantly high on meth or weed or whatever, so he's out of work, and always forgetting to do stuff, like pick me up.

"So Sasha's like, 'Have you tried getting him help?' But my mom's been dead for years, and if Dad went to rehab . . . what if

Social Services found out? God knows what'd happen to me. I'd probably wind up in foster care."

"Wow," said Diego.

"I'm so sorry," I said.

"Yeah, I thought she was, too." Scott glared at Sasha. "But a couple weeks later, she cornered me and asked if I could swipe some of my dad's meth for her. I said, no way, and offered her weed instead, but she insisted on meth. She said I'd be doing him a favor, putting a dent in his stash. 'Besides,' she said, 'don't you need the money?' I refused, and then she started going on about what a shame it'd be if he kept doing meth, and someone found out about it—"

"I didn't mean it like that!" Sasha finally interjected. "I wasn't blackmailing you. I was just trying to help."

"Bullshit," said Scott. "You were only trying to get what you wanted. I confided in you, and you used it against me."

"You're wrong!" Sasha's expression darkened. "You have no idea what you're talking about." I glanced at Priya, whose arms quivered as she gripped the chair next to me.

"So that's why you sold her the Ritalin, then," I said to Scott. "So you'd be selling her something, and she'd keep her mouth shut."

"Exactly," he said. "And now she wants to kill me over it."

"That's not true!" said Sasha.

"We're not going to kill you," I said to Scott.

Sasha gave me an incredulous look. "He's trying to twist my

words around. I never meant it that way. He just wants to make me look bad to make sure one of *us* dies instead."

But I didn't think Scott would make all of that up. I believed him. "What do you mean, 'one of *us*'?" I asked Sasha.

"Well, you know. Us. Our friends." She pointed between me, Robbie, and herself. "But it can't be one of us. It *can't* be." Robbie put a protective arm around me, like he agreed. Heat radiated from him, nearly suffocating me.

Priya released the chair and took a step forward, balling her trembling hands into fists. "In case you haven't noticed, you're not in any sort of majority." Sasha bunched her eyebrows, and a rock settled in my gut. "It's three versus three, and I say it should be one of you to die."

Her words shattered my heart into more pieces than any bomb could. We'd been best friends all our lives, up until a couple of months ago. But *it should be one of you to die* looped in my ears as I stared at her, tears brimming my eyes.

How had it come to this?

But before I could say anything, before I could try to reason with someone who until recently had been like my sister, Priya's eyes fluttered shut, and she collapsed in a heap.

2 MONTHS AGO

DECEMBER OF SENIOR YEAR

Priya never showed up to school today.

I waited on her front stoop in the morning so we could drive in together as usual. I desperately needed her advice. Last night, Robbie told me he received a full scholarship to play on Georgia Tech's baseball team. It was a big shock—he barely expected to get recruited, let alone a scholarship. But apparently they felt like they'd discovered a hidden gem. Robbie couldn't be more thrilled—they'd churned out nearly a hundred MLB players, and he finally earned his dad's respect. But after I finished jumping up and down with him, covering his face with kisses and congratulating him, he did the unthinkable.

He asked me to come with him.

To Georgia freaking Tech.

I was floored. I loved him, and I wanted us to be together—but I always figured that if we ended up in different cities, we'd date long-distance, reuniting over winter and summer breaks. We each knew and respected each other's career goals, and that was supposed to come first.

At least, I thought it was.

Caught off guard, I babbled incoherently about how I'd already had a list of schools in mind, but said I'd look into their music program when I got home. "They have a great program, I promise," Robbie had said with a grin. "And I looked it up—tuition is half the cost of USC. Your dad'll be happy about that. We can even move off-campus at some point to save you money. And hey, you can come to all my games, too."

Dread bubbled in my stomach—any program of theirs wouldn't match those at my dream schools. And when I Googled Georgia's Tech's offerings late last night, I quickly discovered they had no music program to speak of. None. Nor did any college within a fifty-mile radius.

But Robbie wanted me to come with him—to be together long term. To *live* together. He was serious about us. Part of me was elated. But my music . . . how could I drop all of my plans like that? Worse, how could he expect me to? He knew how much I wanted to go to music school. But would I lose him altogether if I said no? Was following him to school something I should consider?

Hence needing Priya's advice. She was the one person I ever confided in, who knew all of my dreams, and how much work I'd done to accomplish them. If there was anyone who could talk some sense into me, it was Priya.

But she didn't come outside when I rang the bell or knocked

on the front door. Her car was in the driveway, but the two-car garage door was shut, so I couldn't tell if her parents were home. Her parents always let me in if they got to the door first, so I guessed they'd already left for work. Did Priya go with them somewhere? She ignored my texts and Google chats: *Where are you???*

I kept checking my phone between classes. It wasn't like her to ignore me, and I kept expecting some explanation to light up my screen. The longer my messages went unanswered, the tighter my stomach twisted.

I swung by Sasha's locker on my way to physics. Amy and Maria huddled next to Sasha, watching something on her phone, tittering. Sasha and Amy were decked out in their cheerleading uniforms for tonight's football game.

Sasha caught sight of me and stuck her phone in her locker. "Hey, lady, what's up?" She stretched out a cheek to kiss the air on either side of mine. "You coming to the game tonight?"

I wiped sticky gloss off one of my cheeks when she turned back to her locker mirror. "Umm . . . I don't know. I have orchestra practice."

"Oh, well that's good. They learned my new songs, right?" *Her* new songs? I nodded, watching Maria's face fall. The orchestra had finally learned all of the new singing numbers. I'd never composed music to lyrics before, and it ripped me from my comfort zone. But I was especially proud of the haunting, mournful melody Juliet sings after discovering Romeo is dead. It showed off my range brilliantly alongside the other samples I'd be sending to colleges. So I took extra time to make it absolutely perfect to use it as my fifteen-minute recording from the play, along with the full PDF of the composition. Maybe if it blew the admissions boards away, they'd deem me worthy of a scholarship.

Maybe I'd get to go to my dream school after all.

"Yeah, they sound great," I replied. "Hey, have any of you seen Priya? She missed our calc exam second period, and it's not like her to—" I paused when the three of them exchanged furtive glances. "What is it?"

Amy adjusted one of her curls. "Priya's probably going to be out for a while." She cringed, biting her lip.

"Poor thing." Sasha pouted, twisting her tube of lip gloss closed.

"Why?" I asked. "What happened?"

"She bit it at practice last night," said Amy.

"Literally," said Sasha. The three of them erupted into giggles.

"Oh my God," said Maria, "stop it, that's horrible."

An uneasy feeling settled in my stomach. "What exactly happened?"

"Ugh, it was a disaster." Sasha rubbed her lips together. "She couldn't do a basic tuck flip."

"A *basic* tuck flip?" I said, raising my voice. "Off someone's shoulders?"

Amy wiggled her fingers. "Mine."

I glared at Sasha. "You know she sucks at balance stunts— why would you let her do flips off someone's *shoulders*?"

"Hey." She slammed her locker shut. "It's not my fault she's a complete moron." She set her hands on her hips and stuck out her chin, ready for a retort. "She's had weeks to learn that stunt."

How could she say that? Heat coursed through my veins as the warning bell rang. But concern for Priya trumped my anger. "So what happened to her? Is she okay?"

"It wasn't pretty," said Sasha.

"And probably still isn't," said Amy. "It was a hard fall." She frowned. "It was actually pretty scary."

"Ugh, I'm so glad I didn't see it in person," said Maria. "I would have thrown up."

"Well, you freak out at the mere mention of blood," said Sasha. My fingers and toes went numb. There was *blood*?

Maria shuddered. "True."

Sasha glanced at her watch. "I don't want to be late. Good luck at orchestra practice. I hope they're on point." She grabbed me for a quick hug. "Just three weeks left until opening night!"

I banged on Priya's front door for the umpteenth time. Her parents were still at work, but I spotted her peeking through the blinds in her bedroom window on the second floor. "Priya!" I yelled at her window. "I *saw* you up there. C'mon, let me in!"

No response.

"I just want to make sure you're okay! I heard about what happened."

No response.

"C'mon, Priya! It can't be that bad. So what if you have some cuts and bruises?"

No response.

I stood back from the house and contemplated checking the

windows to see if any of them were unlocked. "I'm not leaving until I talk to you!" Squeezing behind the hedges next to the front walkway, I tried the living room window, but it was locked. "Priya! You don't have to hide—"

The front door lock clicked, and the door creaked as it opened slightly. I scrambled past the shrubberies, back to the front stoop. "Will you shut up already?" said Priya.

"I just wanted to . . ." I trailed off when I saw Priya's face. Her upper lip had been split, and a few stitches crisscrossed down the middle. Her right cheek was covered in deep purple bruises. I couldn't see the rest of her—she wore a long gray sweatshirt over black leggings. "Oh my God, are you okay?"

Defeated, she opened the door a bit wider. "What does it look like?" She made a whistling sound when saying "does," and I caught a glimpse of her front teeth—or lack thereof.

I clamped a hand over my mouth, holding in a gasp.

"Yeah. Come in." She stepped aside so I could walk in, and led me to her bedroom. It'd been forever since I'd come over, since we always hung out at my place. Posters of David Thurston and old-fashioned diagrams of illusions still lined her walls, and her bookshelves were crammed with magic books and fantasy novels.

When she sat at her desk, I sank onto the edge of her bed. "Does it hurt?" I asked.

"No, Amber." She covered her mouth when she spoke. "I literally fell on my face and knocked out my two front teeth last night, and it doesn't hurt one bit." I strained to make sense of her words through her new lisp.

"I'm sorry. Of course it hurts . . ." I paused when the tears pooling in her eyes spilled down her cheeks. "Will they be able to fix it?"

She dropped her hand and ran her tongue over the empty space where her teeth had been drilled down to nubs. "Yeah. The teeth broke in half, but they're going to cement on a bridge with fake teeth. Supposedly nobody will be able to notice anything changed."

"Oh, good. That's great. Still, that must have been scary."

"Ya think?" she shot back, her eyes narrowed.

"I'm sorry. I was just—"

"Just what? You just wanted to come over to see what a freak show I am, right?"

My brow furrowed. Why would she think she's a freak show? I'd think it's pretty normal to fall while attempting a difficult flip stunt. It was rotten luck that she landed splat on her face, but nothing about the situation made her a freak. "Of course not. I was worried about you. I'd never think that about you."

"Well, *she* does. All the time. Sasha's constantly reminding me how I'm ugly, incompetent, a geek, a horrible cheerleader, and a fat useless moron." I stared at her in horror, my mouth agape. "I heard her tell Amy I was a freak when she saw . . . when she saw . . ." She motioned to her mouth.

"She . . . she called you a *fat useless moron?*"

"Not exactly . . . she writes these nasty comments on my Facebook and Instagram posts for everyone to see. 'Aw, Priya, you're so pretty in pictures.'" She scoffed. "Like I'm ugly in real life. And everyone knows what she means."

My lungs seized up. I'd heard Sasha say stuff like that before, but I thought Priya was just being overly sensitive. Sasha had been so nice to me, so helpful, I didn't think she *meant* to be mean.

"After a while, it got even worse," Priya went on. "She'd comment with links to makeup that would hide my zits, or dieting advice. Everyone likes all her comments, and some of them even chime in with their own 'tips.'" She made air quotes. "'Oh, Priya, you should wear your hair down like this more often so it covers your face.' Or, 'Ever heard of Photoshop?'"

"No," I whispered.

"That's not even the worst of it." Oh, God. "Someone took a video of me at cheerleading practice yesterday . . ." She choked back a sob. "Sasha didn't take it, obviously . . . someone else must have sent it to her. But she shared it publicly on every platform, under the pretext of a fucking safety lesson for cheerleaders. As if she was doing it to help people. And it's going viral."

"What?" My stomach curdled like sour milk. Sasha hadn't mentioned that earlier. Priya grabbed her phone from her desk, scrolled for a moment, and tried handing it to me. I winced and leaned back. "I don't need to see it. I . . . I believe you. I'm so sorry, I had no idea—"

"I know, I know. You don't use social media. You're the only person on the freaking planet who doesn't use social media." I'd deleted my accounts after Maggie's death, afflicted with PTSD, terrified I'd see something I wouldn't be able to unsee.

Just like Maggie had.

"Why didn't you tell me what she was doing?"

"I tried. You kept rationalizing away her jabs . . . the ones you saw for yourself."

"I . . . I didn't realize—"

"And I know how triggering social media is for you. So there I am, trying to still be friends with her, like a complete idiot, because I still wanted to be friends with you. And you know what? I don't even care anymore. I'm done."

I shook my head, unable to comprehend her words. "What do you mean, you're done?"

"I'm done," she repeated. "With all of it. Starting with cheerleading. I already quit."

"But you can't quit now. You've worked so hard . . ." But I glanced at her busted lip and swallowed hard.

"Oh, please." Priya shook her head. "I'm quitting cheerleading, and I'm quitting Sasha, and I'm quitting *you*."

My heart went numb. "What?"

"You heard me. I can't do this anymore. I can't compete for your time." My mouth opened and closed a few times as I struggled to find words. "Let's just face it, Amber. We've drifted apart."

I stood. "No. No we haven't!"

"It's like you're in your own little bubble. All you care about is your play, and your perfect friend, and your perfect boyfriend. You chose them over me. And I've always been there for you. But I can't stick it out any longer."

My eyes watered. I couldn't believe what I was hearing. "Priya . . . I know you're upset about the video . . ."

"It's not just the video. Honestly, I should have done this

months ago." Oh, God. She must have been bottling this up, and nothing could stop the explosion. "But I didn't want to lose you. And I did want to be on the cheerleading squad. I wanted to live out my pipe dream, just like you were living yours. I wanted you to be proud of me for coming out of my shell. I wanted to be friends with whoever you were friends with, so we could be best friends together, always." She choked on the word "always," tears slipping down her face.

"And it's not just that she was awful to me. She made me *do* awful things, too. I drank at school when I didn't want to. I stole an exam for her. I bullied Phil Pratt to try to fit in, and then he brought a freaking gun to school—"

I grabbed for her hand, but she pulled it away. "That wasn't your fault. You didn't bully him, Priya. It was one time."

"What if that was his breaking point? Maybe if he thought even dorky Priya Gupta could insult him like that . . . well, maybe that was his last straw. What if he went on a murdering spree, and I was one of the people who'd made him feel like crap? All of that blood—maybe even my own blood—would be on *my* hands."

"But he didn't!" I shook my head—I had no idea this had been weighing on her so heavily. I was the one who encouraged her to be fun and silly around Zane, which led her to taunt Phil. If anything, that was *my* fault. "Why didn't you tell me any of this earlier?"

"When?" she cried. "When could I? Sasha's *always* around. And you're never online, and you suck at texting. If she's not around, you're hell-bent on focusing on your music. And honestly, I wasn't sure you'd choose me over her."

I wiped the tear slipping down my cheek. "I thought she was a friend. A friend to *both* of us."

"But you saw her yelling at me! You saw it!"

"I thought she was just cracking under pressure, or high, or something." But stress and drugs didn't excuse what Sasha was doing to Priya.

I'd been selfish these past months. I got my wish to score the play, the most popular girl in school befriended me, a baseball jock fell for me, and I was considered one of *them* now. For the first time in forever I felt part of a group, accepted by people I always considered "above" me. But I'd deserted the person who truly mattered, and let them steamroll her. It had to stop. I couldn't lose Priya over this. I couldn't let her continue getting hurt.

"I can stop hanging out with her. Right now." My voice shook. "She has to go through with the play now, anyway—"

Priya slapped her desk. "*There it is.* It's always about the play, or what Robbie wants, or what Sasha wants, but never about what I want. Don't you see that? It's never about how I feel. It's too late. I want my sanity back. I'm done with you. With all of it."

No. This couldn't be happening. She couldn't mean this. I couldn't lose Priya. "I swear, I'll stop talking to Sasha."

"You won't just walk away. I know it." Priya shook her head. "You're so ingrained in that group now. That never happened for me. They won't miss me at all."

"I'd miss you. Every day. You're my best friend, Priya."

"No I'm not. *She* is. She took that honor months ago. And I've had enough. I'm done."

22 MINUTES LEFT

"Priya!" I scrambled to her side after she hit the floor.

Diego rushed over as I turned Priya to lie flat on her back. She'd been shaky and off-balance for a while, but I thought it was out of fear, and maybe the heat. I knew about her blood sugar problems—I should have been more insistent that she eat something earlier. This was all my fault. *My* fault.

In a panic, I stood and grabbed a pepper shaker from the table. "Should we put this under her nose?"

Diego took it from me. "What, pepper?"

"Yeah. You know. To wake her up."

Diego shook his head and handed it back. "That's not a thing. You're thinking of smelling salts, which we don't have."

"Well, we have to do something!" I threw the pepper shaker across the room, and it shattered against the fireplace, pepper spilling everywhere. "This can't be happening." My stomach clenched, and I swallowed hard. *It should be one of you to die.* I couldn't have understood Priya properly. The heat must have been muddling my brain. Sure, we'd had a falling-out, but she couldn't mean she wanted me to *die*. Tears blurred my vision.

Diego wiped his own forehead and glanced at the shattered window, a panic-stricken look on his face. "I didn't think it'd get this hot. How is it so damn hot in here?"

"Something must be wrong with the boiler," suggested Robbie.

"Robbie, break the other window," I said. "Let's try to get more fresh air in here."

He nodded. "It's worth a shot."

"Priya, wake up." I gently shook her shoulders, and her head lolled feebly from side to side. "Dammit, I told her to eat something. She's hypoglycemic."

"Maybe it was a combination of that and the heat," said Diego as Robbie dragged a chair to the intact window, lifted it over his head, and bashed away.

He hopped aside in time to avoid the glass raining down and waved his arms like a lunatic, trying to circulate the air. But the windows were so small, and the room was so hot, it wasn't helping. Everyone looked exhausted, and we were all sweating profusely.

Panic racked my body, and I trembled despite the heat. There was no way out of here. There was no way to get Priya to the hospital. There was no way that door was opening until the hour was up, and we still had around twenty minutes left. What if the heat made us all pass out?

"Maybe she'll die," said Sasha, "and we won't have to kill any-one."

"Holy shit, Sasha," said Diego.

Sasha frowned. "I'm just saying"—she pointed toward the camera in the china cabinet—"if they see someone die, maybe the timer will stop. Besides, you heard her. Priya totally meant she wanted me to die. She's ready to become a murderer."

"You're one to talk." Scott straightened his back against the wall. "You were the first person to suggest killing someone." He tapped on his chest, glaring at Sasha.

Sasha threw out her arms. "That was only to save the rest of us."

"Bullshit! You were just afraid I'd rat you out." As the two of them hurled accusations at each other, Priya coughed, and her eyes fluttered open.

"Priya!" I grabbed one of the last glasses of water from the table and handed it to Diego, who helped Priya sit up and tilted the glass at her lips, helping her drink. "Quick, let's get you something to eat." I stood and started toward the table, where the platters of chicken and roasted veggies, salad, yams, and deviled eggs sat untouched.

"No," Priya croaked, gripping Diego's sleeve. "I don't want anything *they* gave us."

"I'm sure it's fine," I said.

"What if . . . what if it's poisoned?" she whimpered.

A helpless feeling washed over me as I scanned the food. Priya had to eat *something*. "Does anyone have a granola bar? Trail mix? Something like that?"

"Oh!" Diego exclaimed. "Amber, I have a Snickers bar in my backpack." He motioned toward where he'd been sitting when this mess first started.

"Won't all that sugar just make her crash again?" I asked.

"Snickers is fine," said Priya. "I just need something quick."

"Hell," said Robbie, "we might not be alive by the time she'd crash again." A pained look crossed his face.

"Right." I rounded the table and unzipped Diego's backpack, digging around. "In the main compartment?"

"No, the one in front," Diego said. "It should be—" He took a quick intake of breath as I unzipped the front compartment and felt around for the familiar shape of a candy bar. There were like a gazillion pockets in this thing. I turned the bag upside down and shook it until a Snickers bar fell out, and tossed it to Diego over the table. He fumbled to catch it, looking like he was about to be sick himself, and glanced toward my feet as he unwrapped the bar and handed it to Priya. I set down his backpack and stooped to pick up a bunch of pens, pencils, and an index card.

Wait, that wasn't an index card. It was a Polaroid. I froze.

My heart stilled as I inspected it. It was from the winter ball last year, the selfie we took together.

I could feel Diego's eyes on me now, but I couldn't avert my gaze from the photo. He carried this with him all the time. Had he dropped it into his bag, never to look at it again? Or did he look at it often? The edges appeared worn, like it'd been handled quite a bit. And he seemed nervous that I'd find it.

But maybe it meant nothing.

I glanced up and met Diego's gaze. Oh, God. The way he looked at me now—it wasn't nothing. He watched me like I could tear his world apart faster than any bomb could. I used to have such a crush on him before my family's world collapsed. Before I thought he found me worthless. Before he thought I hated him. We'd let our own misguided assumptions drive us apart. Did this mean that Diego liked me all this time? How many years of lost chances did this photo represent?

I glanced at Robbie, who watched Sasha and Scott scream at each other. He met my gaze and gave me an exasperated look, like he couldn't believe the two of them. I never thought it possible to have feelings for two different people at the same time. It felt like teetering over the edge of a lakeside cliff, unsure whether to step back to safety or leap and enjoy the thrill, without knowing what waited under the glassy surface: a deep pool of water, or jagged rocks. How the hell was I supposed to know if I should take the plunge?

After slipping the photo back into Diego's bag, I rounded the table and kneeled next to him as Priya leaned against the door and nibbled on the Snickers bar. Her chin quivered, and she wiped her nose. Diego took my hand for a moment, and my fingertips seemed to ignite, confirming my suspicion. There was something there. Without a word, he stood to join everyone else by the windows.

"Priya . . ." I focused on her. "I'm so sorry. You'll never know how sorry I really am, because it's, like, an infinite amount. I never, ever wanted to lose you as a friend. As my *sister*." She scrunched her face at the word "sister," tears flowing freely as she swallowed her chocolate.

"I didn't mean that." She finally choked out between sobs. "I don't want you to die." Relief settled on me like a blanket. But would things ever be right between us again?

"You know I love you," I said. "I never wanted to choose her as a friend over you. I never meant to hurt your feelings. And maybe . . . maybe I was too scared to see the truth. You know, because of what made Maggie think she had no other way out. I was in denial that it was happening again." I shook my head and glared at Sasha. "But it should have made me fight harder to protect you. I was a coward. And I'm so, so sorry."

"I know you are. And I should have told you how I felt earlier. I should have shown you what she was saying. It's my fault, too."

"No, none of it was your fault." Just like none of it was Maggie's fault. If I'd been there for Maggie, she would have had the help she needed to fight back. Now I was going to make sure I was always there for Priya. "I'm going to make it up to you, I swear it. I'm going to get you out of here alive, and make sure she never—"

"Enough already!" Diego yelled at Sasha, breaking up her argument with Scott, making me and Priya jump. "Scott's right, you were the first one to suggest killing someone."

"No—"

"Yep. We all witnessed it. But the more time you two waste arguing, the more likely it is we *will* have to kill someone."

"It's already too late," said Sasha. "We already have to kill someone, and you know it."

"You know what?" I climbed to my feet, curling my hands

into fists. "I think if we do need to choose someone to die, it should be whoever showed the least regard for everyone else's life."

"Oh, please." Sasha waved at the air like she was brushing away the idea. "Enough with the noble bullshit. Let me tell you something. When there are five minutes left on that timer"—she jabbed her finger toward the fireplace—"you're going to want to kill someone, too. You're going to want to do whatever you can to save yourself."

I wiped my upper lip. "Maybe. I don't know what's going to happen. But at least I wanted to give everyone in this room a fair shot. And so did Diego, and Robbie, and Scott, and Priya. We all wanted to figure this out, but all you could think about was making sure it wasn't *you* who died."

She scoffed, but I went on. "And it's not just about tonight, in this room. You constantly hurt people to make sure you come out on top." I threw Diego a meaningful look.

Sasha's face went stony, like I'd dug a little too close to home. "That's not true."

Diego caught my gaze and balled his hands into fists. "Yes it is. You'd do anything to get better grades than me."

Sasha scoffed. "Like studying my ass off is really hurting anyone."

"Seriously?" He raised his voice. "Have you really forgotten all the ways you've tried to sabotage me?"

1 MONTH, 3 WEEKS AGO

DECEMBER OF SENIOR YEAR

I took my usual seat in physics near the window, crossed my arms, and rested my forehead against them. I hadn't been able to sleep a wink after Priya cast me out of her life. What was I going to do? How could I get Priya to forgive me? Scarier still, how was I going to confront Sasha about what she'd done, and the hurt she'd caused?

"Hey, babe." Robbie sat in Sasha's usual seat, kissed my temple, and wrapped his arms around me.

"Oh, hey," I said, surprised to see him, but happy to get a much-needed hug. I nestled my cheek into his shoulder, breathing in his musky scent, holding him tight.

"Is something wrong?" He could always sense when I was upset.

I sighed. "It's . . . everything." I didn't have time to tell him about Priya now. Besides, I had to figure out *how* to tell him. Sasha was one of his best friends. He might take her side out of sheer loyalty; they'd been friends forever. Had he ever even seen her cruel streak? "I'll tell you later."

"I'll be here." He kissed the top of my head. "Hey, did you get my texts last night?"

I had, but I'd ignored them, too heartsick to interact with another human being. Instead I'd snuggled with Mittens, who chivalrously endured my endless sobbing, and blasted movie scores all night like it would somehow lift the cloud from over my head. "Sorry, I went to bed super early. The sleep deprivation is real."

He chuckled. "I feel you. So I wanted to see if you applied to Georgia Tech yet?"

My body stiffened. He must have felt me cringe. "Um . . . yeah." As I pulled away from him, my cheeks pulsated with heat, and Robbie's jaw hardened as he scanned my face. He knew I was lying. "No," I whispered. I'd been putting off this discussion, too afraid to crush him.

"But you're going to, right?"

"I don't know. The thing is . . . Georgia Tech doesn't have a music program."

"I thought they did."

"No, they don't. They have this music technology program, but that's not what I'd need—it's more of an engineering program."

He blanched. "Oh. I didn't realize."

"Yeah. Well, you know I want to study music, to become a film score producer. USC and Berklee have the best programs—"

"But you can practice music anywhere, on your own. Or you can hire a teacher."

I frowned. "Wait, what?" I'd poured my heart out to him about wanting to study music. About Dad pressuring me to apply to cheaper schools. He knew how important this was to me. Where was this coming from?

"You don't need some stupid music program," said Robbie, and my mouth fell open. "You're already so good at it—"

Boom. I jumped. Diego dropped his heavy backpack on the desk in front of me and glared at Robbie. Robbie saw his expression and glared right back. What was *that* about?

"Hey, Robbie, scoot," said Sasha, hovering over him. "Don't you have Spanish now?" I pursed my lips and fought against the rage threatening to unleash in her direction. I couldn't believe I fell for her nice act. Robbie leaned close and muttered in my ear, "We're not done with this conversation."

"Clearly not," I retorted, and glared at him as he left the room.

"Hey, lady!" Sasha took his place at our desk and tried to kiss the air next to my cheek, but caught my expression. "Um, are you okay?"

"Just fine and freakin' dandy." I opened my bag, pretending to search for something.

Sasha stared at me like I was an alien life-form until Diego slapped his homework on his desk. She glared at him and cleared her throat as she shuffled through her homework. "Question five, question five . . . the answer is fifty-eight point two kilograms," she said just loud enough for him to overhear. I glanced at her paper—she'd scrawled 63.5 kilograms under question five, not 58.2. Sure enough, he turned the page and scratched his head. "Geez, Amber, that one was so easy. Get with the program."

As she flipped through the pages, searching for another chance to make Diego second-guess himself, I stressed over Robbie. Maybe he was right. I'd learned piano and violin at such an early age, music was like my primary language. Did I really need to learn anything new at school? I could keep building my online presence, get jobs scoring small, independent films, and work my way up from there.

No, no, no. What was I thinking? I couldn't let Robbie win me over. I couldn't apply to Georgia Tech. Everything I did was for my music. Everything was set in stone: I'd apply to my dream music programs, get an internship at a film score production company, and make the connections I needed to become an assistant sound producer, or even a composer assistant. I'd had it all mapped out since I was in eighth grade. I'd never second-guessed this path.

Until now. Robbie swooped in with those irresistible dimples and kisses, making me feel safe and protected, flattering me with attention, and planning for a future together. How could I give that up? How much would it crush him if I said no? The thought made my throat constrict.

"Alright, everyone," said Mr. Greenwood, snapping me from my thoughts. "Today's going to be fun. We're going to have an egg-drop competition!"

"What, like we did in middle school?" Sasha asked.

Mr. Greenwood shook his head. "Not exactly. The principles in this experiment—momentum, impulse, and impact force—are what engineers and car manufacturers use to help people survive major car accidents. They apply the laws of physics when designing things like airbags and seat belts. Now, this is going to be an extra-credit project. You'll be able to add up to three points to your grade for the quarter. So those of you with a B can move up to a B plus, and so forth." Sasha leaned forward, biting her lip. "You'll need to build a structure that acts as a safety net for your egg. Keep your egg safe from a half-meter drop, and you'll get half a point. One meter, one point. One and a half meters, one and a half points. And so on. But you have to build this structure with nothing more than ten sheets of paper, a meter of masking tape, and a pair of scissors. And you'll only have twenty minutes."

Seriously? How were we supposed to keep an egg from cracking with a few measly scraps of paper? As the class let out a chorus of groans, I glanced at Sasha, my lab partner by default, who gave me a confident grin. Relief flooded my chest. Of course she knew what to do. She sure owed me one.

Or fifty.

Or a best friend.

"Let's mix things up today," said Mr. Greenwood. "Instead of working with your usual lab partners, I want you to pair up with the person sitting in front of or behind you." My stomach sank. *Crap.* So much for getting Sasha's help. Mr. Greenwood paced the room, making sure everyone knew who they were paired up with. "So Sasha, you're with Jason. Amber, you're with Diego."

"Yes!" Sasha whispered. She leaned close to my ear. "You have to make sure your egg breaks."

"What?" I whispered back. "Are you kidding me?"

"You have to! This could be my chance."

"Hell no." My grades were suffering, and colleges would see our first-semester grades. These extra points would really help me out.

She threw a glance at Diego, who was gathering his things to join me. "Please?!" She gripped my hand, her eyes bugging. "We both ace every exam. I'm just a few decimal points behind him."

"Now, come get your supplies and pass in your assignments," said Mr. Greenwood, tapping on the empty tray on his desk.

Diego dropped his backpack next to Sasha's seat. "I'll get everything."

"Okay, thanks." I handed him my homework. Once he left, I frowned at Sasha and lowered my voice. "I'm not sabotaging my own grade so *you* can be valedictorian."

Her jaw hardened. "Oh, come on, Amber. Don't be a little bitch." I flinched at her tone. "You know how much this means to me. All you have to do is balance a sheet of paper on top and 'forget' to secure it with tape." She made air quotes at the word "forget." Diego shuffled over to our desk. "Just do it," Sasha growled in my ear. "Just fucking do it—"

"Hey." Diego dropped our supplies on the table, strands of black hair flopping over his downcast eyes. I gripped the table, my heart racing. She'd never talked to me like that before. Did I even know anything about who Sasha really was?

Sasha's expression transformed again with a beaming smile.

"Hi!" she said, about three octaves too high. "Sorry, let me get out of your way." She picked up her things and practically launched herself at Jason, her new partner.

I rubbed my lips together, my heart still pounding as Diego organized our meager supplies. We had a short stack of paper, a roll of masking tape, and hot pink plastic scissors.

"So," said Diego, "I think the best approach will be to create a bowl with some of the paper, and crumple the rest to provide a cushion." His tone was cold, and his gaze didn't meet mine.

"Um . . . yeah." I stared at him, baffled. Was he mad at me? "Yeah, that sounds like a good idea—"

"Okay, good. So I'll take care of it. You don't have to do anything."

"What? Why?" Oh, no. He must have heard Sasha. She was currently hunched over her stack of paper, already taping sheets together. When Jason reached for their scissors, she slapped his hand away. "Diego—" I began.

"Don't bother. Here." He slapped half the stack of paper in front of me. "You can crumple each of these." Then he pulled the stack back. "No, on second thought, I'll do it. Wouldn't want you hiding something heavy or sharp in any of them."

My heart clenched. "Diego, I wouldn't do that," I whispered. "That was all Sasha. I didn't agree to sabotage anything."

Diego folded a sheet of paper, getting to work on an origami bowl. "You know, it's funny. I always wanted to give you the benefit of the doubt."

I watched him fold, a helpless feeling spreading through my gut. "What do you mean?"

"Nothing. Never mind." He clamped his lips shut and kept working on his bowl.

"No. Say it," I prodded. "I want to know."

He let out a deep exhale through his nose. "Well, remember that time last year when you interrupted our Science Olympiad meeting?"

A lump formed in my throat. How could I forget? I was so terrified Diego saw Priya slip the folder with the biology exam answers back onto Mrs. Tanner's desk. But the exam came and went, and Priya, Sasha, and I thought nobody was the wiser. Sasha got her perfect score, Priya got away with it, and I got stuck with a heavy load on my conscience.

"Yeah, I remember," I croaked.

"I thought maybe I had the wrong idea. I thought maybe Priya was late handing in a homework assignment or something, and was embarrassed she hadn't turned it in on time." I bit my lip and said nothing, watching him fold and unfold the piece of paper until the side of a square bowl took shape. "But then Mrs. Tanner handed back the test the next week, and she mentioned how she was planning to curve the grades because it was such a hard test, but she couldn't because someone got a hundred percent."

Oh, shit.

"And I saw the look on Sasha's face," he went on with a bitter chuckle, "so pleased with herself, and I knew she'd gotten the perfect score. And fine, she's crazy smart, so it was plausible. But then I saw the look on your face . . . red as a tomato."

I stared at the desk's surface, where students had etched their names, initials, and crude messages over the years. "If you knew what she'd done . . . why didn't you call her out?"

Diego shook his head as he folded the final piece, completing the bowl. "I rationalized it away . . . I thought, maybe you were upset because you got a bad grade. And I wanted to believe you were better than that."

Each word coming from his mouth tore my heart into a thousand tiny fragments. I clasped my shaking fingers under the desk. I wanted to be someone he admired. Someone he respected. What he said about me when he apologized to me, when he agreed to help me film the play—I'd never felt so *seen* before. I couldn't stand to lose that.

"Diego—" I cleared my throat, unsure what to say. "Please believe me . . . I never wanted any part in that. Priya already stole the test." I whispered so softly I could barely hear myself. "She regretted it right away, and I was just trying to help her put it back."

"She stole it for Sasha?" He crumpled a sheet of paper into a ball and taped it into the inside of the bowl, still refusing to look at me.

"Yeah. But Priya's parents . . . they're extreme. If she got in trouble for cheating, she'd be homeschooled for sure. I had to help her. And just now . . . well, that was all Sasha. She's desperate to beat you."

He crumpled the next piece of paper into a ball, glaring at the back of Sasha's head. "It wouldn't be the first time she did something underhanded."

I gave him a flabbergasted look. "So why haven't you said anything? Why haven't you tried to stop her?"

"Why haven't you?" he shot back. I rubbed my lips together, unable to meet his eyes. "You're the one who's friends with her. Anyway, I think you should've been more careful picking your friends. Because they clearly don't give a shit about you."

18 MINUTES LEFT

"You're always trying to sabotage me." Diego hurled the accusation at Sasha like he'd been repressing it for ages. "Remember the egg drop?"

Sasha fixed her gaze on him, the syringe mere inches from her reach. "Oh, it was some stupid extra-credit assignment. So what? You're going to kill me because I wanted a few bonus points?"

"It wasn't just the bonus points," said Diego. "You cheated on that bio midterm last year. Remember? The one where the grades should have been curved."

Sasha's eyes widened for the tiniest moment, and she glanced at Priya, whose mouth dropped open.

"You're not the only one she's tried to sabotage." When I piped up, Sasha threw me a baffled look. "Remember last year? The flyers you created for your class president campaign?"

Sasha rolled her eyes. "Oh, please." But there was a tremor in her voice.

"Wait, what did she do?" said Diego.

"She tried spreading fake news that Jason Goding stole class funds." I tried ignoring Sasha's glare, with which she was clearly attempting to burn a hole through my skull. "But I dumped them in the trash."

"You're kidding me." Diego shook his head, while Sasha crossed her arms and poked her cheek with her tongue. "That's some pattern of behavior. You're a cheat. A liar—"

"You guys," said Robbie, who'd started piling the rest of the drawers in front of the fireplace. "A little help over here? We need to finish stacking shit."

I nodded. "Sure."

"You really think that's going to work?" Sasha asked Robbie. "You're willing to bet all of our lives on it?"

I frowned. "We have no choice."

"Yes we do! We don't know what's going to happen when that thing blows." Sasha mirrored me, pointed at the fireplace. "We don't know how strong it is, how powerful. Even if we stack everything in the room against it, it could kill us all anyway. Why are you so willing to take that chance?"

"Because everyone in this room deserves a chance!" I screamed back.

"If I had to choose between six people dying and one person dying, I'd choose one person! Every time!"

"Even if that one person has to be you?" I said. She opened her mouth to respond, but I cut her off. "And what if we kill some-one, and the bomb goes off anyway?" I said. "You're trusting a psychopath to keep their word that the rest of us will get out of here alive."

Sasha retorted like she'd already thought that through. "But killing someone is the only chance we've got to stop the bomb from going off. Are you really willing to let that bomb blow you to pieces? Do you have any idea how much that'll hurt? Your body will literally be ripped to shreds, and if it isn't, you'll be burned to a crisp. You really want that?"

"No . . ." I clutched my throat. "But there *has* to be another way."

"I think we should choose someone," said Diego.

My breath caught in my throat. "What?"

"Choose someone, but not necessarily do it yet," said Diego. "We *are* wasting time. Let's pick who it would be, get that over with, and then keep trying to figure this out until the last minute."

"But then it might be too late!" said Sasha.

"Or the last five minutes, whatever," said Diego. "But let's get this part over with now so we can move on."

Sasha crossed her arms and nodded. "Okay. Fine."

"So how're we gonna pick who dies?" asked Robbie.

1 MONTH, 2 WEEKS AGO

DECEMBER OF SENIOR YEAR

It was do or die time.

I gripped my violin tight, swallowing the nausea that kept trying to creep up my throat, watching everyone in the orchestra tittering around me. Jason was so nervous he kept dropping his horn. We were gathered in the cafeteria, all wearing matching black skirts or pants and white collared shirts, waiting for our cue to file into the auditorium. The drama club was backstage putting the finishing touches on their elaborate costumes and makeup.

All the work I'd done over the past year led to this moment. Our dress rehearsals over the past week had gone well save one or two minor mishaps, but none of that mattered. Only tonight mattered, because the first deadline for my college applications was midnight tomorrow. Tonight was the night I needed to get my recording. So tonight was everything.

I glanced toward the door to the hall, willing it to open,

willing Robbie to come in and wish me luck before the most important performance of my life. But no dice.

"Alright, everyone," said Mr. Torrente. "It should be any moment now. I just want to say how proud I am of everyone here. Putting on a full-length production is no small feat!" He launched us into a round of applause. "Yes, Amber?"

I lowered my trembling hand. "Can I say something to everyone?"

"Of course. This is your show."

Clearing my throat, I stood, clutching my violin to my side. All eyes were on me. Oh, God. Playing an instrument in front of a crowd was one thing. Speaking words was a whole other story.

"I just . . . I just wanted to say thank you. Thank you, Mr. Torrente, for letting us do this show instead of our annual winter concert." He gave me a little bow. "And thank you all for spending so much time practicing. I know it wasn't easy to learn something completely new. And maybe it wasn't as exciting as our usual rendition of 'Rudolph the Red-Nosed Reindeer.'" A few people chuckled. "So thank you for taking a chance on this, and for putting up with me."

"Thank *you* for creating such an amazing score!" I whipped around to see Sasha striding toward us, looking like a modern-day princess of Verona in her sleek, glittery periwinkle dress. Asher, our Romeo, joined as well. They paused next to Mr. Torrente, and Sasha smiled at me encouragingly, her eyes sparkling, like she was blind to the resentment in my own. I'd been avoiding her ever since my falling-out with Priya, but since we were both so busy prepping for the play, she hadn't noticed. And my brain couldn't handle both the chaos of wrapping up rehearsals *and* confronting Sasha for what she'd done to Priya. The pressure of everything made me feel constantly on the verge of collapsing.

"I think the music is stellar," said Sasha. "We've got a full house tonight—the auditorium is packed—and I can't wait for everyone to hear you guys. Way to go, Amber!" My God. How could she be so nice to me, and so vile to Priya? *How?*

Someone in the orchestra whooped, and the rest of them broke out into applause again as a fluttering sensation swept through my chest. As Sasha mingled with people in the orchestra, wishing them luck, Asher approached me. "Awesome job on the score."

"Thanks!" I forced a smile onto my face. "And you make a pretty amazing Romeo. Are you nervous?"

"Nah." He waved me off, then grimaced. "Well, okay, maybe just a little, about the balcony scene. But seriously, thanks for only making me sing once."

I tilted my head. "You didn't want to sing?"

"Oh, geez, not at all. That's Dan's and Maria's deal—I usually go for whatever role has the least singing." He laughed. "When Sasha said you'd insisted on adding singing parts, I wanted to puke." My blood went cold in my veins. "Don't get me wrong, they came out great. But we were all a little nervous you were going to totally mess this up . . ."

His words faded into background noise as I gaped at Sasha, who chatted animatedly with Mr. Torrente. That bitch. She told me the actors wanted the singing numbers. She said they'd switch to *Grease* if I refused. But it was her call all along. She didn't even tell them about the singing numbers until after auditions. Until *after* she already landed the lead role. Until it was too late. And once she knew it was hers, she made sure she'd be able to show off in front of everyone.

She lied to me to get her way.

Worse, she lied to *everyone*.

As I ran my bow over the violin's strings, my eyes fluttered past Mr. Torrente to the glowing faces in the audience. I didn't need to watch my fingers—I could play this piece backward with my eyes closed.

After all, I'd composed it. I'd composed the music for the entire play. It was the hardest thing I'd ever done—not only did I have to write the music for a full-length play, but I had to make it easy enough for a high school orchestra to play without any gaffes, and without any bassoons or harps—not to mention our only horn player, Jason, was a total dimwit. But it was done, and after hours and hours of composing and practice and rehearsals, we'd finally nailed it.

I tried not to think about how Sasha nearly ruined everything. I didn't want any bitterness to come through the music soaring from my fingertips. Tonight—this music—it was all that mattered. And I had to stay strong.

I could make out a few familiar faces toward the front of the audience. Mom stared at me with laser focus, beaming with pride. And since Sasha's Juliet was currently mourning Romeo's death and was about to kill herself, Mom looked like a psychopath grinning in a sea of sadness.

The seat to Mom's right might as well have been empty—Robbie looked bored out of his skull. He hogged Mom's armrest, resting his head in his palm, his expression glum. Sometimes his face glowed from the light of his phone screen. If Mom were at any other play, she would have slapped the phone right out of his hands, but she seemed too mesmerized to notice.

On Mom's other side, Dad wore his usual guilty expression. I wished he didn't have the constant cloud of not being able to pay for my education hovering over his head.

Another familiar face grinned up at me from the center aisle. When I met Diego's gaze, he offered two thumbs-up from behind his camera's tripod. Despite what happened in physics the other week, he'd kept his promise. I stifled a smile and focused on my sheet music again. I had to pay close attention now—my solo was coming up. And this was the part I'd be sending in to colleges. My heart fluttered, and I took a slow, deep breath.

The rest of the orchestra silenced. I watched Mr. Torrente for my cue, and a thrill rushed up my spine as I ran my bow over the strings. The vibrations from the violin under my chin coursed through me, floating into the air to mingle with Sasha's voice, our mournful melody filling the room with grief and longing. I glanced at the first few rows of the audience again, gauging their reaction. They watched with rapture, leaning forward in their seats, fully engaged as Sasha pretended she was about to plunge a dagger into her chest.

But then Sasha's voice went all raspy, and she coughed.

She *coughed*.

I refused to stop playing. This was the only night I could get this recording. There were no do-overs. I glanced back at the stage. Sasha opened and closed her mouth, like she was trying to time the right line to my music. But she was supposed to have stabbed herself in the heart by now, and the orchestra was supposed to jump in for a crescendo as she died.

I swallowed down my panic and kept playing, nodding at Mr. Torrente to conduct the orchestra to join in as planned. But all the viola players were gaping up at Sasha, and Jason Goding was too busy scoffing to play his horn.

The orchestra became a din of confusion as half of them joined in, while the other half ogled at Sasha. Finally, Sasha simply pretended to stab herself and fell backward, fake dead.

My God. Sasha ruined everything. *Everything.*

And I just wanted to die.

17 MINUTES LEFT

I inhaled sharply. We were really going to choose someone. This was really happening.

"How the hell are we going to figure this out?" Priya pulled herself to her feet, but after a woozy wobble, plopped down on the nearest chair. "I don't want to die. And I . . . I'm my parents' only child. This would crush them."

"It'd crush any of our parents," said Diego. "My dad . . . after everything he's done for me . . ." He shook his head and brushed back the hair falling across his forehead, clearly holding back tears.

"And my dad . . ." Robbie knelt like a catcher behind the mound, gripping his head. "God, he was so proud of me when I got that scholarship. So many of Georgia Tech's players end up in the majors. I can't *die* now. This is so fucking unfair."

"It really is." Sasha jumped in the fray. "I have so much ahead of me, too . . . I got into Brown!"

Diego gave her an exasperated look. "So? I got into Harvard. We all have things going for us." Sasha locked her steely gaze on him, and opened her mouth to say something, but I cut her off.

"At the rate we're going, none of us are going anywhere!" I said. "We'll all be dead in less than twenty minutes. We've all got parents who don't want us dead. We've all got plans. None of them matter any more than the others. Not Harvard, or Brown, or your sponge, or your baseball scholarship." Robbie's jaw hardened, but I ignored him. A lone tear trailed down my cheek.

"Maybe *some* matter more," said Sasha.

"No! The last thing we should do is compare each other. There's no point system, where Harvard is worth ten points and a baseball scholarship is worth eight points and—" I stopped short when Robbie furrowed his brow as I rated baseball less than Harvard.

"See?" I pointed at him. "Exactly! It's not fair to anyone. Nobody's future is worth more than anyone else's. Nobody's *life* is worth more."

Robbie chortled.

"What?" I said.

"Well, I mean, really? *Nobody's?*" said Robbie, motioning toward Scott.

My hands shook with anger, and I balled them into fists. "You can't be serious."

"I just . . . I think there's a difference between some people."

"Oh yeah?" Scott glared at him. "What difference?"

Robbie rubbed his neck, shifting his weight from one foot to the other. But he couldn't backpedal out of this one. "A difference between someone who's going to leave their mark on the world, and someone who's going to be a fucking drug dealer."

"I agree," said Sasha.

"Screw you," said Scott. "You don't know anything about my life."

"Wow." I shook my head at Robbie and Sasha. "I can't believe you two. All you care about is yourselves. You push people around to make yourselves feel better, and make everyone around you feel this small." I held two fingers an inch apart. Robbie folded his arms and stared at the ground. Could he possibly feel remorseful?

"You traitor," said Sasha. "How dare you turn against *us*?"

Scott slapped his good leg. "Oh, like it's treason to say anything against Queen Sasha! My life might be worth shit, but you are the definition of shit. The epitome of shit. The bacteria that fester on shit—"

I rested a hand on Scott's shoulder. "Nobody's life is worth shit. Not yours. Not hers." We all made mistakes. Just because Scott made some mistakes, like getting high in school, or selling Sasha his Ritalin—his life wasn't worthless. God knew I'd made plenty of mistakes myself. But I refused to be defined by my mistakes, or let Scott be defined by his. Even Sasha deserved a shot at proving she could do better. It wasn't our mistakes that defined us, but how we learned to overcome them. Everyone should have a chance to overcome theirs.

"Maybe not," said Robbie after a moment's hesitation. "But don't we have to choose *someone*?"

I stormed at Robbie, fists clenched. "All you care about is saving your own skin."

"That's not true at all," said Robbie. "I want us both to get out of here alive."

"Oh, sure!" I chortled sarcastically.

He gripped my arms and shook me. "Of course I want that! What's the matter with you?"

I struggled out of his grasp. "Robbie, I have never known you to care about anyone's future but your own."

His eyes widened.

"That's right. You knew all I ever wanted was to get into music school. But as soon as you got your scholarship, you made me feel like I was *betraying* you by choosing music over you. Suddenly your future was the only thing that mattered. But you don't get to choose my future. And you don't get to choose who lives and who dies tonight." I pointed at Scott. "He is a *person*. With hopes and dreams of his own. They might not be as ambitious as yours, but he's got every right to pursue them. Just because you don't know him or what they are doesn't make it any less true."

Robbie gawked at me, seemingly unable to find words. But Diego nodded along. Priya crossed her arms and stared at the bomb, her lower lip trembling. I still had about fifteen minutes left to convince everyone. There was still time.

And then there wasn't. Before I could move, Sasha rushed the table and grabbed the syringe, then raced toward me, pointing the needle straight at my chest.

1 MONTH, 2 WEEKS AGO

DECEMBER OF SENIOR YEAR

I found Robbie the morning after opening night of the play at his locker, laughing about something with Zane, facing away from me. I tightened my grip on my binder and approached him, ignoring Zane. "Where were you last night?" He spun, and his smile slid off his face. "After the play. Where were you?"

"Ohhhh." Zane shoved Robbie's shoulder. "Someone's in trouble."

I gave him a disgusted look. "Ugh, shut up. Can you give us a minute?"

"Sure, sure." Zane patted Robbie on the back and sauntered off toward Amy and Maria, who were hunched over Amy's locker mirror.

Robbie slammed his locker shut. "Can you not embarrass me like that?"

"Embarrass you?" I hugged the binder to my chest. After Sasha flubbed the most important scene, we got through the rest of the performance without any more snafus. But the damage was done. And when our friends and families gathered backstage afterward, I scanned the crowd for Robbie. I needed him to hug me and reassure me that it'd all work out in the end. But he didn't show.

"How do you think I felt last night?" I said. "I worked so hard on that play. I was expecting you to come backstage afterward. Instead you just Irish-exited on me."

Robbie scrubbed a hand down his face. "Didn't you get my flowers?"

"Yeah, my mom gave them to me. But I should have gotten them from *you*."

"Well, I had to go get some sleep. We have a big game tonight. It's the league championship—"

"Seriously?"

The truth was, missing the afterparty only scratched the surface. Ever since he won his scholarship, all he seemed to care about was his games, his goals, his future. But he pressured me to apply to Georgia Tech with such determination, I figured he had to care about me; otherwise he wouldn't bother. But not coming to congratulate me, to comfort me, to say *anything* to me after the play confirmed my suspicions. He didn't care about me. Not really. Not the way I thought he did.

I brushed my side bangs back. "I've been to most of your home games this season. I always run from rehearsals like a maniac to get there in time. *And* I come out to celebrate after. You couldn't have sacrificed a little bit of sleep for me this one time? You couldn't have gone out of your way to be there for me just this once?"

"I went to the play, didn't I?"

"You were staring at your phone half the time!"

"I'm sorry. It's just . . ." Robbie slapped his palm against his locker. "Couldn't you have told me the truth?"

I tilted my head, confused. "What are you talking about?"

"About school. Georgia Tech. About you not wanting to come with me."

My stomach clenched, and I took a step back. "Is that why you left? Because you're *mad* at me?"

"No, it's not that."

"Then why?"

"Because I had to get out of there! I had to get away from the thing you're choosing over me!" He pressed his fist against his lips, and his eyes darted at everything in the hall but me.

My expression softened. "I . . . I didn't realize you cared that much."

"Of course I do! I fucking love you!" He yelled it so loud the people around us scattered and stared. Oh, God. That was the first time he said those words to me. It was the first time any boy had ever said those words to me. I never thought my first time would come with an f-bomb, but there it was, reverberating in the air, echoing in my ear canals. "I thought we had this all planned out," he went on. "I thought you'd come to school with me, and we'd be together."

My breath hitched in my throat. This double standard was so unfair. I never thought of baseball as something he was choosing over me. It was his dream before he ever met me, and it would be unfair to talk him out of it to follow me to music school. I always wanted to support him. But he was pressuring me to abandon my lifelong dreams. If this argument flipped on its head, he'd choose baseball over me in a heartbeat. I didn't doubt it for a second.

"We never decided that," I said. "You just assumed it. I never agreed to go to Georgia Tech. You know I want to study music."

"Yeah, but I thought you'd study it there."

I shook my head. "We've been through this. Georgia Tech doesn't have a music program. I need to go to USC, or Berklee, somewhere with a great program where I'll be able to make connections—"

"You can make connections anywhere! Everything's online now. You can write and play music anywhere."

"That's not how it works! You don't know anything about how the film industry works. I'd need the right internships, the right production assistant gigs. In person."

"Not necessarily." Robbie clasped his hands behind his head. "Why aren't you trying harder to make this work?" But I couldn't just wave a magic wand and make the industry work differently. That was like me saying he could prance into USC and demand a spot on their baseball team—and throw in a full scholarship, thank you very much.

"And besides," he went on, "you have your whole life to have a music career. Most baseball players only play until their late thirties. But you can play music whenever."

He couldn't be serious. There was no guarantee I'd live long enough to put my dreams on hold like that. Maggie's life was cut short before it even started. "No way. I'm not putting off my plans for that long. Who's to say what'll happen to me in twenty years? Ten years? *Tomorrow?*"

"Oh my God. Nothing's going to happen to you."

I threw out my arms. "How can you know that? What kind of God complex do you have? I don't understand why I'm the one who has to throw my plans away, because what? Because you got into school first? Because you're the *guy* in our relationship?"

"Oh, so you'd rather throw *us* away?"

"That's not what I'm saying!" I couldn't believe he was trying to make me feel guilty about this. That he didn't deny either of those reasons. How could he be so selfish? So *manipulative*? As soon as he asked me to come to school in Georgia with him, I should have known we were hurtling toward our expiration date.

The warning bell rang, but he ignored it. My face screwed up as I fought back tears. He stepped close and leaned his forehead against mine, gripping the back of my neck. "Amber . . . we can figure something out."

My heart swelled. Maybe I was wrong. Maybe he'd be willing to give long-distance a shot. "Really?"

"Yeah, of course. We could get you private teachers. I'll help you find them. And you can make any connection you need online."

No. I closed my eyes, and a tear escaped, rolling down my

cheek. Robbie grinned—he mistook it as a tear of relief.

"You know what?" he went on. "This is a moot point if you don't even get in. We don't have to decide anything now. Why don't you apply and see what happens? That'll give us time to figure something out." He still didn't get it. He still thought the world revolved around him. It was his way or the highway.

But my road forward was *mine* to pave.

The final bell rang, and he kissed me gently. "We'll talk about this later, okay? And you'll apply?"

I nodded, too hurt and frustrated to say anything. A rock swelled in my throat. I had to leave before the floodgates opened. I tugged his arms down and whirled, dashing down the hall before he could see me bawl in full force. I rounded the corner and slammed right into Diego. I sprang back, and my binder flew from my grip, papers scattering across the hall.

"Whoa!" He caught his balance in time.

"Oh my God, I'm sorry." I let out a nervous laugh, but traitorous tears trickled down my cheeks.

"I was just looking for you." Diego frowned and touched my arm. "Are you okay?" I inhaled sharply—it was like electricity shot up my arm and through every vein in my body.

I wiped at my face, which pulsated with heat. "I'm fine, yeah." I stooped to gather the papers around my feet, and he scooped up my binder. The last stragglers darted around us to their classes.

"What happened?" Diego asked, his brow furrowed.

I grabbed the binder from him while wiping my cheek with my other hand. "It's nothing. We've got to get to class."

"Class can wait," he said. "I want to make sure you're alright."

I hugged my binder and backed into the locker behind me, banging my head softly against it. I shook my head, not even knowing where to start. "I'm just tired. I'm tired of trying to make everyone happy, and doing the exact wrong thing. I'm tired of doing the best I can, and it's never good enough. I'm tired of being *manipulated*. I'm tired of failing so miserably. I'm. Just. Tired."

"First of all, you're not failing miserably." Diego slipped off one of his backpack straps and dug around the main compartment for something. After a moment, he pulled out a USB drive and offered it to me. *My recording.* "Not at all. Your music is beautiful. Keep writing music like what you performed last night, and you'll make people happy every day for the rest of your life."

My heart clenched. How did he do that? How did he make me want to simultaneously dissolve into the tiles and leap into his arms with a few simple words?

"But she screwed it up. I was going to send the recording of that scene, and she screwed it up."

He grinned. "Well, you still can."

"What do you mean?"

"I recorded the dress rehearsals for practice, remember?"

My heart leapt. I remembered spotting Diego setting up in the back of the auditorium, and assumed he was calibrating the equipment for opening night. I didn't realize he recorded the whole thing each night.

"Right before her cough," he went on, "when there was a pause before your solo, I swapped in footage from the last dress rehearsal. Really, you can't tell anything went wrong. So you can use any of it. You could send them the whole thing if you wanted to."

"Oh my God." Fresh tears spilled down my cheeks as I took the USB drive, my fingers grazing his. "Thank you," I whispered. "Thank you so much."

"No problem. *You* did great. You deserve this." He took another step, closing the gap between us. My breath caught in my throat as he reached out and wiped my tears away with his thumb. I touched his hand to brush him away, but instead our fingers entwined. I was sure he could hear my heart drumming madly. He leaned closer, his face mere inches from mine, and my lips parted, wanting this, wanting this so badly.

But I flinched back, my head banging against the locker. No. I wasn't a cheat. I couldn't do that to Robbie. He might be acting like a selfish prick, but he deserved better than me cheating on him. I couldn't let us end that way.

Besides, how would a relationship with Diego ever work? Dad would be crushed if I started dating the boy who flicked the domino starting the chain reaction that ended his career.

Diego took a step back, looking hurt. I wished things could be simpler—that I could be with a boy who made sure I knew my own worth.

I wished I could erase the past year. But I couldn't erase what I'd done.

At the same time, I couldn't let my world completely fall

apart. I had to fix it, starting with my music. That's what started this whole mess of a year. I couldn't let it be for nothing. I had my recording now. I wasn't going to let my dreams slip through my fingers. I was going to send this recording to my dream schools and see whatever the hell happened next.

16 MINUTES LEFT

The thing about being trapped in a room with five other people, a bomb, and a syringe of lethal poison is that at some point, shit's going down. No matter how frantically you claw at rationality, how desperately you cling to common decency, you eventually give in to your basic instinct to survive.

I'd tried to hold it together this whole time. But when Sasha gathered a fistful of my dress in one hand, gripping the syringe with the other, fear and shock mingled in my brain. Her thumb hovered over the plunger. She was really going to do it. She was really going to stab me with that needle. People around me shouted for Sasha to put the syringe down, but I couldn't make out what they were saying as adrenaline blasted through my veins. With nowhere to go, flight wasn't exactly an option.

So I had to fight.

I wound my arm back, readying to punch her in the face, but caught myself in time. *No, no, no.* If I prompted her to stab me with the needle in self-defense, it'd all be over. I couldn't resort to violence. My emerald dress clung to me as sweat trickled down my back. It was too hot to think straight. What should I do? How could I get a grip on this situation?

Sasha's eyes flamed, and she clenched her jaw, her lips puckered like she was holding her breath. She could so easily plunge the needle into my arm and push in the beige liquid, but she was hesitating. I glared back, almost daring her to do it. Would she really try to kill me? Would she be able to live with herself after? I stepped forward so our faces were mere inches apart, fighting against every impulse urging me to wrestle away from her. Sasha's arm wavered, and the corners of her eyes crinkled as she grimaced.

Finally, she let out a frustrated growl and released my dress. "Why are you making this so difficult? Why can't you let us choose Scott and be done with this? What's it to you if he dies?"

Air whooshed from my lungs. Maybe she didn't have the gall to murder a friend after all. "He doesn't deserve to die," I said. "Can't you see that?"

"Well, none of us deserve to die." She licked her lips, shifting her weight on her feet. "So if you don't want it to be Scott, and you'd *never* choose Priya or Robbie, it'd have to be Diego, right?" Sasha approached Diego and raised the syringe. Diego backed between the china cabinet and fireplace, eyes wide. He had nowhere to go.

"NO!" I shrieked. "Don't touch him!" The words came out more passionately than I meant them to.

Sasha spun to face me, tilting her head, like she was trying to piece together a jigsaw puzzle. Suddenly her eyes brightened, and the corner of her lips crept up. "Oh my God." No. There's no way she could know the truth. I waited with bated breath for her next words. "I knew it. You like Diego."

There it was. Out in the open, in front of everyone. My feelings exposed, hovering like smoke that threatened to smother me. Every red blood cell in my body swarmed to my cheeks as Robbie stiffened beside me. I glanced at Diego, who watched me from under the strands of dark hair falling over his forehead. I said nothing as the timer tick, tick, ticked down.

"Is that true?" asked Robbie. Oh, God. I squeezed my eyes shut as though if I squeezed hard enough, I'd wake up from this nightmare. This couldn't be happening. We couldn't have this conversation right now. My pulse crashed in my ears like bass drums. "Amber. Is it true?"

I opened my eyes to see worry etched across Robbie's face. Every fiber of my being wanted to deny it. But I was a horrible liar. "We've got to find a way out of here. That's all that matters." But my non-answer said everything.

His jaw tightened, and he balled his hands into fists as he turned to Diego. "What the hell, Spongeman? You trying to steal my girl?" Shit, shit, shit. This was exactly what I was afraid would happen tonight, and now it was happening when we absolutely did *not* have time for it to happen. Diego's eyes widened, but he clenched his own fists and held his ground as Robbie stepped toward him.

I leapt in front of him and pressed my hands into his chest. "Robbie, stop it," I yelled. "If we don't survive the next fifteen minutes, none of this matters." I felt his breath hitch as his eyes flicked toward the bomb. He'd always assumed the life stretching ahead of him was limitless. But now I needed him to focus on surviving this one hour. We all did.

"So what do we do?" Priya perched on her chair, hugging her knees to her chest.

Robbie wiped his hand down his face. "Well, I'm not gonna stand around waiting to get blown apart. We've got to pick someone."

"But how can we choose?" asked Priya. "We can't agree on anything!"

"We could do rock-paper-scissors," Scott suggested.

Sasha burst out laughing. "Right. We're going to decide who gets poisoned to death based on rock-paper-scissors."

"Well, why not?" Diego finally peeled his eyes off me. "It'd be fair. Leave it up to fate."

"Fate?" Priya visibly shuddered. "That means . . . that means it could be . . ."

"Any of us," I finished. "It means it could be any of us."

Sasha shook her head. "That's ridiculous."

"Is it?" My heart pummeled my rib cage so hard it was like it was trying to escape. What if it were me? What if I lost at rock-paper-scissors? I *always* lost at rock-paper-scissors. I was like the

Murphy's Law of rock-paper-scissors. But Sasha's sense of entitlement was abhorrent. This was a fair way to choose. "It's the most logical thing I've heard so far."

"No way. It could be me." Sasha wiped her tear-stained cheek with her palm. "Or Robbie!"

"Why shouldn't it be one of you?" Priya shouted.

"Shut up!" Robbie pounded his fist on the table. "We're spinning our wheels again. Let's try rock-paper-scissors." I let out a breath of relief that despite everything, he was focusing on something other than Diego and me.

"Tournament style?" Priya suggested.

"Yeah, but the opposite," said Robbie. "We'll pair up, and the winner of that round drops out. Loser moves on to the next round."

Diego rubbed the back of his neck. "Yeah, that actually sounds fair."

Robbie narrowed his eyes at him. "Maybe you're *actually* not the only smart one around here."

"I never insinuated I was."

"Alright, alright," I said. We didn't have time for them to go at each other's throats. "Let's focus. How do we do this randomly?"

"There's no time to organize anything." Robbie raised his hand and flapped his fingers in a beckoning motion. "Come on, who's against me?" Everyone was silent. Nobody moved. "Christ." He knelt next to Scott. "You and me, man."

"Fine." Scott released his ruined leg and cracked his knuckles. The rest of us huddled around them. Priya pinched her lips.

I squeezed Robbie's shoulder, silently wishing him luck, but he ignored me. "Best two out of three?"

Diego folded his arms. "Seems fair."

Robbie nodded. "Okay. Ready?" He and Scott pounded their fists against their palms. "Rock paper scissors shoot." Scott covered Robbie's rock with paper. Robbie stood, a vein in his neck bulging. "Bullshit! You hesitated for, like, a half a second."

"I did not!" said Scott.

"He went the same time as you!" said Priya.

"No way, I saw it, he waited," screamed Sasha. Soon everyone was shouting so loud, I couldn't hear myself think through the din.

"Stop it!" I shouted, gripping my ears. But nobody paid me any attention. Robbie clenched Scott's black T-shirt in his fist, and Scott howled in pain. Diego grabbed the back of Robbie's shirt and yanked him back.

"Get off me," said Robbie, tugging himself free from Diego. He spun and wound up to punch Diego.

"Stop!" I threw myself between them, extending my arms like a catcher between a base runner and home plate. "Stop it! Everyone shut up! Shut the hell up!" Everyone stilled and stared at me, except for Scott, who hunched over, his bad leg angled strangely, sweat streaming down his cheeks.

"We need a better way to make this random," I said. "How about . . . how about we draw straws instead?"

"Less room for cheating?" Priya asked.

"I didn't cheat," Scott grunted, pulling himself to sit flush against the wall again.

"*No* room for cheating," I said, ignoring him.

"Are there straws anywhere?" Priya edged open one of the smaller sideboard drawers we'd left in place.

"I haven't seen any," said Sasha, scanning the dining table. "Dammit, Amber, we're running out of time."

"You think I don't know that?" I said. "Stop reminding us how little time we have left and *think*."

She huffed and eyed the fireplace, where the bomb's timer was hidden. I glanced at my watch. Thirteen minutes. *Focus, Amber. Focus.*

I drummed my fingers over my lips, scanning the room. "There!" I dashed to the sideboard next to the door. There was a small vase of bamboo incense sticks. I yanked them out, dripping lavender oil all over myself. "Eight sticks," I said as I wiped my slick hand on my dress. "We only need six." I discarded two of them on the sideboard. Turning from the group, I snapped one of the sticks in half and shuffled them, leveling the top tips. I spun to face them, gripping the sticks with both hands. "One of these is snapped in half. You guys pick. Whoever picks the short stick . . ." I swallowed hard. "Well, you know. And if I get left with the short stick, it's me. Fair?"

"Fair," said Diego. Everyone else nodded. We gathered at the end of the table next to the huge brass mirror covering the wall, as far from the bomb as possible.

"Alright," I said, "who's first?"

"Ladies first?" Scott suggested, motioning for Priya to approach.

She approached me and bit her lip, fiddling with her sleeve as she stared at the sticks. "Come on," said Sasha, "we don't have all night here."

She glared at her. "I'm not gonna lie . . . I hope you get the short stick." Sasha's eyes widened. Priya exchanged a glance with me.

"Way harsh," I whispered, flashing her the smallest of smiles.

"She's got it coming, don't you think?" She bit her lip again and took a step closer. "Listen . . . I'm sorry about everything. I just wanted to make sure you knew that before . . . before this is over." Her voice cracked, and she choked up as she gave me a hug.

I hugged her back with my free arm, my fist clenching the sticks caught between us. Relief mingled with fear in my chest, and I struggled to fight back tears. Maybe I finally got my best friend back. But in another instant, I could lose her all over again. "I'm sorry, too," I whispered into her ear. "Love you always."

"Love you always." She backed away with a stick in her grip—one of the long ones. She gave me a tight-lipped smile and turned around.

"Who's next?" I asked. I now had a one-in-five chance of being left with the short stick.

Sasha didn't hesitate. "Let's get this over with," she muttered to herself. After examining the bunch of sticks for a moment, she plucked the one closest to her. It was a full-length stick. My breath caught in my throat. One-in-four chance. She closed her eyes in relief and backed away, clearly lacking any sympathy for the four who were left—not even for her best friend Robbie, who watched her with narrowed eyes.

He approached me, his shirt stained with blotches of sweat, and my heart plummeted. Oh, God. If only love came with an off switch. Despite his selfishness, he was the boy who got me through one of the hardest times in my life, who made me feel adored and protected. What if he pulled the short stick? My lungs felt like they were being sapped of air even though I was still breathing. But he didn't move to take a stick. Instead he gave me a pained look and glanced at Diego. "Is it true?"

"Does it matter? Seriously, does it?"

"What's that mean?"

"You know what it means. You know we're going in two different directions. You're going to school to play ball. And if I manage to get out of here alive"—I waved the sticks under his nose—"I have my own dreams to see through."

"But—" He clenched his jaw, and then let out a low growl. "I know. I know you do. I never meant to make it seem like yours were less important than mine. I just—I assumed we had time—"

"Come on already!" said Sasha.

"Shut up!" Robbie snapped at her. She pursed her lips and crossed her arms. "I just wanted us to be together. That's all I was thinking about. And now we might both die before either of us has a chance to do *anything* . . . and I've been such a jerk."

Yeah, he had been. But at least now he seemed to understand. Everything could end in the blink of an eye. Life offered no guarantees. We both glanced at the bamboo sticks. We had to get on with it. He had to choose. "Better get this over with."

He nodded and swallowed hard. Finally, he pinched one of the sticks, and pulled it free from my grip. It was a long stick.

"Oh, thank God," I breathed. But there were still three sticks to go. It was down to Diego, Scott . . . and me.

Diego approached next. When he met my gaze, a million questions hung between us. As he pinched one of the sticks, his fingers brushed against my clenched fist, sending a shiver of goosebumps trailing up my arm. Without breaking eye contact, he inched the stick from my grip. He was safe. With one last look, he twirled the stick between his fingers and backed away without a word.

Two sticks left.

There was a fifty-fifty chance I'd be the one to die.

Tremors rippled through my body as I tried to stay strong. I couldn't panic. Not now. But my hands visibly shook, and a lone tear escaped and trickled down my cheek. Priya let out a sob.

Robbie gripped the back of his neck. "You know what? This wasn't a good idea."

"Maybe it'll be Scott," said Sasha.

"Are you willing to risk that?" Robbie screamed.

Sasha pointed at me. "She's the one who risked this. We could have killed Scott twenty minutes ago. We could have been out the door by now, on our way home. But she wanted to be all *noble*—"

"I wanted to give everyone a chance to survive," I said, cutting her off. "I wanted to get us *all* out of here."

"We can still do that!" said Robbie. "This straw game is ridiculous."

"You're just panicking," said Sasha, "because now your girlfriend's at risk. Ex-girlfriend. Whatever. Fair's fair. We've got to finish this out."

"You've got to be kidding me!" Robbie screamed at her. While they argued, Scott and I stared at each other. He gripped his stomach where Sasha had kicked him, and sadness and fear swirled in his eyes. "Fair's fair," I said, my voice shaking as I knelt next to him, my shoes crunching on shattered glass.

We stared at the two sticks. Then he whispered low enough for only me to hear. "I don't want it to be me. But I sure as hell will be sorry if it's you, Red."

I let out a nervous chuckle. "Likewise."

"Well." He pinched one of the two remaining sticks. "Here we go."

18 DAYS AGO

JANUARY OF SENIOR YEAR

Mom was waiting on the front stoop when I got home from school, which was weird—she hated the outdoors, and always jumped at the smallest buzzing noises. She usually spent the afternoon editing someone's manuscript in the kitchen, papers and notecards scattered across the table as she peered at her laptop, refusing to be interrupted by anyone except Mittens, who took up permanent residency in her lap. I pedaled up the driveway and walked my bike into the garage.

"Amber, c'mere," Mom called as I hung my helmet from the handlebars.

"What's up?" I looped my earbud cord around my fingers as I joined her on the front stoop. "What're you doing out here?"

"Waiting for you."

Mittens sat next to her, licking his black paws. I plopped next to him and patted his soft head. "Why?"

She tilted her head toward the front door. "Well, you know how your dad's between gigs right now. He's been in one of his moods all day. And I wanted you to see this before he did." She handed me a thick envelope. USC insignia decorated the corner. "It's thick."

"I already know." I hugged the envelope to my chest without opening it. Mom raised her eyebrows. "They sent the email last week. I got in."

Mom beamed at me. "Congratulations, honey. I didn't know to expect good news yet. It's pretty early, isn't it?"

I plucked at the edge of the envelope, refusing to meet her gaze. "I applied early decision." USC had only launched their early decision program last year—it meant the plans would be binding if I got accepted. But I'd known USC was my top choice for years. They had one of the best—if not the only—undergraduate film score programs in the country. And after my argument with Dad, and after Robbie tried to manipulate me into following him to Georgia Tech, I didn't want to be tempted or forced to go anywhere else.

But it meant lying to Dad.

It meant I'd be in debt up to my eyeballs.

But it was my life. My choice. And I'd take responsibility for it.

Mom tilted her head. "Early decision . . . this sounds familiar. Doesn't that mean you can't apply anywhere else?"

"Yeah. Well, I did. Every school's deadline is different . . . it's complicated. But I have to pull all my other applications." Including the one I begrudgingly submitted to Georgia Tech. I tried not to think about how Dad would be annoyed by the wasted application fees, since he'd paid for my state school applications. Mom had slipped me her credit card—the one she sparingly used for the occasional purse or pair of shoes—for the rest, and told me she'd handle Dad if he put up a stink.

Her brow furrowed. "So you *have* to go to USC now, right?"

"Yes." I cringed against the impending explosion. But her face broke out in a wide grin, and she wrapped her arms around me. "Oh my God! My little girl's going to be a famous movie composer!"

My laugh caught in my throat, where it felt like a rock had lodged itself. "Seriously? Aren't you mad at me? I lied to you. To Dad."

Mom sighed. "True. And we'll have to talk about that later." I gave her a sheepish look. "I know Dad wanted you to go to a state school, but . . . you only have this one life. You don't get a redo. This is it, kid. And you're the only one who can decide how you want to live it."

"I know. That's why I applied early—I knew I'd regret it forever if I didn't try." I rotated the envelope in my hands and stared across the street, watching the Johnsons' sprinkler flinging water across their front yard, creating a radial green gradient that faded to dull yellows and browns. "Did you decide how you wanted to live your life?"

Mom tucked her chin-length hair behind her ears. "I don't want to say this the wrong way . . . I loved staying at home with you and Maggie, raising you, being there for you, watching you grow up. I would never, ever consider that a mistake. But yeah, Amber, I had dreams. I wanted to be a screenwriter in LA."

My eyebrows shot up under my bangs. "Seriously?"

She nodded. "Yep. I think wanting to be in the movie biz must be in the genes. But the point is, I chose not to pursue those dreams for myself. Maybe it wasn't the right decision, maybe it was. But I got to decide." She tapped her chest. "I decided to be an editor. I decided to stay at home with you guys. And I loved every moment . . ."

As she trailed off, Maggie hung between us, heavy in the air, darkening our conversation. "Maggie didn't get to decide," I said. My chest tightened.

"No. Maggie didn't get to decide." Mom held a hand to her brow, blocking the sun. "She got into Yale, you know." Her voice trembled slightly as she pet Mittens. "Pre-med."

My eyes widened. Yale had been her dream school. "I didn't know that."

Mom nodded. "The acceptance letter arrived the week after she died. Another full scholarship. She could have done so much more with her life. It was all laid out before her, ripe for the taking. But . . ." She trailed off, watching the sprinkler across the street.

"But they killed her."

Mom gripped my knee. "No, honey. She got sick."

Anger rippled through me. We hadn't had this conversation in years, but the fury felt just as fresh as it did back then. "They *made* her sick. Nothing was wrong before they got to her."

"That's not how it works. The doctors said it's not . . ." Her

319

own tears cut her off. Instead of continuing the argument, she clasped my hand, and we both stared at the Johnsons' sprinkler in silence for a long time. Finally, she wiped her cheeks and cleared her throat. "Either way, it proves all that matters is health and happiness. You have your health. Now go after your happiness. And don't worry about Dad—he's still freaked out about losing his business, but he'll come around. He wants you to be happy just like I do."

Suddenly the front door creaked open, and Dad slipped out. He cleared his throat awkwardly. "She's right, you know."

Mom rolled her eyes. "Were you listening through the door this whole time?"

He grunted, digging his hands into his pockets. "Maybe not the whole time." He'd clearly been listening the whole time. "And listen . . . whatever school you choose—er, already chose—and whatever financial burden you take on . . . that's your choice. And you never have to apologize for not being your sister." He still couldn't say her name out loud. "You'd only have to apologize if you tried to be anything but yourself. Clearly . . . this music thing you've got going on . . . that's what you're meant to do. You'll be fine."

"Aw, Dad . . ." I beamed up at him. "Well, you know, I *did* get a scholarship from USC."

"What?" said Mom.

"Not a full scholarship or anything. Just a quarter of tuition. But it's something."

"Well, that's fortunate." Dad stuck his hands in his pockets.

"I still want a yacht when I retire. So I expect you to get filthy rich in LA."

I guffawed. "Anyway," said Mom, throwing daggers at Dad with her eyes, "Grandma left you and Maggie a small college fund. It's yours. Now, it'll only put a dent in your tuition, but between that and the scholarship, we can do this. We'll cosign any loans you need. And we won't let you starve when you graduate."

I scoffed. "Who says there's no money in music?"

Mom put her hand around my shoulder and gave it a squeeze, squishing the cat between us. "Every record label in the country since the internet, hun."

"FYI, the record labels are doing fine. And so are the movie studios." I tore into the envelope, careful not to rip USC's emblem. I pulled out the top sheet of the packet and tilted it toward Mom.

"'Congratulations,'" she read aloud. "'We're pleased to offer you admittance to the film score program at USC.'"

13 MINUTES LEFT

Scott pinched the long stick, and his shoulders slumped in relief. The long stick meant life. The short stick, the one left in my grasp, meant someone would stab me with the syringe and push the plunger. Bile rose from my stomach, and the floor spun under my feet. It took all the strength I could muster to keep my legs from buckling.

"I'm so sorry—" Scott started, but his brow crinkled as he stared at the stick in my outstretched hand. "What the hell?"

I glanced down. It was a long stick. Not the short stick.

"What the absolute fuck?" Robbie asked. Diego looked at me in wonder.

My eyes darted between my incense stick and Scott's. They were the same length. Nobody drew a short stick. "Wait. How . . . ?"

"You cheat." Sasha stared at me accusingly.

"No!" I exclaimed. How could we all have pulled long sticks? "It was a fair draw, I swear."

"You were buying more time, weren't you?" said Sasha.

"No, no, no. I swear, I didn't cheat. That'd only be *wasting* time." I spun and scanned the sideboard. "See? Here!" I grabbed the half of the stick I discarded earlier. "I definitely broke one of the sticks in half."

"But . . ." Sasha examined her stick. "Where'd the other half go?"

"I have no idea!"

Diego grabbed the short stick from me and examined the broken end. Then he scanned the floor around my feet. "This is bizarre. You're sure you counted out only six sticks?"

"I'm positive! And the two extras are still on the sideboard, see?" I pointed at them. "I don't know where another stick would have come from!" Sasha still glared at me, and I glanced from face to face, searching for support. "I swear, I had nothing to do with this." Everyone wore confused expressions. Everyone except Priya.

Realization dawned on me. As she watched my expression change, her eyes widened, and she folded her arms—not in impatience, but as though to hide something. "Oh my God," I muttered.

Priya shook her head, but said nothing. What should I do? I knew what she did. But if I ratted her out, everyone would choose her to die for sure.

Sasha glanced between us, cocking her head. And then she

spotted it. "You little bitch!" She threw herself at Priya and grabbed her wrists. "Roll up your sleeves."

Priya wrestled to break free from Sasha's clutches. "No!"

"Roll them up!" Sasha yanked at Priya's sleeves, making a ripping sound as she freed half a stick from one of them. "Ha! Looks like your magic tricks aren't so freaking magical."

Priya burst into tears as she backed against the wall between Scott and the sideboard, her shoes crunching on the broken glass. Scott stared up at her with a baffled expression. A matching incense vase with bamboo sticks sat on that sideboard. Of course. That's how she got a stick to swap. And that's why she hugged me. My chest tightened. Did she mean what she said at all?

Diego tugged his fingers through his hair, gripping his skull. "How did you know which was the short stick?"

"I didn't." Priya's words bubbled through her tears. "I wasn't going to swap anything if I'd pulled a long one. When I felt it was short, I . . . I . . ." She demonstrated pulling an invisible stick from her sleeve with the same hand.

"Oh, for Christ's sake." He paced to the door and rested his palms and forehead against it. "This is ridiculous."

"You're a cheater!" yelled Sasha.

Priya narrowed her eyes at Sasha, like she was one to talk. "But not at anyone else's expense. This way, nobody would pull the short stick, and we could figure out how to get *everyone* out of here."

"All you did was waste time," said Sasha. "We still have to choose."

Robbie scowled at Priya. "And you pulled the short stick. It has to be you." He pushed past me toward the syringe.

"No, wait." I reached for his wrist, but strong arms grabbed me around the waist from behind. Sasha was pulling me backward. "Get off!" I shrieked.

"You're the one who made the rules," she said into my ear.

"No!" Priya shrieked, backing against the door. "Please, don't!"

Diego came to his senses and lunged at Robbie, gripping the back of his shirt and pulling him backward. The seams in Robbie's collar ripped, but he elbowed Diego in the stomach, spun, and shoved Diego's chest, easily overpowering him. "Get off me, man!"

Diego grunted as he slammed into the mirror, and Robbie headed for the syringe again.

"No! Wait, I have an idea! There's still time." I clawed at Sasha's arms, trying to pry them from encircling my waist, but she was too strong, too determined to let Robbie end this. My hair fell in my face as I met Diego's gaze. "Stop him!"

Diego grabbed the chair nearest him and dragged it between him and Robbie, creating a barrier. Meanwhile, I dug my fingernails into Sasha's arms, but she wouldn't budge. "Please! Let me go!" Desperate to stop this, I mimicked Robbie and elbowed Sasha as hard as I could, connecting with her rib cage.

"Aaugh." She made a gurgling noise and loosened her grip for a moment, and it was enough. I propelled myself forward as Robbie kicked the chair toward Diego. Diego didn't yield. I hurtled past

Priya and Scott on the other side of the table, sidestepping the only chair blocking my path.

I rounded the table, rushed between him and the syringe, and threw out my arms as Robbie finally shoved Diego out of the way. "Don't!" I couldn't let him try to kill Priya. This wasn't how this was supposed to go at all. "Please don't do this."

Robbie screwed up his face, lines deepening in his forehead. "She drew the short stick. Rules are rules."

"I have an idea." I licked my lips, scrambling to find logic I could work with. I had to figure this out. "I know how we can get everyone out of here alive. I really think this could work."

"What is it?" asked Diego.

I lowered my voice, darting a glance at the webcam in the china cabinet. "We fake a death. We pretend to inject someone with the poison. We pretend we've done what they want us to do. And we see if the timer on the bomb stops."

"Yes!" Priya breathed.

Diego raised his eyebrows and nodded. "That's brilliant. I can't believe we didn't think of it before."

"We didn't think of it because *this one* keeps making us panic." I motioned toward Sasha.

"It's worth a shot, at least," said Scott, glancing at the syringe. The corner of his mouth quivered. "No pun intended."

"We only have, what"—Sasha glanced at her watch—"twelve minutes left now? And that thing"—she jabbed her finger at the bomb over my shoulder—"that thing's going to kill all of us. And I'm not going to let that happen."

Sasha lunged toward me, but then she hesitated. She'd have to reach past me to grab the syringe. All I had to do was lean back and snatch it from the table. The moment stretched for what seemed like an eternity. Sasha's chest rose and fell. My fingers tingled.

And then I moved. I threw myself at the table, closing my fingers around the syringe. I couldn't let any of the liquid out. Diego tackled Sasha, crashing onto the table over plates and glasses and silverware.

As I backed away from them, the syringe felt heavy in my grip, like I was carrying the weight of all of our lives in my hands. It was such an all-consuming weight that I didn't notice Sasha break free from Diego and barrel toward me. I tried dodging from her path, but she threw herself at me and grabbed my calf before I could escape. In the moment I was airborne, I reflexively threw my arms out and braced for impact before slamming onto the floor. The wind was knocked from my lungs, and the syringe rolled across the hardwood floor, bumping into Robbie's shoe.

He knelt and picked it up.

"Robbie!" I gasped, lifting myself onto my elbows as Sasha scrambled to her feet. "Don't let her get it—"

But Robbie approached Priya, his expression pained. She backed hard into the china cabinet, the glasses and porcelain inside clinking against each other in protest, but she had nowhere to run.

"Robbie, no!" I shrieked.

"I'm sorry," said Robbie. "But she pulled the short stick."

Sasha nodded encouragingly. "That's right. Do it."

"No!" I shrieked. "You're not a murderer."

"None of us are murderers," said Robbie as he gave Sasha a wary look, the syringe shaking in his fist. "But someone has to end this. She drew the short stick. It's the only fair way."

Priya shrank against the china cabinet, tears rolling down her cheeks, raising her trembling hands. How could I get him to drop the syringe? We were running out of time—I didn't have time to convince him of anything. But I had to fix this. I had to—

The pepper spray. I had pepper spray in my purse. Mom made me carry it around after the grocery store serial killer went berserk. I kept my expression blank. I could surprise Robbie with the spray and make him drop the syringe without doing real damage.

I could see my purse, three feet away, still next to Sasha's chair. Robbie and Priya stood near the fireplace. I had to keep him talking, keep him from stabbing her, while I somehow retrieved the pepper spray.

"Robbie, hear me out." I lowered my voice to a whisper. "My idea could work. We'll fake a death. We'll see if the timer stops. We'll know once and for all whether killing someone stops the bomb."

"That won't work!" said Sasha.

"Shut up!" I refused to break eye contact with Robbie. "You're not a killer, Robbie." I collapsed onto my knees next to Sasha's chair, like I was begging him to reconsider, and edged my purse under the table with my knee. "Don't do this. She's my best friend."

Robbie narrowed his eyes. "What, should I kill him instead?" He nodded toward Diego, who took a huge step back and tripped over Scott's outstretched leg. Scott yelped as Diego tumbled backward and fell onto his butt. *No.* This was exactly what I was afraid of. Robbie hated Diego now, and would have the perfect excuse to get rid of him on account of saving *my* life. I couldn't let him stab Diego with that syringe. I couldn't let it end this way.

But I couldn't panic. I said nothing, and while everyone watched Diego clamber to his feet, I fumbled with my purse's clasp under the draping red tablecloth and rummaged through it with shaking fingers.

"No, it has to be Priya," said Sasha. "We agreed to the rules. She drew the short stick. *And* she tried to cheat her way out of it." Robbie raised the syringe over Priya's shoulder, but hesitated, biting his lip uncertainly as my fingers clasped the familiar cylinder. Was he contemplating who I'd hate him less for killing?

Priya raised an open palm toward Robbie, like she could block the needle from penetrating her skin. "Please, don't kill me. *Please.*"

Robbie's arm trembled more than ever. Priya sobbed, staring at the needle inches from her skin. He met her eyes and scowled. "Dammit!" He spun and rushed Diego, slamming him against the wall by the neck with one hand and gripping the syringe over his shoulder with the other.

"No! Don't do this, Robbie." I stood, hiding the pepper spray in my clenched palm. "You're letting them win."

Robbie scrunched his brow, the syringe shaking in his fist. "Who?"

"Whoever put us in here!" I wasn't sure what I was saying—I just needed to distract him long enough to spray him. It was hotter than a sauna in here. So hot. It was hard to focus on what I was saying. "They wanted one of us to become a killer. They wanted to turn one of us into a monster. Are you going to be that monster?"

Beads of sweat lined Robbie's furrowed brow. "They want all of us to *die*! They put us in here with a bomb!" Robbie positioned his thumb over the plunger. Diego was breathing hard, gaping at the needle inches away.

"No, you're wrong." I edged closer without tearing my eyes from Robbie's. "They're testing us, trying to get us to turn on each other, kill each other. And you're falling right into their trap! You're letting them prove that all you care about is yourself." I was screaming now, my entire body trembling. "Let's try my idea."

"We've tried enough!" Sasha cried, staring at her watch. "If we don't kill someone now, we're all going to die."

Riled by her words, Robbie tightened the grip on the syringe and lowered it toward Diego's shoulder. Diego's eyes widened in fear. "No!" I rushed forward, aiming the pepper spray at Robbie's eyes without shooting. "Give me the poison."

He flinched. "What the hell is that?"

"Pepper spray," I said. "And I *will* use it."

"You're insane!"

"You're the one about to poison someone!"

"I have to! I have to do this!"

"Robbie. Don't give in. Prove them wrong." I enunciated each word, fighting to keep the tremor from my voice. "Prove that you're willing to give a damn about anyone else." A look of sheer agony crossed his face. We'd been driven to the depths of insanity to fight for what we thought was right. He wanted to save five lives. I was arguing to save six. But he thought trying to save six might get everyone killed.

Which was more right?

Suddenly he lowered his arm and dropped the syringe on the table. "Fuck!" As Diego slid down to the floor in relief, Robbie shoved the nearest chair against the wall and kicked it repeatedly. A vein in his neck bulged, and he released a guttural growl with each kick.

Sasha covered her ears and screamed, "What are you doing?"

"Dude, I don't think murdering the chair counts," said Scott.

With one last kick, the chair finally splintered. Robbie collapsed next to it on the floor, buried his face in his knees, and let out heaving sobs. Everyone watched in silence, shocked by his outburst.

I glanced at the syringe, the needle gleaming on the table where Robbie dropped it. My eyes met Sasha's across the room. We both froze for a split second. And then we lunged.

14 DAYS AGO

JANUARY OF SENIOR YEAR

"What the hell is your problem?" Sasha slapped her notebook on the table across from me, making me jump.

"Shh," said the librarian, Mrs. Burr, peering at Sasha from behind her desk. Sasha rolled her eyes.

I plucked out my red earbuds and paused the track I was working on. "I don't know what you're talking about," I whispered.

"Bullshit," she grumbled, folding her arms. "You've been avoiding me ever since the school play. Are you still mad I flubbed that song? I said I was sorry . . ."

I quirked an eyebrow at her. I still hadn't figured out how to confront her about bullying Priya, or lying about the school play. I could just tell her off—but would she listen? Or would she just deny everything? Probably the latter.

And then she'd turn me into her punching bag, too.

I couldn't let that happen. I had to think of some other way to get through to her without giving her a chance to simply slither away and ridicule me in hissed whispers.

Each time I saw her, I remembered how she'd laughed at Priya for knocking her teeth out. I'd see Priya covering her mouth in pain and humiliation. And I'd think, *I did that. That's my fault.* Whenever I tried talking to Priya in the halls, or in class, or outside her house, she'd bolt in the other direction. No matter how many times I texted her, she ignored me. I'd racked my brain for a way to get through to her.

So I hadn't cut Sasha from my life, but held her at arm's length. If I could get Sasha to apologize to Priya, and if I could mend her wounds, maybe Priya would let me back in.

My knee bounced under the table. "It's not just about the song. I . . . I've been upset since then. So I haven't felt like partying—"

Sasha screwed up her face. "Why? You got the recording you wanted—"

"Shhhhh." Mrs. Burr shushed us so hard spittle flew from her lips. She glared at us, and so did a few other people at the neighboring tables.

"Oh, for Christ's sake." Sasha stood and rounded the table to sit next to me, glaring at Mrs. Burr all the while. Leaning close, she whispered, "The recording came out great. I mean, for the most part, right? You submitted your applications on time. Isn't that exactly what you wanted?"

"It's not about that. I've been upset about what happened to Priya."

Sasha cocked her head. "Nothing *happened* to Priya but Priya.

Besides, her teeth look even better now than they did before." Sasha ran her tongue over her own front teeth and frowned, like she was dissatisfied with them. "Lucky bitch."

"Nothing about what she went through is lucky!" I rasped. "You made fun of her constantly. You hooked up with the guy she liked and didn't warn her off."

"Hey, that's not on me. I liked Zane for years. She's the one who tried to get her paws all over him." I raised my eyebrows. So she *was* jealous of Priya. I never realized she liked Zane so much; I figured whatever was going on between them was casual.

"Either way," I said, "that didn't give you the right to post that video of her falling online for the world to see."

Sasha rolled her eyes. "But it didn't zoom in on her or anything. You couldn't even tell who she was."

"But *she* knew. We all knew. Why did you always need to take her down a peg? You already won the popularity contest. You were already dating Zane. You're already best at everything. Didn't you see how much you were hurting her feelings?" I *had* to get her to see the light. To see that she owed Priya one hell of an apology.

Part of me was convinced she'd come around. Despite her manipulation to get those singing numbers out of me, she'd convinced the drama club to let me score the play, and did so much extra work to make it happen. She nudged Robbie to ask me out. She invited me to all of her parties, and befriended me without question. She was clearly capable of kindness.

But another part of me was worried she was a narcissistic bitch. That she was only decent when it benefited herself.

Sasha's eyes got all misty, and finally, she whispered, "I'm not best at everything."

That's when I knew I couldn't convince her.

Of everything I said, she'd latched on to the bit about *her*. But how could the queen of everything think so little of herself? I tilted my head. "What do you mean?"

"You don't . . . you don't know what I've been through. The pressure I've been under. You have no idea—" She blinked furiously. I'd seen her mother pressure her to focus on her schoolwork. But that was no excuse for the lies, or the bullying. "For the past few years I've worked so hard to get into Harvard. I still haven't heard back. Even after everything I do, it's never enough."

"Sasha, you're going to be successful no matter what school you go to. You've already gotten into Brown, and hell, you'll probably get into Harvard. And even if you don't, you'll be fine. I've never met someone so driven in my life, and I'm pretty damned determined when it comes to my music, so that's saying a lot."

"That's why I love you." Her lips flickered into a smile. "You're the only person I've met who reminds me of, well, me."

Her words hit me like a thousand bricks to the forehead. I was nothing like Sasha. *Nothing.*

Or was I?

I gripped the edges of my laptop as the reality of what I'd done flooded my mind. I hadn't bullied or manipulated anyone in my quest to score the school play. But I betrayed my parents' trust— and my teachers' trust—to sway the drama club with booze. I drove away my best friend, and let her be bullied. I lied to Dad and applied early decision to USC. Yes, I'd gotten into my dream school. But at what cost? What if I'd become more like Sasha than I realized?

"Hey, guys." Maria collapsed in Sasha's abandoned seat across the table. "I've been looking for you everywhere—"

"Girls!" Mrs. Burr's face was now bright red, and it looked like she was about to spontaneously combust. "If you don't keep it down, I'm kicking you out!"

Sorry! Maria mouthed.

"Oh, hey," Sasha whispered, releasing my hand. She rubbed her eyes like she was tired, trying to rid them of tears. "I've been meaning to ask you when we're gonna stock up for next weekend. Zane's parents are out of town again." Her words flitted in and out of my ears as I reeled from the truth. What had I done? I had to fix this.

"There is no *we*. Unfortunately," said Maria. "I'm going on that stupid cruise with my family next week, remember? I'll be gone for two weeks; they're pulling me out of school the week after President's Day, too."

"Dammit, that's right!"

"Why is that a bad thing?" I asked Maria, though Sasha's words repeated on a loop in my mind, like a recording I couldn't turn off. "You get to miss a whole week of school. And a cruise sounds amazing."

Maria scoffed. "Yeah, it's *amazing* to be stuck on a boat with your parents and grandparents and annoying cousins for two whole weeks." She groaned. "My mom's got all this lame stuff planned for all of us, too . . . origami lessons, water aerobics,

Escape the Room. Ugh. Besides, we're almost done with Brewster forever. I don't want to miss that much of our last few months."

"You won't miss much if we can't get our hands on some booze," muttered Sasha.

Maria pouted. "Get Nat to pick some up. She's coming home this weekend, right?"

"Who's Nat?" I asked. The familiarity of the name prickled the back of my neck.

"My big sister," said Sasha. "And no, she's not anymore. The actress she's understudy for has the flu, so she's taking over her performances for the next few days. Can't you snatch some booze for us before you go? Just a few handles?"

"Are you kidding me? After last month?" Maria shook her head. "No way."

"What happened last month?" I asked, my mind still reeling.

"Oh, gawd, how do you not know this?" said Maria. "We did a booze run at the Chesterfield one Saturday morning. I'd heard my dad say he was keeping a few extra handles of Jack Daniel's in the supply closet, and I wanted to snag one. So this bitch and I went in there"—she thumbed at Sasha—"and she let the door close like an idiot."

"Go to hell," Sasha said with a smirk.

"We were stuck in that closet for a half hour until Mom came to open up."

"Thank God it wasn't longer. I was so bored, I thought I was going to die," said Sasha. "If I had a gun, I literally would have shot myself. Anyway, I have to pee. Be right back."

She left, leaving Maria and me alone at our table. "The things she'll do for booze." Maria rolled her eyes. "I'm not getting grounded again because she wants to get plastered. I miss when she'd make you get it for us."

I frowned. "I only got booze for the drama club."

She chortled. "Right."

My eyes widened at her reaction. I thought of how Sasha lied to both me and the drama club to get those singing numbers she wanted. What if . . . "No."

"What?"

I leaned forward and whispered, "That time she said the drama club was coming to Zane's party, but then they didn't show up . . ."

Maria rubbed her lips together. "I don't think I should—"

"Tell me!" I rasped.

She rolled her eyes again. "Alright, fine. She never invited them. She laughed about how gullible you were. That you'd do anything to score the play."

"But . . . at the winter ball . . ."

Maria shook her head. "Asher and Dan don't even drink."

I remembered Asher setting his untouched cup on the piano. It felt like someone had kicked me in the stomach. Bile shot up my throat, and I clasped a hand over my mouth.

"Oh, don't worry," said Maria. "She loves you for giving her the chance to beat me." Her words came out sharp and bitter. "She was always so jealous that I got to play the lead. I know that's why

338

she agreed to let you score the play. So she could finally be the star." She made jazz hands. "And then you went and added those stupid songs, and she got to sing after all."

Oh my God. Maria didn't even know Sasha was the one who wanted the songs.

Sasha tricked me all along. The booze. The play. The songs. Priya. She'd betrayed me at every turn. It was no wonder she'd warmed to me so quickly—she was *using* me. She pretended to be kind, when she was vile. She pretended she was helping me, when all she wanted was the limelight for herself. Why did she even set me up with Robbie? Maybe she only wanted to pull him and Zane apart, so Zane would spend more time with her.

Now I knew the truth. Sasha couldn't be reasoned with. She was a liar. A fraud. She'd destroyed my friendship with Priya, and she nearly destroyed everything I worked for.

Someone had to stop her. Someone had to make things right.

And it had to be me.

9 MINUTES LEFT

I reached the syringe first. It was slick with Robbie's sweat. I brandished it at Sasha, and she backed away, her eyes widening.

"Why?" I asked, choking back a sob.

"Why what?" Sasha hissed. We'd run out of time because Sasha repeatedly sent us spiraling into panic mode. We could have found a way out of here if we'd worked together the whole time. But she was so selfish, we weren't even a half hour in before she was suggesting who to kill.

"Why are you like this? How are you so willing to kill someone? I just need to understand the mechanics behind how your brain works, because I don't fucking get it," I snarled. Sasha's jaw clenched. "And it's not just tonight. Even out there." I jabbed my finger at the door. "You'll lie, cheat, betray your friends . . . you'll do whatever it takes to get your way.

"But why? Why are you like this?" I was yelling now. "You were already Ivy League–bound, but you took drugs to cheat your way to the top. You were already salutatorian, but you wanted to sabotage Diego. You were already captain of the cheerleading squad, but you ridiculed Priya and made her feel worthless. You were already director of the drama club, and you lied to *everyone* to steal the limelight."

Her mouth dropped open.

"Yes, I know what you did. I know how you manipulated me, and the whole drama club, so you could be the prima donna you always wanted to be. That's why you suspected Maria first, right? Because you basically stole the lead role from her!"

Sasha's wide eyes got moist and red. She must never have expected me to find out the truth.

"And I could go on and on. You'll do whatever it takes to beat everyone else at literally everything, even if it means hurting everyone around you . . . even if it means hurting *yourself*! Why? What the hell is the point?"

"Because I couldn't be the one thing I wanted to be!" She clasped her mouth and shook her head, and the corners of her eyes crinkled like she was about to start sobbing. "Since I was four years old, I spent hours and hours training to be an Olympic gymnast. My mom quit her job to be my coach. And when I qualified for the national championships, I thought I was destined for a gold medal. It was everything I lived for—*breathed* for.

"And then I got into that horrible car accident and busted my leg. I had to give it all up. All that time my mother and I put in . . .

all of it was for *nothing*. After that, I wasn't sure what I wanted to do, or who I wanted to *be*. It was like I didn't know who I was anymore. You have no idea what that's like. To lose everything in an instant. None of you have any idea."

I remembered that time Sasha's mother caught us playing Fortnite, and asked Sasha how she could waste any more of her time. Now it all made sense. "So then . . . you wanted to be the best at *everything*."

"Wouldn't you?" Sasha spat. "I'd spent all those years focusing on just one thing, and look where it got me."

My heart hammered in my chest. I wanted to kick myself for not figuring this out sooner. Maria and Amy mentioned her car crash that first day I'd asked Sasha to score the play. It wasn't just pressure from her mother. It was because she'd lost everything she once strove for. How had I not seen it myself?

But it still didn't explain one thing.

Priya beat me to the punch. "That doesn't explain why you treat everyone like shit."

Sasha's moment of redemption went as fast as it came, and her expression turned to stone. "Didn't you hear anything I just said? I did whatever I had to. And dammit, I'll do whatever it takes to get out of here alive. Whatever it takes."

Wow. It was one thing to have lofty goals—admirable, even—but it was another to intentionally crush everyone else to achieve them. My blood boiled as I glared at her. Despite the pain she'd endured and dreams she'd lost, she didn't care about who she hurt, whether in here or out in the real world. If there was anyone who didn't deserve to walk out of this room, it was her.

"Well, now you're going to listen to me." I glanced at my watch, the syringe tight in my grip. Eight minutes left. "We're going to figure this out. Together."

"No—" Sasha took a step closer, but I waved the syringe from side to side, and she backed off.

"Listen. We're going to give this one last shot before we take someone's life. We're going to try my idea, or so help me God, the next person to flip out on me is going to get this poison in their bloodstream and that will be that."

I didn't mean it, of course. But they didn't need to know that.

How the hell had it come to this?

All of my life, I blasted movie scores into my skull, attempting to make everyday life more dramatic. Now I stood pointing a syringe at the people I once called my friends, wishing more than anything I could get back to my mundane life. This wasn't how things were supposed to happen.

Priya took a quick intake of air, her eyes darting between Sasha and me. "So how do we do this?"

"We'll act this out," I whispered. "We'll pretend to inject someone. They'll drop to the floor and convulse and stuff, and the rest of us will freak out and pretend it's real."

Sasha crossed her arms and laughed her haughty laugh. "That'll never work!"

"Shhhh," I said. "Keep your voice down."

Scott flicked Priya's leg and motioned for her to bring over the nearest chair. She dragged it over. "Help me up," he said.

"What're you doing?" I said.

"I'm not sitting here like some useless moron anymore."

Priya and Diego each grabbed one of Scott's arms and helped him stand. He gasped. "Oh, God. Fuck." But he stayed upright. He hobbled on his good foot, using the chair like a crutch under his arm while letting his bad foot hover above the floor.

"You guys." Sasha pointed at the china cabinet to the right of the fireplace. "This isn't going to work—" A bunch of us cut her off with sharp shushing noises. She lowered her voice, but barely. "Oh, please, they can see us talking. They probably know we're up to something. And they'll see if you don't push down the plunger!"

"Whoever does it can hide it from the camera," said Diego. "I'm sure they won't see. That's no high-res camera in there. We'll check their pulse after they stop convulsing, make it convincing." Robbie still sat on the floor rubbing the tears from his face, but he didn't argue.

"Exactly," I said. Priya and Scott nodded.

Robbie rubbed his lips together, contemplating this for a moment. Finally, he nodded and stood. "Let's give it a shot. But we have to move fast."

"No!" Sasha stomped her foot. "You idiots! We're all going to die!"

But everyone ignored her. "We'll know one way or another before the timer runs out," said Robbie.

"Yeah," agreed Diego. "We'll have to expose the bomb so we

can see if the timer stops." That would mean carefully lifting the stack of drawers and pulling out a few of them, so the timer would be visible again. "C'mon, it's out of view of the camera." Robbie joined him at the fireplace.

"What if it does explode? Doesn't that defeat the whole purpose of putting it in there?" Sasha continued her protestations to nobody in particular. "This won't work."

"Shut up!" Scott shout-whispered. The rest of us ignored her.

"Who's going to fake die?" whispered Priya, ignoring Sasha.

Scott stepped toward me, scooting the chair along with him. "Dammit," he yelled, giving me a pointed look. "You assholes have had it out for me from the beginning."

I nodded slightly and raised the syringe, aiming the needle toward his left biceps, keeping the syringe out of the camera's view. "Sasha's right. It's too late now. This is the only way out. We have no choice!"

Diego carefully lifted the top couple drawers as Robbie slid a few out near the top of the stack, lowering the bomb. The timer was now in clear view.

"I'm so sorry, Scott," I said, trying to sound convincing. "I never wanted to do this—"

"This isn't going to work." Sasha tugged at her hair. "We only have five minutes left!"

"On the count of three," I whispered to Scott, "lunge at me. Then fall."

Scott furrowed his brow, pretending to look angry. "You can't do this!" Then he added in a low voice, "One."

"Do it!" cried Robbie.

"No!" Scott shouted, hobbling closer. Priya shrieked and knelt near the door, covering her eyes.

"Guys!" Sasha cried. "If this doesn't work, they won't believe us when we kill someone for real. Then we'll all die anyway."

I ignored her. "Two." I drew my arm back, like I was readying to stab Scott, feigning fear that he was about to tackle me. "Get away!" I screamed. "Don't come any closer—Sasha, no!" Before I could say three, before Scott could lunge at me, Sasha launched herself at Scott, wrapping her hands around his throat. Taken by surprise, Scott toppled back, and Sasha sailed with him, maintaining her grip.

Robbie rushed toward them—whether to help or to stop her, I didn't know—but tripped over a chair, blocking anyone else from interfering. Sasha bared her teeth and grunted as she struggled to hold Scott down. At nearly six feet tall, he usually could overpower her, but with his oxygen supply diminishing, and the pain of his injured ankle, it seemed he couldn't find the strength. He clawed at Sasha's wrists, his eyes bulging as his face started turning purple, and he made gagging and gargling noises as his lungs strained for air.

My mind flashed back to Maggie's death. Her purple face. The gurgling in her throat.

Everything seemed to happen in slow motion.

And then everything happened at once. Diego and Priya leapt over Robbie's sprawling form and hauled Sasha off of Scott.

"What are you doing?" Robbie climbed to his knees and

shook Sasha by her shoulders. "We had a plan! We might've had a chance!"

"It'd never have worked!" Sasha cried. "Don't you see that?"

Robbie released her and backed away. "We could've pulled it off. How would they know Scott wasn't really dead?"

"Since when are you willing to risk that?" she cried as Diego helped pull Scott to a seated position. "We could just kill him and be done with it! Why the hell are you on *their* side now?"

"Because I'm not a complete monster!" Robbie yelled.

Sasha's face fell, and her eyes widened. "And I am?" Her voice wavered and cracked. Robbie's silence spoke volumes. He just stood there shaking his head, like he suddenly realized he didn't know her at all. Tears brimmed in Sasha's eyes. "You think I'm a monster."

"You are!" Priya and Diego screamed in unison.

"You are a fucking monster," Scott said hoarsely, massaging his throat. "You've been hell-bent on killing me since this started."

"And me," said Priya.

Diego shook his head. "And me."

Sasha gripped the sides of her head. "I only wanted to get out of here alive."

My heart clenched. Despite everything, I almost felt bad for her. She was finally starting to realize how terrible she'd been, but it was too little, too late.

"All you ever think about is yourself," said Priya. "You should be the one to die. You're wicked. You always have been."

"No—" Sasha started.

"You're so mean to me, all the time. You posted that video of me falling for everyone to see the most humiliating moment of my life!"

"And you blackmailed me about the worst thing in my life," said Scott.

"You tried to sabotage me every chance you got," said Diego.

"And you manipulated me," I said. "Did you ever really want to be my friend? Or were you just using me—laughing at me behind my back—the whole time?"

"Oh, please." Sasha crossed her arms as a tear dropped onto her cheek.

"Don't 'oh, please' me," I shouted. "You're a *bully*. Did you know my older sister died by suicide because she was bullied?"

Maggie. Her purple face. Her gurgling throat. The empty pill bottles.

That utterly helpless feeling that sucked the air from my own lungs.

I remembered being in Maggie's room, after the 911 dispatcher talked me down from my panic and instructed me to turn Maggie onto her side. I'd hunched over her, watching her face, watching her life leave her. And there was nothing I could do. I couldn't save her. I wasn't good enough of a sister to save her.

"She's not moving," I'd said to the dispatcher. "*Please*. What do I do?"

"You just keep hanging on, okay? An ambulance is on its way. Help is on the way. You just . . ." Her voice had faded into the background as I glanced at Maggie's open laptop. Making sure she didn't fall onto her stomach, I stretched and grabbed it. She'd been looking at Facebook.

Numbness shot through my heart at the first comment, from a girl named Natasha Jane: *I can't believe they still let you go to Brewster High. You're such a waste of space.*

A comment on a political link she shared: *OMG look at you trying to look smart. Fake news!*

A comment on a makeup tutorial link she shared: *Too bad nothing could fix your ugly face.*

A photo comment on one of Maggie's selfies, with Maggie's face superimposed on the body of an old, shirtless, overweight man.

Another lone comment: *Why don't you just kill yourself?*

My stomach clenched as I read the messages of hate filling her timeline. It was the same girl, time after time. Sometimes other girls chimed in, agreeing with her, liking her comments, egging her on. But it was mainly Natasha. I scrolled back over the months, unable to go back far enough to see when it started. It'd been happening for ages. I never saw any of it in my news feed—Maggie must have blocked me from her timeline. Why she didn't block Natasha or any of these other people was beyond me.

This must have been why she was so surly over the past year. I thought she was too busy to hang out with me. I thought she didn't want anything to do with us, her family. But the truth was, she was being bullied. She was in pain. And I had no idea. Why didn't she ever say anything? I could have been a friend to her. Mom and Dad could have helped her. Why did she keep this from us?

"I'm sorry, I'm sorry, I'm sorry," I sobbed, hugging her limp form in my arms as sirens blared outside my house.

But I would never be able to comfort her. I'd never be able to take back what those bullies said to her. I'd never be able to help her.

She was gone.

Now Sasha stood in front of me, eyeing the syringe in my grip. Sasha, another bully, who'd tormented Priya; blackmailed Scott; tried to sabotage Diego; manipulated me; ridiculed so many others. Her eyes widened from my revelation, but she said nothing.

"Some girl wouldn't leave her alone," I said. "She bullied her on Facebook, like you bullied Priya. Only Maggie . . . the forensic psychologist said she showed signs of depression. We didn't realize at the time. We missed the signs. But she was too sick when it all became too much. She couldn't stop herself when she thought dying was the only way out."

Sasha gave a great sniff. "Well, that's her own fault."

"No, it wasn't! She was sick . . . !" I was shrieking now, my voice shaking from years of pent-up anger for that horrible girl who tortured Maggie. Robbie watched me with wide eyes and a slack jaw.

But now I couldn't stop myself. "She couldn't help that she was depressed. And if she didn't feel like the whole world was against her, maybe she would have asked for help. But people like you don't care how you're affecting anyone else. All you care about is making yourself look perfect, and feeling better than everyone else. Just like tonight, all you've cared about is saving yourself. You're a cruel, selfish bitch. Just like your sister."

Sasha's face scrunched in confusion. "Wait, what? My *sister?*"

"Your sister was the one who bullied Maggie, wasn't she? I saw your expression when you saw Maggie's pillow with her name on it. You recognized her name . . . because your sister is the one who bullied her to death. Natasha Jane. Nat, right?" I'd finally made the connection when Maria mentioned Nat's name in the library. "Natasha and Sasha." I scoffed. "Real cute."

Robbie blanched. "Holy shit, Sasha. She's talking about *you.*"

What? Every hair on my body stood on end. Sasha's face crumpled, and she said nothing.

No. That wasn't possible. "What do you mean?" I looked between them, waiting for one of them to answer. Neither of them did. Sasha was almost hunched over, shaking her head at Robbie. He glared at her like she was a stranger who'd spit at him. "What the fuck do you mean?" I demanded.

Sasha gripped her throat like she was about to throw up. "Robbie, please."

But Robbie went on anyway. "Sasha changed her Facebook name to Natasha Jane after she broke her leg in eighth grade. That's her full name. Then a few months later she deleted her account for a while."

Priya's jaw dropped as she connected the dots. I stood in place, numb, unable to believe what I was hearing. *Sasha* killed my sister? It was Sasha all along? "I . . . I don't understand," I said. "I thought Nat was your sister."

"Natalie. Her name is Natalie." A tear created a glistening path down Sasha's cheek. "We always hated how similar our names were. Natalie and Natasha. So she went by Nat, and I went by Sasha. But I didn't want my old gymnastic teammates to find me after the accident. I was so angry . . . so *mortified* . . . so I unfriended them and changed my name online for a while."

After everything I already knew Sasha had done, she was even worse than I ever imagined. "You . . . you killed my sister," I said. Every part of my body shook. "You tormented her. Tortured her. Drove her to think there was no other way out."

"I'm sorry," Sasha said. "I'm so sorry. I didn't realize she was your sister until I saw the pillow on her bed. I never put it together before. She only used her last initial online."

I remembered that. It was because she didn't want our parents finding her profiles. "How . . . how the hell did you even *know* her?"

Sasha wiped her eyes. "I met her at one of Nat's parties one weekend my parents were out of town. I was in eighth grade. I still had my cast on, and I didn't know many people, but I . . . I wanted to fit in. So I . . . I . . ." She trailed off, but I knew where this was going.

"You teased her. So you'd look cool, even though you were only an eighth grader."

She nodded. "And then for some bizarre reason she friended me back on Facebook. It was like she was *asking* for it."

"Bullshit," I screamed at her. "You're fucking *evil*." Even after she knew her nastiness had led to one girl's death, she'd bullied Priya.

"No," she said. "I'm sorry, I'm so sorry—"

"No you're not," I said. "If you were sorry, you'd never have been so mean to Priya. You got sneakier about it though, didn't you? Teasing her with those backhanded compliments. Ridiculing her when you thought nobody was listening. But you were bullying her . . . and you *knew*. You knew how devastating the consequences could be, and you did it anyway!"

"Priya . . ." Sasha clasped her hands as though in prayer. "I'm sorry, okay? I'm so sorry for everything." But Priya only crossed her arms and shook her head.

"Are you saying that because you mean it?" said Robbie, a tormented look in his eyes. "Or are you saying that because you're afraid to die?"

Sasha screwed up her face, lost for words. Even her best friend had turned against her.

"I don't buy it for a second," said Scott.

"So someone do it already!" said Priya, glancing at the bomb's timer. "We have less than two minutes left."

Sasha shook her head and backed against the brick fireplace, a step farther from us, but a step closer to the bomb. She had nowhere else to turn. "No. Please . . . I'm sorry." But for what, exactly? She had so much to be sorry for. The red timer blinked beside her. One minute fifty-seven seconds left. Fifty-six. Fifty-five.

But nobody came to her defense. Not even Robbie. "I'll do it, Red," Scott said with a rasping voice. He extended his hand toward me. "Help me up. I'll do it. I won't ask you to kill your friend."

"Holy hell." Robbie crouched close to the floor, covering his face with both hands.

After a moment's hesitation, I took Scott's hand and helped him stand again, letting him put his arm over my shoulder so I could help him cross the room. "She's not my friend. Not anymore." I swallowed the bile rising in my throat and clamped my lips shut, struggling not to throw up. One minute thirty-eight. Thirty-seven. Thirty-six.

"I got it from here, Red," said Scott. I released him and stepped back, and he hobbled the rest of the way toward Sasha. Sweat dripped from his face, the blood from his forehead cut dry now, but sheer determination led him forward.

Sasha uttered a strangled cry, her eyes frantic. "Robbie, please! Don't let him do this!" But Robbie didn't stand to stop him. Diego was suddenly next to me, wrapping his fingers around mine.

Before another moment could pass, before he could change his mind, Scott shoved Sasha against the wall and raised the syringe, pressing the needle against her bare shoulder while holding her in place. His thumb hovered over the plunger. She let out a guttural shriek. "Please! No!" One minute twenty-seven. Twenty-six. Part of me wanted to bury my face in Diego's chest. But I had to watch this. I had to see how this ended. One minute twenty. Nineteen. Eighteen.

"Scott! Do it!" cried Priya.

"No!" Sasha screamed. She hugged herself around her stomach, unable to move with Scott pressing the needle against her skin. She pressed back against the bricks so hard it was like she was trying to dissolve into them.

Scott cringed and squeezed his eyes shut. He wasn't a murderer. But to save the rest of us, he was willing to become one. He cried out as he stabbed down, the needle disappearing from view, and Sasha shrieked as he pressed down the plunger.

The room was silent. Scott opened his eyes, a stunned expression on his face. Liquid trickled down Sasha's arm. We all stared. Sasha sobbed and slid down the brick wall as her legs gave out from under her.

"Did you stab her with the needle?" said Diego.

"Of course I did." Scott inspected the syringe and noticed some of the liquid on his fingers. "Ahh!" He threw down the syringe and frantically wiped his hands on his shirt. Diego raced to the table, picked up one of the cloth napkins, and used it to scoop up the syringe. He rotated it in his grip, his brow furrowed as he shook his head. Finally, he used some of the cloth napkin to push at the end of the needle. He let out a breath with a whoosh. "Whoa."

"What is it?" I asked.

"It's a retractable needle." He grinned at me. "It's totally fake."

"Holy shit, man." Robbie rubbed his hands over his hair. "I could've sworn it was real."

I threw my arms around Diego. "It's fake, it's fake. It wasn't real." Priya ran to us and joined in the group hug. We all laughed and cried in relief.

Scott held out his damp hand like it was contaminated, but grinned from ear to ear. "Thank God." Then he grimaced in pain and let himself drop to the rug. "Some sick prank that was."

"It's over," said Priya. "It's over." We disentangled ourselves from Diego so we could hug each other.

Robbie took the syringe from Diego and inspected the needle. "I dunno, you guys. How do we know the liquid inside wasn't really poison?"

"It's obviously a prop," I said. "It's fake. It's over." I gave him a hug, but his arms remained limp as he examined the syringe over my shoulder.

Diego leaned toward the bomb, the red glow from the timer illuminating the inside of the fireplace. "Uh, guys? The timer hasn't stopped." My stomach clenched. Oh, no. This was supposed to be over. We survived, and now we could leave.

"How much time is left?" Priya asked.

"Fifty-eight seconds."

"What if the syringe was broken or something?" asked Robbie.

"That's not how syringes work," I said. "The needles don't just retract into the barrel. It's a fake."

"I don't know." Robbie shook his head. "I don't want to be blown to bits because the syringe didn't work right."

"Oh, right." Sasha scrambled to her feet, teetering from the shock of nearly being poisoned to death. "But you were willing to let *me* die." She lunged at the table for a napkin.

"Wait, what are you saying?" I asked Robbie.

"What if we still have to kill someone?" he said.

"No!" I screamed. "It wasn't real. Don't you see?" I grabbed the syringe from Robbie, pinching it between my fingers and raising it like it was evidence at a court hearing. "It's a prop. It's over. We all get to walk out of here alive. The timer will run out, and nothing will happen. None of this is real."

"It is real, it is!" said Sasha, scrubbing the napkin against her skin so fiercely her skin was already red and raw. "I have to get to a hospital." The red timer blinked. Thirty-nine. Thirty-eight. Thirty-seven. "The bomb is still ticking down. Someone has to die. But it's not going to be me." She threw down the napkin and raced to the chair Robbie had annihilated earlier. She yanked one of the legs clinging to its frame by a few splinters, and it detached easily.

"Wait!" Priya approached the china cabinet with the camera, waving her arms over her head. "Turn off the bomb! The poison didn't work!"

Sasha raised the chair leg over her shoulder like a baseball bat. "No, stop!" I cried, raising my hands. "Sasha, it's not real."

"Oh, shut up," Sasha cried, her whole body shaking with fear . . . or fury. "How can we know for sure the syringe didn't malfunction? That the poison's not slowly killing me? You think you're right about everything, that you're so high and mighty— everyone's fucking savior." She shifted her wide-eyed gaze to the bomb. "Well, guess what? I'm not dying in here. Not because of you. Not because of *anyone*." Twenty. Nineteen. Eighteen.

"You're not going to die!" Diego shouted. But Sasha ignored him, her eyes darting around my face like a rabid animal. I'd exposed the truth about her. Her drug addiction. Her manipulation. Her lies. Her murder by bullying. Now everyone knew she was far from perfect. And it was all because of me.

Thirteen. Twelve. Eleven.

Without hesitating another moment, Sasha barreled toward me, pulling back the chair leg. I recoiled, scurrying backward, but before anyone could stop her, she brought down the chair leg hard. I tried to sidestep the blow, but the table blocked my path, and the wood cracked against my bare right shoulder. Pain shot down my arm as blood streamed from where the jagged edge sliced my skin. I shrieked as I tripped and fell back onto the glass shards. One of them slashed my left palm. It felt like every part of my body was on fire.

Oh, God. She was going to kill me.

Fear clawed at my throat as I scuttled backward, ignoring the sound of people screaming, ignoring the searing pain of the cut on my palm as I used my good arm as leverage. All I could think about was getting away from Sasha. As she pulled back the chair leg to take another swing, clearly aiming for my head, Priya sprinted toward us from behind and slammed into Sasha, shoving her backward.

Determined as ever, Sasha quickly regained her balance. Her face twisted in fury as she reeled back to take aim at Priya.

What happened next, I never could have predicted.

As Sasha leaned forward to swing the chair leg, Priya bent and scooped up the nearest shard of glass she could find. And Sasha's mouth formed a silent O of surprise when the shard sank deep into her belly.

5 SECONDS LEFT

Everyone watched the deep red stain flower across Sasha's light red dress as blood spread from the stab wound. She dropped the chair leg, and her aghast stare shifted from Priya to the glass shard protruding from her belly. No. *No.* This couldn't be happening. This wasn't supposed to happen.

Just then, the red timer blinked to zero. And nothing happened. Because of course it didn't. The bomb was fake all along.

Priya finally released the glass shard and stepped back, a dazed expression on her face, like she couldn't believe what she'd just done. Her wide eyes trained on the bloodstain blossoming across Sasha's stomach. "I had to. I had no choice. She was going to kill Amber." I gripped my shoulder Sasha had bashed with the chair leg. It was swollen and bright red, and warm blood streaked down my arm from a deep cut, but I could still move it.

"Holy hell," Robbie croaked.

Sasha lightly touched the end of the shard with shaking fingers and winced in pain. "What . . . what do I do? Please, what do I do?" Before anyone could answer, her knees buckled. Robbie caught her before she hit the floor and gently lowered her onto her back. Blood bubbled from the stab wound, and Robbie reached for the glass shard.

"Don't touch it!" I scrambled over to them, trying to avoid cutting myself on more glass shards, and knelt next to Robbie. "She might lose blood faster if you do." I glanced at Diego. "Right?"

He exhaled slowly, considering it. "I don't know." He stared at Sasha in shock. Nobody moved. Nobody knew what to do.

A trickle of blood ran from the corner of Sasha's mouth down her cheek, mingling with her sweat. Oh, God. That had to be bad. "No . . ." Robbie whimpered, hovering over her.

Sasha focused on Robbie with glassy eyes, her brow creasing from concentration. "I'm not . . . a monster. I panicked . . . I'm sorry."

Then her gaze trained on me. "I never meant for your sister to die. When I found out, I thought maybe she accidentally overdosed . . ." She paused to take a ragged breath. ". . . maybe it wasn't really suicide."

I shook my head, tears blurring my vision. Being in denial didn't make what she did to my sister any more justifiable. "You knew. You deleted all of your comments. You deleted your accounts."

"I didn't know. But I was afraid . . ." She gasped, something gurgling deep in her belly. Her fingers hovered over the glass shard, like she wanted to pull it out but was afraid to touch it. Her fingers trembled wildly as she clasped my hand. "I never meant for . . . for . . ." She opened her mouth to say something else, but all that came out was a wheezing sound. Her eyes were glazed and unfocused.

"Sasha." I gripped her hand with both of mine, despite the searing pain in my arm. Despite everything she'd done—bullying my sister, torturing Priya, and even trying to kill me just now, I didn't want her to die. Everything she'd done, she'd done out of fear. Maybe she truly was sorry. "Stay with me, okay?"

"I never meant for . . ." She tried again. But the next moment, her eyes stared blankly toward the ceiling. Her left arm flopped to the floor beside her, and her right hand stilled in mine. We'd never know what she was going to say. She was gone. Just like that. Gone. Robbie howled as Priya turned, hunched over, and threw up in the corner next to the fireplace.

"No. Sasha, no. Stay with me." I shook her shoulder. Her head lolled with the movement, and her eyes remained open. "You weren't supposed to die. Nobody was supposed to die." She would never get to say goodbye to Zane or her parents after all. This wasn't supposed to happen. I failed. Everyone should have gotten out of here unscathed, but I failed. How did this happen? How the hell did this happen?

I jumped at a ripping noise to my left, sending another wave of pain rippling through my arm and chest. Diego tore one of the plastic bottles from the bomb. He gave a sniff, then raised the bottle to his lips for a swig. He swilled the liquid in his mouth for a moment. "Flat ginger ale."

"Holy shit," said Scott. "So, now we know. None of it was real."

"Holy shit," Robbie repeated, shaking his head at Sasha's limp form.

"No," I confirmed, my voice monotone. "None of this was real. Nobody was supposed to die."

"I had to. I had to," Priya repeated over and over. She sank next to the fireplace, next to her own pool of vomit, wrapping her arms around her knees. "I had to. I had to. She was going to kill you. She was going to kill *me*. I'm sorry. I had to. She would have killed someone if I didn't."

"Shut up!" Robbie cried. "Just shut up."

I knelt next to Priya and wrapped my good arm around her. She gripped me back hard, and her whole body shook fiercely. "I'm sorry, I'm sorry," she repeated over and over.

"It's not your fault," I said. After a year of torture and ridicule, Priya finally stood up to Sasha tonight. But she'd be forever traumatized by it. "None of this is your fault. You're right; she would have killed me. You saved my life, Priya. You did what you had to—"

The sound of a door slamming out in the restaurant made everyone turn toward the large oak door. I scrambled to my feet, clutching my right shoulder. Footsteps grew louder as they approached from the other side. I glanced at my watch. Eight thirty. We held a collective breath as someone fumbled around outside. "Oh fuck," said Robbie. "Are they going to kill us all now?"

My veins throbbed with anticipation. "It wasn't real. They wouldn't hurt us." I crossed the room and rested a bloody palm against the oak door. Should I shout out to whoever was out there?

"Who the hell did this?" Scott asked. The lock made a scraping noise as the key was inserted.

I backed away until I hit the table.

We stared at the door as the lock clicked, and the door opened. A young man, perhaps in his mid-twenties, with shoulder-length matted brown hair tied back in a ponytail, stood on the other side. A rush of cooler air followed him into the room. I instinctively took a step toward it. He held a large pink box, and shock registered on his face as he stepped into the room. "Holy crap, it's hot in here—"

"Who the hell are you?" asked Robbie. He barreled toward this man, growling as he ran. The stranger's eyes widened in surprise. "No!" I yelled, blocking Robbie's path.

"Why not?" Robbie cried. "Who are you? Why did you do this?"

The young man crinkled his brow. "Do what? I'm just here to make a delivery, dude. From Sweet Cakes." He held the box out to Robbie.

"Yeah, sure you are," Robbie fumed.

"Whoa," said the deliveryman, eyeing my shoulder and blood-streaked arm. "What the hell happened to you?"

Robbie took the box from him and shoved it into Diego's

hands. He turned back to the deliveryman, ignoring his questions. "Who's this from?"

"Lemme take a quick look." The deliveryman took a tablet from his bag and scrolled down the screen. "It was paid for with cash. Let's see . . . they would have had to leave a name for the delivery . . . yep, here we go. Meagan Abbie ordered two dozen cupcakes from Sweet Cakes and left instructions—"

Robbie grabbed the tablet from him. "Gimme that." He scrolled back down to the instructions and scanned them, his eyes widening as he read.

"Who's Meagan Abbie?" asked Diego. I shrugged, frowning.

"What does it say?" asked Priya.

Robbie read aloud. "'Deliver the two dozen cupcakes to the Chesterfield at 121 Sherborne Lane at eight thirty p.m. It's a surprise, so don't arrive earlier. The front door will be open. Leave them in the back room next to the bar—the key is next to the bar register. Please don't skip this last step—otherwise our party will be ruined.'"

The deliveryman plucked his tablet from Robbie's grip. "I thought the instructions were bizarre, but here you are." The crease in his brow deepened as he took in the shattered windows. "Hey, were you all locked in here?" That's when he noticed Sasha's body. "Oh, shit! Is she . . ."

"Yeah," said Robbie. "She's dead. Mind calling the cops?"

The deliveryman whipped out his phone.

"There's no signal," I told him as Diego set the pink box on the table and opened it. "You have to go outside."

"Got it." He raced out the door and left us alone again.

Diego peeled off a note taped to the inside of the lid, unfolded it, and scanned the two lines. He glanced at me, his expression a mix of relief, sadness, and shock, before reading aloud. "'Congratulations on getting through the last hour. Now you all know who you really are.'"

4 HOURS AGO

I spent the last hour getting ready for my guests.

It didn't take as long as I thought it would. I biked home after school, grabbed two duffel bags from my room, threw them in Dad's car, and drove to the grocery store a couple towns over to pick up enough precooked food to make this dinner party look plausible—a couple rotisserie chickens, roasted yams and veggies, a platter of deviled eggs, salad mix, and a couple bags of bread rolls. I was nervous it'd look sketchy to keep my gloves on while shopping.

But I didn't want to get my fingerprints all over everything.

Not that I intended for anyone to die. That wasn't the objective of this little experiment. But if we happened to do any damage to the Chesterfield while trying to escape, Maria's parents might try to find out who was behind everything, and I didn't want to get busted for the most epic prank in Brewster history. Without proof, nobody would suspect innocent little musician Amber Prescott. But I figured I couldn't be too careful.

Nobody seemed to notice my unnecessary gloves, and I used the self-checkout line and paid with cash. So far, so good. Everything else was in the duffel bag, so my next stop was the Chesterfield.

I parked a couple blocks away from the restaurant so nobody would notice Dad's car near the entrance. Getting everything into the restaurant was the tricky part. The Chesterfield's back entrance was in a narrow alleyway, and if a neighbor spotted some stranger entering the code when the restaurant was supposed to be closed for two weeks, it could raise some eyebrows.

Dammit. I was probably overthinking this. For all anyone knew, I was staff coming to check on the place. My nerves had been going haywire all day. Everything had to go perfectly tonight.

I pulled my faux-fur-lined hood over my eyes and snapped the clasp under my chin. There were a few people milling around, but everyone stared at their cell phones as they walked. I slung the duffel bags over my shoulders and hauled the grocery bags to the restaurant in one trip, grunting at the weight. I'd seen Maria enter the lock and security codes plenty of times when I was the lookout for her and Sasha as they snuck in to swipe booze. Once I got the back door open, I typed the security code into the beeping panel near the door. Maria's parents closed the restaurant whenever they went on vacation. I didn't have to worry about anyone raining on my parade.

In fact, that's how I got this whole idea—it was in the library, when Maria recounted how she and Sasha locked themselves in the supply closet during their last tequila run. All the locks in this place must have been ancient. Sasha's words replayed in my head: *If I had a gun, I literally would have shot myself.* Like suicide was something anyone should ever joke about.

But it made the idea for this little prank pop into my head, and I'd rushed off and spent the next two weeks turning the idea over and over, scheming all the little details, figuring out how I could steer the conversation in the room so that ultimately, everyone would turn against Sasha. Everyone would choose her to die. It'd be the perfect way to teach her a lesson, to get her to understand how she treated everyone around her—and to prove I was nothing like her.

And once I mailed out the invitations, there was no going back.

I hauled my bags through the kitchen and out to the main dining room. The door to the private back dining room was already propped open. I dropped everything on the floor next to the fireplace and switched on the light. This room would be perfect. It was big enough to spend time searching for a way out, but small enough to make everyone feel claustrophobic. This needed to feel scary. This needed to feel *real*.

I slung my jacket across one of the chairs and fished my phone from my purse, scrolling through my movie score playlists. My battle music playlist seemed like a good fit for the occasion. I was readying for a battle of sorts.

After popping in my earbuds and slipping the phone into my back pocket, I let out a shiver, rubbing my gloved hands together.

It was chilly in here—Maria's parents probably turned off the heat to save energy while they were gone. I found the thermostat out in the main room next to the bar, switched it on, and adjusted it to the low seventies.

Back in the private dining room, I unzipped the first duffel bag and pulled several platters with matching concave lids I'd found at HomeGoods. I wasn't sure if the Chesterfield had platters with lids, and I'd need to cover at least a few trays so the bomb and syringe would be hidden when everyone first sat down. After a bit of hunting, I found a tablecloth, more fancy platters (with lids!), baskets for the bread rolls, plates, silverware, glasses, and pitchers—everything I'd need to make it look like a convincing setup for a dinner party. The rotisserie chickens smelled delicious. They'd be cold by the time everyone showed up, but it wasn't like anyone would notice. And at least Priya would be able to eat something if she needed to. I shook some steamed veggies onto the platters with the chickens to complete the dish.

After I laid out the rest of the food and filled the glasses with water, I unzipped the second duffle bag and set the most important items on the biggest platter.

The bomb.

The syringe.

And the envelope.

At first, I envisioned using a prop gun as the fake weapon. But after what happened with Phil, I couldn't bring myself to buy any sort of gun—not even a fake. Besides, there were too many ways a prop gun could go wrong—namely, it'd be too easy to know it was fake. With a syringe of poison, all I had to do was make everyone think one drop could kill them. Like hell Sasha'd want to risk testing it.

So I'd ordered the fake syringe with a throwaway Amazon account, and it looked like the real deal. It was almost too easy. If my parents found it in my room, I could always claim it was a toy from when Maggie played doctor. I'd never be able to pull that excuse with a prop gun.

I switched on the Bluetooth timer I'd fastened to the bomb last night and set the domed lid on the platter. Then my stomach dropped. If I didn't have a signal down here, would the Bluetooth timer work? It wouldn't need a signal or Wi-Fi or anything, right?

I set aside the lid and pulled my phone from my pocket. As usual, there was no signal in the Chesterfield. The timer was set to one hour and two minutes. I'd need that two-minute head start— it'd look a little suspicious if I tapped something on my phone at the same moment I lifted the lid. I opened the Bluetooth timer app and stared at the timer on the bomb as I hit Start. The timer began ticking down. I let out a relieved breath, reset the timer, and replaced the lid. I might be able to pull this off after all.

My next challenge was the door. I needed to get the door to swing shut once everyone was in the room. The door automatically locked when closed, which I'd first learned when it locked behind Robbie and me, right before our first kiss. I pulled the brass key from the keyhole on the outside of the door. I'd need to leave it on the bar for the cupcake delivery person to grab once it was time to let us out. I bit my lip, scanning the room. Was there another key hidden anywhere? What if the delivery person didn't show up? Then we'd really be trapped.

Hiding a spare key inside the room was too risky, though—if someone found it, the whole prank would end early. I'd have to risk going without it.

I tested the inside lock with the door open to ensure I'd be able to let myself out after testing the door, and stuck the key in my other back pocket.

Now I had to test swinging the door shut from the table. If this didn't work, I might have to call the whole thing off. I'd bought a spool of dark brown nylon rope online. Like Diego once told me, you really can find anything online. The brown rope blended into the hardwood floor and the Oriental rug, and was barely noticeable. Hopefully it'd be strong enough for me to loop around my ankle and yank the door shut from my place at the dining room table. I'd already fastened one end of the rope into a noose for my ankle. When my parents went grocery shopping last weekend, I'd practiced wiggling the noose onto my foot and kicking my bedroom door shut. At first, it seemed impossible, but wearing peep-toe shoes helped me feel the rope with my toe, and it seemed to work.

The large oak door swung open toward the bar outside. The plan was to tie one end of the rope to the doorknob, and carefully run the rope to the table under my seat. After wiggling my foot into the noose and tightening it, I'd extend my leg and slam the door shut. But this oak door was a hell of a lot heavier than my bedroom door. I let out a deep breath. If this didn't work, the rest of it would be moot, and I'd need to pack everything back up and haul it out of here. Not to mention the supposed scholarship winners would show up tonight to no host, no Amber, and no idea what the hell was going on.

After setting the noose under the table where I'd be sitting, I unspooled the rope until I reached the door and measured out enough length to run slack down the door and across the floor so nobody would trip over it.

Hopefully.

I cut the rope with scissors and tied that end around the doorknob, making it loose enough so I could slip it off after the door shut. I'd have to race to inspect the door before anyone else could get to it, slip off the rope, and hide it somewhere. I glanced around the room. I could throw it under the dining table. With the red tablecloth draping near the floor, hopefully nobody would spot it. But that seemed risky. There was also a sideboard running along the wall next to the door. Ah, even better—I could kick the rope under the sideboard. Nobody would find it there.

Hopefully.

Sweat broke out on my forehead, and I wiped it with the back of my hand. There was an awful lot of hoping going on here. I didn't like depending on luck. So many things could go wrong. But it was too late to chicken out now.

I sat in my chair to give this a practice run. Without too much effort, I got my foot into the noose and made a circular motion with my ankle to kill the slack in the rope. I shot my foot forward. The door slammed behind me.

I grinned. This might work after all.

I reset the door and rope setup and did a few more practice runs. I'd have to wait until everyone was seated and talking to kill the slack—otherwise someone might trip over it. But if I moved fast . . . if I waited for a moment where everyone was distracted . . . this could work. After the final practice run, I reset the door one last time and inspected my handiwork. The rope blended almost perfectly with the grain of the oak door. If you didn't know to look for it, you wouldn't spot it. Then I set the old brass key on the bar for the cupcake deliveryman to find.

Now for the finishing touches. Of course, there would be no host tonight, so I taped a sign to the host podium near the front entrance directing everyone to the Winona Room, with an arrow pointing toward the private dining room. Then I fished a battery-powered webcam from my duffel, set it on the top shelf of one of the china cabinets, and covered it with a red cloth napkin. A red light was barely visible underneath. It wasn't actually streaming a recording anywhere, of course, but nobody would know that.

Next, I removed anything that looked remotely valuable. I replaced the delicate crystal in the china cabinet with regular glassware, locked the cabinets, removed the keys, and carefully carried out the crystal vases on the end tables, hiding everything under the bar. While I didn't think Maria's parents would trace this back to me, I also didn't want my prank to cost them a fortune. I'd considered different venues—the school, the town theater, places like that—but I couldn't think of anywhere else with an isolated room with no reception. I still had some babysitting money saved up from the past few summers I could anonymously mail to Maria's parents if shit hit the fan. Hopefully it'd be enough to cover any damage.

Last, I set the place cards with each of our names on each table setting. I assigned myself the seat closest to the door, where I dropped the noose. Scott would sit on the other side of the table, opposite Sasha. If I knew anything about her, she'd give him hell for being there. When everyone focused on them, I could kick the door shut.

And the rest of it would play itself out.

Hopefully.

What worried me most wasn't the door, or the timer, or any of the technical elements of this prank. It was me. I was orchestrating a play of my own, where I was the only performer. And I was usually a crap liar. Did I have what it took to pretend this was real? Otherwise I'd be stuck in a room getting hate from five people for an hour. Would I be able to hide my feelings for Diego? Otherwise Robbie might flip out on him and ruin this whole prank. Would I be able to steer the conversation the right way, so this would all end how I hoped? Otherwise, who knew what would happen?

I stuffed the empty plastic bags from the grocery store into my duffel and slung it over my shoulder. I didn't know for sure if this would work. But with a prop syringe and fake bomb filled with ginger ale, nobody would actually get hurt.

Ah. That reminded me. I still had to clear the room of anything . . . sharp. Dangerous. I dropped the duffel and opened the drawers of the china cabinets, scooping up any knives I came across and transferring them to one of the silverware drawers in the main dining room. Then I dragged the decorative brass fire-place tool set out into the main dining room as well.

Like I said, I didn't want anyone to get hurt. This was a psychological exercise, not a death sentence. A lot could happen in an hour when you think you're facing death.

I wanted Robbie to know his dreams weren't automatically worth more than a girl's. Faced with tonight's impossible choice, he'd finally understand that you can't place a value on someone's life or ambitions. And the ticking bomb would show him that time is not guaranteed.

I wanted Diego to stop letting people sabotage him—and to stand up against someone trying to take the easy, immoral way to the top. Tonight I'd help him call out Sasha for her cheating ways. Tonight we'd take a stand together.

I wanted Scott to see that certain secrets were too dangerous to keep. By putting him in a high-pressure situation with Sasha, I'd show him how unstable she was. He'd finally understand the consequences of selling her drugs, and how wrong he'd been to play coy with her secret.

I wanted Priya to see I still loved her like a sister. She might've ignored my calls and texts, but tonight she'd be a captive audience. I'd stand up for her against Sasha at every turn, so she'd see how much I truly cared about her. Part of me hated the thought of putting Priya through this, but she deserved getting revenge on Sasha more than anyone. And if everything went to plan, hope-fully Sasha would apologize to her. . . .

Because most of all, I wanted Sasha to see what a selfish bully she was, and to expose her malice, her lies, her manipulations. After my conversation with Maria, I realized why Sasha's sister Nat's name sounded familiar. It must have been short for Natasha Jane—the girl who tortured Maggie online. Sasha recognized Maggie's name that night in her room. I saw the shock in her eyes. I knew she knew the truth. But then she went and tortured Priya despite knowing the deadly consequences of bullying.

I couldn't save Maggie's life. I couldn't save her from the bully who hounded her. But I could save Priya from any more of Sasha's vitriol. And tonight I'd teach Sasha the thing she should have tried the hardest to perfect: empathy.

Tonight I'd kill several birds with one stone. By steering the discussion as we navigated this impossible choice, I'd teach everyone their lesson.

At the beginning of the hour, I'd encourage everyone to work together to find a way out. It would be a test of sorts to see who would choose compassion over fear, who'd choose life over death, who'd be selfless—and they'd all see each other's score. I'd suggest everything we could do to survive this together—while showing them nothing would work.

Ultimately, we'd have to choose.

So eventually, people would start panicking. It was inevitable. I was willing to bet Sasha would panic first. And whenever that happened, I'd be her foil, steadfast in my determination to keep everyone alive. I'd orchestrate the conversation to force out each person's inner demons, so they'd all come to understand their deepest flaws, and hopefully, overcome them.

And in the end, I'd try to unite everyone against Sasha. If everyone tried to guess who locked us in, I'd show how Sasha had wronged each suspect. But the people she'd wronged the worst would be in the room. I'd reveal how she'd bullied Priya, sabotaged Diego, bought drugs off Scott, manipulated me. I'd expose each of her secrets, one by one. Maybe when people finally said "no" to Sasha Harris—even Robbie, someone she assumed would always take her side—she'd finally see the error of her ways. Tonight, we'd all get our revenge. And once she braced for the needle to pierce her skin and poison to flood her veins, once she knew her actions had consequences, she'd turn things around.

Sure, this might have been a little over the top. There were probably a zillion other ways I could have taught everyone their lessons.

I guess you could say I had a flair for the dramatic.

But teaching Sasha a lesson would take more than words. People like Sasha and Natasha weaponized words to ruin people's lives, but swatted them away like gnats. She was deaf to all but her selfish goal of perfection; no amount of lecturing, screaming, guilt-tripping, or rational discussion would elicit change.

Some people can't see the light until you shutter them in darkness. Sasha needed to see for herself that her own selfishness would be her downfall.

Tonight she wouldn't be able to bully herself out of the room. Tonight she'd see herself for who she was. Tonight would take care of everything in one fell swoop.

And it'd only take an hour.

35 MINUTES LATER

I leaned on the back of one of the police cruisers, wrapped in a light blue fleece blanket from one of the ambulances. A paramedic had cleaned my wound, which wasn't as bad as it first seemed, and wrapped my shoulder and upper arm in gauze. My jacket was still inside; we couldn't touch anything in the crime scene. It finally stopped pouring, but it was still drizzling, and my damp hair clung to my face and neck. I shivered as two paramedics lifted Scott's stretcher into the back of one of the ambulances.

The other ambulance would be for Priya, but the police wanted to question her first, and had told the rest of us to get fresh air outside. Would she be arrested? Last I saw, she sat at one of the red booths in the main dining room, talking to one of the police officers.

Oh, Priya. I never meant to turn her into a murderer. A fresh wave of nausea rocked my stomach, and I almost keeled over and vomited at the thought. What had I done? What the hell had I done?

Before I could lose it, I sucked in the cool air. Breathe in. Breathe out.

Several police cars lined the street behind the ambulances, their flashing lights pulsing blue and red on the brick buildings. The sidewalk in front of the restaurant was blocked off, and two burly cops stood by the door to supervise, making sure none of us left the scene yet. They all seemed confused as hell. As far as they could tell, we were all victims of something . . . but what? A plot to murder one of us? A practical joke gone wrong? Although we had trespassed and damaged the restaurant, we were invited with no idea the invitations were fake, and once we were locked in we had no choice but to try to find a way out.

Another ambulance was on its way for Sasha, but the crime scene photographer had to finish his job first. I vaguely wondered where they'd bring her. It's not like you need to go to the hospital if you're already dead. Would they bring her straight to the morgue? Was the morgue in the hospital? I wasn't sure where they took Maggie after I'd called 911, because my parents made me wait at Priya's while they went . . . well, wherever they went with Maggie's body. Now I wondered where Sasha would go. I somehow managed to stay on my feet without collapsing into a heap of regret, and felt like I was encased in a giant vat of cold jelly—completely, utterly numb, and barely able to support my own weight. Breathe in. Breathe out. All I could do now was keep breathing.

Robbie sat against the building under the awning next to

Diego and his family, texting someone—probably his mom or dad. Whenever his eyes darted my way, I pretended I'd been watching the cops, or the paramedics. I never meant to break up with him at the party; maybe part of me wanted to give him another chance once he understood his dreams weren't worth more than mine. But like I'd feared, he found out about my feelings for Diego.

Diego's parents were the first to arrive. His dad had practically trampled the cops, demanding answers, while his mom clung to Diego. Neither of them seemed to understand their son was never in any real danger.

At least . . . he wasn't supposed to be.

I'd been so careful. So careful. I cleared the room of anything dangerous. I'd played out the scenario over and over in my mind beforehand, practicing how to steer the conversation. And for a while, things went according to plan. I revealed secrets I wanted to reveal, made points I wanted to make. But then the conversation got away from me, and the hour unfolded differently than I'd imagined. I'd forgotten what people can be capable of when they're desperate. I couldn't have predicted something would go wrong with the boiler, driving us mad with heat. I couldn't have predicted Scott would fall and break his ankle. I couldn't have predicted a glass shard from a broken window would be used as a lethal weapon.

I couldn't have predicted any of it.

But I was responsible for all of it.

My throat constricted, making it hard to breathe as Diego detached himself from his mother and headed over to me. "Hey."

He leaned back on the cruiser next to me as his parents interrogated the cops. "How're you holding up?"

"I don't know," I managed to choke out. "I keep thinking I'm going to wake up, and this'll all have been a really bad dream. I can't believe Sasha's . . ." I couldn't finish the sentence. I never imagined anyone would die tonight. That was never supposed to happen.

Diego put his arm around me, careful to avoid my wound, and pulled me close, resting his temple against mine. "I'm so sorry about what happened to your sister. I never knew she was bullied like that."

I sniffed. "After the news spread, Nat—well, Sasha—combed through her social media comments and deleted all of them. I should have spoken out about what I saw, but my family was in shambles." In retrospect, I should have done more to call out Maggie's bully. But I was so scared to be bullied myself. And maybe if mental health wasn't so stigmatized, Maggie would have come to us for help. Maybe none of this would have happened.

"Right, of course. And I'm sorry you lost your friend tonight."

"She wasn't my friend. Not in the end, anyway." I shook my head. "God, I really had no idea it was her all along who tortured Maggie. But still, even knowing . . . I didn't want her to *die*."

"You tried so hard to get everyone out of there alive. You were the one voice of reason in that whole mess. And you know . . . you were really brave . . . braver than any of us."

A tear finally slipped down my cheek, and I shifted to look at Diego. He gazed at me with those copper eyes, filled with so much admiration and . . . could it be love?

It made me want to dissolve into a puddle of shame. The only reason I seemed brave was because I knew the whole thing was fake. I didn't think anyone was going to die, at least not until the heat became overwhelming and I realized we could be in real danger. That's when I'd started to panic—especially after Scott fell. But by then, we were in too deep, and there was no way out until the hour was up and the cupcake delivery person set us free, anyway. I had to see it through. Otherwise it'd all have been for nothing.

But that's exactly what I should have done. I should have pumped the brakes. I should have stopped everything when things started going awry. This was all my fault. All my fault.

"I'm sorry any of this happened," I said. "I'm so sorry."

Diego touched my cheek. "None of this is your fault. You did everything you could." He leaned closer, and the truth threatened to burst out, that I was the one behind this, that this was entirely my fault. But before I could speak, his lips were on mine, both of his hands cupping my face, and it was like every nerve ending in my body lit up.

It made tearing myself away from him that much harder. My heart imploded with grief as I pulled back, placing my hands on his chest so he couldn't tug me close again. I didn't deserve him. And I could never be with him now.

Sasha was dead because of me.

She would never get to redeem herself. She was gone forever.

I doubled over, letting out fierce sobs. "I'm sorry . . ." I managed to croak out. "I'm so sorry."

Diego scooted closer and silently rubbed my back until my

face was drenched with tears, and I had to sniff back snot. At one point he disappeared into the empty ambulance to grab me a bunch of tissues. I must have looked like a blotchy mess, but that was the least of my worries.

"Oh, God." I hiccupped after I blew my nose. "Sasha is dead. *Dead*. No matter how selfish she was, no matter how mean she was to Maggie, she didn't deserve to die like that. And what's going to happen to Priya? Will she be arrested?"

"It was self-defense." Diego drew circles around my shoulder blades. "Well, maybe not self-defense, exactly, but she did it to save you. I don't think she'll be in trouble. The real murderer is whoever put us in there."

I screwed up my face and stared at a break in the clouds where the stars peeked through, shaking my head slightly. The sky and I ran out of tears at the same time. My body trembled against Diego's as two paramedics appeared in the doorway, wheeling Priya on a stretcher between them, her cheeks streaked with dried tears. When Priya spotted me and Diego, she let out a sob and wordlessly held out her arms for me. She wasn't handcuffed. Thank God. I sprinted over and enveloped her in a hug, ignoring the paramedics' protestations. She clung to me as we cried into each other's hair, and I squeezed my eyes shut, wishing I'd thought of any other way to get her back. But I didn't. This was our reality now. Somehow, we'd have to come to terms with it.

Finally, Priya released me and wiped her nose as Diego joined us. "Are you okay?" I threw a worried glance at one of the paramedics. "Is she okay?"

"She's fine," she huffed, tightening her messy bun. "It's just a precaution. We should get some fluids in her and run some tests. And you're Amber, right? You're coming with us." She pointed at my shoulder. "That needs stitches."

"Wait," I said, "I need to talk to the police." I knew what I had to do.

"You can speak with them at the hospital."

"No, now." It couldn't wait. I couldn't risk chickening out. I didn't trust myself anymore. "Can I just talk to Priya for a minute? Please?" The paramedic's nostrils flared, but she nodded and stood a few feet away with her colleague.

"What happened?" I asked Priya, glancing at the police officers talking near the door. "What did you tell them?"

"Everything." She hiccupped. "But the police want to question me more at the hospital. They agreed to wait until my mother gets there. But Amber . . . I *killed* her. I killed Sasha. My life is *over*."

No, it wasn't. I'd wanted to seek justice for Priya—to help her get revenge on a bully. But Priya didn't need my help. She was a badass who could stand up for herself. She'd dropped toxic Sasha from her life, and dropped *me* when I became a shitty friend. And she'd saved my life tonight. I wouldn't let Priya get in trouble for what she did. I'd never be able to take away the trauma of tonight, or the blood that would forever stain her hands. I'd never be able to take away the memory of stabbing another person, or the nightmares that were sure to plague her for years.

But I could turn myself in and tell the police the truth. That I set all of this up. That none of this was Priya's fault. That she only

killed Sasha in self-defense, and that I was the one who should go
down for murder. If I got arrested, I'd probably never go to USC.
I'd never score movies. I'd never see my dreams come true.

I'd prioritized those dreams above all else over the past year—
over Priya, and our friendship, and her pain. And now I'd caused
her even more agony, and I couldn't risk letting her get in trouble
on my account. I had to do what was right for my best friend. This
much, I could do for her.

I gripped her shoulder. "You saved my life. You did it to defend
me. They're going to see that. None of this is your fault." I took a
deep breath and forced the next words out. "It's my fault."

"No it's not—"

"Yes it is. It is literally my fault." I lowered my voice so only
Priya and Diego could hear, and my stomach clenched as I spoke.
"I did this. I locked us all in there."

Priya's eyes widened. "*What?* But . . . how? Why?"

"No." Diego shook his head, taking a step back. "You can't
be serious."

"I . . . it's a long story. I might've gone a bit overboard with the
whole bomb thing—"

Diego guffawed, gripping his hair. "You think? Holy shit . . ."

Priya's mouth was agape. "I can't believe this. I can't believe
you would do this."

"Wait, let me explain . . ." I swallowed hard. "I just kind of
lost it when you didn't want to be friends with me anymore." I
took Priya's hand, and she let me. "You're like my sister . . . and
I couldn't bear to lose another one. I blamed myself. I turned a

blind eye to your pain, and what Sasha was doing to you. So I wanted to make it up to you."

"But why this?" Priya gripped her throat. "Why did you do *this*?"

The paramedics started back over, and I held out a finger. "Wait! Five more minutes." I couldn't let Priya go to the hospital without an explanation. "Please. She's not in immediate danger, right?"

The paramedic raised two fingers. "You've got two minutes." She shook her head at her colleague.

I turned back to Priya and Diego and lowered my voice. "I mainly did it to get revenge on Sasha. So we could *all* get revenge on her. I never meant to *kill* her. I just wanted to teach her a lesson. She's so damn selfish; I knew she'd want to kill someone first. I thought I could use that—and expose all the horrible things she's done—to turn everyone against her." I laughed bitterly. "It turns out she did even more than I thought."

I'd always planned to reveal how Sasha bullied Priya despite knowing what happened to Maggie, thinking it would seal everyone's decision to choose her. But I had no idea Sasha *herself* was the one who bullied Maggie.

"But," I went on, "I thought if everyone chose her to die, she'd finally see how horrible she was. I thought I could get her to change . . . to apologize. And I figured that would be worth one hour of fear—one hour of thinking this might be the end—because that hour would end years of abuse for everyone.

"But I never meant for anyone to get hurt; I didn't think every possibility through. Scott falling, the glass, the heat . . . and I didn't think people would be so eager to stab each other with that syringe." I glared at Robbie, who sat against the building, holding his head in his hands. "I thought, at the very worst, someone would try to inject the poison, and of course, nothing would happen. It'd suck if it happened before making the point to Sasha, but everyone would realize the whole thing was a prank, and the delivery guy would eventually let us out.

"But I never for one second imagined people would think it was real even after the fake poison dribbled out everywhere. I thought for sure everyone would realize it was all a joke. I was an idiot—I'd cleared all the knives from the room ahead of time, and I never thought people would try to use other things to kill each other, or to choke each other . . . I didn't think of everything."

Diego folded his arms, clasping his mouth. "My God." I couldn't read Priya's stony expression.

"It was stupid," I said. "I'm stupid. But when I was planning this, it all made perfect sense . . ." I shook my head and tightened the blanket over my shoulders. "Anyway, that paramedic is going to have a seizure if she doesn't get you to the hospital. And I have to go tell the cops before my parents get here." I started toward the nearest police officer, my feet crunching over gravel on the sidewalk.

"Wait, wait." Diego grabbed my arm. "What are you going to say?"

"I'm going to tell them what I did. That I was behind this. That this was all my fault." I glanced at Priya, who stared at the white sheet draped over her lap, deep in thought. "I can't let Priya take the fall for this. I'm the one who put us in there."

Diego wiped his upper lip. "Maybe you don't need to. Maybe they wouldn't find out the truth. Like I said, I don't think Priya will be in trouble." I stared at him with my mouth slightly open, aghast. I couldn't believe that even after learning the truth, he didn't hate me. That he didn't want me to get in trouble. "You did it to stop Sasha from hurting people. Granted, it was a pretty messed-up way to go about it. But you were trying to stop a bully."

"But I was the bully tonight." I jabbed a finger at my chest. "I *have* to tell the truth. Even if Priya doesn't get in trouble . . . it's my fault she'll have to live with this for the rest of her life."

Priya's expression softened. "But . . . your intentions weren't evil. And if Sasha hadn't lost it at the end, like the selfish brat she was, and if I didn't . . ." She clamped her lips for a moment, like she was holding back vomit. Even after Sasha was dead, Priya would never take her side over mine. Like a true friend. Like how I should have sided with her all along. "Anyway, you never meant for anyone to die."

I scrunched my forehead. That was the same as saying Sasha didn't mean to kill Maggie. But in a way, she did kill her. Even though Maggie was already sick, Sasha was her last straw. Instead of relief washing over me at Priya's words, I felt an overpowering guilt. Sasha had died because of my actions. Priya might have been the one who stabbed her, but if I didn't set up this horrible prank, if I didn't trap everyone in that room, one more human being would still be alive on this planet. My actions caused her death, and no matter her flaws, no matter what she did to my sister, and to Priya, killing her wasn't justified. Even Sasha deserved a chance at redemption, and I snatched it away from her. This was all my fault. If I'd torn down Sasha's future, why should I get to build my own?

It'd be so easy to let myself fold into Diego's arms and be Priya's best friend again and be done with this horrible night, the secret tucked away in each of our hearts as we each went off to college and accomplished our dreams.

But I couldn't take the easy way out.

And that was it. That was the difference between Sasha and me. We both had made mistakes. We both had caused others pain to get our way. The difference was that when she understood the consequences of her actions, she didn't stop. She kept bullying. She kept lying.

But I was going to stop. I was going to set things right.

"No. I have to turn myself in. I did this. I can't just stay quiet and hope this goes away. I have to confess. If I try to get away with this, I'll be just as bad as Sasha. This was *my* fault. I have to own up to it. Hopefully . . . hopefully they'll see I didn't mean for this to happen."

"Amber"—Priya grabbed my hand again—"whatever happens . . . I want you to know you'll always be my sister. No matter what." That was what I wanted most from tonight. And it was all I needed to know I was doing the right thing. I hugged her again, until the paramedics took her away from me and lifted her stretcher into the ambulance. Once the ambulance pulled away, I trudged toward the police to turn myself in.

"Wait!" Diego called after me, and I froze again. "I have one question. Who's Meagan Abbie? You know, the person who ordered the cupcakes?"

I brushed my bangs aside and tucked the ends behind my ear. "That was my sister's name. Maggie was her nickname."

In a way, maybe this was all for her. I wanted to prevent people from hurting anyone else the way they hurt Maggie. But the last hour was born out of anger, desperation, and revenge . . . and now I had to find forgiveness.

I had to forgive people like Sasha, who crushed others to feel better about themselves. I might never know if Sasha was a true narcissist, but if so . . . maybe she couldn't help the way she was. I had to forgive Maggie for taking herself from this world, when she could have asked for help, and when none of us were ready for her to leave. But she wasn't being selfish. She was sick. She was sick, and I wasn't there for her when she needed me.

I was the selfish one. In my quest to redeem myself, and get revenge on Sasha, and regain Priya's friendship, and all the rest of it, I'd put everyone through hell.

Now I couldn't be selfish anymore. No matter how hard it would be, no matter how much trouble I'd be in, I had to do the right thing. I had to face the music, even if it meant I'd never write music again. Even if it meant giving up my spot at USC. Even if it meant I'd never see my dreams come true.

And hopefully someday I'd learn to forgive myself. But that would take a hell of a lot longer than an hour.

AUTHOR'S NOTE

Suicide is the second leading cause of death for people ages 10–24—yet four out of five teens who attempt suicide have shown clear warning signs. If someone you know is struggling, **you can make a difference.** You can get them help.

Here are some of the warning signs that can help you determine if a friend or family member is at risk:

- Talking about killing themselves, feeling hopeless, feeling trapped, having no reason to live, being a burden to others, or feeling unbearable pain.
- Looking for ways to end their lives (e.g. researching methods online).
- Withdrawing from activities, family, and friends.
- Giving away prized possessions.
- Saying goodbye to family and friends.
- Being excessively moody, aggressive, depressed, or anxious.
- Sleeping too much or too little.
- Increasing their use of drugs or alcohol.

If you are having suicidal thoughts, please know that it's not a sign of weakness. Know that it's not your fault. And you are not alone. There are people who love you and would miss you terribly, and there are people who can help.

If you've had suicidal thoughts, or know someone who displays the warning signs above, please don't keep it a secret. Please reach out for help. Contact the National Suicide Prevention Lifeline at 1-800-273-TALK (8255). You can also learn more at www.suicidepreventionlifeline.org.

ACKNOWLEDGMENTS

I spent the last hour staring at this blank page, wondering who to possibly thank first. My path to publication was long and twisty, and so many people helped me along the way.

First, I want to thank *you*. Thank you for choosing this book and spending your time with my characters. It still blows my mind that anyone wants to read my words, and I'm so grateful that you did.

This book would not be an actual book without my talented editor, Catherine Wallace. Thank you for loving and championing this story, and for making my dreams come true. You're a true character development genius, and your guidance made this book sparkle. Working with you has been such a delight, and I can never thank you enough. Thanks also to Christina MacDonald, my keen-eyed copy editor; Alexandra Rakaczki, my production editor; Vanessa Nuttry, my production manager; Shannon Cox, my marketing director; and the rest of the team at HarperTeen, EpicReads, and HarperCollins, for all your hard work getting this book into readers' hands. I'm so thrilled *All Your Twisted Secrets* found such a supportive home.

To literary agent extraordinaire, Jim McCarthy, thank you for also making my dreams come true, and for so fiercely loving this story. You are an absolute joy to work with. (And I continue to be amazed by your lightning-fast responses. Seriously, you're the best.) Thanks also to my foreign rights agent, Lauren Abramo, the team at Dystel, Goderich & Bourret, and all the subrights agents advocating for this story overseas.

To illustrator Evgeni Koroliov and the designers at Harper-Collins, Corina Lupp and Alison Klapthor, thank you for designing such an incredibly stunning cover. I've spent *way* too much time staring at it!

To my film agency, the Gotham Group, and film agent Shari Smiley, thank you for championing this project in Hollywood. Thanks also to AwesomenessTV for optioning this project, and to Melanie Krauss and Brin Lukens for loving this story. I can't wait to see what the future holds.

To my author BFFs—Shana Silver, Mike Chen, Hannah Reynolds, and Dan Koboldt—your friendship means the world to me. Thanks for letting me vent and for generally keeping me sane on a daily basis over the years.

To all my CPs and beta readers—Shana Silver (my brainstorming buddy who confirmed my idea for an ending would be a "delicious twist"), Sonia Hartl (my first reader, whose brilliant feedback made me rewrite every flashback chapter), Hannah Reynolds, Mary Elizabeth Summer, Brianna Duff, Rebecca Phillips, Dannie Morin, Annie Stone, Kimberly Moy, Erica Boyce—and my mother-in-law, Linda Urban—thank you so much for your input and words of encouragement. Thanks also to Kate Brauning, Kaitlyn Johnson, and Laurie Dennison for your help with the pitch.

To everyone who blurbed this book—R.L. Stine, Lisa Unger, J.T. Ellison, Mike Chen, Kimberly McCreight, Kaira Rouda, Wendy Heard, Eileen Cook, Kim Culbertson, and Rachel Strolle—thank you so much for your time, generosity, and kind words. I've so admired your work over the years, and it's surreal that you even know who I am, let alone read my words and liked them. Having your support is truly an honor.

I'm so grateful to my friends, old and new—Chris, Alyssa, Ranjini, Sarah, Hartley, Carolyn, Kenna, Ed, Melanie, Danielle, Jennifer, Merida, Lauren, Wendy, Karen, Alexa, and so many more—you know who you are—my coworkers at BookBub, and author groups the Clubhouse, Submission Swamp, and Not-Secretly Agented, plus the fellow debuts I've bonded with, thank you so much for your friendship and encouragement. I'm thrilled to have you all in my life.

To the early readers, book bloggers, librarians, and booksellers—and to my street team's earliest members—I'm so grateful for your support and enthusiasm for this story.

To my favorite film score composers Howard Shore, John Williams, Hans Zimmer, Ramin Djawadi, James Newton Howard—as well as Lin-Manuel Miranda—thank you for bringing hours and hours of joy into my life, and for inspiring Amber's dreams.

To J.K. Rowling, thank you for Harry Potter, and for providing an escape into such a magical world. Growing up with Harry got me through some rough times, and I will always appreciate that.

To all my family and in-laws, thanks for always cheering me on and being so excited to read my stories! Grandma Gloria, you're going to love this next part. (And I love you.)

To my cat, Kitty, thank you for being the perfect little writing buddy. Yep. Just thanked my cat. Don't judge; she's the best, and she was the inspiration for Amber's cat, Mittens.

To my parents, Mark and Lorri, thank you for always believing in me, for supporting my dreams, for reading everything I write, and for introducing me to Harry Potter (in the most hilarious way). I love you. Sorry I started dating before I was 47.

To my husband, Bryan, thank you for literally everything. Words cannot express how grateful I am for your endless encouragement, love, patience, and support every step of the way. I couldn't have gotten here without you, and I'm so happy we're on this adventure together. I love you so, so much.

Sometimes I think back to my time as a teenager, when I felt ostracized and alone. And now I look at this list of names—these people who've loved and supported me over the years—and my heart is so full. To readers out there in middle school or high school who feel bullied, isolated, or manipulated, please know that **you are not alone**. One day you will find your people, and it will get so much better than this.